The
Hollow
Stones

Chapter One

How many thoughts can you have in the last thirty three seconds before you die? How many memories pass through you as a feeling, before your heart stops beating? What images pass behind your eyes as you close them? What is your life, if not a memory, held ever so gently by the current of time?

I remember so clearly now, looking out over the flat plains that led to the sea. The land was so green, so fertile. You could see the energy as it rose from the grasses, the smell of life infused the senses. Life was everywhere, and the aliveness of it was palpable.

The understanding of our world was different then. The people saw life as a joyous celebration. There was not want, nor was there fear, for the rulers made sure the people were cared for. The land and the people were as one, harmony and understanding between the two. The people took what was needed from the land and offered gratitude in return.

But as all things are, it could not stay that way, for the nature of life is to change, to cycle. No matter the strength of those that work with the elements, life will have its say. Life must experience itself in all forms, and peace is only one form. So without my knowledge of what was to come, the pendulum of peace was starting to swing in the other direction, my life would soon be something I did not recognize.

I was just a child when my memories started. At that point I did not know I was different than the Others. The Others were the other group of beings that lived with us. They helped us and in return we took care of them. Their needs were greater that ours, as they had to consume the plants that grew on the planet to survive. They did not seem to know of life in the same way as my people did, they had no memories. As a child I played with the their children in the fields, we played the games of children and chased butterflies, we would run til we could run no more, falling exhausted onto the sweet grass below us. Life was a constant adventure. My world was safe, I had no idea what fear or loss were. Love was the world I lived in. Endless discovery, constant curiosity, it was a perfect life. On the days when I would go out with my parents, I would see the people courteously greet my parents with a bow of acknowledgment, and a big smile. I knew my Father was a person in a great position, many people came to him everyday, to consult him. He was a man of great knowledge and held the respect of the people. My Mother was very beautiful and moved with elegance and grace. She spent a great deal of time with the people, teaching them better ways to do things, and helping them plan and create great celebrations.

My Mother would sometimes take long journeys to the mountains beyond the sea. She told me one day she would take me to meet her family there. I wanted the adventure, but I did not want to leave my Father. I loved my Father. He was always there, ready for a game. No matter what he was doing he would stop and be part of my life, even if just for a moment, before he had to return to what he was doing. He was a great man.

The home where I lived sat high on a hill overlooking all the land. The homes were different colors and made of different kinds of stones, depending on what your needs were. The healers lived in green stone, the masons lived in white stone. I lived with my parents in an home that was created of shimmering stone. The stone would change its hue as the light changed. There was a glow that emanated from the walls at all times. It was the color of pearls from the sea. Bright sunlight would make the colors dance across the surface of the white stone.   On days when the color was strong you could walk through the color and feel its energy move within you.

My parents had told me that when we first came to this place, we were not as we are now. We were lighter, not so dense, we could move on the air, with the speed of thought. Light would bend toward us as we moved. The breath of heaven still descended towards us. As time passed, and we adapted to this new world, our bodies became heavier, denser.   We could not move in the same manner, it became much more difficult to move about. We required energy from the planet to support our bodies, and we could not create our children in the same way. And so it is, that I am the last true princess of our people, the last one to come from the chambers, deep inside the mountains.

The coloured light that dances across our walls contains the energy of our ancestors, it stays with us, it is our memories, it is how we can still help the skies to rain and grain to grow. It is the energy of our essence, if it were to disappear, we would die. It is how we regenerate. We live in the energy of our ancestors. Each night as we rest, we dream ourselves into being. We remember who we are, so can awaken and know ourselves. It is our connection to the source.

I have seen how the babies of the Others have cords that attach them to their Mother. Our cords are made of coloured light, and they connect us to the All. The One source that is the source of everything.

We were different from the Others. When we breathe, we do not require the oxygen from the air, we require the light in the air. Our nourishment comes from touching the land, sitting with the trees and swimming in the sea. We are made of the elements of this planet. It was the only way the ancient ones could create their children.

They failed many times before they found the right balance of energy, so that the children of their memories could be born. They could no longer put their thoughts together and create a new life, they had to use substance and then, vibrate life into it.

That is how they discovered the chambers. The place deep with the heart of the earth. The place where a single thought reverberates through time, and back again. It is the place where the ancient ones could imagine the next generation into being. Where their thoughts could become The Ones they loved. Their children were brought to being with songs and thought. They were truly children of the earth, with hearts that were formed from heavens breath. I am the last child to be this way. The earth has gotten too heavy, too dense. My parents tried to create another child, but the chambers would no longer respond to their songs. The light of the heavens cannot penetrate the walls to breathe into the elements. So I am the last of my kind. This is what I was taught to understand in my youth. I was taught that, I would have my childhood to do as I pleased, to learn the value of the land and the people. To learn to be. To learn how the Others loved, and to learn how my people loved. For I am a child of two worlds.

I retain the memories of my ancestors, the knowledge of what is, and how to be. But I am also a guardian to the Others. The Others were created for my kind. The Others of this planet came from need in the time of seeding the planet. These people do not have the memories, or the understanding that they are all one. They see themselves as one unto themselves. They do not seem to be able to feel each other as they feel themselves. It is difficult to understand how they are. They do not need to go to the chambers to create the memories of themselves, so that children can be born. They come together, man and woman and out of that, a child is born. I do not understand how it is, that they are but they have great love, and it is through that love, that they find the all.

Last night when I was asleep, I dreamed of a beautiful being. She was light and as she moved, colors would dance all about her. She came to me, calling my by name, Aeiya. She motioned for me to come with her, but I did not know where she was going. She did not speak to me, but I could hear her talking, she took me on a journey, through my own memories, she told me it was time. I wanted to go with her, but I would not leave my parents. She has much to teach me. I felt she was a part of me. It is hard to explain, I did not understand.

In the early morning hours, my Mother came to me. She asked if I had dreamed of The One. I knew she was talking about the beautiful being I had seen in my dreams. I told her yes. My Mother told me it was time for me to go on a journey. She was going to take me to the sacred mountains, the mountains where I was created. There I would meet The One and the rest of the ancient feminine. She could tell by the look on my face that I

5

was not fully understanding what she meant. She went on to explain.

The planet where we live is a balance of energies that could not be manipulated too far in either direction, not to masculine and not to feminine. If that were to happen, it would become unbalanced and fold in upon itself. We, the royal family were the keepers of these energies. We made sure the rains fell and the sun shone in the right amounts. The Others had to be cared for, they would not survive on their own outside of our protective walls. I had no knowledge that the land we lived on was protected by an energy field that came from the stones on the royal ground. My Mother explained to me that the planet beyond the walls of the field was very unstable and too harsh to live in. So they created a field that was anchored in five different spots to protect all beings under it. The ancient ones, kept the field balanced and those of original creation, kept it anchored. I needed to learn how to do this, so I would go and live with The One for the next cycle of my life. There I would be taught all that I needed to know, how to watch over the land and its people. I would learn how to continue to keep peace on the land, how to understand and work with the energies of the planet so a constant and continuous flow could be maintained.

I did not have a singular concept of time. For me, time happened in two different ways. Ours was a people that lived for thousands of years. My family however did not die in the same way as the Others, our energy got thinner and thinner til we merged with all that was around us. No longer could we consciously guard anything, nor could we partake of the life of those around us in the same way. We could still communicate through the essence of energy though. We could offer help and wisdom through whispering to the stones and the stones would offer the vibration to the royals. So all that ever were, still are, however they are in a formless form. We feel them as our memories. They have become part of the field that protects our land.

Preparations were made for the journey to The One. I was very sad to be leaving my Father behind. I did not understand why he could not be with me. I understood he had to be here for the people, to solve any disputes, but I would miss him greatly.

My Mother told me that, The One and the energies of the ancients were a gathering of feminine energies. The memories of how to understand and assist the planet were only passed down through the feminine beings of our race. It was the feminine that represented flow and continuity. Merging and creation. The masculine represented, structure and stability, solidity and the action. Both energies were needed to maintain the field, but the feminine was the very memory of the ancestors. It was understood long ago that for us to survive, no one being should have all the memories. So it was that the masculine received some memories and the feminine received the rest. This created an existence where we would have to come together and share, be mutually supportive and cooperate. And so the nature of all creation was placed within the feminine and nature of structure was placed within the masculine. In that way, there was balance.

My Mother and I were ready for the journey. I was excited and sad at the same time. I watched as my Father moved towards me, I could not see his face, it had been shaded from the sun sitting at his back. My Father always moved, with great sureness and love. He did not miss a step. He came towards me and pulled me into his arms. He held me close and I could feel him missing me. I was special to my Father, not just because I was his only child, but because I was so much like him. I was always taking on challenges, I had a love of life that many times put me in places I should not have been. I had been dangerously close to the field that guards the Others many times without knowing it. Never once did my Father discourage my behavior with fear. It was always explained to me, that my behavior's have to consider the Others and how fragile they are. If we were to do something to upset the balance then we would be the cause of life losing love. I was raised to understand the Universe has an energy that connects us, and if that link is broken in one spot, it will weaken everything else. So my actions were always put into perspective as it would affect the whole.

I kissed my Father and he smiled as he always did. He said the time between us did not exist and that we would be together again in the blink of an eye. All I had to do was breathe him in and he would be there with me. He also told me to listen to The One, because that way, I could come back sooner. The One was important to us all and one day I would be just like her. It was my destiny.

So off we went. I waved good bye to my Father and watched the love emanating from him fade as time and distance folded together, creating a veil my eyes could not penetrate.

Travel for my Mother and I was part physical and part thought. We had retained some of the abilities of the old ones. We could travel great distances with thought, but only for very short periods of time. We could not maintain the necessary frequency to hold our denser bodies, for extended times. So we passed through space, by collapsing time. The journey to the sisterhood, although by distance was long, was made relatively short by manipulating time. My things, which were being physically transported over the great land bridge, would take a few weeks to arrive.

Lemuria our great Island was totally surrounded by the sea and completely cut off from the sacred mountains at times when the sea would rise and portions of the land bridge would disappear under the water. Travel was always appropriately timed in advance, so no one was lost to the sea or stranded on the few tiny islands that protruded above the water. The land bridge was blocked when it was accessible, by a mirror like energy field. It was the only thing that protected the people from the great beasts that roamed beyond the sacred mountains. There were also dangerous creatures that swam beneath the surface of the great sea. Travel in small boats was forbidden as many of the common people had been taken when their boats were overturned. Harvesting the sea was not necessary as everything they needed was grown in the fields. But the Others had a great spirit and curiosity, they always wanted to know what was beyond the boundaries of the energy field. It is horrible that many of them lost their lives, to satisfy their curiosity. But this is how we came to know so much of the dangers around us.

There were great birds that flew in the skies, and would take a man for their meal. So when crossing the land bridge all people wore special clothing to disguise themselves as part of the land. A protective cloak, that contained a numbing potion. If the birds tried to take anyone, the taste would not be pleasant and the numbing potion would cause their wings to fall to the ground. Once the potion wore off, the birds were free to fly once again.

After crossing the great land bridge, we arrived at the flat lands just below the sacred mountains. I had never seen anything that seemed to reach so far into the sky. The clouds were lazing about on the great cliffs of stone. I did not think it possible to ascend to the place we had to be. Mother said The One lived up by the peak, in a small valley that gathered the morning sun. Their temples looked out over the land bridge and the protective shield of our island. Mother said it was the easiest way for The One to make sure all was well.

As we approached the base of the mountain I could feel the mountain breathe us in. A sort of welcoming, It was watching us. Mother sat and offered a few words to the mountain. The mountain reached out and blessed my Mother, it felt like a warm embrace, the energy was like the suns rays, but they moved through and beyond the boundaries of your skin.

I could see rising out of the ground a stone that had been carved with special symbols. Mother said it would be our passage upwards to the temples. The symbols were a language only spoken by the Sisterhood. The words were not meant for communication between beings, instead they were sounds that would activate the elements in the proper sequence, to allow us to rise.

Mother began to sing very softly at first, as her voice rose, the symbols seemed to move, to vibrate a little. With each round of sounds she would raise her voice a little more and a little more, changing the tone and the tempo. The symbols started to vibrate very quickly, as they did, a mist appeared through the solid stone beneath us. As it enveloped us, I could feel myself moving, but I could not see a thing. In moments I could feel solid stone beneath my feet again, but this time we stood on the peak, across from the temple of the sun, the home of The One.

I was in a place I had never been in before, I had feelings inside myself that I could not describe, I could feel things all around me that seemed to be trying to merge with me. I clung to my Mother, for the first time in my life, I felt unsure of what was happening. I could see a light emanating from the temple. It was getting brighter and brighter, a beautiful golden pearlescent light. I stared into the light, looking for its source. It did not hurt my eyes but it overwhelmed them, finally when my eyes thought they could take no more, The One stepped out from the darkness. The light was The One.

Mother grabbed my hand and moved forward to greet the bright golden light. As we got closer the light changed form appeared as a beautifully mature woman. Her hair was long and pulled back. She was tall, taller than most, her eyes were slightly larger than everyone I knew, but they had a compelling ease to them. Something about her made me want to run to her. I felt as though in her presence, nothing could go wrong. She was the very essence of time, but looked at me with grace. I will never forget the first time I saw her. Seeing her and feeling her were the same thing. She was Mother to us all. I could feel a thread running through all the feminine energies I knew, and it led back to her, back to The One.

I was introduced to her very formally. There were the names and the proper stance, and last but not least, the expression of my energy. I could see The One was pleased. After all this proper pomp, we were invited into the temple, to rest. The journey had been short in time, but long in energy. I was tired and so was my Mother. A good rest was welcomed.
I was placed in a large white area that glowed with a golden tinge. The walls didn't look solid but when I touched them my hand did not pass through. This is where my Mother had once stayed when she was in training and her Mother before her. The One had initiated all the feminine energies in my line. Now she would initiate the last one. I wondered what would happen to her after that? Was that her only purpose, to train the initiates? Who was she really? Why did she feel so familiar? My mind raced, with each thought I could see a pattern ripple through the gold tinging on the wall. Was I doing that? It looked like the ripples that happen when you breathe on still water. I was fighting to stay awake, to try and match my thoughts with the reverberating ripples, but the call of my dreams was too strong. I drifted off with the speed of one breath, allowing myself to be taken by the magic of the sacred mountain.

Morning came, the rays of the sun passed over my body, like gentle golden caresses. I was excited to get up and go explore my new surroundings. There was so much to discover. Magic happens here. Magic is the rhythm here, not the exception. I loved the unexplained events that would happen at my home, I would spend endless hours and days looking for explanations. When I could not find any satisfactory answers, I would always ask my Mother, magic seemed to be her department. If I asked my Father, he would say to ask my Mother. My requests for resolution were always met with the exact same answer. One day you will know. That is all my Mother would say. I knew that day had come. For it seemed all magic sprung from the peak of this sacred mountain, and the light beings that lived here.

I left my white walls and went outside. It was early and the mists were rising upwards from the valley below, the air was cool, but very very clear. The mist looked like wisps of smoke, following an invisible master upwards and disappearing into the clouds above. Long thin fingers reaching to the sky, in a slow rhythmic undulating dance.

How long I stood there watching the mist, I do not know, but I was jolted back to my present space and time by a tap on the shoulder from my Mother. My Mother smiled at me and told me to be careful of the mists, they can steal time, she said. The mists are outside of our understanding of time, and if we become the mist, our time can be stolen from us.

My Mother was always explaining everything and explaining nothing at the same time. I would listen intently, knowing she was right, but never knowing why. With a flick of her finger we were off. The mists held me no more. Life on top of the mountain was awakening and I could feel the stir and pulse change. Why was this place so different than home? At home the sun rose and the people awoke, here it seemed the other way around, the people awoke and then commanded the sun. I hoped I would find answers soon. Patience was not something I had time for.

We strolled across the courtyard as the sun began to split the mist with its rays. The sun felt so good here, as though it shone through you, and not on you. As we moved through and around the various women, my Mother would nod her head towards them. She was warmly received here. This is a part of my Mothers life, of which I knew nothing. She had rarely mentioned anything of her time here. Just as the mist shrouded one's vision of the next mountain, I almost felt as though I did not truly know my Mother. The woman I had loved everyday of my existence, was starting to appear very different to me as we moved into her past and my future. I felt as though I was grasping to keep time congruent in a place where time is conflicted. I could not describe what I felt, only that I felt it. It made me unsure of myself. A feeling that was unfamiliar to me.

We joined the other women at the temple of the sun, to honor it as it rose. To thank it for its warmth and to ask for wisdom in its rays. One of the women started to sing and the song was picked up by another then another, till the song was being sung in waves that seemed to pass around us as it spiraled upwards. If you looked into the rays of the sun that were squeezing between the mountains, you could see the energy of the song cause little patterns in the light. Even the grass below my feet seemed to respond by standing straighter. The sound moved through my body, warming me. The sound seemed to spread out from the women through the ground and through the air, moving in rhythmic pulsing, spiraling waves. I could feel the vibration pumping through the ground. These beautifully unusual women sang words that I didn't understand, I had never heard these words before but they haunted my soul like an echo from an ancient life.

The words disappeared as the rise and fall of the harmonies seized my mind, I could feel myself moving, faster than light, I moved through the darkness. As I turned my head there were streaks of light passing down the sides of me. Ahead was a planet, it was a blue planet. I was going so fast I was afraid I was going to crash into it. I was panicked and tried to stop myself. As I struggled I could feel myself start to fall, I was falling fast now, through the atmosphere towards the planet. I knew I would die, I could not prevent impact, I could not regain my levity.

The ground approached me fast, I knew it was going to reach up and grab me, I closed my eyes and waited for the pain, then, I felt arms around me, holding me tight. Something had plucked me from my free fall. I was afraid to see who had captured my fate. I slowly opened one eye, as if it would only be half a problem if I looked with that one eye. Standing there, staring back at me, was The One. We were on this planet, this earth, but we were not on the top of the sacred mountains, we were on a long flat plain, with a great span of beach between us and the sea.

At the edge of the plain where the beach overcame the grasses, were many large rocks, and caves. Some small animals were scurrying about. The sun was low in the sky, and different than the sun I knew. It seemed to be shrouded by dust. It was having difficulty forcing its rays to the surface of the planet. This earth seemed to be trying to protect herself with dust, as though she was hiding from the cosmos, not quite ready to present herself to her sister stars. I didn't know what was going on. The One gently placed me on the ground, and steadied me. My legs were weak, I felt as though the ground beneath me was trying to shake me to its surface. I looked at The One, she could see the questions in my eyes.

"Lets walk together, shall we?" she said.

So we crossed the rocks, til we could feel the sand below our feet and turned to walk down the beach. The One then told me the story of our beginnings. As she spoke, her voice pulled me into her memories, I could see through her eyes, and feel her heart beat, I could feel all things through her, she and I were one.

"We are on this planet that you know as home, the planet where we live

11

now, but this was not always our home. We came from the stars, out there. See there, it is known as the belt of Orion. Our planet was dying very quickly and we had to find another place to live, to create life and to give life back.

Our home had been thought of as rebellious, and non conformist. The other planets in our system did not want us, so we had to look elsewhere. We waited as long as we could and sent many ships to find a new home for us. In the end our people divided up into four groups and left for four different star systems. It was not long after that, the light in our home planet went out, she took her last breath and was silent.

This planet was still trying to form, she had not created her identity yet. She was but a child, energetic and full of wonder. But not yet formed and settled. With a world in such turmoil, we were not sure we would survive here at first. We tried to encourage her by calming her energies, but it was far too taxing for us. We were almost destroyed. In desperation we returned to our ships, and prayed to the All for assistance. We were shown the elements of this planet. That the crystalline structure was in place, but not fully formed. However, we could use the energy of the not yet formed structures to create a safe space, an area which could be protected from the growing pains of the earth. So we searched the planet for a spot where we could live and a spot close by in which the energy could be anchored and projected. It brought us to our current locations. Inside these sacred mountains, are the crystals of our birth, the sacred chambers we used to grow our population.

You see this earth is magical, it has many pieces of the universe all together here in one spot. It is as though the All wanted to create a great library of all its accomplishments and creations, here in one beautiful garden. So it created this planet with bits and pieces of everything else it has created. It took all those pieces and breathed life into them so they could grow, and become life themselves, and then, find their own way. There are elements here of our own planet, and all the other planets we know of. This planet is the culmination of creation. It is the essence of understanding. The basic structure of all known things, exist here, and if you look with the right sight, you can know the entire universe from this spot on which you stand.

This planet holds all the potential that is held within all planets in all dimensions. When this was understood by the population of the universe, a great coming together of the beings within multiple dimensional realities was held. It was decided, because this earth is the energy of creation, important species that were in danger or dying in other places, would be brought here to seed this planet for future generations. For some worlds, saving one species, would mean saving a whole planet.

We were concerned that we would be asked to leave, so the planet could be used as an incubator, but it was decided that we would be charged with guardianship of the diversity of species. We were asked to watch over the growth and development of the new life. We agreed.

So they came, some worlds offered many species, some worlds only brought one. This planet was seeded with a diversity of life that is not known in the rest of the Universe. However, in the beginning, much did not survive. The earth was too volatile, she would role and turn, protesting the very request that she nurture life. Over time though, she has matured and come to understand that she is unique, and that she has something to offer that no other does, and so as she calms, she has embraced life. The ships still arrive from other worlds, they bring the necessary species for the existence of their world, here to us for safe keeping. When the time is right, they will return to harvest their kind, to return the life to their planet that they entrusted here to earth. So we are the guardians here. We inform the other worlds of the progress of their investments.

This is the nursery, and we are here to tend it. It is our responsibility and our honor. We share our energy with all species here, and it offers the same in return. We have grown together, in a literal way. There is no boundaries between our energies, and this is something you will learn a great deal more about. However as with all things there is a cycle, birth, growth, decay and death. Our species, our people are now in its final stages. Because of the rejuvenatory energy here we are the last of our people. You see me and think I am different than you, but this is only partially true.

I and a few of my sisters have retained our original vibration, we still exist in the same dimensional form we came here in. This is because of the crystal chambers here, they constantly recreate us, in our original form. If we were to leave this mountain, we would soon pass through dimensional time and grow old and our appearance would change. The sisters anchor the energy that protects your island from the species we are guardians over. Yes if you were to go beyond the shield you would discover a world full of diversity, beauty and great violence. As with all birthings there is pain.

The diversity of species that were brought here live in harmony, but it is the same level of harmony that the planet is experiencing. These species feed the energy of the planet and in turn she feeds them. They experience need, and she responds. She has truly taken on the responsibility of Mother.

As these species grow and develop, they have started to create new species on their own. There is a blending of dimensional realities happening here, as these species grow and adapt with and to each other. Some of the species have merged together creating a whole new species, this in turn has caused a healing on their home planets. What happens here, affects this planet as well as where they came from. It is a direct line of energy from the species to the originating planet. It is why it is so important for us to care for this nursery. Well that is enough of our history for today. We need to be getting back to the others. I am being called by the sister of the gardens. You will awaken back in your bed. We will continue our lessons at another time." With that she disappeared and I could feel myself falling again. I did not like that feeling, it was uncontrolled and almost violent. I could feel my insides contracting painfully as I opened my eyes. My vision was blurry, but I could see the white walls around me, and my Mother sat on the edge of my bed. I started to shake and shiver. I did not know what was happening.

Mother placed a cover over me, "Don't worry, it will be over in a minute. It is a reaction to crossing dimensional time. You body is a little too dense to handle it well the first time. It will get better every time you go. Just rest now." She placed her hand on my cheek, and the room went dark. Asleep I fell, exhaustion set in. Rest became me.

I awoke the next morning, rested, but restless. I knew now, that I had come here, to become that which I am. My life would never be as I had known it. It is why my Mother did not tell me what lay ahead, she knew I would not have come. She also knew it was my destiny and I could not escape it. It is always best to meet your destiny when it calls, delayed destinies, are sometimes not survived.

With that I decided, to escape, to go to the mountain itself, to be gone before anyone could find me. I slipped through the pre dawn darkness. Across the courtyard, behind the temples to the walls of the mountain itself. The scent of the night clung to the moss as I ran my hands across the damp wall. Then it was total darkness, it was the opening to the mountain. As I peered into the depth of the lack of light, I knew it was the way to the chambers, the chambers where I and the other had come to life. I could barely see, but something was pulling me, I could see tiny particles of light dancing in the air far below me. Almost imperceptible dots of color, moved to the sound of their own song. A song I was starting to feel, but could not hear.

I moved forward, finding my footing on the path that would lead me below the surface, away from the sun that was starting to awaken the light of day. Slowly I went forward, placing each foot carefully. I was trying to memorize my way, in case I needed to make a sudden escape. I was not sure if I felt anxiety or anticipation, but it made my senses come alive.

As I descended, the light grew brighter, the path started to flatten out, and the walls grew moist with dew. I could see faintly in the growing light. Above me were the sharp rocky indents on the inner walls of the mountain. The space went on forever and I could hear the echo of my breathing bouncing from the walls to the ceiling of the cavern.

I stopped breathing, the echo stopped. I took a long deep breath, and let it out slowly, the sound undulated through the cavern like the mists snaking their way towards the sky. As I moved along the path I played with the echo, it was a living thing to me, part of myself, the part of me that is hidden, my hidden breath, I could almost see it in my mind, what my shadow would look like, it would be me, but not me. I was completely lost in my own imagination when I heard it. A breath exhaled, it was loud and it was close, and it was not me.

Fear stole my breath from me, as I backed up against the wall on the opposite side of the sound. I did not know what was there. The wall was cold and it held me hostage, I could not move. I had never felt terror like this before, I had been warned and I had not listened.

I heard the breath again, even closer this time, it seemed to be right above me. I could feel a set of eyes piercing the faint light, and striking my body. Something was watching me, breathing towards me. I did not want to see, but I could not stop myself from looking.

An invisible image forced my vision upwards to the rocky crag just above my head. I saw movement. I wanted to run, but in that instant I could not remember where to go. I tried to move very slowly down the wall, edging closer to the light I could see below me. As I moved, it moved. It was my shadow, I thought my imagination had come to life. Every move I made was mirrored by the green eyes that pierced through the darkness, and plunged into my soul.

What felt like a lifetime passed before I reached enough light to see what was following me. I now understood, how fear holds you captive, the more you fight its grasp, the more you struggle, the tighter it holds you. I had two choices, I could run and hope to make it somewhere, or I could look at the fear that was holding me hostage. I took what could be my last breath and I slowly raised my vision upwards. There was just enough light for me to see the outline of a large creature. It was staring back at me. I tried to meet its gaze, but fear over came me once again. I lowered my head and tried to shield myself from my fear. My fear had a strong smell, it was permeating the cave, it reminded me of the fermentation process that some of the Others put their food through, to make it more digestible. There was a putrid rotting smell to it. It was making me ill.

I had to do something, I could not stay and I could not go. There was no one to help me and I was too far away for anyone to hear my cries. I had to face this thing, this creature.

I moved slowly towards the light, away from the cold walls of the mountain. I could see the creature following a path downwards, coming towards me. It was much larger than I, covered in fur with large teeth, long sabre like fangs. Tan in color in the front and it faded to faint stripes in the back. It moved slowly, purposefully, never taking its eyes from me.

It crouched closer to the ground as it approached me, all I could do is pray the way the Sisterhood had prayed. But I knew nothing of prayer, nothing of bringing the sounds of the earth to my song. I did not know the language of time. I wished I had not run into the night. I wished I had faced the things I knew would come. I wished my Mother was there at my side.

Then I felt the damp warmth. The creature was so close I could feel its breath, I was too afraid to open my eyes for fear of what I might see.

"Open your eyes", I heard spoke in a soft voice. The shock of the voice made me lurch forward. I opened my eyes to see one of the sisters. She was tall and I could feel her holding me up as my knees once again found their strength.

"Before you is this great beast, it is how you would appear if you had been a creation of this planet. You would be strong and stealthy. You would move silently through sound. You could be dangerous and powerful, yet soft and yielding. You would feel the movement of all things around you. You would travel far and experience much, for you have created a beast that has both strength and stamina. It is a beast that is solitary, it finds safety in its own strength. It finds its answers through, watching. Stillness allows it to understand its world. It prefers a vantage point from above.

The Mother will be pleased. This beast is of your own creation. It is the essence of your soul come to life as the part of you, that you have yet to know. This illusion, is one of the ways you can walk on this earth beyond the boundaries of the shield and not be harmed. You are the beast and the beast is you. You have but to think of this form and be transformed to it. No one will recognize you, and you can pass unnoticed." I did not understand, how I could have created this being? I knew nothing of energies or elements. I was not one of the sisters. But Enaka heard my thought, and smiled.

"Here in this place, the place of your birth, the energy of creation is strong. It is why we chose to build the chambers here. This earth has many different lines of energy, but this is place the energy of creation flows like a great river. It comes from the center, where her heart spins and her loves pushes outward. It is one of the four points of creation. Within your thoughts, there is a special place. A part of your mind that does not know boundaries, it is called your imagination. It is the part of you that never stops creating. This part of you is the piece of your soul that amplifies the images you feel and projects them into what you experience as reality. It does not amplify your thoughts, only the images that you cannot explain with words. Life cannot be contained in words, only in images. You must remember this well, so when you take your place as ruler of guardians, you will always create from images, not with words. Words have vibration, but they are not pure. They can mistakenly transmit false images, and create false realities. Images are created of what you feel, and they are of a pure frequency, so the reality they create is stable. Realities created of words, will in time return to chaos and fall in upon themselves. Stability is created from expansion, all images expand and build upon themselves."Enaka smiled again, she knew I was not truly understanding what she was saying.

"I am the sister of connection, I connect the images, so that reality can create itself. I hold them in one spot so they can attract each other, within a single vibration. A dimensional frequency, is created from multiple images. Once those images materialize, physical reality is born. Understand?"

I shook my head. She smiled. As I started to speak the creature disappeared instantly. I new it had something to do with what Enaka had told me, but I didn't care, I wanted to see the sun, and breathe the light back into my being.

"Have you ever seen the Others make there cloth? They use individual fibre and place them together in a pattern the moves them over and under, and over and under. That is weaving. If it is done properly it creates a very strong cloth. Creating reality is like that. However, instead of using fibers, you use images merged with thought. Does that make it a little easier for you?

I nodded. At that moment I would have said or done anything to get out of there. She took my hand and led me out to the courtyard. I collapsed onto the grass and fell into a deep sleep. I dreamed of my beast, my great cat, I am walking through the underbrush in a great forest. I am alive. I awoke once again within my white walls, as I looked around and adjusted to being back in my body, I could see an image over in the corner on the wall. I rose and walked over to see what it was. The image was of the great cat standing by my side. It was so detailed it looked real. I touched it, and it felt alive to me but it was only an image.

I felt revitalized, and strangely connected to this place now. I felt as though it was not only me in my body, but the others as well. I could feel more clarity now than before I had descended into the belly of the mountain.

I sat back on my bed, trying to make sense of all that was going on. It was my life, and it was happening to me, but at the same time, it felt like I was playing a role in another life and it was happening to someone else. It was then that my Mother entered the room. She seemed so light, like she was lit from within. She came to me and put her arms around me.

"I am so very proud of you. You passed the first initiation. You created yourself. You gave your feelings an image, and then created that image. Now you have a way to explore your world, beyond its boundaries. You must promise me one thing. " I nodded my head willingly.

"You must never tell anyone of the creature you created. It is our tradition, in the sisterhood, that no one will know. Not even your Father knows of my creations. You must promise.``

Again I nodded exuberantly. I was not sure I would want to tell anyone, I wasn't sure anyone would really believe me.

"Now," my Mother started. "Get ready, we are to celebrate. You are the cause of our celebration. Many never learn to create from their feelings.

Many have not passed the test. But you my child have brought great joy here to this place. Now our lines will carry on. Go get ready, join me outside, and we shall dance!"

All my questions were swept away, with the single thought of dancing. I loved to dance. Being of the Royal family, we did not dance often. Even when we did dance, it was controlled movement, we could not dance what we felt. We could not feel the dance.

Within moments I was outside standing by my Mother. The One stood by the standing stones at her temple, she nodded to me, acknowledging my accomplishment, then she nodded to my Mother. Then with the rise of her hand music started to emanate from the colors that grew inside the crystals. It rose and fell like a ribbon of rainbow. Other women appeared with instruments, they started to play in harmony with the crystals and energy started to dance from the top of the mountain. The dancing light descended in a wave of color falling on all things. As it did, everything came alive, the plants the sisterhood, the stone and the crystals, everything was a dance of light, it moved within its own rhythm, and each rhythm was merged into the next. The rhythm of the movement infused me, it was moving me, I fell into the pulse, the beat, I could feel my sisters dancing within me as I danced within them. We were one. There was no separation. The energy spread beyond the boundaries of the temples, beyond the mountains, and beyond the sea. We spread around the earth, expanding outwards towards the stars. Everything was a dance. A dance of light, a dance of sound, a dance of love. The dance became ecstatic. Taking us on journeys through space and time. Carrying us to the places we needed to experience most. I descended to the earth, the great Mother that was below my feet. As I did, the great Mother let me in.

I could see deep inside the earth, at the very center, was her beating heart. There was a single tiny point of light spinning so fast you could not really see it. You could not define it, but the image of a spinning sphere is what was formed in my mind. It spun faster than light could travel. It spun so fast it forced the planet to turn. It appeared to pull into itself the whole universe, and then push it back out through the planet in a constant flow of light. Light that was so bright and moving so fast, you could not see it with your eyes, you could only feel it with your soul. The earth was alive, it had a heartbeat, it was conscious, it saw me and I saw it. It engulfed me in love. The light that I could see was the energy of love. Light is love I thought? As I looked around me, everything was light, all the planets, the stars, the very fabric of the universe, it was all light. It all seemed to know I was looking at it, and I could feel it looking back at me.

I understood then that with every breath we take the entire universe passes through the heart of the earth and is pushed outwards, passing through everything that the earth is. We are constantly renewed by cosmic

18

dust. We are educated by the universe itself. The universe's only wish is for us to know, we are the universe, cause it is in this way that the universe can experience itself through us. We have to be open to the flow, we must be the flow, we are flowing through all things. In that tiny speck of time, I felt the universe as me. Then it was gone.

The sound of the music danced back into my perception, as my consciousness floated back to the temple. I took my body and danced with wild abandon for the rest of the night. I had never felt so alive, so safe, so awake.

Chapter Two

It was late in the morning, but it was still too early., My eyes awakened to the sound of my Mothers voice as she sat on the edge of my bed and gently nudged me awake.

"Come on, open those sleepy eyes of yours. We have one last day together and then I must leave."

I was awake then, " What? Why? You are leaving? Aren't I going with you? Is my training over already? You can't leave me here alone! I was pleading with her. "

She smiled and replied. " It is time for you to become who you are. You cannot do that in my shadow. You must know your own strengths and weaknesses. You must follow the path we all have followed. All of us. You will be safe here. The Mother will not let anything happen to you. If you are to take your Fathers place one day, you must know who you are, to help those that need you. You have great knowledge, but it takes great wisdom, to make a great leader. It is all there in you, now you must learn how to call it forth from you. Your life is for the good of the all. "

I could feel the tears start to flow. I had never been away from my Mother. I did not know what life was without her.

"Come on, lets make the most of our day. Get up, get ready we are going to the well. You will like it there. Many stories are told around the well, and the well remembers them all." Mother and I left the area of the temples and followed a path that took us down the side of the mountain. We came out to a small area that overlooked the plains below. We could see forever. As I looked out, I could feel the wildness of it. I could see the huge beasts lumber slowly through the grasses, stopping to eat, then raising their heads to watch, then eating once again. Giant birds with wings as large as the temple flew in the sky. They seemed to glide effortlessly, never moving their wings, but spiralling upward and down, on the wind. I had never seen the outside world before. In that moment I could not understand why it was forbidden to venture there. I wanted to see the animals closer, I wanted to touch them. I needed to touch them. My Mother could see my energy pulled in that direction, she knew what I was thinking.

"You must never go there in this form. You would be destroyed. Crushed by the huge beasts, or eaten by those that prey on the beasts. Our bodies are not designed to be part of that world. We are fragile, delicate, compared to the rest of this world. We are so tiny compared to them.

There is a promise you need to keep, it is the only promise I will hold you too. You must make this promise to me now. You must promise to keep the original promise. The promise we made to be guardians of this planet. We do not own any of these other beings. They are not for us to keep or to have. The are all gifts to this place, to be held in trust, til they are needed on their home planet. The day will come that their home will call them back. It may be the difference between the life and death of that planet, as to how we care for them here. You must promise to watch over them, make sure they stay in balance, and do not let one eliminate another, for all are equally important. This planet carries the blueprint for the whole of the universe. This is the spark of life, and that does not belong to any one species. A spark will go out, if it does not feel the freedom of the wind against its soul. We are visitors here, and have been allowed to make it our home, you must never allow harm to come to this place. Do you understand?"

The severity in my Mothers tone, was new, I had never heard her speak so seriously before. It forced me to pay attention. I did not like her being so serious, it did not feel right to me. As I looked around trying to avoid the intensity of this conversation, it struck me that there was no well. My Mother had said we were going to the well, and there was none to be seen.

"Mother, where is the well?" My Mother laughed, instantly I relaxed.

"Ah, yes the well! Tell me, my dear daughter, what do you think a well is?"

"A well is a long deep hole that holds water." As always I was very proud of my direct and articulate response. With smiling eyes that outshone the sun, my Mother responded to my definition of a well.

"Yes, you are right, that is one kind of well. But there are many kinds of wells, depending on how you define a well. The well I am talking about lays here before you. It is the great plains. It is a well from which an incredible amount of diverse life forms spring. A well can hold anything. A well is simply a place that holds potential. A place you can draw that potential from as you need it. Your heart is a well for your love. Your mind is a well for your thoughts. And your soul is a well for your wisdom. There are many types of wells my child."

As I looked out over the plains once more, I let my mind drift to home, to my Father. I missed him. I wondered if he knew of this place, and if he knew what happened here. Why were there only women here? Did the men go somewhere for their training? I knew I would learn these things in time, but I thought if I had the answer now, it would make everything so much easier.

I started to ask these questions of my Mother, she cut me off. " All things will come with time", she said.

I knew there was no use in pursuing my line of questioning. No one had ever been able to get my Mother to answer a question she wasn't ready to answer. Even my Father could not coax her into a reaction if she did not want to offer one.

We sat quietly watching life unfold. It was mesmerizing, so much right in front of me, I never knew. How could all of this have been hidden from me? Was I not paying attention? Maybe I just never realized the world was bigger than me. A scream yanked me from self obsessed day dream. I turned to my Mother, she motioned for me to look on, at the scene unfolding below us.

The animals were very disturbed and agitated, they start to run, then stop, then run again. It was as though they thought something was there, but were not sure. One of the smaller ones, a baby, moved towards a small hill, cautiously it moved forward. It sniffed the air as it went. Its Mother called to it, trying to get it to return. As the baby got close to the hill, something stirred and the baby, lay on the ground, it was surrounded by tiny beings.. The being held sticks in their hands. They looked a little like the Others, but they did not act like the Others.

"Why, why are they doing that?" I was almost in tears. I wanted to save that baby. I could not understand the desire to kill another being.

"They eat the flesh of the beasts. They are not like us and they are not like the Others. They were created differently. They have a long journey ahead of them. That will take time and learning."

The Others were a very passive gentle people. They ate the fruits of trees and the plants that grew in the earth. I could not imagine them killing and eating the flesh of another.

I could smell that stench of fear, wafting up the walls of the mountain, coming off the valley floor. The rest of the animals had bolted, the Mother was still crying after her baby, to afraid to stay, but not wanting to leave the lifeless body, to the tiny men. I could feel her pain. It was a savage act. Why would one being kill another being, it made no sense? I was so disturbed. I demanded my Mother do something.

She said no, it was not up to us to upset the balance, only to keep the balance. The tiny men were a species that were brought here from another planet. That planet was a troubled planet. Many wars and much death. It was a planet where the inhabitants still tried to control one another. She said the men were really worse than the animals, they killed when they did not have to. Life meant nothing to them, unless it was their own life. I could not understand that. Confusion covered my face. My Mother saw that and took the opportunity to tie the loose ends together.

"You can see as you look out there, this planet is a beautiful place. It is full of life and diversity. There is no other place in this universe that can claim this many species. The sight, the smell, the energy here is something you would not experience elsewhere. We are grateful to be able to live here. But we are visitors to this place. The animals and the men that you see out there, are more a part of this place than we are. They were brought here as energy structures, and the raw materials were put in place to create life. They have known no other existence than this one. They are made of this planet, even though they are all children of the stars. They are all evolving together, at the same pace. They have created a community, a system of life that is so intertwined, it is dependent on one another. If you were to remove one species now, the other would suffer in some way. They are the matrix of this planet. They have created a weave of energy that feeds the planet as the planet feeds them. Earth can see herself through all their eyes, and can understand she is alive and aware. She did not have self awareness before these species were here. You could say that, just as a Mother matures when she has children and her focus moves from herself to the child she has to care for, this is what has happened to the earth. All these species are her children and she has calmed herself and settled herself now, so the beings that live upon her surface are under her care. She is self aware and aware of others. She sees it as her role as protector and caretaker.

Our role is to help her balance her energies until she is fully stable, to make sure that other beings do not come from other places and take advantage of this bounty. This earth is a record of the history of the universe. It is meant for all to learn from, but none to destroy. This is something you must understand, it is not up to you to change the earth's decisions."

I nodded my head. I did understand, but I did not like what I understood. But it was not for me to change the way it is. For I could not change anything, without destroying something and all things have their place in history.

"If our existence was known to the world out there, we would upset the balance. We carry the memories of where we are from, we have knowledge of how to force change. Our life is not a natural existence, it is a controlled existence. That is why we have the shield. We are safe there and our energies are not allowed beyond the shield to influence the others." But what about the sisterhood? They do not have a shield and their energy is so much more than us. They must effect the whole world?

Ah, my Mothers smile, I loved my Mothers smile, it was The One thing that always, always made me feel like nothing in this world was wrong. Her smile would move through you and you could not help but feel her joy. Her smile this time was a knowing one. I knew she would only tell me so much, but it would be enough to quiet my curious mind.

"Yes, they do affect the whole of the world. But the sisterhood is different. Their energy is merged with the energy of the planet, they are conscious of her needs before their own. If you were to try and find where

24

their energy started and this planets stopped, you could never find a line to determine that. The sisterhood are the original beings that came from the home planet. They are in the same state. Their bodies have not gotten any denser. It is one of the reasons they live so close to the sky, where the energy is light. They have no need for protective shields, cause they cannot be seen by the Others unless they allow themselves to be seen. The eyes of those born to this planet, cannot perceive such light bodies. Animals can sense them, but cannot see them physically either. They are very special beings and you must always remember it is the greatest honor to be accepted by them as a student."

My Mother and I sat there for most of the day, talking, hugging, basically just loving one another. Thinking about it later, I felt so much of our words were spoken as though we were already apart. That made me feel very uneasy. I was tired, and drifted off to sleep quickly.

I awoke with a scream piercing the darkness. I looked around, my eyes grasping for a bit of light. I was feeling very panicked, and then I understood, it was my own screams that awoke me. I was not sure if I had dreamt of the scream or if the scream had actually leaped from my lips. I pushed myself up against the wall and wrapped the blankets around me. The feeling lingered. I tried to gather myself, to remember what the dream had been. It felt so important. I needed to see those images again. The putrid stench of fear again, I felt as if someone's eyes were upon me. I was sure the walls were getting closer, moving in on me. I cried out, but there was no response, I could feel something grasp my throat, it was squeezing, I could not move.

Mother burst into my room, she brought the light with her. There was nothing there in the room, no hands around my neck, no frightened being to create the stench, no reason I should feel the way I do.

Something was wrong, very very wrong. I could feel it, I could almost touch it, it was so real. I just didn't know what it was. Mother stayed with me for the rest of the night. Sleep did not return easily, I could not shake the feeling that someone had been there, watching me, touching me. What had happened to my world? I no longer felt safe in it? I just wanted to go back, to the life I knew. I knew that life would never be the same again, never as right as it was. Deep within me, I knew, I would spent the rest of my life looking over my shoulder. Trust was gone, the only problem was, I did not know who had stolen it from me.

I opened my eyes to the color of grey. I had never seen the mists this heavy. I could barely see across the courtyard. As the women moved about you could see the trails they left as a void in the fog. As I watched, it looked liked shadows were being left behind, left to find their masters, as they snaked their way back towards their target. The mist was both ominous and comforting at the same time. I suppose it represented my new life that way. Either direction could be taken, if chosen.

Mother was standing across the courtyard saying her good byes to the sisterhood of women she had known for most of her life. I watched her as I always did. So graceful and sincere. Elegance in action. My Mother had a way of pulling people into her, so that they felt comfortable. She was a natural choice to care for the people, great compassion and empathy. Often my Mother knew what the people needed before they did. She would act on her feelings, and changes would happen long before there was ever conflict. I believe it was my Mothers willingness to trust what she knew, that made our world so harmonious. Needs were taken care of, so exaggerated desires did not develop. In that way, my Mother moved our world forward. There were days as a child I had wondered if Mother had gotten up early, just to make sure the sun would shine.

Mother was ready to go, and I did not want to let it happen. With grace as always she was able to comfort my fears, at the same time she let me think I was making the decisions. I held her, kissed her, and said good bye. She seemed to float into the mist and disappear, as she headed toward the absence of time, that would allow her to re enter the world at the bottom of the mountain. I did not know it then, but it would be the last time I would ever see my Mother.

Chapter Three

I screamed out in pain. Why did I let her go, why? My Mother had disappeared. It made no sense. Where would she go? Why would she disappear? There was no where for her to go. I couldn't understand. I wanted to go after here, but there was only one way down the mountain, and I didn't know how to make it work. I didn't want to come here, and now, my Mother is gone and I can't go home. I hated this place and all these people.

At that moment The One came into my sight, I wanted to lash out at her. It was her fault that I am here, if it wasn't' for the tradition, that I be trained here, by her, my Mother would still be here, instead of out there, somewhere. What if one of those great beasts got my Mother? What if she is somewhere and needs help? My mind would not stop racing. My thoughts fueled my rage.

"Stop it, and stop it now" The Ones harsh tone, snapped me back to the present moment. How dare she? I am trying to help my Mother. She has no idea, I am going too...........

"You are going to what, harm all of us here, and then try to fix something that cannot be fixed?" "You have no idea what is even going on and you are still trying to lash out in rage? Do you not understand that the rage you are relentlessly flinging about, is hurting everyone here, you have no idea how much pain you are causing all of us!"

"This is your fault, you and some stupid archaic tradition, that I have to come here, to learn nothing from you.. My Mother would be home with me right now, if it wasn't for you and your demands. I am going to find a way out of here, and go home, and you are not going to stop me. Then I am going to have my Father come and destroy this place. You can go live on the plains with the beasts." I screamed at her. I would make it happen, my Father must hate these women too.

The light around The One dimmed a little. It was only now that she understood, my Mother had told me nothing. Nothing of who the sisterhood was, or their role in my life. She had not told me who I was either. My Mother knew how strong willed I was, and had made the decision that if I was to learn anything it would have to be because I knew nothing.

The One approached me and grasped me tightly as I struggled, and then hugged me with all her might. As her energy enveloped me, I struggled against it, I raged against it, but I could not resist the warm golden light washing over me. My mind said it was some kind of trick, that they would bind me til I calmed down. But within moments I collapsed into the energy, I felt safe again.

I was trying to be angry, but the love that encompassed, me, was dispensing my anger and allowing grief to replace it. How was I going to find my Mother? She needed me. It was up to me. I had to fix this thing. I could feel exhaustion, setting in. I had been raging for hours after the news came that my Mother had disappeared. As I lingered in that place between waking and sleeping, I could see The One, aglow in a bright light, telling me, it is not what I think. I could see her, telling me, let it go, there is nothing we can do now. She touched my forehead, and I left the waking world behind.

The next morning I awoke and stared straight up. I had a dreamless night. But I remembered the horror I was living, I didn't want to move, I didn't want to get up, I didn't want to breathe. I just wanted it all to go away, I wanted it to go back to the way it was, I wanted to be that little girl again, running in the fields, feeling the sun on my face. I did not want to know this pain. I did not want to be part of this reality.

I lay and thought for awhile more, but it was getting me nowhere. I could faintly remember The One saying things to me before I fell asleep. I could remember wanting to know what she meant. I also remembered hating her. If I was going to know more, I was going to have to get up. I was going to have to face her and demand to know what she knew. I would do anything to force her to tell me. It was my Mother and I had the right to know.
I got up, got dressed, and went to the center of the courtyard, the whole of the sisterhood was gathered there. They did not move as I approached, no one turned to look at me. As I reached them I pushed through them, I needed to know what they were all looking at.
There in the center of the small circle was my Mothers lifeless body. The One was holding her as she wept. I fell to my knees. I could not believe what I was looking at. I was so afraid to touch her. I reached out, hesitating to touch her face, thinking somehow that if I touched her, she would return to life, and it would all be some kind of cruel joke. But that did not happen. Her cheek felt as it always had, but it was cold, there was no response to my touch. No smile graced her lips. Her eyes did not open. I jumped up and backed away, stumbling as I did. I pushed myself back through the women standing there. I turned and ran, I could not see beyond my tears, I could not feel my body. All I knew was pain, it was tearing me to pieces, shredding my soul. I felt like an injured wild animal, I needed to hide, I needed to be alone. So I ran til there was not enough air to fill my lungs, til my body collapsed. I could feel myself crashing to the ground, I did not care. I wished only for death, I wished for the darkness, I wished life would leave me alone.

When I reopened my eyes, I could feel the pain in my body. I knew I had fallen, but I was not aware that I had fallen such a long way down. I stood there looking up at the steep cliff in front of me, wondering how it was that I was still alive. My leg had taken most of the impact, but was still functional. I could walk, but I had no idea how I was going to get out of this valley with the walls being as steep as they were. The walls were covered in moss and every time I would climb a few feet, I would slide back down a few feet. I tried and tried and tried. I would need much more strength than I had to get out of this.

So I sat, and I cried. I cried from the depths of my soul, for my Mother, for myself, for my Father. I cried til I felt sure I would drown, from my tears filling the valley. I cried all through the night. Then as the sun was making clear its intent to shine, I heard my Mothers voice. I turned sharply to see a wisp of luminance in the pre dawn dinginess.

"My child, my daughter, I am here. I am with you and always will be. We are part of all things and I could not leave this place, with you in such need."

"Mother?" I tried to say as my throat choked out my words.

"Yes, now is not a time for talking, we have to get you out of this situation. Do you remember in those caves, you became the animal which lives inside of you?"

"Yes, but how are you............"

"That does not matter now, we do not have time to discuss this, you must listen to me, for I will be gone in a moment. You must will the animal within you to appear. Feel your fear, stop trying to be brave, allow your instincts to once again become wild, do not think of yourself as human, feel the energy of all that is around, desire with all your heart to be that which you are. Be the part of you that is from this planet, merge with all that surrounds you. Try now, try hard."

I closed my eyes, and tried to focus on the smells around me. The deep musky smell of the night air that still clung to the moss. The earth and the dew on the ferns. I could smell the sweet scents of the flowers above as a gentle wind started to stir in the sun's light. I forgot about my hands and my feet, I forgot that I had long auburn hair, and green eyes, I forgot that my Mother was my Mother, and my Father was my Father. I opened myself to the earth, to feel her heartbeat, then I opened myself to the stars, to those ever watchful points of light, who only dare to allow us to see them at night. I opened myself to the universe and all the beings that exist here, I saw it all as if it lived in my own heart. In that second I felt myself expand to beyond the edges of the universe and contract as fast as I had expanded. In a fraction of the time it takes to breath one breath, I absorbed the whole of the universe, and then I fell silent.

Upon opening my eyes this time, the world shimmered and danced. All of life had a glow that moved in unison, dancing with one another. It was wave after wave of light, interwoven so intricately, you could not see where one thread started and another ended. The rocks knew the moss grew upon it, and the moss knew the flowers grew just above. All things were beings of light, and constantly flowed in and out of each other, carrying pieces of this and that back to the self. Nothing stood still, it was all vibrating light.

I turned, very excited, wanting to share this with my Mother, but she was gone. As I looked around me, I could feel the difference in my body, I felt strong, and alive. I could sense things I had never sensed before. I looked down and my feet had been replaced with paws. I was the giant cat.

I wasted no time, I wanted out of the valley. I jumped but fell. I tried again. I seemed to have plenty of strength but no coordination. I then realized, I could not be in this body and use it like I was walking upright. The power of this body, comes from walking on all fours, it has a very different center of gravity. So I tried to get out of my thinking mind, and allow the part of me that just knows, to operate my cat body. With one powerful lunge, I was out of the valley. I started back towards the sisterhood. I was able to cover so much ground so quickly. This was like no experience I've ever had. This cat body did not think or plan, it moved through energy, everything was a vibrational experience. The scent of a bird flying above came to it as a vibration layed out as an image. The sound of the distant waterfall, fell upon its ears and its thirst was automatically triggered. As we approached the waterfall, it looked just like the image that had been created in the great cats mind. How was that image created when I had never seen that waterfall before? Every single detail, every rock, every plant. Before we approached, the cat quieted its energy, to use its senses fully. Every detail of every bird, rock and flower was in the energetic image before my eyes. I had to wonder why we as people did not see this way? Life would be so much more accurate. If words were seen as energetic imprints, there would be no misunderstandings. We would never have to worry about lies, or deceptions. The image would relay the true intent of the words used.

The longer I was in this body, the more I was starting to understand what I was seeing. Each species seemed to have the same pattern of energy, but each individual within in that species had a pattern that over layed the species pattern. I was soon able to identify, individual birds within a flock, different ferns within the same group, and individual water drops that flowed together to make a river.

If something was hurt or damaged, there was a disturbance in the flow of energy. Over there was a great tree, one of the lower branches was partially severed, so that most of the branch was laying on the ground. A small piece was still attached to the tree but the branch was dying. As I looked at the tree through the cats eyes, I could see what looked like an echo of the branch when it was still attached to the tree. Where the branch had broken off, a flow of thick energy was reaching and moving, like it was trying to help the broken branch back to the tree. The tree seemed to be aware and conscious, and trying to help itself.

Indeed the more I understood this body, the more I was part of everything around me, I could not experience myself without experiencing everything else. I knew them and they knew me, if I needed help they would offer. When they looked at me, they did not see the cat, they saw a light being. They did not see who I knew myself to be, they saw a being that pulses with light and motion.

It was then that a true understanding came to my consciousness. Energy, all this light and vibration that I was perceiving around me was not just what animated the world, it was a language. The energy of one being spoke to the energy of another. No words were exchanged in this conversation, so understanding was not necessary. Knowing is what took place here. I knew what the ferns experienced. The flowers knew what I experienced. A true pure language, where nothing has to be described, for I experience it the same, as The One having the experience.

As I move through the energy fields of all things around me, I instantly know them and they instantly know me as the truth that we all are. The exchange of information is immediately integrated into my consciousness, as though I am The One having the experience. Misinterpretation does not happen in the absence of separation.

As I arrived back at the sisterhood, I stopped just outside the courtyard. I didn't want to go back there, I knew my Mothers body was there. I could not bare to see her empty shell. She was no longer in that body. How do you convince yourself that, the image you have known all your life as your Mother, is not really your Mother?

"Now you know the truth, this is why we did not come for you." I heard The One's voice in the back of my head, like an echo. The One was standing beside me, how did I not feel her approach, I was still in the cat body. I did not sense her. She was something that I did not yet understand. I leaned towards her.

"We knew where you were, and we also knew, you would acquire skills in removing yourself from the obstacles placed before you. The One thing we did not expect was your Mother to still be there to help you. She is much stronger than we thought. I am very pleased to see you found the connection to true power, while you were in the valley. By using the word "power" I do not mean this cat body you are in. I am talking about your tears.

Do you know what tears are?" she asked with uncommon tenderness in her voice.

I did not want to think of tears now. I connected tears with pain, not power. I lowered my head and shook my shoulders.

"Tears are our connection to the seas. If you have ever tasted a tear, you will taste the salt that lies within the tear itself. The salt in your tears are tiny crystals of light. Your tears connect you directly with the power that lies in all oceans here on this planet. The seas here represent the sea of consciousness that this universe floats in. Salt is a crystalline structure designed to heal damaged energy flows. When you cry out from the depths of your pain, you are calling on all the strength and power that consciousness has to offer you. Pain comes from our attachment to non truths. Salt will carry those distorted energies from your body, allowing you to find a new truth. Just as nothing can resist the constantness of the sea for long, tears bring a wave of change with them as well. You must change back to your common body now, go rest. We will discuss many things tomorrow. We will also be honoring your Mother. Word has been sent to your Father. Go now, rest. "

The morning had crept upon me. I did not move, instead I lay still and thought. I felt like I had aged half a lifetime in the short while I had been here with the sisterhood. I knew The One had answers and I had a lot of questions. I knew there were things that my parents had not told me. I knew life was different than I had be allowed to believe. I was ready now. I was ready to know what the world really was. I arose, got dressed, and prepared myself for what I was about to learn. I understood, things would be different from this moment on, and that I was part of that difference, for I would no longer be the person I knew. I had the choice to fight it or to flow with it. I knew well enough that I myself could not force the flow of the river to change, so I had to learn to navigate its waters.

I walked slowly and purposefully toward the temple, I knew The One was in there waiting for me. Truth, was there waiting for me. I was afraid, but the need to know overruled my fear. There is no fear worse than the fear of death, and I now knew, that death is not real. So I knew, no fear is real. I pushed back the temple doors, and in flooded the light. The One sat in the farthest corner, there is a small opening there, overlooking all of the land. In midsummer the light of the sun, comes forth, illuminating the whole temple, setting in motion the energy that turns the wheel of time on this planet.

I sat directly across from her, leaning up against the cool strength of the temple walls. Looking out over the land, was mesmerizing. There was a flow that happened there that did not happen inside me. The land held a knowing, which I did not possess.

"I am going to tell you a story, it is the story of how this earth is now. It is the story of who you are. It is the story of what is to come. Let me tell the whole story before you speak. I will answer all your questions, but sometimes, if you wait, questions answer themselves. We came to this place from there, the place known as the Belt of Orion. It is a grouping of worlds that have very different cultures and understandings. Our world did not readily conform to the will of the Counsel of Worlds. So when the light of our planet started to dim, no help came from the counsel. We were not welcomed into the arms of our sister worlds. So we left, we left to find a new world to call home. The population was divided and we went in many directions. Some of us found another home planet and some of us did not. Here on this planet we were able to make a new life for ourselves.

In the beginning the planet was not settled. It would crack and swallow mountains whole, then vomit up the remains in other places as rivers of red lava that would set fire to the little water that had formed. It was a hot place. Had we been of your body, no one would have survived. The air was not breathable, there was no food. It was desolate, but not much worse than the home we left.

We the sisterhood, and a few others, knew the ways of the universe and how to work with the energies that could mould the land, cool the planet and let the water condense. With cooperation with the planet, we came to an agreement, we went to work to create a world that could be inhabited. We would help her stabilize in return for residency. The lands stopped cracking and falling, fire stopped falling from the sky, the mountains stopped moving, and over time more and more water came to the surface, bringing rich nutrients from the belly of the earth.

When the earth had settled enough we found the spot you call home, and created a life for ourselves. At first we did not realize that we would not be able to recreate ourselves and grow our population. We did not understand that, being able to birth our children was a gift only our home world supported. Here we quickly learned, in this place we would live and die. The energy was too dense to allow us to create new life from our being.

We began to feel it would have been better to stay on our own planet, to die in our own space. To go through all this, to come to this place only to find we could no longer create. Creation is what we are, but that was taken from us here. It was a very dark hour when the Ancient Ones reached out to the others of our kind for knowledge, for guidance as to how this life ending problem could be changed. Their plea was answered in a memory from our home worlds. We were to use our power of creation, to construct chambers, deep in the belly of this mountain. Planets, just as the beings that live on them, have their place of creation. The place where they create themselves from. Here in our bodies, it is at our chest, the Others have the point where the cord is attached to their Mother, all things have that point of creation. That point of creation is what allows structure to enter into time.

When we came to this mountain, we could feel how time is distorted, it is not as stable as the planet was. It was still fluctuating. It took a great deal

33

of searching, but we found the right stones, and the right crystalline structures. We thinned the walls to the exact frequency that was needed. Then we started trying to create life.

We realized very quickly that the vibrations that were placed in the hollow stones were only vibrating one way. It was was pushing outwards all the energy we gave it. We are not solely external beings. we had to find a place that would reverberate the vibrational pattern back into the chambers so there was a constant pattern of energy expanding and contracting at the same time. That is how we came to the present location of the chambers. There were many many failures. Many parts of ourselves were lost. But as we continued to try, we found that within the vein of time we were able to create a stable frequency. The more stable the frequency became, the more encouraging were our results. Then one day, from the two energies in the chamber, a third formed. That third energy stabilized and our first child was born.

Instead of celebration, we were concerned. This child was not like us. The body was denser more solid, light did not emanate from it the way it did from us. It was different, but we loved it with all our might. We continued to try and create ourselves in the chambers, but we were never able to succeed in creating our life forms here the way we created them on our home planet.

Then one day, the ships came, the Counsel of Worlds came to this planet. Because of the position of the planet and the stability we had been able to co create, it had come to the attention of the counsel. Many of the worlds in this universe and others were in a state of decay. The Counsel had decided that this earth was the best choice for seeding. We were given the choice to become planetary guardians or to leave.

We had been here so long, to leave would devastate us. So we chose to stay. We were told that this world was to become a universal library. A library of living species. Many of the worlds that were in a state of decay would bring species here in hopes that they would thrive and they could return at a later date to claim them and re populate their planet. Some worlds would have only one species, other worlds would bring many. It was our job to watch over the species and to make sure they grew, to provide for their needs, but not to interfere with the direction that their growth took them. It was a matter of allowing their creation to evolve naturally.

You see, all planets have a delicate balance of energy that keeps them stable. The species that live on the surface of the planet are as important as the mountains that run like spines across a continent. If the guardians of the planet do not care about the balance, at some point the balance will tip and the planet will start to destabilize. When there are many stones piled on top of each other, it only takes removing the wrong one, to bring the whole pile down. Since we had established communication with the planet in the process of stabilization, we were able to work with her to create a balance of species.

And so the ships arrived with the species. The world was seeded, and life started to grow everywhere. There were species of green that were anchored to the earth, and animals that walked upon it. Great beings that flew in the air, and sang out with their voices upon the wind. It was truly glorious. Life was thriving. As time passed it became a problem to keep the beasts apart from us. Lives were lost and beasts were killed. It was decided that we would retreat to the island and place a protective energy shield between us and them. We could pass through it and cross the land bridge to get to the birthing chambers when we needed too.

A long time passed on the island and the ancient ones became very weak. They came to the realization that they could not live in the dense energy of this planet. Another place would have to be found, where the energy is lighter and they could be off the surface where the energy is the heaviest. So we built the temples here, at the top of this mountain. But it was too late for the old ones, they were too weak, they did not recover and eventually they left us.

We the sisterhood are all that is left of the original people. We came here when we were very young, and it is here we will die. This mountain, and the chambers below are located in the energy of the vein of time, so we can go on for a very long time yet, but we cannot leave this mountain, or we too, shall move beyond the veil of this world. We are coming to the point in the story now, where there is a severing. In the history of all worlds, there is a point where, a decision is made that will create not just one world but two worlds within one world, at that is the beginning of the world that now is.

The earth was thriving, many species roamed the earth and all but a few, were doing well. We had learned how to create life in our own people. Everything appeared to be well. Life was peaceful. Then the Warriors came. The Warriors came from another star system, their worlds have been at war with one another for a very long time. They do not know anything other than war. Life for them is about power, not creation. They knew earth was thriving and they thought they could come here and take what they needed. They came and took many species that did not belong to them. This angered the Counsel.

It was decided by the Counsel that all species must contain a coding system that allows only the original donating planet to claim their species. And so that started the process of coding the species. We had to work backwards with each species. The coding sequence had to start here with this planet. All species carried the code for Earth. Then they carried a code that stated whether they walked, flew or swam. Whether they had fur or scales. Finally each species was coded with the energetic sequence of their home planet. The coding allowed an immaculate identification process to protect everyone's interest, but it also did something else. Species that were similar, started to breed, and create different species. We did not interfere, for that was our agreement with the counsel.

We had been so occupied with the coding process, we hadn't noticed that the warriors had infected some of the females of the Others with their essence. Later when the children were born, we thought nothing of it. We thought because they would be raised here with us, that they would be as we were, but this was not to be.

The violent nature of the warrior was strong with these children. We offered them all that we had. We educated them in our ways. We taught them how to work with the species. We raised them as we raised our own. Nothing seemed to be enough. They had all they could ever need, but that was not what they wanted. They wanted to change the coding on the species so they could control them. They wanted to separate the people into groups and force them to do specific types of work. They had a need to control all they touched.

In your home, there is a library of knowledge that you are not aware of. It is instructions how to work with time on this planet, how to fluctuate it so that you can use it to travel from world to world. Having this knowledge allows you to bypass, the known laws of earth and to exist outside of them. This was the only knowledge they were not allowed to have. It was felt that if they could understand these instructions and use them, they would be able to devastate other worlds, and devastate this one in the process. So they were forbidden access to your home. But they refused to listen.

Many attempts were made to access the knowledge. Some were partially successful, but their bodies are not energetically compatible with the knowledge to complete the process. That is the reason, this mountain, has been kept hidden from them. They have the knowledge that there are birthing chambers, but they do not know where they are. If they were ever to discover the chambers, they could destroy this world and everything in it. The chambers would alter their energy enough that they may be able to attain their goals.

Because of the disrespect for our civilization and the repeated attempts to steal the knowledge, we could no longer tolerate their presence. An entire world was at risk, because of a small group of others, and their insatiable need for power. The decision was made to banish them from the protective shield. In the end they promised to abide by our laws, but what was decided could not be rescinded, so we sent them off to survive amongst the wild species, in a harsh and unpredictable world.

We mourned the loss of them, we did not think they could survive, but they did. They turned to killing other species for food and shelter. Their number grew over time and the knowledge we had given them was used to create their own structures. In a land far toward the rising sun, they now live and thrive. They are strong in numbers and have much resources to make them powerful. There have been wars among their people but in the last while a woman has risen to unite them, a woman that was born here in Mu. She is The One with the most knowledge, and she has a good understanding of energy. Although they look like you, they are not like you. At their core, they seek to possess that which in not theirs to possess. They seek to destroy that which they cannot conquer, and they seek revenge on Mu for being banished.

The time has come for them to try to take over this land, and your people. This is why you were created in the chambers. You were created with the knowing that it would be for you to stop them. You have more knowledge and understanding of energy than your Mother did. You were created stronger than your parents. You were created to understand how they think, so that you can defend the planet and our agreements with the Counsel. In the time to come, many of the species will be harvested. Beings will come from their home planets to retrieve their property. You must honor this agreement. We will train you in all that we know. It is why your Mother brought you here earlier than planned. She felt something was about to happen and the only way she could guarantee your safety, was to bring you here. She gave her life to save her people. It is your turn now to do what you must, to save your people. "

My head hurt. This other race of people, I had never heard of them, Father had not mentioned them, not once. Why, if I am to defend my people, why would he not tell me? I knew eventually ships would come to collect the species, but why did The One make it feel as if, something horrid would occur if the species were not here to collect? So many questions, but no idea where to start. How could I ask what I needed to know, in a way that would make sense? I decided just to start asking and see where it took me.

I took a deep breath and looked up. The One was gone. Where did she go? I did not see her leave? I have questions, she said she would answer them. Why did she leave now? I took another deep breath and tried to compose myself. I was not ready for the task before me. I did not want to be the bearer of this burden.

Chapter Four

Outside the sisterhood was gathering to honor my Mother. There, her body lay under a veil of flowers. Butterflies were flitting all about just above her. I was in such pain over the loss of my Mother but the scene where she lay was so peaceful, almost hopeful. Trying to determine what the truth was at that moment, was very difficult. I was not sure what life was trying to tell me. My insides were all tied up in knots but the world around me seemed to rejoice in the fact that my Mother had existed. It was more of a celebration and a grand send off, than a painful memory. I could feel that familiar feeling coming up in me again, that feeling that I wanted to run. But I chose not to. It would not be respectful of the honorable position she held within the sisterhood.

Throughout the day, songs were sung, and stories were told, not only of my Mother but of legends far past. Legends of how we came to be who we were. The stories were interwoven with the songs, to create a great web of beingness and to tell of my Mothers place within it. My thoughts were with my Father. He must be in such pain. Did he know we were celebrating her? I wished he could be here, but I knew it was not possible.

We danced and sang long into the night, and when it was over, and everyone else had gone to bed, the low flames of the fire still danced to celebrate my Mother. I heard a prayer dance into my thoughts,

Mother of time
be here unto me
Passages of mind
be clear unto me
With love and grace
no fear you shall see
Heart to heart
shall never be without thee.

I did not know where it came from. I could feel it as much as hear it and from that moment on, I felt a peace settle into me. I sat, mesmerized by the fire, held by its enchanting glow into the night. I could feel the love of my Mother, gently holding me, cradling my emotions. She was preparing me for the next step in my life. I knew that my childhood was over and I was to stand on my own now. With her love surrounding me like a protective blanket I steadied myself to embrace my future.

The clear blue indigo skies, gave shape to the mountains as I opened my eyes. Infrequent soft white clouds danced around one of the peaks in the distance. The birds sang and trees strained to get a little closer to the sun. The world was vibrantly alive. I felt so much better than I had expected to. I was aware of my Mothers passing, but it was more like a memory than the gash through my soul that I had felt the day before. My place in time had shifted.

My training would start in earnest now. It would be a constant seesaw between learning and testing. I knew The One would want to be sure of my understanding of new skills. She always spoke of the future as if it had already happened. That was a little hard to understand.

The One had a powerful presence, but I felt safe within it. In my struggle to understand her, I knew there was no way I could, at least not yet. I had wasted so much time trying to figure something out that was not important. I had learned this valuable lesson, it is not for me to know everything about The One. That is just not possible. So I decided to see where not knowing would take me. To not fight so hard, perhaps it is a possibility that she knows something I do not. So I will place one foot in front of the other and try to learn what it is the sisterhood will teach me. With that thought The One appeared and motioned for me to stand. I stood and followed her to the smaller temple just down the hill. Whenever I entered one of the temples here, the feeling was not that of going into a building. It was more the feeling of entering a different world, a world that existed in its own time, that is what I felt in the temples. Going from one temple to another was very disorienting, and had caused me at times to misstep and stumble.

"This is the Temple of the moon. It exists within the time of the soul. It deals with all energies that command water. It calls to the emotions, and will grant visions of what is to come. Memories are the domain of the moon. Who you have been in other times and who you are to become. For your lives happen along the same thread of time, and you can travel back and forth between them. When you learn to do this you can bring knowledge from one life to another. You will not be granted this privilege until you understand what your lives are. Many other abilities stem from these understandings, but you will learn those as you go."

With that she turned and walked out, again motioning for me to follow her. We went back up the hill to the main temple and entered there.

"This is the temple of the Sun. It commands the energies of fire, structure and movement. The sun is the balance for the moon. The sun represents that which can be seen, what is illuminated and that which is predictable. Men are of the sun, women are of the moon. The sun allows you to see the power of things, and how the use of that power will change structure. The light of the sun activates the energy that travels through the web of life on this planet. The energy of the moon, holds the memory of the web intact, so that the sun's energy has somewhere to travel. Do you understand?"

I nodded my head.

"Good, This is what I want you to do today. I want you to go back and forth between the two places. In the temple of the moon, I want you to create a memory, then in the temple of the sun I want you to move that memory forward. Then I want you to see the web of life that exists because of your memory and destroy a piece, go back to the temple of the sun and see how the energy is affected if that one part is removed from its place. Alright?"

I really wasn't sure what she was saying, but I didn't want her to think I didn't understand. So I repeated back to her, what I thought she was saying.

"You want me to create a memory. Does that mean I have to create a story that is not in the present time?"

"You could think of it that way. Yes."

"Then you want me to take the creation point of that story and expand it through the web of life to the present point. This way I can see how following a certain path, creates a certain story. Then you want me to change something along the way, so that the story has a different outcome than previously. And you want me to do that while going back and forth between the two temples. Is that right?" I gave her my sideways look, that always conveyed curiosity contained within acknowledgment.

"Yes, that is what I want you to do." She acknowledged my look. That pleased me.

Immediately I went to the Temple of the Moon to start creating memories. I sat near the dark pool of water. The mystery of this pool had captivated me since I had arrived. You could stare into the black bottom for a long time and nothing would happen. Other times you would stare for a short time and the water would start to stir. Tiny ripples would dance across the surface of the water or little whirlpools would spiral their way downwards. The pool was unpredictable. I enjoyed it immensely.

As I sat I wondered how The One expected me to create a memory. I already had my memories, they were already created. I can not undo what is done. As I stared into the blackness of the pool, the water stirred. I kept my focus, I just kept thinking, create a memory, create a memory. Suddenly I was back home, I could hear my parents talking. My Father was concerned that my Mother wanted to take me for training earlier than expected. My Father was protesting, my Mother told him it was necessary and he would understand later.

I wanted to know what would happen if I ran away and I hadn't allowed my Mother to take me to The One. So I ran, I ran to the farthest point of the land I could find. I hid and I waited. Time was different in my imagining, it passed much faster. The next thing I knew I was back standing in the main courtyard of my home, everyone there was dead. I was horrified as I looked around, I was starting to panic. A short distance away a woman stood with her back to me, she had long dark hair and she seemed to be The One giving orders, I knew she had done this and I wanted to see her face, but time pulled me, fast and hard, I was back in the temple of the moon.

Part of me wanted to get angry, to rage, to react to what I had just seen, but my directions were to get to the temple of the sun now, and try to change it. I ran as fast as I could to the other temple, I didn't want to lose what I was seeing or what I was feeling. The images of everyone I knew laying dead, horrified me. I couldn't seem to move anything, one image was stuck in my head.

In the temple of the sun, there was a deep pit, walled in by smooth cut white stones. In the belly of the pit, was a fire with great flames. The flames reached towards the sky like they were the sun itself. The energy here was not a calm energy, it was active, almost to the point of agitated. I climbed down into the pit and sat back from the flames, I could not take the heat. I focused on one spot, the flame was going from orange to red to purple. It was hypnotic, as I allowed it to pull me in deeper and deeper. I could hear a voice, I was not familiar with this voice, it was a woman, and she sounded like she was commanding someone. Everything was black , but then changed in a instant to brilliant yellow. As I adjusted my eyes, I could see I was back in the courtyard of my birth. My Mother and Father were standing there, the woman with the long black hair is the voice I heard, she was commanding my Father to give her control of Mu.

I ran over to my Father trying to warn him, what was about to happen, but they could not see me and they could not hear me. I was frantic, I had to stop this. But how? The One said to pull a piece out of the web. What did she mean? How can I pull a piece out of the web? I tried yelling and screaming. I tried to physically move this evil woman. Nothing worked, I was there, and yet I wasn't. I had to watch the whole thing play out. I watched my parents be struck down, and then the orders were given to kill everyone else. It was over, I had failed.

I went back and forth like this, all day. I tried everything I could think of, and I kept failing. I kept seeing the same scenario over and over again, til it ceased to be real. I was having a hard time connecting to what was right in front of me, it wasn't real. I had seen it so many times, I just didn't react to it, I couldn't change it anyway. In that instant, I felt myself being yanked from my position by what felt like a giant cord in my back. I was pulled hard and fast out of the courtyard, out beyond the land of my birth, out beyond the boundaries of the planet, it kept pulling me and pulling me til I was in complete darkness. There I was, in nothingness. No sound, no light. I tried to look at my hands but there was only darkness.

"What do you fear most?" a voice pierced the silence.

I snapped my head around to see where it was coming from, but it seemed to be coming from everywhere.

"What do you fear most?" it repeated.

I don't know, I responded. Who are you? What do you want? Where am I? I was scared, but I didn't want whatever it was to know that.

"I want to know what it is you fear most? Then I will tell you where you are."

"I don't know what I am afraid of, nothing, really." I was determined to be brave.

The darkness resounded in laughter. "You are really going to try and be brave right now? You have nothing to fear in this place, I am you, I am the part of you that you battle and fight the most. I am your fear."

What is that supposed to mean? My fear is in me, not what this place is.

"Fear is a place, a place where everyone goes. It is a dark place. A place of unknowing. A place of insecurity, a place where you don't think you have any control. You can get lost in fear and never find your way home if you do not learn how to find the path out. Right now you are afraid, very very afraid, and the more afraid you become, the deeper into the darkness you go. There is only one thing that can take you from here to the web of light."

"What is it?" I asked, not really expecting a response.

"Do you understand that you cannot have two experiences at the same time? You cannot feel two things at the same time. You may look at many things in front of you, but you only perceive one thing at a time. What do all these statements have in common?"

I rethought everything I had just heard, the only common thread was, Time and oneness.

"Time and oneness are the common thread here."

"Ah, yes, you are right." What is time?"

I knew the answer to this. " Time is the space that occurs from one event to another." I produced that answer, feeling quite proud of myself.

"Most people think that is what time is, yes. But time is an entity unto itself. Think harder. What is Time?"

I gave a few various other answers, none were right.

"You are very inventive with your answers, and have a great ability to stretch your imagination, that will help you greatly on your quest. But I will tell you what time is, and you will have to discover the rest for yourself. Time is the current of emotions, that flow through dimensional space. Without feeling there would be no time and without time you would not know reality in the manner that you do. There are ways to control time, but you cannot do that until you have mastery over your emotions. There are only two emotions in your reality, all the rest are different variations of the same thing. If you wish to change your reality, you must change time, but you cannot change time til you know how to alter what you feel. When strong emotions are felt it is like punching holes in time. This creates a slight vacuum, a pushing or a pulling. Think of it this way. You are familiar with the sea by your home. Well the sea is like time, the individual drops are the emotions that make up the sea. Can you control the sea? No, but you can jump in and displace some water. If you were to jump into the middle of the sea and the sea was absolutely still in that spot, you would create ripples. By the time those ripples met the shore, they would be huge waves. Do you understand?"

I nodded my head and continued to listen intently.

"Now if you just jumped into the waves, you would not make much of a difference. So learning how to change time is like that, you need to pick a point where the emotions are most in need of change, and you can only change them with Love. You must make a vibrational connection with what ever or whoever it is you are trying to change. Now, I want you to think loving thoughts, and see what happens"

I focused on my parents and the love I had for them, I closed my eyes and tried harder, and harder till all I could feel was love. It flowed from my heart and I breathed it back in, it permeated all my senses. At some point I stopped thinking about love and I became love. I no longer envisioned the physical appearance of my parents, all I could see was love in front of me. Then I could perceive light. With my eyes open now, all I could see was the light that stretched out in front of me. As far as I could see, the light formed what looked like spider webs. The webs were made of light. There were places where different threads came together and formed a ball of light, and from that point, many threads would lead off in different directions til there was another crossing point that created another ball of light.

It was incredibly beautiful. So much light, it was almost hard to look at. I wanted to cry, all I could feel was love. As I looked down, I realized I was no longer me, but I was a ball of light in the web. I followed the thread out from the center of my light and it led to so many other points. The points all looked the same but they were all different. I knew them not by how they looked, but by how they felt. I realized at that moment what The One had meant when she got upset with me for my rage, and how I was hurting everyone, not just myself. I could see that whatever I was feeling would travel along the web to the intersecting points of light. My emotions would then continue along all the threads that expanded outward from that ball of light.

I remembered being a child and playing for hours with spider webs. I would try to just touch one far corner and not have the whole web shake. I never succeeded. That one touch would always set off a chain reaction. I learned that the ability of the web to move with the smallest touch, is what allowed the spider to survive. The tiniest vibration alerted the spider to a potential meal. The flexibility in the web allowed it to move with the breeze and hold so many raindrops after a rain.

If we were all connected by these webs of light, and the webs of light are suspended in a river of emotion, then time is created by our reaction to the events of life. If we never reacted to anything, our perception of time would cease.

"You are right. That voice was all around me again."

So, what keeps time in place? I would think that if time is created by emotion, powerful emotions would speed time up, or slow it down, what makes time feel like it is constant?

"The same thing that holds everything else to the surface of your planet. There is an energy that pushes inward towards your planet. It allows everything to stay in its place, it allows you to breathe the air, it allows the water to stay its course. Everything on your planet has its own energy and its energy is tied to everything else, so it all stays in the same place in the same time."

"So if I want to change time, all I have to do is collapse it, by deconstructing the emotional vibrations that hold it in place". I was feeling very comfortable, having a conversation with nothing.

"Yes!, Lets go back to the sea. If you wanted to change the flow of a portion of the sea, all you would have to do is put a big rock in the water. It would change the flow in that place, and leave the rest of the sea uninterrupted."

"So if I want to warn my parents of what is about to happen to them, I have to disrupt the emotions between them and their death." I was still focused on saving my parents.

"That would allow you to warn them, but not to prevent their death. Your parents at that point are at the intersection where two time lines meet, you cannot affect one without affecting the other. What you are saying would be correct if it was only your parents involved. But this moment in time, is a fated moment, that has a long lead up to it. It has many more threads attached to it, not just your parents. Do you understand?"

"Yes I think so. You mean not all moments are just moments. There is a sequencing. Moments are grouped together and the only way to affect the end is to affect the beginning."

"Exactly, the thing to remember here is, everything travels along threads, and sometimes those threads cross over one another. When they do that, it means more than one person's fate is involved in the same event. The people involved in that event have travelled together in many lives, and their paths will continue to cross long after this life is done. It is very important for you to know this, trying to affect a crossing point like this can lead to very unexpected outcomes. Have you thought about travelling beyond this point on the thread to see what happens after your parents death? There are no accidents, it may be that your parents have chosen to die."

"No, absolutely not, they would never do that. They would not leave me." With that burst of emotion, I was back in the Temple of the Sun, feeling the heat of the flames on my skin. I had to get out of there.

I left the temple as quickly as I could so as to not bring attention to my discomfort with the suggestion that my parents chose to die. That was so ridiculous. Who was that voice anyway? It did not know what it was saying.

I sat down by the stream for a time, soothing my hot skin in the cool breeze. I let myself relax into the sound of the flowing water. I had no idea what had just happened to me. Where was I? What was I really looking at? Did we really just live in a giant spider web? If we did, was there a giant spider out there? I always had more questions than answers. My Father called me the curious creature. I missed him so much right now, and I couldn't wait to go home.

The sound of the water, flowed over me, like it flowed over the rocks. I just couldn't wrap my head around what I had just learned. Life in threads, groups of moments, deconstructing time. How could any of this be useful to me? The thought that I may have the kind of life that I would have to use this stuff, did not please me. I just wanted to live my life and be happy, was that so much to ask?

I watched a little black bird with a red patch on his throat, playing in the water. He would hop from rock to rock, at times snatching something from the air. I started to pay more attention to what this little bird was doing. There seemed to be a rhythm to it. I moved closer to the rock so I could see what he was snatching in the air. All around, in the pools of water that got caught against the rocks, were insects. They were emerging from the water to take flight in the air. The bird had to time it just right so that he could catch them before the breeze caught their wings and they were off. The problem the bird had, was knowing which pool to be at, when the insects emerged. He would spend most of his time in the middle and raise his head, close his eyes and then move very quickly one way or the other. He seemed to feel which pool the bugs were emerging from.

I wondered if I could slow down time and allow the little bird to get more bugs. I focused on the bird, I let the sound of the water carry me. I was trying to separate the thread of time that the bird was on, from the thread of time the bugs were on. At one point the birds movements seemed to slow down and then speed up very quickly. When that happened I could feel the great joy in the bird, and the fear in the insects. They seemed to know the bird was waiting for them. But they didn't have much of a choice. If they stayed below the water, they would drown, above the water, they would be a meal. The bird in his joy, could feel the movement of the insects, and the rhythm they had, even if the insects were not aware of it. Once I could feel the joy the bird felt I was able to make his time move slower or faster. The key was to feel exactly as the bird felt. In a way it felt as though I was the bird. But I was the bird looking at the bird.

"That is exactly how it is done." whispered The One, she did not want to disturb the bird.

She snapped me out of my moment of being the bird, and I landed, plop, back in my body. I must have looked a little confused cause she started to laugh. The One was such a mystery to me. When I thought there was no pleasing her, I would find out I was doing the right thing.

" I am understanding this concept of time more now. But I must ask you about the web of light. It looked like a giant spider web that formed through the entire universe. I understand how lines of light that meet at a crossing point can affect both lives but why is everything strung together like that?" I asked The One as we both continued to stare at the little bird.

"Ah, you are expanding your thoughts, this is good. The web of light is just that. Millions upon millions of threads that intersect and come apart. Each one crossing over at a vital point in the development of the being who walks on that thread. Have you ever noticed that change does not often happen without the assistance of someone else? Yes you can come out here into the forest and watch the little bird and learn, but the change that prompted that came from the voice in the darkness. Did it not? The web that you speak of is the way we grow through dimensions. You were not always as you are now, and you will change over the many lives that you still have to live. Change is brought about through understanding what it is that you experience. You then apply this new understanding to your life, thereupon making different choices and piloting your life in another direction. When you understand this, the next natural step is to understand that you are The One that creates these experiences so you can learn to understand them. How do you think you send out a signal to all the necessary players in your theatre of life, so that you can create the drama of your experience? Some experiences require a large number of players so that you and they can learn their next lesson.

Every lesson you need to learn has a specific vibration. When the time is coming near for you to have this experience, your subconscious knows this and sends small signals to you. That creates a feeling in you. That feeling may make you uneasy, anxious, or even curious. That feeling in you sends out a vibration along the threads just like all the other feelings you have. When the feeling you are sending out travels along the thread and it finds someone else that is supposed to participate in your experience, that being's thread starts to vibrate at exactly the same speed as your thread. This identical vibration draws you toward each other so that the experience can take place, and both of you can learn. So the web of the universe is the same as a spiders web. Touching anywhere on a spiders web will send a vibration to the spider, alerting it that something may be caught in the web. But the spider knows the difference between the wind creating a wave in the web, or a fly vibrating with panic. The spider is tuned to the vibration of panic. It is the vibration that announces food has arrived. Specific vibrations pass specific messages. You just need to learn the language of energy. Are you understanding all this?"

I nodded my head yes. As The One was talking, I could feel her words form images in my mind. I wasn't sure if she was doing that, or I was indeed, learning the language of vibration.

"Come, you have had plenty enough for today, time for stories and rest now. If there is time later we will speak of the rest of the sisterhood and what it is we do."

That is what I had been waiting to hear. There were all these women wandering around here, but no one seemed to be doing anything.

I relaxed in the evening, looking out over the mountains, watching the suns rays weave their way through the peaks as it was on its descent. Time did seem slower now, that I was calmer. There were moments when it almost seemed to stand still. I could often feel my Mother's energy around me. I wondered if she visited Father too. It would be harvest time now. The fields would be golden, the children would be playing in the long grasses, and they would be getting ready for the Festival of the Harvest.

I waited to see if The One would be visiting me or not, but something happened and there was a gathering of the sisterhood. There were many loud whispers and hushed concerns. I knew it was something to do with me. I could have gotten close enough to hear them if I had wanted to, but, I was tired of eavesdropping just to find out something horrible was occurring in my life. I decided if I was supposed to know, then The One would tell me. I just didn't want to grow up any more than I had, at least not on this night. Tonight I wanted to remember running in the fields and playing with the other children, feeling the long grass as it brushed against my cheek. Falling into it and looking up, the grass was so long it looked like tall trees against the blue sky. I just wanted it to be the way it was before, just for tonight. And that is just the way it was.

Chapter Five

I rose before the sun was up, today I wanted to watch life unfold here on the sacred mountain. I had never really watched the sisterhood as they went through their routine. Every morning as they rose they did their prayer to the sun, but after that I had no idea what they did. Even though I had met all the sisters, I only knew of the Keeper of the Gardens and the Keeper of the Flow. I wondered if they were all keepers of something and if so, what?

So today, I would be an observer. That is, if I was not interrupted and sent on some journey somewhere. As the sun started to glow behind the distant clouds, the sisters gathered for prayers. Sitting and watching them, I could feel a pulse in the energy as they prayed. The energy was so much stronger when they came together and acted in unison. After prayers, they dispersed and returned to their homes. In a short period of time, they started to emerge, and I realized they did not have the same glow to them as when they were doing morning prayers. They seemed more, well, solid. There were times when I felt like if I touched them, my had would pass right through them, and there were times when they looked just like me. That was baffling for me.

As I sat and watched, or moved among them, I realized they did not speak much during the day, they went about their business, nodding as they passed one another. It was more common for them to converse with The One, than with each other. The other curiosity I noticed, is each one would visit the Temples of the Sun and Moon, then to the Temples that sat in the west and the east. Each sister followed the same pattern but at a different time of day. Here there was a rhythm within a rhythm. Each sisters pattern was part of the larger pattern of all the sisters. They never rushed, nor did they slow themselves. They moved at a constant speed, usually with their head in a partial bow. Low enough to see the ground but high enough to see each other. After watching them for most of the day, I felt as if they walked the same steps in the same pattern each day as the sun rose and fell. Moving rocks, tending gardens, adjusting the flow of water, maintaining the fires. It all looked so normal, but it was performed with ritualistic understanding.

As night fell, we all gathered in the center of the courtyard. This was the time for conversation and the telling of stories. This was when the sisters would relax and enjoy themselves, this is when laughter could be heard echoing through the valleys. Night brought the cover of darkness, under which I had the opportunity to experience the personality of the sisters.

I continued to watch them and they were very different again, spending time relaxing, sharing stories from their day, remembering stories and getting into lively conversations about how to improve the energy of things. There was a hint of competition in the air, as though the challenge to do their daily routine in a more efficient way, was always in the offing. Just how far could they push themselves, and still keep life balanced.

The mood was a happy one, as it usually was. There seemed to be no concern of the passing of time here on this mountain. In fact time was never mentioned. There was never the thought, we have to get this done before sundown, or we can't do that til tomorrow. I had never realized that so profoundly as I did now. There was no concept of time here. Is that why none of the sisterhood ever died? What was this time thing all about anyway? It felt as though all my teachings are about time. I just did not see the importance of time. How is time relevant in anything?

"Ask someone who has run out of time, if it is relevant." The One's voice flowed over me like sand running through my fingers. Her voice felt like a warm caress at times. Like all you ever needed was to hear her speak and life itself would be fulfilled. I turned to look at her and started to say I did not understand. She looked back at me with a knowing gaze.

"Time is wasted on the young, for you have not yet lived enough to understand the power of time. Time is one of the great paradoxes of the universe, cause it is not a constant. Time does not belong to all planet or places. There are planets that do not have time. Then there are planets that come and go so swiftly, they never get old enough to know time. You can perceive time as both your friend and your enemy, but it is neither. You give time great power over you, but it has none. Time is what you pray for, but it cannot be given. Time is the greatest illusion of all. For time is an individual construct of ones own mind. From the point at which you enter this reality, you are spoken to as if time is your master, and you will spend the rest of your life, trying to overthrow it. Then when you are old, and time has been stolen from you, you will wish, you hadn't wasted so much of it."

I listened intently as she spoke. Sometimes she would take long pauses between thoughts as though she was waiting for the energy to formulate into words, so she could speak again. This was one of those moments.

" Here on this planet, time is held in place by gravity, the energy that keeps your feet on the ground. But gravity is always in a state of flux, so time is never truly consistent. You have days when you feel like you could fly, and those days seem to fly by. Then there are the days when you are so heavy you cannot move, and those days drag on. You are altering time, because you are altering you personal gravity. As you may have guessed, gravity is directly affected by time and time affected by emotion, what you are feeling individually and in combination with everyone else, creates the only constant that gravity will know. Gravity is dependent on a balance of emotions. If everyone was joyously happy on the same day, it would effect gravity tremendously, to the point, where you could start floating about in the air. The reverse is true also, if everyone was to feel devastated on the same day, the pressure and weight of gravity could force you to the ground."

With that there was another long pause. I sat and waited respectfully, I knew this was important.

"The most important thing about time is it can only exist in this moment. There is no such thing as time in the past, nor does time exist in the future. Time is created with every breath you take, every thought you have. This is why you literally leave a thread behind you that is a collection of moments in your life. If you did not have this, you would not be able to think of what you did two moments ago. So you track time with thoughts and emotions together. If you try to think of a time when you just had thoughts with no emotions, or emotions with no thought, you will never remember it, because it is not tracked on your thread. It takes thought and feeling together to generate the energy of creation. And that energy becomes a dot of light on your thread of continuity, because thought and feeling together create potential. Potential is what the universe is made of. Creative potential is how all of life functions. So as you create time through feeling, the direction that time goes in can be manipulated with thought. Thoughts and feelings are polar opposites, but you can consciously bring them together to form a spiralling energy, causing time to stand still." She continued, "Do you know what makes people age?"

I shook my head, I did not understand aging at all. I had seen people grow old, but the people that we watched over, the Others, grew old much faster than my kind, so I had no understanding of how aging would affect me yet.

"Aging happens when there is a resistance to time. Regrets of time, wishing time away, desire for more time. It has always fascinated me how the Others have created a concept of time that does not exist. If they truly understood that time is something they created themselves and they could manipulate for themselves, they would not behave as though it existed outside of themselves. They seem to see time as a controlling factor in their lives, and the truth of the universe is time does not exist if you do not believe in it. For it to exist you must construct it, and to construct it, you must believe in it. Do you understand what I am saying?"

I nodded my head so heartily, I banged my chin on my chest. This made The One smile a grand smile.

"We the sisterhood exist outside of time. We understand what time is, but we are not bound to it. The beings on this planet operate within the boundaries of time, but the planet herself does not. The spinning light at

51

the center of the planet is timeless, and there are places on the planet in which it is easier to access the timeless energy of the spinning light. This mountain top is one of those places. From here you can pass through the center of the planet and come out on the other side. There are many places on this planet like this, but not all vibrate in the same sequence. Some vibrate in a manner where time past can be accessed. And there are places where the time to come can be accessed. The planet is very aware of the creation of her potential, so for her, she is already there, all you have to do is find the right thread to experience that. Although your eyes cannot see it at this point, there are points of light all over the planet, they vibrate in different sequences, each sequence can take you to a different place. All the sequences vibrate outside of time. To see them, you must train yourself to let go of time. Once you can identify the sequencing, you can alter your own vibration to match, then choose to travel on, in or through the light of the planet. Tomorrow, I want you to spend the day becoming aware of how many thoughts you have that are in some way attached to the passing of time. Even though you don't think you have a concept of time, you do. I want you to be aware of that. Understand?"

I nodded my head and I started to speak, but she got up and left. I remembered thinking when I first got here, that she was a very rude person. She would walk away from me, halfway through a conversation, and never excuse herself. I was now starting to understand, that, because of my constant need to know, she was preventing me from wasting her time and mine. Wow, there it was right there, my construct of time. I was realizing, that before I went through an experience, my questions were only speculation. Answering speculation, was not something she was willing to do. She wanted to deal with real questions that resulted directly from experience. I was very good at discoloring reality with perception.

I was getting tired, so I wandered off to the world of dreams, with great anticipation of applying myself to my new task in the morning.

My dreams were very bright and colorful but I have no memory of any particular images. I did wake up with a sense of busyness in the dream. I was more tired upon waking than I had been when I went to sleep. I could only believe that I had been active all through the night. As I rolled over in my bed, I could feel a very warm breeze, much warmer than usual. I loved the way the air danced over my skin. Playing upon the surface, tugging gently at me to rise. Catching a few strands of my hair and lifting them upwards, as the top of my head tickled due to the movement. The warm air moved and played within the space, bringing to life anything that was light enough to dance. The interplay between the seen and the unseen was magical. For a time, that which did not have life was alive, and experienced movement in a dance of color and flow.

I needed to get up, the day was moving along and I was not part of it yet.

So I rose and got dressed. As I was getting ready to go out, I thought about the idea of NEEDING to get up. Why did I NEED to get up? I followed the thought to being another time construct. There was truly only one need for me to get up, the idea that I would run out of time in the day, that I would miss the day, if I did not get up. I then wondered if all needs were based on time constraints? How did we know we NEEDED something based on time. If we need something based on time, we must be using the concept of time to create a limiting perception between ourselves and something else? As I continued to follow my thoughts about time as a boundary, I could see that we used time as a form of structure. A physical thing to confine us within boundaries. I don't have the time, not now, later would be better. So many statements were running through my head, most of them I had heard from my parents. I even remembered The One saying, "If there is time later.............."

Time is a self imposed imaginary boundary, most often used as an excuse to not use the time we have. I was discovering that time was not used to create a flow to our lives, but instead it was used to erect a bunch of walls meant to separate one event from another. Time had nothing to do with flow. We used time to stop flow. We used time as a memory marker, so we could hold on to the moments that had some kind of significance in our life, whether those moments were happy or painful. I wondered if we were to let go of our perception of time, if all the memories we had would come flooding into us, or if we they would pass through us. Was our concept of time something we created so that we could end these lives and move on to others? From the point we are born we entertain the concept that we only have so much time. The less time we think we have, the faster time moves. How is it that we actually believe time to be something that stops us when we are The Ones who create the concept of time. All day long I thought and thought about time, till I felt like I was just going around and around on the same thought.

Time doesn't exist, unless we create it. The second we stop believing in time, it collapses. Aha, that is how Mother used to be everywhere at once. At least that is how it felt. No matter how far away I was, she would show up if I was doing something I should not have been doing, which I was most of the time.

But how do you let go of time? How do you collapse it to be where you want to be?

I had pondered so long, I needed a nap. The part of me that thought, hurt from so much thinking. So I lay down in the sweet grasses overlooking a lush green valley below. I watched the tall trees sway in the breeze and the birds rise and dive, on upward swirling energy. It all had a rhythm, it all acted independently of each other, but in absolute flow with one another.

The questions were endless as I let the scent of the sweet grass carry my soul to another place, another time. I left the constraints of my body behind. I floated out, out beyond the mountains and toward the sea. I could see the beings in the sea move and play, they looked like great golden energies in the blue green water. The mystery of the sea drew me into it. It is a place where I cannot go.

With that thought I descended at a rapid pace, I felt as though I would crash into the waves and be devoured by one of the creatures. I waited for the impact, but never felt it. From behind closed eyes, I could determine the light had faded some. I opened my eyes to discover I was well below the surface of the water. The light of the sun filtered through, catching the movements of the beings that lived here.

They moved in an undulating manner, moving their bodies back and forth in a way that mimicked the waves themselves. Some of them had the same movements as birds and seemed to fly through the water. So much life, another world within a world. I wondered if time lived in the sea. Was it marked in the same way? Was my perception of time the same as those with wings that flew through the water? I was starting to think that time was such a strange concept. That is had no meaning. It was so silly to let our lives be ruled by time. The more I thought about time, the less I was able to grasp, that it existed. I wondered if The One knew what I was thinking? My being jerked and lunged, I did not seem to have control over my motion. In a second I was aware I was back in my body, but I was not in the sweet grass. I was in the middle of the courtyard, on top of the mountain. The One was standing over me smiling.

"You are very lucky no one stepped on you." She could not contain her laughter. "We were all going about our daily chores and you just appeared from no where." She smiled again as she pretended to be surprised. "Where did you come from?"

I smiled back, knowing she was very pleased with me. I shook off the tingly feeling from my skin and stood up. I was doing as you requested, thinking about time. But the more I thought about it, the less sense it made to me. I was at the point of believing time couldn't possibly exist, and all of a sudden I was here. What happened?

"My dear sweet child, you collapsed time, of course." The words moved effortlessly through her smile. "Your Mother was a master at it, and I have often wondered if you would have the gift as well. I can see you are on your way to finding it. Now you may want to go and rest, the first few times you succeed in bypassing time, your body may have a little reaction."

I had to admit, I suddenly felt exhausted. I went to my room and lay on my bed. I waited for sleep, but the questions that kept rifling through my mind, would not allow it to rest. If I collapsed time, why was I not able to see the landscape around me as I went from the sea to the mountains? Why did I appear out of nowhere? Why don't I remember feeling the movement? I was there and then I was here. I was having a very difficult time comprehending what had happened. It felt more like something that was done to me, not something I had done myself. I couldn't see how anyone could learn to control that happening, not even my Mother.

As I lay there trying to go to sleep I could feel The Great Mother's warmth. This comforted me. I could feel my energies starting to calm and my body was letting go of its stress. A soft sweet voice gently wafted into my mind.

"So many of you that try to find the truth of reality never do. Do you know why?"

I could feel myself answer the very soft feminine voice, "No."

"Well that is because you are trying. You are all so beautiful, the most elegant states of expression, and yet you struggle so valiantly against nothing. Reality is just that, it is what is. But you refuse to accept what is and you create so many layers that do not even exist. Your reality then exists in the illusion that you have imagined. You exist in non existence. Why is this? So often you only discover reality at the time of your death, for that is the moment when all your layers are peeled away, They must be peeled away to allow you to return home. You were not born with those layers, and you cannot return with them. You discovered a new part of reality today. You discovered a truth about time. Time is constructed as you grow. It is merely part of an agreement the beings of your kind have made, so that they can participate in a mutual reality. Today you moved beyond that mutual agreement.

Many have tried and failed, because of trying. What you discovered today was, time can only be bypassed by moving into it so far, that it ceases to exist. No, you do not become time, you actually become timeless. Those that have failed to do what you did today, have lacked one piece of understanding. Eliminating something in your reality doesn't mean you resist or ignore it. You cannot make anything go away by thinking it is not there.

The way to make something change is to absorb it into yourself so deeply that it is transformed by you. You consumed time at a faster speed than it was moving, so you created a gap in it. When you created that gap, all parts of your reality ceased to exist for the amount of space that you were timeless. This is why you could not see anything around you. There is an agreement on this planet, time and space are joined. So if there is no time, there is no space. When there is no space, nothing is there to fill that space up. So many people try to understand concepts by expanding themselves towards the concept, but that will never allow them to fully understand anything. The only way to know the truth of the concept is to yield to it. To allow it in to your consciousness in a way that it becomes a part of you. This is how the understanding of the concept can then be retrieved from your experience, through the process of your thoughts. I do hope this has answered some of your questions. It has been delightful talking to you. Sleep now, child of the universe, know that I always see you."

As my eyelids became to heavy to hold, I could feel the Great Mother releasing me. The great feminine energy herself had spoken to me. How I had felt safe and warm in the cradle of her voice.

The next few days were relatively uneventful. I was grateful for that but felt anxious as well. The pattern for me here, was the quiet before the storm. I was never sure how bad the storm was going to be. There was really no way to prepare for the things that were happening to me. Most of my time was spent thinking and trying to collapse time again. It would seem I was not accomplishing either. I was very distracted by the sisters. Now that I had discovered the pattern of their daily lives, I really wanted to know why. Why they did what they did? Why they did it in that exact same pattern everyday? Why each of them had a singular duty and The One seemed to combine all of the different energies? At times I felt as if my learning was being distracted by my personal need to know.

Discovering how to focus in this light mountain energy was a learning in itself. I had come to realize that is what all of life is about. Energy. I could see it when I trained myself to, but for the most part, I was completely unaware of energy. Energy had no need of drawing attention to itself, as it only works in co operation with other energy. Why did energy not want to be revealed? Why did it hide behind what the eyes can see? Do we only live on one layer of life? The Great Mother had told me of the many layers people like to create. I had started seeing my life as having to have experiences to interrupt my thoughts. Thump! I heard it and felt it at the same time. Something had just fallen on the top of my head. I looked up to see what had happened and there were several small furry creatures in the trees above, staring down looking at me. I looked around on the ground beside me and there was a large seed.

Did they throw that at me? The look on their faces was one of joy and playfulness. Why would they want to throw things at me?

"Probably because they know you spend far too much time in your head and not enough time in your life".

Once again The One appeared from nowhere. I really wished she would stop doing that, it made me a little nervous.

"The mind is a wonderful tool, but that is all it will ever be. You will never learn anything from it for all it does is try to tell you what it is you think and feel. The mind thinks, it does not know, and if you think you know, you do not truly know. You can only know from doing, not from thinking. Tell me something, do you think your way through life or do you feel your way through life?"

I felt like this could be a trick question. So I thought about it. I really did not want to answer at all. The One spoke again.

"Reach out and touch that leaf there, yes, that one right there. Now tell me, what did you just do?"

"Well I touched the leaf because you told me too."

"That is right and what was your experience."

Hmmm, well it was soft and moist, and furry. It was cool, but firm, it felt alive. I looked at her expectantly, hoping that answer would please her.

"That is very good and very descriptive, so, was the experience in you mind?"

Was it in my mind? I am not sure I knew how to answer that, so I reached out and touched the leaf again.

"I feel the leaf with my fingers, that is where it starts, my fingers give me the information I need to understand the leaf, if it feels warm or cool, if it is soft or hard. From there it feels like the information travels to my mind. In my mind the experience gets changed into words and then I can think about it in words." Wow, I had never realized that was the process before, I had always just assumed my experiences were thought about.

"That is right, the mind only recycles the energy that comes from feeling. Now tell me, can you experience the leaves without turning that experience into a thought process?"

Why, why did The One always do that. I got the right answer, couldn't she be happy with that. There was always another step, with her. Well I had better try, or she is not going to leave me alone.

I reached out and touched the leaves, but the experience went right to thought. The more I did it, the faster, the feeling was turned to thought. It did not seem possible to have the experience now, thought started happening in anticipation of the feeling.

"There now you understand the purpose of the mind. It rides upon the waves of experience, but it will never be the experience. The mind is there to judge the feeling. The problem is the mind cannot feel so it can never know what feeling really is. Because of this, you can never rely on the mind too much. The mind doesn't really know what it is talking about. The mind will spend its life with you, it will never leave you and it will talk to you constantly. However the mind will always be in a state of assumption, for it cannot know life, for it does not experience life, its thinks words are the same as feelings, and if you trust the words more than the feelings, you will never learn to trust life. You must constantly remind yourself, do you think life, or do you feel life? Is life something you touch, or is life something you see? Each experience is real, but on very different levels of truth. The life that you see is a non experiential life, it is an opinion of what life is. In a thinking life, you cannot truly discover the truth. Truth is not something you can see, it is only something you feel. Not much of what you perceive can be seen, but all that you see can be perceived. You have had the experience of the great cat and how it sees the world around it. It does not look with its eyes, it sees with its senses. To see the truth of life, you must not look with your eyes, you must perceive with the senses. Do not allow words to to tell you what it is you perceive, for truth is much more than words. If what you perceive can be described in words, it may not be truth. Do you understand this?"

It was a lot to take in, but yes I did understand. I thought to my time as the cat and how I was able to see the world around me with such accuracy. I could see in a way that I have never been able to experience in my own body. I understood now, this was because I filtered everything I experienced through my mind and then bound the experience with words. I nodded very excitedly at The One. She smiled and instructed me to go about my day experiencing life, but not bind the experience with words. This excited me, I had permission to roam and discover. These were always my favorite things to do. To see what is under the leaf, or to discover what is over the hill. I loved to wander, it was the most exhilarating feeling, the feeling of not knowing. A pleasant anticipation.

As I wandered about, I touched everything, I absorbed the texture, the color, the smell. When words would start to explode from my mind in an attempt to distort my experience, I would stop them. The world was a completely different place without words. As I pursued my mission, I found I became a part of the world I was experiencing, I was no longer an observer. I could feel what the plants felt, I could hear the wind whisper, I was the flow of the water, I could feel it flow through me as it flowed through the mountains. If I put my hands on the Earth, I could feel her heart beat. I could see through the eyes of the great beasts and they could see through mine. I was part of the great pulse of life, we were in unison. Life was so much easier when I stopped trying to think about it, when I flowed with what is, and let go of trying. Thinking created a wall of separation between me and my experience of life. I did not want to do that anymore. I wanted to feel me, in my life, and know I was not alone. Why had I spent so much time thinking my mind was right, when in truth it knew nothing?

My experiences that day could not be described with words, nor did I want them to be, it would have diminished them too much . I now understood, so much of what The One was hoping I would discover. All of life is connected and waiting for me to experience it. Understanding only comes through experience. Everything has a language, but we are the only beings that use words. Words spoken without feeling, have no meaning, they cannot be perceived, they can only be heard.

This day had changed my life, I would never be the same again. I now truly understood, both the power of words and that words have no power. It made me understand that the whole of life, exists within a paradox, everything has many levels of understanding that can only be experienced. If you do not ever question your words, you will never experience your reality.   I was happy, so happy, I could feel my life now. I was alive. I was part of reality, and it was part of me. I spent many days, wandering, exploring, discovering life as it is, without, thinking about it. I could not imagine wanting for more, as I allowed myself to be carried by the love that was the shared experience of life itself.   It was so all encompassing, that at the end of the day, it was hard to return to reality as I used to know it. It would be easy to get lost in the sensual experience of life, but I knew that would not be what I was allowed to do. For now it was enough to know, the differences between the two levels of truth. I could escape to reality any time I needed

Chapter Six

The One was walking toward me, she had one of the sisters by her side. She motioned for me to meet her.

"This as you know is Eawannu. She oversees the energies that create the structure of life. I would like you to spend some time with her and learn what she does. It will give you a better idea of how to maintain your world when you go home." With that she turned and walked back to the temple.

I did not know any of these women particularly well. My interaction with all of them had been pleasant and cordial, but for the most part I spent time on my own, learning as I could. But I knew there would come a time, when I would be learning from each of the women. Not that I was supposed to learn to do what they did, but more that I was to learn, why the did what they did, so I could ask for help if I needed it.

I joined Eawannu as we walked down the path leading to the valley floor. We exchanged pleasantries and talked a little about the sisterhood along the way. The sisterhood, were all beings of the Orion system. They had existed long before their home planet was in trouble. They had warned their leaders and pleaded with the people that the time was coming when the great light of the planet would burn out. But by the time anyone started to listen it was too late. When Earth was found the energy here was very different than it is now.

"The energy in the beginning was very very light, very little gravity, we were able to move about anywhere. As time passed, the energy here became heavier and heavier, those that were born here, their bodies became denser and denser, to be able to withstand the weight of gravity. We found our home in the mountains. Each day, each one of us must spend time in the mountain, in the energy that comes from the planets light. The spot in the mountain where you went to, it is not far from the birthing chambers. We placed the chambers there to be in direct line with the energies that run through the planet to both sides. It is within this energy that time ceases. Time can be manipulated within this column of light, to go forward or backward. The structure of the energy there is the closest thing we could find to our home planet's energy and it is the reason we still exist."

"Eawannu, what happens when you die? I know what happens when my people die, but you are so different. Where do you go? "

"Well that depends on how we die. If someone should suddenly extinguish our light, we are absorbed back into the All that is. We return home just as you, your Mother or your Father would. However if we are consciously choosing to leave, and transform into something else, that is exactly what we can do. We could choose to become part of the plant life here, or the mountains, or the waters. We can stay here if we want, and become part of the energy that creates life. "

"How can you do that?" I asked with genuine curiosity.

"Well I am about to show you something. On this planet as is on all other planets that have so much diversity, there are levels of creation. Seeds do not just grow, nor does the rain just fall. There is a discussion at another level between all the elements and the energies that create the structures of life, to decide what is best for balance."

My face must have been contorted into a look of puzzlement, cause she smiled at me and lifted a large leaf, there to my surprise, was a ball of bright light, just hovering. It was a beautiful golden light with a swirl of other colors, fading in and out. Eawannu spoke to it and it hesitated in coming out. With a little encouragement, the light came out into sight, and I could just barely see a form inside the light.

"This is one of the very many beings of light, that create the patterns in energy that give the energy structure. There are many different beings, and that is all they do. They organize patterns of energy that create a structure that will support growth. They use the energy of chaos to create organized energy. You see, because this planet is a great library, any one of the worlds can come and harvest their investment at anytime. It is my job to make sure that the pattern of the species they harvest can be grown again and again. Because energy works in patterns, growing just one species in one spot, may not be the best thing for the species. It can be that the structure of one energy, can help and support the structure of another energy, so different species can live harmoniously together, in a mutually supportive way.

The other things these craftsmen can do is blend structures. They can pull a little energy from this and take a little energy from that, mix it together in a new pattern and work with it til it is self supporting. That is what I am. My Mother was one of these beings, and she fell in love with my Father. I am a creation that exists because of their ability to blend structures. Something that you will learn as you get to know all of us, is that none of us are pure of blood. We were outcasts on our home planet and not well respected. But here we have been essential to the existence of life."

I nodded my head, but it was bursting with questions that I felt would be inappropriate to ask. So instead, I asked what the little light beings name was.

"They all have names but they are not names as you know them. They are a specific vibration of energy, that is connected to the patterns they create. If you wanted to put words to what this little one does you would call her Leafsails.

The vibration her name created hurt my ears. I tried to duplicate it, but I could not. The little light being seemed to take pleasure in my difficulty in pronouncing a name I am sure she thought was simple. The movements and gestures made Eawannu giggle. The longer we spent in the energy of the little golden being, the more Eawannu became like her. She seemed to be aware that I could see her changing, so she abruptly ended our session with the little light and we moved on down the valley.

"That was a little light being, and she has very little structure herself for all the structure that she creates. I am going to show you a completely different being now, but they do something very similar. "

We came to a steep cliff. As we approached the edge and looked down, I was not sure I could see where the bottom was. I could feel the cool musty air rising from below. The feeling in the air was very heavy. I felt heavier here, like my feet were hard to lift. Each step took effort. I could feel the presence of something, I did not however know what it was.

"These beings here are of the oldest of beings. They helped the planet itself form. The structures they create are solid and strong. They work directly with the elements to shape the planet so that there will be a surface for other beings to walk upon and for the plants to cling too. These beings exist in a different form of time. What we see as death, they do not experience. For them death is transformation, into another form, merging with other elements. All of the beings here, and there are many, they write the patterns that structure is built upon. It is those very patterns that create cycles of time in the earth, when the rains come and when the winds blow. These patterns determine the shape of the petals on the flowers. Without these beings, life would be chaotic. It is their job to turn chaos into predictable patterns. Over time some of these patterns will be stitched together to make new patterns. This is how new species are born. It is how all beings develop and grow. Creating new patterns, allows all things to become more than they were. However becoming more, is not always a good thing if a species is not prepared to understand, experience and be responsible for it. But this is part of the pattern too. Patterns also decide the cycles of growth and decay. Decay within a species is not always death, sometimes decay is a form of negative growth, a way for a species to see what is not beneficial to them. Decay is not always physical. Sometimes it happens within the realms that are most hidden. The realms of feeling or thinking. This is where decay is most dangerous, because it is not always acknowledged as such.

Many worlds have fallen because of this kind of decay. But all of this is part of the pattern making of these beings. It is as life should be, here in this place. There are many beings that would spend their lives trying to break free of patterns, and the breaking free becomes a pattern in itself. Patterns are what life is, and knowing how to use them, that is what we,

The Wisdom Keepers spend our lives doing. Every time a new pattern is born, there is a different way to work with it. Life itself is in a constant state of birthing, so we never run out of work to do.

What The One wants you to understand is the patterns within yourself, and how to work with those patterns to become the whole of who you are. Once you understand your own patterns, you will be able to understand the patterns of the whole. It is one in the same. The same patterns happening on different levels. Within this realm, these patterns define reality. There are other patterns in other realms, but for now, this one is the only one you need to master.

The All That Is, is patternless. All patterns flow from that. A thought is a pattern, a color is a pattern, a feeling is a pattern. Time is a pattern. Space is a pattern. To be able to move within these things, you must know the structure and cycle of the pattern. Within the sisterhood, I have achieved a great understanding of patterns, so I work with all the beings that are pattern painters and pattern stitchers'. They bring patterns together in such a way that life is both what we perceive to be alive and what we don't normally think of as being alive.

As you go forth now in your lessons, it is essential that you start to see the patterns. It is only by seeing the patterns that you can interrupt them, long enough to reshape reality. But always remember, a pattern that has been interrupted will go back to the original pattern very quickly. A pattern can only be changed if it is stitched into place with another pattern. Always be able to see the beauty that is around you, but the truly wise person knows, beauty is only the pattern of pleasure. A pleasurable pattern cannot be created without the experience of joy. As you experience this life, all these beings are helping you to create your reality based on the pattern of your thoughts and your feelings. Your thoughts whether they be happy or sad, have a pattern and patterns will always seek themselves out. What I mean by this is, if you are unhappy, you will be attracted to other beings and places of unhappiness. Patterns are most secure, when they exist within other patterns just like themselves. Just like shapes. Triangles create beautiful patterns when arranged with other triangles, and the same is true of circles within circles. Triangles do not always fit with squares, or squares with circles. It is part of the nature of the universe. You can always know the truth of the nature of something, by what is around it. Beware any being that professes good will but has the need to protect themselves. This would indicate mental decay, what they are saying and what they are thinking is not in alignment, anything not in alignment is in a state of decay. Are you understanding these teachings?"

My head was spinning but, as she spoke I saw images. Images of beautiful elaborate patterns that created flowers and the creatures that walked on the earth, even patterns that the sisterhood formed with their prayers. So my answer was yes, I did understand what she was saying, but I did not truly understand how it all worked. It would take a great deal of working with patterns to understand how the patterns worked.

Eawannu, suggested we return to the mountaintop, and the rest of the sisterhood. On our way back I tried to see the world as one big interactive pattern. Eawannu continued to explain that some patterns are also dependent on other patterns. The patterns move within each other and could not exist without each other. Like the moon that pulls on the water, gently rocking the earth back and forth, helping it turn on its axis. Patterns within patterns. The earth as a whole was patterns within patterns but not all patterns were directly dependent on one another, they were dependent on the cycle of a much larger pattern. With practice I would start to see the patterns. The learning was to be aware of the patterns and to watch for them. This in itself would allow me to see them.

We reached the mountain top just as the sun was passing behind one of the majestic peaks for the last time before darkness fell. I felt at peace, but at the same time I could feel constant motion. It was as though the patterns of the world that were driven by the sun, were slowing down as the sun descended for the day. As the light returned in the morning, I would try to feel if its energy generated the movement for all the patterns to come alive again. I was not sure I would ever be able to see my reality in the same way again, knowing that I was part of a greater pattern. My pattern was the cause of other patterns. How would it be that I could choose to create patterns that were beneficial to this place? I would not exist if I did not serve a purpose.

That night as I slept, I was drawn into a beautiful dance of exquisite patterns. They moved and flowed, swaying to a beat that only they could hear. It was hypnotic, each design moving in perfect unison with every other design. Everything in its place and all with purpose. As the dream progressed I could see my own pattern and how I fit with other patterns. How my life was intertwined with the lives of so many others in ways, I could not decipher. At that moment I knew my life had purpose, although I did not know what that purpose was. Knowing there was purpose, made all of this easier. It made me understand that perhaps we are supposed to go forward not knowing the specific pattern we are part of, lest we may try to change it. I knew I must learn all of this as well as I could. It would make my part of the pattern flow. Then I would be able to return home. Home to be with my Father.

Patterns, patterns, patterns. For a long while this is all I did. I would wander through the sisterhood and move through the valleys sitting in stillness till I saw the patterns. I searched for the patterns so much, I almost lost the ability to see without patterns forming. Seeing the patterns brought me great wisdom, and understanding about how everything following a pattern also follows a predictable course. Change is brought about, because of an interruption in a pattern, or healing is brought about, due to rearranging of a pattern. I was understanding my world from a very different perspective, but one that made a great deal of sense.

Chapter Seven

The day that Eluna approached me, it was raining. Eluna as I had learned was Goddess over the waters. She put the tides in to place, with the help of the moon. She created a course for fresh water to flow over the land. She separated the salt water from the fresh water, so that different beings could exist in separate environments creating more diversity.

"Fresh water will always flow to the sea, but the sea is the source of fresh water. There are those beings that need the sea to survive. Their bodies are very dense and their movements are undulating, the salt in the water does well to support them. Then there are other beings that need fresh water cause there bodies create so much salt that there is a need for dilution. Water is a source of life for all beings on this planet. Water allows movement, flexibility, suppleness. Without water, things would dry up and disintegrate. Water is the pattern that holds the other elements together. Lets go down to the river, it is where you can learn the best.

"I loved the river, the sound was so constant. The sound would carry you wherever you wanted to go. There was always a slight breeze at the river, too. I was not sure if the breeze stirred the river or if the river stirred the breeze, but it was one of my favorite places to spend time.

The rain had stopped which made it easier to travel to the river. As we approached, I thought I heard the river speak to Eluna. Whatever the voice was, it was there and then gone. Its pace seemed to slow, and time seemed to change. My body, felt as though the river was running through it. The rhythm of the river was flowing through my being. As it did, I could see all the waterways on the planet, how they were all interconnected, how they all ran together, to the sea. The sea was like their Mother and they ran constant patterns of leaving her, living their life and then returning home to her. The nature of water was cyclic. It never stayed in one place but it never left that place either. Each drop of water was individual but it was not aware of its separateness from the whole. Even the fresh water experienced itself as the sea, as vast and unlimited, even though it may only be a tiny drop. It had no awareness that it was separate.

Eluna spoke," That is right, even the tiniest drop, contains the whole of the sea within it. Of all the elements, the consciousness of water is the most similar to what you call consciousness. It is aware at all times, but does not exist within the rules of time, for it is never still. Even as you may see a puddle after the rains, it does not mean it is still. For the water of that puddle is either nourishing the earth below it, or it is returning to the sky.

Water is always in motion. Water can take any shape or form, for it adapts to whatever tries to contain it. If water is contained within a vessel for too long, it will die and it will no longer be good. However if it is returned to its home, it will be revitalized and resurrected. The water of this planet is the same structure as The All That Is. Your body may be dead, but when you return to the All, you are resurrected in spirit. This is the nature of water and because it is such, it is also the greater part of the nature of your body as well. The gift of water is the absence of separateness. Memory is established in water and solidified in substance. Now try to pick up some of that water there."

I had tried many times to hold water before. With my bare hands, I was able to scoop water up, but never to hold it indefinitely. It would leak out, sometimes a drop at a time, but it would always find its way back to the earth. I tried many times, but never was I able to hold onto water.

"Nor will you ever be able to hold onto water. For water is the essence of softness, it is so flexible that it has great strength. Water can cut holes in mountains, and move entire landmasses. All water needs to accomplish anything is, persistence. Water gives the pattern of structure its fluidity of motion. It allows for one pattern to flow flawlessly into another. For there is the water you can see and then there is the energy of the water, and that cannot be seen with your eyes, it can only be felt. The water that you can see is the perceptual image of the energy of the universe. Of all the species on this planet, it is the creatures of the sea that are most like us. They do not understand what water is. Although they rely on it for their very lives, they do not understand that water is water. All other species will seek water out, to drink, to bathe to find food, for all other species are being of the realm of air, but water creatures live in a world within a world. They represent who you are deep within yourself. They show you, that there is another you that exists in another realm, a you that exists within emotion. Water is ruled by the energy of the feminine, and it shows you that feminine energy is powerful, deep, unstoppable, and goes to places that the masculine fears to follow. Water is the creative element, the energy that gives structure its flow. On this planet, life ceases to exist, where water cannot be found. The gift of water is, that it can carry the essence of all other things, within the space that it carries itself. Water has a structure that can adopt or absorb all other structures. Thoughts and feelings are all absorbed by water. The parts of you that hold the most water are the most affected by your thoughts and feelings. When you are angry, you push your emotion outside of yourself and the water in other beings will absorb your energy. Always be aware what is going on inside of you, because you are very easily received by the water of others. You know now, what I say to be true, do you not?"

I nodded my head. I watched Eluna as she moved. She moved with the fluidity of water. One part of her would lead and the rest would follow in one constant motion. Moving from one place to another, she seemed to flow across space, as opposed to walk within it. There was no wasted motion, no rigidity in her. Just constant fluid energy in action. There was a instant that I thought I could see her pouring herself back into herself. But that only lasted for a moment.

Eluna settled herself in a small quiet pool of water a ways away and motioned for me to join her. I was happy to get into the water, I loved the water. It brought me peace and joy, to be supported and surrounded by it. I slipped into the water, and found a comfortable rock to sit on. Next to Eluna I could feel the magic of the water outside my body, communicating with the water inside my body.

"You remember the healing baths that are located in your home?"

I nodded, thinking of my home. High up on the hills a short distance from my home, lies the Alaria, that is where the healers live. This is where the baths lay that are cut from different colored stone and a small stream runs from bath to bath in one continuous motion. No matter what the injury, if someone were to go through a specific sequence of baths, the injury would be healed within a days time. I remember spending time there with my Mother. I would watch as the healers would strike the side of the bath causing a ripple of sound to go through the water. Other times a melody would be played over and over, til the waters would stir, and shapes and symbols would form on the surface of the water.

There were other baths where beams of wood passed through the water and there were drums attached to the ends of the beams, when stuck the vibration would go through the water as well as the person in the water. Masters of the drum would play for hours and people would be healed. The healers had created a beautiful sanctuary, where even the smallest whisper, reverberated through the walls and baths. I loved spending time there, to hear the music and to feel the vibrations. One of the old healers told me that every persons body has its own song and sometimes when they got sick, the body forgot how to sing the song correctly. The healers helped remind the body of the proper melody, and the body would then heal itself. Water was one of the few mediums that could be used to communicate with the body, and to help it remember how to sing its own song.

Eluna continued as she settled into the embrace of the water, "The water feels the heartbeat of the earth at all times. The flow of the water follows the pace of that beat. Each being on this planet is attuned to that beat. The song of the being is a personal melody, that rhymes in time with that heartbeat. It is a pulse that is dependent on the beat, without it, it would lose its momentum."

She then started to sing. It was a beautiful melody, that carried us both. Its rhythm flowed up and down and as she sang, small ripples started across the surface of the water. I could feel tiny tingles running up and down the surface of my skin. The ripples grew larger and turned to spirals that would form and spin in one direction then form and spin in another direction. I could feel myself getting sleepy, I tried to keep my eyes open but soon enough I was lulled into a dream that took me backwards in time. Back to a time when my Mother and I hiked into the hills behind the Alaria. We sat there listening to the songs and the beat of the drums. We lay back in the grass and watched the skies above. It was a happy time, before my heart knew of troubles. I then drifted back to the river, to my body, and to Eluna. As I awoke my body felt as it did when I was younger. It took a few moments to realize I was no longer that child. I was completely aware of my surroundings, but my body was somewhere different, in a different time. As Eluna ceased her rhythmic tones, the water ceased to dance and my memory of my body as a child faded. I turned to her for an explanation.

"Your body always wants to be in a state of wholeness, of happiness, of maximum joy. The water flows through your memories, certain rhythms will bring your memories to the surface. If the song you are singing matches the beat of the earth when you were a child, then those memories will return. Wherever that song took you, is when you were happiest. That memory, if appropriate can be locked in to the current frequency of your bodies rhythm. Is that a reasonable explanation?"

I understood her words, but not the experience. So I did not say yes or no, I just stared at her. I was still trying to comprehend what had just happened and how real it felt. My Mother was just right beside me. It has been so long since I have seen her, how could that have been so real? I started to cry. Eluna decided I needed some time alone, so she quietly slipped out of the river and disappeared beyond the trees, on her way back to the mountain top.

I stayed in the river. I wanted to go back to my Mother, I wanted to feel her at my side again. I wanted to be happy like that again. I started to get angry at my Mothers death. I still did not have all the understanding of what happened. No one had really told me what happened to her? In fact no one had really told me anything about my home, or how my Father was doing? I hadn't been told when I could go home? Nor had I been told what it was I was really doing here, only that I needed training. I could feel the heat rising in me, I wanted answers to all these questions. I was going to The One right now. I was going to demand answers. I was ready to know, and I deserved to know.

When I returned to the Temple, The One was waiting for me, under the calling stone. She knew I was wanting answers. By the look on her face she was going to give me answers. Suddenly I wondered if I was ready to hear what she had to say. What if I didn't really want to hear what she had to say? I was second guessing my decision, but it was too late, I was here now. She invited me to sit by her and asked if I really wanted to know what happened. I didn't think I was going to be able to make my head move. I was trying to nod, but nothing was happening. My neck was seized and I felt it would break if I forced it. I tried to relax, that helped just enough to free up my neck, and I nodded ever so slightly. The kindness on her face, told me, what she was going to say would be difficult for me to hear. Now, I knew I didn't want to know.

"What I am going to tell you, is going to be very hard for you to hear. You know very little of the history of your existence here, and sometimes history is what is needed to make a story complete. I will do my best to offer you the whole story. I will answer your questions at the end, please let me get it all out first, then I will fill in the blanks that are left. When your Mother left that day, she knew she was going to die. Your Mother always knew. It was part of her path. When she descended the mountain they were waiting for her. She did not resist, and she did not fight. Your Mother has always had the gift of seeing life as a pattern and with that comes the responsibility to know how best to guide the pattern for the betterment of all. Your Mothers death is the reason you were brought here ahead of schedule. She knew she could stop the war that was coming with her own death. Yes I said a war.

Long ago, when we were still adjusting the frequency of the birthing chambers, a group of us were born, we knew from the beginning they were different. What we didn't know was how different they would become. It has been very difficult here, the creation of our kind, has led to the creation of another kind. This other kind does not live in harmony with all life. They are a group of beings that are very angry at themselves and one another. They eat other beings and seek out how to control everything in their path. They create devastation and destruction wherever they are. They are led by a woman, and that woman was your Mothers sister. I believe your Mother told you they had been seeded by warriors from another world, but that is not true. We are The Ones responsible for this creation. The day that your Mother was created, there was only supposed to be one child, but there were two. This happened many more times, and from early on it was obvious these children were on a different path. They would hurt small creatures and hurt one another. We tried to teach them, that their behaviors was not the way of our people. We tried to show them, hurting others would only result in hurting themselves. But they did not learn.

As they grew, we became very aware that they were thriving on this new planet. They were stronger in body, and ate large quantities of food. Your Mothers sister was raised within the royal family and because of this she knew of the knowledge that only the royal family can have. The knowledge that allows us to change time.

She searched for that knowledge. She would go and tell the others like her that she was going to change everything, when she found the knowledge, she would change time to get rid of our kind and she and her kind would take over the planet. There was no stopping her. She thought nothing of hurting people to gain information of the knowledge. One day she killed another in her desperation to try and find the knowledge. Her behavior and the behavior of her followers could no longer be tolerated. She was putting an entire society at risk. So the decision was made to banish them.

When your Mother had been chosen to join your Father as a royal, her sister declared she would have her vengeance. The rage has been growing in her for a very long time. This group of people were taken on a long journey to the other side of the mountains. A small community was built for them and they were left there to fend for themselves.

Guards were placed in two positions on the return journey, for it had been predicted that they would try to return, however they never did. A very long time has passed and they have grown their numbers. They have expanded to many different places. They are truly the first society of earth. But they live without understanding or caring of their actions. They believe they can take what they want without repercussions. They are dangerous to themselves and all other beings on this planet. They are in a constant state of war. They do not understand that war upon another, is war upon oneself. They are a fledgling society, and they will kill everything in their path, till self destruction falls upon them. Have you heard all that I have said? Take a moment, collect your thoughts, then ask your questions, and know I will speak the truth to you."

All I could think about, was my Mother being killed. Someone else took the life of my Mother. I could not understand this. People died from accidents or old age, their life was not taken by another. I had never heard of this. And why would my Mother not fight, why would she just give her life away? What is war? I did not know of this either. None of this made any sense.

Why would another being take my Mothers life? How can a life be taken? I don't understand how that is possible?

"In your life, here, on this planet, you have not known violence of any kind. There has been no reason for you to suffer this. It took a very long time for our society to come to the wisdom in knowing true power is peace. But this was not always so. All societies go through many growth stages in their development. The most common sign of a society in its infancy is violence. The need for violence comes from the great fear that you have been separated from your source. It comes from the fear that you are not loved. When these things happen, you start to think that you are somehow less than everything else and if you are going to be anything you have to prove this to yourself by means of violence. They assume something is not given so they choose to take it. It seems so unnatural to talk of this now, it has been so long since our society has lived in this way. Violence is not just a physical act. Greed, competition, isolation they are all examples of violence. But the others, cannot see past their fear, and that fear turns into self loathing and self punishment, and from there is turns violent, the violence that is felt towards the self is turned outwards towards others. These beings are only capable of seeing their world through their own eyes, and what is going on inside, gets projected outside, and that is when the greatest self deception happens. They stop seeing what is and start seeing everything they feel as a projection onto life outside themselves. If they are feeling angry, they see it as others being angry with them, then they feel the need to retaliate against their self delusion. The more they believe that what they feel inside is coming from outside, the worse it gets, til they train their children in infancy to believe everything is external. The problem will get so bad in a society that people stop believing they have any power of their own and they start to believe that all power is a form of control placed upon them by external forces.

  Long long ago we had a process in life where, the talents of the people could be purchased with currency. The gifts that were naturally occurring in us, were not shared, they could only be given in exchange for pieces of beautifully carved stone. At one point in our history, the carved stone was considered to be of such importance that millions of us were killed and enslaved because of it. It was only when most of us were dead that the ones who held the stones in such high regard discovered they could not function in their world without the talents of everyone. Then our world started to change. They could not eat the stones, nor did the stones know how to heal them, when disease ravaged our world. It took a very long time for our world to understand, that the people of the world are what is truly valuable. It is the love of the people that power the planet. Life is an energetic exchange, if you take it to far from its balance point, all life will cease. "

  "I still don't understand. If those other people are over there, why did they come here, and why did they kill my Mother?"

  "This is an act of jealousy on your Mothers sisters behalf. Her intention was for it to be an act of power. When your Mother died willingly, it took that power from her, and enraged her even more. People who seek power, have no understanding of what power really is. Now what is happening, is this, in your Fathers weakened distraught state, Orla, your Mothers sister, has returned to your home to comfort your Father. She is pretending to be someone she is not. She had planned on overtaking your home, and killing all that stood in her way. However she rethought her plan and decided to become deceptive, and to take advantage of your Fathers innocence."

I was trying so hard to understand what I was being told but I just could not fathom it. These concepts of deception and violence, it had never been a part of my life, and I just did not comprehend why people would become like that. Isn't it better to have all the best in people, and not to force the worst to come out. How can anyone possibly be happy if they are spending all their time thinking about how they can control someone else? Why would you want to control someone else? I did not understand, it hurt my head to think about such things. I gathered my thoughts and looked at The One, there was a question I had to ask, even if I did not want to hear the answer.

" You said before that I was created for a reason, this is the reason isn't it? What is it you think I am supposed to do about this? I know nothing of this woman? I do not know how to be like her. Is she going to hurt my Father?"

The One's eyes grew soft, and her energy grew quiet. She came and sat beside me. She took my hand and placed it in hers. "You were created to take your Mothers place. You must try to bring reason to your Fathers mind. You are being trained here and now, to protect the knowledge at all costs. We made agreements with all of the other worlds. We agreed to protect and grow their species, we must honor that agreement. If she gains the knowledge of the immensity of the harvest to come, she will with hold the species and she could cause war beyond this planet. For the other worlds to be able to come and harvest their seeds, the portal of time must be opened beyond this world. There is a special stone that holds the power to do that. This is the knowledge that Orla seeks. You are here to stop the horrors that could be. You will need to use everything you have learned to protect the knowledge and to keep her from ruling our people. When you are finished here, you must go home and take your rightful place as overseer of the people. That is the only way to prevent her from destroying everything we have created."

I had heard the knowledge spoken of many times, but I never gave it too much thought. I was not really aware of what it meant. But I felt now that there was more to it, than just opening a portal. So I asked The One, "Is that all the knowledge does, or is there more?"

"The knowledge is what brought our people here. The knowledge would allow Orla to change time. If she can access time, and learn to collapse it, she may also be able to understand how to traverse space. Time and Space are inseparably linked. One will always lead into the other. Knowledge of one, brings knowledge of the other. With her desire for power and control at all costs, she will do whatever she must to find the knowledge. If she learns how to use the knowledge she could cause a great deal of death and destruction to many worlds. This must not happen. It would change all that we have known. Above all else, you must not allow access to the knowledge."

Where do I find this knowledge?

"Most of the knowledge is within you, you are different than Orla, you are born of a different body. So the knowledge is passed to you. Orla cannot access the knowledge through herself, but she knows of the sacred stones that were passed to us from the ancients. The first part of the knowledge is encrypted within the stones that are kept in the secret place in your home. The second part of the knowledge is kept here in the belly of the mountain. The third part of the knowledge will be shown to you when the time is right. Right now Orla does not know this location, if she finds the knowledge, she can find us. This is why she must never find it. Do you understand this."

I understand. But my soul did not. I could understand that this woman would do anything to gain the knowledge. I could understand that there was something in her that did not feel connected to any others or to herself. I could understand that I had been created to try to stop all of this. What I could not do, was feel anything. I was numb. I did not feel life within me at this moment. It was too much information, and none of it made sense. I understood the words, but not the meaning. I probably never would, it was not in me to desire control of others through power and violence. I understood that I would have to fulfill my duty without the understanding of what drove her. For now though, I needed to rest, I needed to lay down and be alone with my thoughts. I simply could no longer sit there and deal with this calmly.

I thanked The One for telling me all of this, but told her, I needed some time now. She nodded and said "Of course, take the time you need"

I left quickly, returned to my white walls, lay down on the bed and stared straight above me. I did not expect sleep to come, nor did I want to move. I just wanted to let all that information create images in my mind, so they could start a dance that would play itself out. I was hoping if I could see the words as images, somehow it would make more sense. Maybe if I could see the people as actors in a play, it wouldn't feel real. I could watch it from a distance and see the role I played. I just wanted there to be space between the words I heard, and the feelings that were starting to well up inside of me. That screaming, panicking feeling, like there was a wild animal loose inside my skin, and it was tearing me to shreds as fast as it could, trying desperately to get out. The pain was not in my mind, it was screaming at me from every inch of my skin, to get out. In that instant everything went dark.

Chapter Eight

I could hear the sound of water, in a constant and steady drip. I didn't want to open my eyes and see my white walls again. I didn't want to want to see my reality. So I lay there, with my eyes closed, counting the beats of my heart, trying to distract myself from thinking. The wafting scent of mold and damp earth, caught my nose. I suddenly realized I was not within my white walls. I had no idea where I was. I opened my eyes to complete darkness. It took a moment for my eyes to adjust but when they did my surroundings lit up like lines of light on fire with a greenish blue flame.

I looked around scanning for life, but all that was there, was a large open cave, far below the surface of the earth. The temperature was constant and the path where I lay had been well trodden. As I looked down I did not see my feet, but large paws covered in beautifully patterned fur. I was the inner cat again. In my distress, I must have called upon the being from which I draw my strength. But where had the cat brought me? Why was I here?

I rose on all fours and moved about the open area. The many scents revealed the story. All of the sisterhood had been here. There had also been many others over time, but their scents had faded to the point where they all meshed into one. The sisterhood had been here recently though, very recently. I could see the path continued further below the surface. I was here now, I needed to know where here was. I followed the path downward. As I left the openness of the cave, the walls seemed to close in on me and the path narrowed in between steep damp walls. The smell here was strong of the earth, almost overwhelming. Up ahead I could see the walls led into another opening. There seemed to be a slight glow that was coming from beyond that opening. I approached very cautiously, all the cat senses were on alert. When my senses were on high alert, my vision increased. My heart was beating faster, my breaths came in short powerful bursts. I crouched ever so slightly as I entered the opening.

What I saw, was not what I expected to see. I knew immediately, I was in the birthing chamber. This is the spot where I was created, where most of my kind on this planet were created. This cavern was large and very open with a high ceiling.

I could feel my fur standing on end, there was an aliveness to the room. An audible pulse, but the pulse was melodic, rhythmic. It was as though there were some being that took breaths of music, and created melodies as they breathed back out. In the very center of the room were three magnificent chambers. These chambers reminded me of the chambers back home in the center of the concentric circles of water, the hollow stones. Those chambers were used by the musicians to alter and amplify the sounds they created. These chambers were created of pure whole crystals and there were many symbols carved into them. The chamber in the middle was very tall and crystal clear. It was so clear that at first I did not see it and I walked into it. The vibration from my collision sent a a sound up the side of the crystal wall that changed as it ascended. When the vibration reached the very peak of the dome, a burst of light was released.

The walls of each chamber were hard and solid but where each chamber joined to the middle chamber, the solid structure was completely intertwined. The solidity of the structure turned into thousands and thousand of threads of light, clear light and red light on one side and clear light and green light on the other side. It appeared to move and flow, but to the touch it was strong like stone. You could not stand close to the chambers without feeling a pull to enter them. My instincts told me to stay out. I knew intuitively if I was to enter something would alter me, and I could not be returned to myself.

I could feel a pulse from below my feet, that traveled up through my body. I reached out and put my paw against the pure clear crystal before me. The energy from below created a sound as it travelled through me and into the crystal. As I changed my thoughts the tone and tempo of the sound would change. I was able to create a melody, by creating a sequencing of thoughts, and repeating them. I could feel the energy building in me as I repeated the sequence faster and faster. I closed my eyes to concentrate. Trying to keep the same thoughts rotating as fast as I could I opened my eyes and inside the chamber a large ball of light was forming. It was white with many colors inside of it. The rhythm of the colors followed the rhythm of my thoughts. The more I concentrated the larger the ball got.

The light started to reach towards the paw I had against the surface of the chamber, as it touched me, powerful energy surged through me, so powerful I could feel pain. I tried to pull my paw from the surface of the crystal, but it was held by the light. I pulled til it felt like my paw would come off, the more I pulled the more painful the energy became. With every movement a surge of energy would penetrate me. I fought till there was no fight left, at that moment I saw my paw fade and my hand appear. There was no strength left in me. The light let go of me and I fell to the cave floor. I had never been in so much pain before, I thought I would die. I curled myself into a ball, closed my eyes and awaited death.

When I opened my eyes, my white walls surrounded me. The One sat on my bed and the rest of the sisterhood was there staring at me. As I looked in their faces I had flashes of memories. They picked me up, I remembered bright lights, I remembered screaming but no one could hear me, I saw my

78

Mother, and I saw me as energy. Then I remembered the pain. Every time I remembered the pain, I could not feel my body. I was afraid of the pain. I did not want to live if the pain continued. Life went dark.

When I opened my eyes again, I could see the faint outline of flames against the dark background. I tried to sit up but I had very little strength. I was in the temple of the sun. It was quiet and comforting. Then I remembered the pain, but that was gone too. I was tired, very tired. It seemed to take all my energy to breathe. I lay back down, it was all I could do, lie still and breathe. In a few moments, I could hear someone enter. It was The One, she moved differently than everyone else. She was sitting on the edge of the platform that created my temporary bed. I didn't want to look at her, it took to much energy. So I lay there, still, just breathing.

"You died. We had no choice but to put you in the chamber to try to revive you. The pain you felt was from re-birthing. The body is never kind when the soul is forced back into it. We did not think you were going to stay with us. It has been many days that you have sleeping. But you are here now. You must rest, it will be many more days, before you are ready to be moving about. I will tell you what it is you wish to know when you are stronger. For now, rest."

I closed my eyes and let sleep take me, but in truth, death would have worked as well.

Days passed my strength returned. I was fine, in some ways I was better than fine. I seemed to have a better understanding of all things around me. I seemed to know myself better. I felt clear, I didn't struggle so much with the uncertainties of life. I knew I had a very specific purpose and I had every intent of seeing that purpose through to the end. The only thing left for me at this moment was to understand what happened to me in the cave. I did want to know, what that was about. I knew there was a lot more to our being here than had previously been explained to me. It was time, The One had the answers. Evening fell upon us and I sat down with her. I knew I would always remember this moment, for the first time I did not look at The One with starry eyes. I felt more as an equal with her now. I was not able to explain that, nor did I try. I no longer saw her as a surrogate Mother figure, or someone that would discipline me. I knew that she had the wisdom, I had not yet acquired, but that at one point she was just like me. A novice. Knowing, yet not knowing. Searching for truth, but resisting at times when the truth presented itself. The rest of my truth would be found out tonight. I nodded knowingly towards her. I was grateful for my life, grateful to her, for she had saved me. The only way I could repay her was to do what I was created for.

I asked her to tell me all that I needed to know. It was time the pieces fit together. I was no longer the same child that had arrived here with my Mother. My thoughts fell silent as my ears opened to receive.

"When we came here the planet was not as it is now. This much I have told you before. Working with her to solidify and calm her was something we had done before. It has been a part of what we do, since time itself began. We of the sisterhood, are not just from the Orion system, we came there from other systems, and to those systems from other systems before that. We move through time and space, helping worlds grow and become. We are part of the All That Is, we assist in its expression of itself. We do this through the implementation of structure and matter.

The form you see us in, is the form that is most pleasing to you. We are beings of light, and we have no true form. At this time, there are endless worlds in endless dimensions that hold life. There are worlds so different from yours that you cannot comprehend them. There are many worlds like this one, which you could call home just as readily. The All wishes to experience itself through different expressions of itself. It needs life to interact to accomplish this. We, the sisterhood, organize and structure life, so that it will grow and thrive.

This planet is different because it is like a large garden that awaits harvesting. It is a seed planet, where many species that would normally have never met, have come together, because of the need of other worlds. In order to make this possible, this planet also had to become a doorway. The birthing chambers where you found yourself, lie in direct line with one of these doorways. When beings come here from other worlds, there are only two ways they can travel. That is through space or through time. All the species that are here to be harvested exist within the realms of space and time.

So we built doorways, some for time and some for space. All these doorways will cycle through being open and then being closed. Each one of them passes through the spinning light at her center. Beings from other worlds will come when the time is right and some shall travel through these doorways to get here. These pathways through the earth create specific energy patterns on the surface of the planet. They can be felt by all residents of the planet, even though the people may not know what it is they are feeling. The people will be very attracted to these spots and will use the energy for their own growth. If the people were to gain the understanding of how to use these doorways before they had evolved into wisdom, the results could lead to the death of many worlds, including this one.

So on each world where we have created life and doorways, we always train a group of people to guard the knowledge. These are people like yourself but there are many others as well. They must carry the wisdom down through the generations, they must teach it to others, and they must protect the doorways. In time when the population of beings have achieved wisdom, the doorways are opened to them and travel through space and time becomes part of their understanding. Travel through space and time before a culture is ready, is like creating an illness and releasing it into a population that has no way of protecting themselves. Sometimes, someone is present when one of the doorways opens and they have powerful experiences of the other realities that exist on the other side of the doorway. They may become great teachers or wisdom keepers in their time. But this is not always true, either. If the population is not developed enough to have open minds, they may become afraid and end the life of the Wisdom Keeper.

Building a planet with doorways, always leads to a very different development within its society. The people that follow Orla, they call themselves Atlanteans, they have knowledge of the doorways, and they will stop at nothing to find them. At this point they have not expanded enough to discover them, but the time will come, when they will be advanced enough to locate them. It is probable this discovery will end in disaster. Civilizations, societies, they are of a cyclic nature, as is the universe. They rise and they fall. This is the nature of all things. This world is different because it has not been allowed to take a natural course, the course of this planet has been manipulated to a great extent, so that other worlds could survive. Until this planet can settle into its own pattern, we the sisterhood must stay and make sure life flows in the direction of naturalization.

I am sure you wonder why I am telling you all of this. It is because you will be born many times here on this planet. Because your first time here, you decided to be born to the path of wisdom keeper, you will return many times born to the wisdom keepers. This will happen repeatedly till the planet returns to a place of naturalization. There will be many others on the same path. Some you may recognize from this time frame as well. You will not be free till the needs of the planet have been cared for. When you start to deal with Orla, it is important to remember, she has the shared memories of the people of Mu. She was one of you. When you meet her, she will feel very foreign to you, because of the path she has chosen, do not let this fool you. She knows the same history as you do. She knows the secrets the royal family guard, and it is her goal to get your Father to tell her, where the knowledge lies. It must be your goal to protect that. Remove it as a last resort, but you must never tell anyone where you have placed it. The people grow weaker as time becomes more solidified. They believe more in the reality they are creating. They forget what is real. Understand this and you will understand how to rule effectively. Now you may ask your questions."

"You speak as if my time to rule is now. But that is not possible for a long time yet. My Father is well and strong, it is his job to care for the people."

"Sometimes surprising things happen, and they happen for surprising reasons. Never assume you know what will happen, all things are possible.

"You also suggested that these Atlanteans will rise to be a great society. Why is this allowed if they are not assisting the planet in naturalization?"

"The concept of time is very different for the planet, it sees naturalization as something that takes places over many many lifetimes. It is in the nature of these beings to rise and fall. All extremes give birth to their opposite, this is the process of naturalization."

"If I am born many times, that must mean I fail many times?"

"Failure and success are limited perceptions of the same thing. One persons success is another persons failure. What is important here, is not your perception of success or failure but the degree to which you are able to communicate the importance of naturalization of the planet as a path to wisdom. One seed that is nurtured properly can feed an entire society."

"So what you are really telling me is to finish my learning here, so I can go home and try to succeed, but fail instead. But none of that really matters cause I will be back to do it all over again anyway?"

"Yes" and that is all she said as a big smile lit up the room as she rose and left.

"Wait, I have one last question, what do the birthing chambers really do?"

That stopped her in her tracks. She was not expecting me to ask that question. Slowly she turned around. I could tell she was trying to formulate some kind of answer by the time she faced me.

"I was hoping you would not ask me that. If I tell you, and I have promised to answer your questions, you realize the answer could put you in great danger? If Orla were to find out that you knew of the chambers, she would take extreme measures, forcing you to tell her. Do you still want to know what they do, knowing this?"

"Yes, even if I don't know, she will think I do, after being here for so long. If she is going to do harm to me, I would like to think it was for a valid reason."

"Do you remember how the children of the Others are born with a cord that attaches them to their Mothers."

"Yes."

"The birthing chambers sit in the energy where the cord of this planet attaches to the All That Is. All of us are attached in some way to where we came from. For some it is purely an energetic attachment, in other it takes physical form. Everything regardless of the structure of it, is being fed by something else. The flow of energy from the source, feeds the planet and allows her to birth herself into existence and then to support the life that is upon her. The energy flow from the source is of course, most powerful at the center of the planet. We however could not go that far down. So we had to find a spot that lies in a vein, that comes directly from the center. That is why the chambers are where they are. The energy that flows through that vein is the pure energy of the potential of creation. In that energy, focused thought can become physical structure. You can move back or forth in time. You can move through dimensional space. Whatever you believe in can be made manifest. All the energy needs is something to work with. When we created you, the practical elements were placed in the chamber. Earth, water and fire, air was already present. Then your parents had to enter the chamber and hold the thought of your creation. They held each other and thought of you as the energy moved through them. If they hadn't held the thought for long enough, you would not be here. The energy flows from the center of the planet and binds to the thought that is in the chamber. If the thought can be created, it then stabilizes time, so that space can be made for structure. In doing this, patterns are created that start the building blocks of physical beingness. As a body is being constructed for you to inhabit, the source chooses a soul to enter the body. A soul that needs the experience that you are currently having. The soul enters and the body continues to build around your energy, eventually cocooning you in flesh. That is how you were created.

It is a much easier process to move through time or space. To do that all you must do is will yourself to the spot you want to go. You must perceive yourself as already there, and you will travel along the appropriate portal to take you there. The energy of creative potential is the energy that births time and space. In this way you think you are born to a place, or that you arrive at a place. All you are really doing is moving inside the mind of the All. All planets have doorways that lead to other places and spaces in time. The chambers are the direct link to the web of life you saw before. That web is not just the web of the beings here on the planet, it is the web of the universe and the mind of the All. Is that enough of an explanation to keep you for awhile? The ever present smile wanted it to be enough.

"Yes, thank you. I am not sure I understand what you have said completely, but I do not feel it is necessary for me to know how to operate the chambers either."

With that The One got up and left. It seemed to take some energy from her to explain all of this to me. I knew she was worried about my knowledge of the chambers, but she knew I had to know. I sat and thought about it all for awhile. Then I walked around and thought about it for awhile more. Then I sat some more. None of it made sense, if I was supposed to do a job, then it mattered whether or not I succeeded or failed, didn't it?

There have been many times lately when life did not make the sense I thought it should. Life seemed to have a sense of its own that I needed to figure out. It was a greater sense, a sense that could not revolve around one person. The sense of life was good for the all, and had little to do with The One. At this point I had to decide whether to let the current carry me, or, to try to push the river. Since the later was rather impossible, I decided to let the current carry me. To carry on with my learning here, and be as happy as I could. I was no longer so sure that life would be better when I went home. I had no specific reason to believe that, it was just a knowing, a feeling that was stirring deep down inside of me.

Chapter Nine

I knew The One saw the life that lay before me, but she would not speak of it. She was always the first to say, "Life changes with every decision, but the nature of the people, that is carved in stone."

I tried to put my future life out of my mind and live in the moment , but this was not always easy. It seemed I could only go so far with any one learning and then thoughts of my home would creep back into my mind. I found myself unable to stop them, so I decided to let them be and allow them to leave as they came. I found if I stopped the thoughts and dwelt upon them, it only gave them the energy they needed to get bigger and bigger. Then they would take over my day, and I could think of nothing else. I tried to imagine my thoughts of home being clouds floating across the sky. Sometimes they move slowly but they are never completely still. Each thought that came into my mind I would place on a cloud and let the cloud carry it away. I also decided to start approaching the women here by myself. To ask them to teach me, so that I would be able to speed up the process. I knew that they knew, they were all going to offer me something. It was just simply time to get on with it. So I approached Tonn. Tonn was more solid looking than the rest of the sisterhood. Her footsteps were not quite as light. She was joyous and steadfast, always very purposeful in her approach to everything. I felt she knew the outcome of all things before she started them. I asked her if she would teach me now whatever it was she was supposed to teach me. She had to consult with The One, but she felt sure we could begin tomorrow. So for today I was free to wander, daydream, and imagine my life into existence.

One of my favorite places was high up on the green mountain. There was a large stream that ran through the forest and led to a waterfall. The water fell over the drop like a heavy mist, spraying all of life below it. Birds would fly through the mist and go sit on a branch, cleaning their feathers. Animals came by to quench their thirst and would always stand in the healing mist for some time, as though these waters in particular held some magic that was of benefit to them. I would go there on this day. I wanted to know why this place felt so good.

The walk was a long one and the day was very warm. The air was quieter than normal, but it was pleasant. I enjoyed wandering about letting myself just be me. I had the feeling that being me was a time limited event. As I rose higher into the mountains, a slight fog appeared. The cool mosses mixing with the warm air, created a light grey blanket covering the forest floor. I could hear the spray of the waterfall up ahead. It was not far now. As I reached the base of the waterfall, I could see many small animals in the area going about their daily business, a few birds flitted about and the descent of the water stirred the air just enough to make the fog dance. This was a magical place for me. Everything here was alive, even the fog. Everything had a personality, the moss, the water, the trees. All things were speaking to one another in a lively happy conversation. All things flowed into and out of each other here, there seemed to be no resistance, just flow.

I climbed to the top of the waterfall to sit by the water at the very edge, where the water leaped from the security of the earth through the air to then reunite with the rocks far below. I perceived this as the point of courage. What if the water never had the courage to jump? What if the earth would not allow it to leave? What if the air did not carry it softly to the rocks below? How would that change this place? How different would it feel here then?

I sat quietly watching the water leap from the edge of the land, trusting that it would be reunited with itself at the end of its fall. The water knew many of the creatures here were dependent on its commitment to separate from itself, so that other species might thrive. Waters willingness to separate itself allowed it to experience air and independent movement, with the security of knowing it would always be reunited after serving this purpose. I could feel the mists of the descending water gently caressing my skin, as though it knew my soul was wounded and needed healing. The mists gathered on my skin til they became drops that formed and ran downwards, pulling my distress from me and returning it to the earth to heal.

I could feel the consciousness of the water, the emotion of water, Water served but one purpose and that was to infuse all life with feeling. Water was the connection between all life forms on this planet, it carries the life of one form to the life of another, allowing us to know we are all connected, we are all one. It carries the wisdom and power of emotion, it allows us to feel what another feels. It is the frequency of life, in liquid form.

I could feel a slight buzzing starting in my center, as the vibrations became more apparent, images started to form in front of my closed eyes. Water was speaking to me. Not in a language, but in images. Shapes and forms, passed in front of my closed eyes. These shapes and forms would then be absorbed by my mind and translated into images. Images of the cycle of life as water knows it. All life here on this planet is touched by water. Water carries the codes of life. It shows us the truth of existence, even beyond the boundaries of the planet and into the universe beyond. Water is the medium from which images of the mind are created. Water is the birth point of form, it is structure not solidified. There are those which can shape water, there are those who can even use water as weapons, but on this planet water is for the purpose of giving form to thought. Then water carries the message of the thought to the other elements and allows them their part in the creation of perception. As long as water is clean and clear so will be our reality. Water also showed me how vibrations, frequencies, are held within water to affect all it touches. A frequency started in water will be duplicated and magnified by water, till the end of the water. Water is like a song, it is something that can hold you, stir you, heal you, and pass through you, however it can never be captured. Water is the nature of who we are. The creatures that pass through these mists, they sing to the water, asking the water to bring what they need. As the water gathers the right energies, it sings back to them. They pass through it and are affected by it. Water has a very clear and defined language, it is the language of vibration. Water holds thoughts and patterns, in a form not easily seen, but easily distributed.

I could feel the water in the stream speaking to the water within me. I could feel myself vibrate as the thoughts of the water moved into me. I had to move into the stream, the water was calling me. As I moved into the stream, my body started to vibrate from within. The sound of the water got louder and louder, as my body shook. I could hear from within my body, the song of the water, as all forms of light and shapes flashed before my eyes. Beautiful patterns coated with colors and lights moved through me like a ripple in a quiet pond. Then it was quiet.

I pulled myself from the grip of the stream. I had never felt so alive. I looked down at my hands. They seemed to be glowing with life and light. My whole body felt like it was exploding with tiny little beads of light. Then the waters told me how they carried the message of the stones to me. The stones are another part of what I am, they are a part of my coding as well. As the water passes over the stones it gathers the frequency of the coding which I am created from. That frequency passes to my body, and the body remembers, as it starts to vibrate in tune with the waters.

I sat by the water allowing it to wash through me. As the moments moved on, I knew it was time to return to the mountaintop. As I was getting up to leave, I thanked the water for the gift it had given me. This is what I heard as a response, "To be alive is to remember."

With that message, I left, and returned to the sisterhood. I could still feel the pulse of the water flowing through me. It was the pulse of all life, not just my life. In that pulse I could feel the memories of all that ever was and all that ever will be. Again, my lesson was, that all things are as one. This time everything is connected through water as it flows through all things, carrying messages from one to the other. Water collaborates with all things. The rain, the seas, the river, they all carried messages from one spot to another. Life around me made more sense, but the more sense it made the more I felt detached from the people I loved. I knew my Mother knew these things, but I also knew, most of the Others did not. I wondered if I would be able to hold these knowings when I went home, or if this knowledge was somehow stronger here? I could not know the answer to that yet. I left this world and entered the dream world, knowing tomorrow, there would be more to learn. The process never ended, it just repeated itself in constantly evolving layers.

Morning came as it always does, and I waited til the light was a certain color before leaving my white walls. I enjoyed the freshness of the air before the light became strong enough to cause it to stir. In those early moments the world seemed still, quiet, peaceful. My world was untouched by the problems I was yet to know. I could always reconnect to that aliveness within me, that by the end of the day, seemed to disappear.

Tonn was up earlier that usual. She seemed excited to take me out and show me her world. Here within the sisterhood, everything was interconnected but there were also definite boundaries between the worlds the sisters lived in. Each one of the sisters was a specialist. She knew of the other worlds but her world was The One she lived in. Tonn was goddess of the land. She was taking me to learn about the land and how it was connected to all other things.

She came towards me, every step was with purpose, and she grabbed my hand, pulling my body forward as she rumbled on. We followed the path that went down the steep descent towards the valley floor. With specific intent from her feet, downward she plunged. There was not a hint of fear in her, the paths were narrow and the drop was deadly, but that was of no matter. Halfway down the mountain we came to a small landing. At the edge of a cliff and the end of the path, we stopped abruptly. She stopped so suddenly I almost ran into her. I could see her gazing down into the valley. Before us lay the beginning of the great plains. Through the middle of the vast fields a river gently wove its way towards the sea. At the edge of the plains were the small hills covered in trees. This is where one type of life met another. Beyond the hills, climbing upward was the majesty and power of the mountain. Bold bare rock formed, thinning out the trees. In this place only the bravest of birds flew, for the winds would slam mercilessly against the cold surface of the stone. Beyond that was the cold frozen white water. There always seemed to be a storm at the peak of the mountain. It was as though the sky and the earth were in constant argument of who was the greater. They would entangle themselves in a blinding white rage. Even the clouds did not wish to go there, however they were pulled into the swirling anger between heaven and earth.

Tonn sat down on flat rock that looked like it had been made just for that purpose. As she rocked her body gently back and forth, finding just the right position from which to speak, I thought I could feel the ground beneath me shift a little. She reached over and placed her hand on my knee, as if to steady me. Then she started.

"Is it not beautiful? All that you can see before you, is held by the land. Cradled by her nurturing support. She gives endlessly to allow for growth and change. Out of her constant love comes creation. For the earth is still, and yet moving in cycles at all times. It is from her body that all other bodies exist. And through her, life knows of itself. For life is a reflection of the love that the All experiences within itself, and that love is expressed through the land. Just as water is the flow of messages, the land is messages in structure. The land supports growth. The land embraces decay and death and breaks it down into its basic elements allowing birth to once again occur. The cycles of the land happen in a different time from the cycles of the water. You do not see the cycles of the land as clearly as you do with the water. Land gives water purpose, and water nourishes land. Without the land water would disperse everywhere and it would not flow in a specific course. The movement of water is dependent on the shape of the land. Even though over time water can reshape the land. Water and land work together to create form and flow. I work with the land to know what it needs for balance. Land holds the nutrients that water disperses for growth. Those nutrients are really just a vibrational message, that activate coding. There are times however that nutrients form in excess or fall into deficiency. If there is no water for the land to call forth, I assist in the shift of frequencies within the earth.

When we arrived and the earth still shook. I spoke with the mountains and the land. I needed to know what would help them to be still. What they needed more than anything was the earth herself to make a decision as to what her balance was going to be. She was still trying to find the right place for all things to be. The earth, she sits on one tiny balance point, and she needed that point to stabilize, for if it didn't, her light would burn out before it was supposed to. So we, the sisterhood, helped the earth find her balance, and then she was free to experience a consistent spin. The land then started to settle, and the waters were washed into place. Once the land was seeded, the right nutrients had to be in the right place for all living things to grow. Sometimes however the land needed a little help to access the right flavors for the soil. Look over there, beyond that bald rock, to the sharp point, the point that has the red tip."

I looked far beyond the plains to the jagged peaks, and tried to see The One point with the red tip. I wasn't sure I had the right one, but I knew I was looking in the right area.

I could hear the rumble from beneath us. It sounded as though the earth was groaning. I feared that I would feel a great tremble next and that we would be thrown from our place, and down the steep sharp sides of the mountain. But the sound started to move from under me to in front of me, and it travelled beyond the plains, over to the peaks on the far side. I watched, and suddenly I could see the sharp peaks tremble, and the one with the red tip shattered. There was a cloud of red dust and the whole top of the mountain slide down to the lower hills.

"There, now the rains shall come and move the red soil to the rivers, and the rivers shall carry it where it is needed, and the living things shall grow stronger. The mountain agreed to shatter, so that life could thrive. It is the only way the land can move. As each part of the red soil is carried by the river, the mountain shall know itself from another place.
Have you ever noticed that water never flows in a straight line?"

I thought about that for a moment, and looked about me. The rivers did seem to gently coil and curve, moving about in the manner of a snake, heading in one direction only to turn back upon themselves. Yes, Tonn was right, I did see that. I nodded my head and pointed towards the river that lay before us.

"Yes, you see, the land knows the nature of water is to be in a hurry at all times. To get where it is going and to get there fast. However the land in its wisdom understands that water needs to slow down to provide nourishment for life. Water could easily destroy all in its path if it flowed too fast, so the land cradles it in a manner that turns it and weaves it across as much space as possible. This allows it to nourish much more of the land so the growing things can thrive and the water can gain more wisdom by going slower.

If you ever must ask anything of the land, know it needs time. It does not react as water does, it is not supposed to. The land holds the structure of time, while the water allows time to flow and gravity is the constant between the two. The land is the place that all else works from. It may call upon the winds for assistance or the waters. Even the flames of fire assist the earth, for all of these elements know the land is what gives them structure. Water births life, land gives life structure. It is in these two ways we know ourselves. The land will not call upon you, however you can call upon it. Make no mistake, because it does not move, do not think, it is not aware. Always show appreciation to the land for the support it offers you. If you do not do this, it may no longer support you.

The earth has its secrets. To know these secrets you must get to know the stones. They will tell you stories of where they are from, and who they were in those other places. The land seems to be all one, but it is not. It is many layers of beings within one. Many beings live within the stones. Although they are not alive in the way you and I are, they are still living beings. and they have stories to tell. It is why our birthing chambers are made from the stones. The stories they tell, are who they are. But I cannot tell you how to work with the stones. The stones choose the people they will work with. They will tell the stories they wish to tell and no more. They may tell me one story and you another story, and both stories will be true. It is how the stones work. If the stones choose you, they will offer you what you need, not all that they have to offer. The memories of the stones come from the stars, and beyond. The stories they tell do not always make sense for this reason. They do not understand the difference between here and there, and their stories are uninterrupted by time. So you must speak with the stones yourself, to know the stories they will tell you."

Then she was off. She rumbled back up the steep path, just as sure footed as she came down. She did not linger, she did not wait, she just moved on. I guess she felt as the land did, time does not wait. It goes forward at its own speed, for it owes nothing to anyone. Just as you are welcome to join the land, but the land does not require you to join it.

I stayed there, enjoying the view, and watching the rocky crags in the mountains come alive with light as the sun followed the path it has worn in time, illuminating all in its gaze.

I thought about the stones that Tonn had spoken of. The stones were mysterious. They had a presence of their own, a life. I would like to know the stories the stones told, but after my experience with the birthing chambers, I was not so sure I wanted to go anywhere near them. I knew sometimes there were veins of different stone that ran through the land. I wondered if those veins were highways of information that carried messages from beyond the stars. I knew the sisterhood remembered life as it was in their home on a planet far away. But I only had one home and that was here on this earth. I wanted to know what secrets other places held. My Mother always told me "There are some things it is not for us to know, and forcing time to tell its stories, could end our story." I knew I must be careful no matter what I pursued, and it was probable that the stones would not talk to me anyway. I had no real reason to know the stories. I had no intention of working with the land. So perhaps it would be alright if I just asked for a story. I would do that in the next day or two, but first I had to find a stone that seemed friendly. One that felt good when I held it. One that felt safe to me.

I waited til the sun threatened to shine no more, as I wandered back up the steep incline of the trail. I liked that place and I would return, but for now, it was more important that I return to my mountain top and the white walls I had come to know as my home. I was tired and just wanted to sit before the fire and enjoy the company of the sisters. I followed the path back to the edge of the temples. It was quiet, much too quiet for this time of day. As I came into the courtyard I could see no one was there. I could not hear a sound, no voices, no movement, no one. I went into the temples one by one, and could not see a sister anywhere. I was not sure what to do, so I sat in front of the fire and waited.

Images of my Father drifted into my consciousness. I could remember a time when I was very small and there was a celebration of some kind, my

Father would wear a band around his head and in this band there were many colored stones. My favorite stone was the one on his forehead, it was a deep beautiful blue with tiny flecks of gold in it. I was always touching it, wanting to play with it. He told me it helped him see truth. And that some day I would wear the band with the stones in it. I remember wondering as a child what he meant by "seeing the truth", for I did not know what lies were then. I still really had no knowledge of the damage that lies could do, I had never had direct experience with them. I did understand lies were things that could steal your time, just like the mists could steal time.

The One stood beside me, her touch shocked me back to the present moment. I jumped, not realizing she was there.

"Where is everyone!" I demanded, still a little agitated from her silent approach.

"The sisters are at the chambers, they are calling upon time for some answers. We had a visitor earlier today. Your Father was here."

"My Father! Why didn't you tell me? Why didn't he wait to see me? Is he Ok? Where is he now?" I started to ask another question, but The One raised her hand to stop me.

"Your Father could not wait, and I am not sure he was ready to see you. I met him at the base of the mountain. Many things have changed at your home since you have been gone. In his grief since your Mothers passing, the Atlantean Queen has been of great comfort to him. He has had a change of heart and will be allowing her to return across the land bridge, ending her exile. He explained to me that the shock of her sisters death, was more than she could bear, and she has now reconciled herself to be a guardian of the people. And so it is that they will be brought together in union, in a short period of time. He requested that we finish your training so that you can return home, to be present for the ceremony."

"What? My Father is entwining with the Atlantean Queen? I don't believe this. It cannot be true." I could feel the heat of panic inflaming my blood. How could my Father do this? Doesn't he know she is not to be trusted?

"Grief affects all people in different ways. Your Father did not bare his well, and now he is looking for something, anything to replace his grief. Orla has allowed him to smile again. But I do believe the smile she offers your Father will bear a great cost. Orla was always able to make men change their course. Orla would not be there if there was not something she desired. So now we will intensify your training. It is essential you return to your home as quickly as possible. Knowing Orla is going to be there, we need to know also that you are well trained and will be safe. Although we did not train Orla, she was able to absorb some of our training through your Mother. They were created at the same moment and share some of the same memories. This is how your Mother knew she must bring you here early. Are you hearing what I am saying!"

She spoke sharply, that was unusual for her. The One could command a small army with a whisper, she did not need to raise her voice. The fact that she did, made me realize there was a greater picture here, that I did not know yet. Something that made even The One feel threatened. I nodded my head quickly and turned and left for my white walls. I needed some time to sort out all that I had just heard. I felt betrayed by my Father. How could he just abandon the memory of my Mother? How could he take in someone he had exiled? What great hold did Orla have over him? These were all questions I could not possibly have answers for at the moment. My fear was that I would get my answers and more, upon returning home.

My dreams that night made no sense. People were running everywhere, and there seemed to be chaos. I saw the great chambers, the hollow stones collapse and Orla reached out to take something from me, and then all was dark. I did not understand the dream, but it frightened me. It frightened me so much, I thought about asking to stay with the sisterhood. I knew I had been created for these moments, but it did not mean that I accepted them. I did not have any training in how to deal with a life that may not be my own. Right now I felt like I was here to serve something or someone, but it was not myself. Knowing that my education with the sisterhood was about to intensify, I thought I may try to take the day and go on my own, somewhere, anywhere. I knew, no matter where I went one of the sisters would come for me. Deep down, I knew I was only trying to put off the inevitable, the return home. It wasn't that long ago that, going home was all I could think about. Now, I didn't want to think about it at all.

Chapter Ten

I went out into the courtyard as the rays of the sun broke free from the mountains and lit up the sacred stones. The sisters were up going about their daily activities but they were quiet. No one spoke or sang. There was no sense of cheerfulness coming from them. Whatever they had discovered the night before, had left them in a somber state. I wanted to know what they had seen, but I did not dare ask. I didn't think I could take much more information at this moment. To find out, could bring more pain, and I was at my limit.

The One emerged, from the temple of the Sun. She was aglow with golden light. To see this gave me hope. I associated that beautiful sun lit glow, with something positive, something happy. Of course I did not know what the truth was, but today, I was going to allow myself to believe in what I wanted the truth to be.

"Your energies are low my child. You did not sleep well?"

No. I responded. I had difficult dreams that made no sense to me. They occurred at my home. I do not feel well. I think I should rest today."

"There is really only one cure for bad dreams and feeling unwell. That is to go to the garden. To spend time there and let the love of the garden heal you. I want you to go with Gnua today. She is the overseer of growth and gardens. She will help you find your balance again. Wander through the gardens with her, let her show you the things that you do not see with your eyes. You will feel much better when you return. "

I complied with a slight nod of my head. Not feeling well, was not a complete truth, but it was how my soul felt.

Gnua was one of the taller sisters. She moved in ways that reminded me of the wind in the summer as it blew the long grasses. The grasses would move in unison, but each movement was delayed by a heart beat. My eyes would see the start of the movement and then follow it through the fields in an enigmatic dance to music that had no beat. This was Gnua. She moved to a silent song, the breeze gently blowing her from one spot to another with no noticeable movement. I liked her, I liked her energy. This would help me today. I am glad The One chose her. Gnua appeared from the Temple of the Moon, gliding silently towards me, I smiled as she approached.

"Do you have a favorite place you would like to go today? Everywhere is a garden." her voice sounded like wind passing though stones as she spoke. I thought about it for a moment, but I really had not developed a favorite spot here. There were many beautiful places, but I had not seen what I would call a garden. So I shook my head and said, "You pick."

Gnua smiled and started forward in a direction I had not gone before. We walked up a path and across a flat topped area of the mountain, then I could smell a sweetness in the air. Before us in a small valley was a pocket of life. As we descended I could see a small river that leaped over a waterfall. The scent was intoxicating, and the color was healing for my soul. My steps came quicker as I saw what lay before me. I reached the valley bottom and placed my feet in the river. Here in this place there was so much joy. I thought I could hear the flowers laughing at me. Small creatures danced about, staring at me as they went. The waterfall even seemed to be happy, as it nurtured all life around it with its healing spray.

"This is a good place. It is full of life. There is balance here, and joy in existence."

Gnua's voice was soft and sweet, like inhaling the scent of fresh sun ripened fruit on the vine, or a beautiful song in the cool evening after a hot day. I wanted to stay in this place and forget about the outside world. I could feel some happiness again, and I wanted to hold onto it.

"Do you know what the secret of the garden is? The secret of a garden is to allow for all possibilities. It is to allow for the rain that falls from the sky and the sun that gently warms with its rays. To allow for the sound of the waterfalls and the breeze that gently spreads the mists. A garden is all about balance. It is a balance of masculine and feminine energies. The understanding that no one thing is better or worse than any other thing. All things have their place and their time. In a garden there are no opinions, no judgments, each being is allowed to be exactly as it is and it is celebrated as that. That is why there is such peace here. Joy comes from the expression of the pure self. All beings are inherently creative, it is their nature. In a garden self expression is the epitome of ones being. There is no higher honor than to express on the outside, what is felt on the inside. The garden remembers this and they celebrate their lives this way.

The masculine and feminine energies of the garden are also its creative essence. See this flower here, see how the petals curve in soft shapes, the petals themselves are smooth and cool, their energy pulls you inward, towards them. Now see here in the center of the flower, see these spikes that protrude out towards the sun. They are more severe shapes, somewhat harsh and they appear to be much stronger than the petals. Now look at the whole plant, the leaves and the stalk that carries it to the ground. The leaves being of a soft shape and flowing in the breeze and the stalk which is stiff and strong to carry the weight of the plant but flexible enough that it does not break. This is the perfect blend and balance of masculine and feminine. Neither energy is more than the other. They are not better or worse than one another, so there is no competition. They are the best at being who they are so that their life together is a good one. These energies work together to create this beauty. There are some plants that have a stronger female energy, and others that have a strong male energy. No plant however is just one or the other. Life on this planet does not work that way.

A garden shows us how to experience our opposite within ourselves. You were born a woman. You look at your image and you see a woman. You see your softness and your suppleness. You see how your long hair flows in the wind. Your perception of yourself is to identify what you see as female. However you also have many male qualities. You have great physical strength and when you choose to transform, the cat you become would be considered male. When you become rigid and defiant, those are qualities of stiffness and are attributed to masculine energy. Yet still you think of yourself as female.

What you see with your eyes is never the reality of the perception. Truth is there to be seen, but it cannot be perceived with your eyes. Truth can only be perceived with your heart. This is what a garden has to teach us.

See that plant over there, it is all spiky and looks like something you would rather not get close too."

I focused on the plant she was talking about and it was almost painful to look at. If anything was to get to close to that, they would have to spend time in the healing baths.

"Let your eyes lead you now and tell me what kind of flower do you think this being has?"

I looked at the plant and tried to imagine it having a flower at all. It looked so fearsome that I could not imagine anything of beauty coming from it. I imagined a flower that was sharp like its spikes, perhaps something that would make your skin burn, and your eyes hurt, with a smell that would make you turn away. As I saw this in my imagination, it appeared on the plant. The plant seemed upset that I would place such a horrid image over it. I thought I saw it pull away from the image I was creating in my mind, as though it was afraid of the image.

"You must release that image, you are disturbing the plant."

With a wave of Gnua's hand the plant leaned forward and produced the most beautiful blossom I have seen. The flower was larger than my head and had a scent so sweet that bees appeared instantly to drink of its nectar. The color of the bloom was so vibrant it seemed to extend itself beyond the petals, in a color infused mist. I wanted to touch it but the image I had created in my mind lingered. I glanced at Gnua, who nodded to me. As I touched the blossom, it felt like the skin of a new child. It seemed to enjoy touch, as the petals leaned towards my hand. So I stroked the petals ever so gently and found myself apologizing to the plant for the offensive image I had created. As I did that, the color of the blossom grew even brighter, and I could feel its energy vibrate slightly as it was released from the petals.

97

It felt joyful.

"A garden is an expression of truth. These are beings of truth and are here to teach us all what truth is. Truth is always right in front of us, but it may not present itself in the form we expect it too. Beauty is an expression of truth, it can be no other way. Beauty can only be perceived when a being's expression of itself is truthful. So beauty as with truth, is genuinely perceived within the senses, not only with the eyes. The eyes are the last sense that should be trusted to receive beauty, but they are the first place to project truth. Come with me."

We walked a little further down the path, just beyond the waterfalls. Just beyond my sight there was a great commotion, leaves were being tossed in the air and energy was shooting out in all directions at the same time. I was not sure what was happening but, that seemed to be where Gnua was headed.

"Crouch down here and watch for a few moments. See those birds there. The male is The One with all his feathers flashing and dancing. The female over there, is paying close attention to him even if she does not appear to be. He does a few dances, and throws the leaves in the air, he flashes his feathers and squawks his love to the universe. The louder and the flashier he gets, the happier he hopes the female will be. This is how Orla and her people are. All the dancing and flapping and showing of colors is really just a deception. It is all so that he can mate with a female. If the female would accept him without that display, he would never do the dance. The female pretends not to care, but what she is really doing, is assessing him from a distance. She wants to know, what lengths she can get him to go to, how much is he willing to sacrifice. The truth in what you are watching is the act of mating. The rest, is an illusion. This is what you need to learn to perceive. If you perceive with your eyes. you can easily be distracted from the truth. The display the male puts on is very elaborate and beautiful. If you were seeing with only your eyes, you would be fooled into believing, that he is making a statement of how much he loves her, what great lengths he is willing to go through for her. While the truth is, they will mate and he will leave. Beauty that can only be seen with the eyes, is usually a distraction or a deception, that leads you in the opposite direction from the truth. Are you listening to me?"

I thought for a moment and then it made sense to me. Yes there are some people that put on large displays, professing their talents or their love, and the reason they are putting on those displays is to convince the people around them that what they say is true.

"Yes that is right. Sometimes they are trying to convince themselves that what they say is true as well. Your understanding of the world around you cannot come from trusting your eyes. Truth is something you experience, not something you see. Now, I have another question for you? Why do you think this garden makes you feel so good?"

I did not like it when the sisterhood listened in on my thoughts, but I guess this time it was for teaching purposes, so I would let it go and try to answer her question.

This question was a little harder. The garden was alive so maybe it was just the energy that I was experiencing. But I knew the answer would not be that easy. All these questions that the sisterhood asked, they were never really straight forward, that is the one thing I knew about them.

"Well I think it is just that there is such a high energy here!" I was proud of myself for being so assertive in my response.

"That is part of it young one, yes it is. However there is a lot more. It is easy to look at the other people around you and see your likeness in them. You can even look out across the plains and see the great beasts that roam and see a similarity to them. The cat you are, tells you that you have a wild nature. But seeing yourself in the beings that create the garden is a little harder? Is it not?"

Seeing myself as a flower, or a leaf? I had never thought about any of these growing things in that way before. How could I possibly be like a plant. I move around I am free. I speak and communicate with others. I am not like the plants.

"All of these beings in the garden are as alive as you are. However they exist in a different dimensional understanding than you do. You see freedom as movement. They see freedom as nutrients in the soil. Freedom for them, means they are with others of their kind, and are healthy, they have a good balance of rain and sun. Freedom for them is being well rooted and stable. Plants are not of a single mind, they do not think independent of one another, their perception of reality, feeds the whole. I can go over there and speak with thatone plant, however the whole of its kind hears what I say. They are of a unified consciousness. Each plant has no perception of being an individual. The beasts of this planet, they are all connected and they understand this, but they also understand that they are individuals within a herd, or a group. Plants do not have this understanding. For the plant beings, all of life is connected as one, but vibrates within different frequencies.

If you were to stand at a distance and look at all the different plants here, you would see a wall of beings. It would appear that there is no separation. However you would see the different shapes and forms that would tell you there are different and separate plants. Different flowers of all colors and shape, and that too tells your mind that there are different beings here, but it is only when you can see the difference that the concept of separateness enters your consciousness. If you had been taught to believe that one being could produce this variety, you would think you were looking at one plant with many different expressions of itself. Do you agree?"

I nodded energetically, for I understood exactly what she was talking about.

"Well that is exactly how the plant beings experience themselves. They are all one, but they vibrate at different rates depending on the expressions of self. But there is no separation. One plant that expresses itself by degrees of frequency. " she nodded her head at me, waiting to see if I understood.

"As you have learned, there are beings that oversee the growth and structure of the plant beings, they have a consciousness that is attached to the plants but also is separate from the plants. So when you wish to work with any of the plant beings, you can speak to the beings that oversee the consciousness of the plants or you can choose to speak to the plant itself. You will have to work with this to see which suits you better. As with the stones and the waters. plants have their purpose and they make very specific contributions to the planet and the other beings on the planet. One of the secrets within the plant realm is that the contributions they make are different on the different levels of vibration that you can exist within. I can see you are a little confused as to what I mean.

When you were born, you were very little and did not know much of this world correct? As you grew, your body changed and you learned more of the world around you. So who you were when you were born is very different from the person that stands here with me now?"

"Yes, I can understand how you change but think you are the same, because you don't see the separation in your own being." I chimed in.

"It is the same with your consciousness. The body that you stand in, here with me now, is made of pieces of the earth. When you leave this place those pieces of earth will be returned to her. Your body is on loan to you. What animates the body is the vibration of your being that exists within the body. As you learn and grow and discover how the other beings of this place communicate, you gain knowledge and hopefully wisdom about the world around you. As you practice and learn further, you can learn to communicate with the beings that do not always appear to have voices. Are you with me? Good.

Since your body is made of pieces of the earth and it is animated by your consciousness. As you learn to work with the elements, you also learn to operate your body differently. You learn that your body can vibrate in a different way from the others. Just as you can change into the cat, not many other people here on this planet can do that. Because you vibrate at a slightly different frequency, you work with the elements that create your body in a different manner.

The most powerful teaching I can give you is that you must understand, your body is made of the earth and is animated through consciousness. Just as you can learn to ignite flame with a thought, or reroute water by moving your fingers, your body must respond to the same commands, because it is bound by the same laws. Your body, is truly the same as the plant beings, it is made of the same elements that the plants are rooted in. Water gives you flexibility, air allows freedom of thought, earth gives your solidity and structure, and fire stirs the energy that makes it all flow together. As you co operate with the earth to make changes with thought, so you also can command your body. This is something I hope you can truly understand?"

I completely understood her words, but it was difficult for me to understand the process of how this would happen.

We sat in silence for awhile, I believe Gnua was allowing me the time I needed to try and tie all these concepts together, before I started to ask questions.

"What I am not understanding about this is, if I am a piece of the planet, why don't I look like the planet? Why doesn't my skin crumble under the sun like the dry earth does? Why do I have hair on my head? Why am I not the color of the green leaves of the plant beings? Things of the earth look different than I. Why is that?" Gnua smiled a very knowing smile as though that is the exact question she expected me to ask.

"Ah very good, a skeptical mind. A skeptical mind is a mind that has the potential for great wisdom. When you say what you are saying, where is your perception coming from? Do you think you do not look like the planet because you are seeing through your heart or because you are seeing through your eyes? What eyes are you seeing through to determine your reality?"

Oh how I despised that. My Mother used to do the same thing to me. Lead me into a trap, where she knew the answer to the question before I asked the question. She used to say "no matter what, the questions you ask, will tell me who you are." I realized in that moment, the question revealed I was using very limited perception to experience my reality. I was living an assumed reality. I was not living in truth.

"It takes great time and training to see truth. Let me give you a hint. When your emotions are stirred by the beauty you see with your eyes, within that, there lies some form of truth. If you see something to be beautiful, but the emotions are not stirred, it is an illusion. It is here in a garden where you will find truth. Here in a natural environment where you learn what beauty really is. It is also here in the garden where you learn who you are. To perceive with the eyes is a trap, all it will give you is an appetite for illusion. However to perceive truth in another, you must look deeply into their eyes."

"Why the eyes? Can you look into the eyes of the beasts and see them as well? Plants don't have eyes to see, so how can you look into them?" My questions were coming in rapid fire now?

"Well the eyes, whether it be people or beasts, allow the light of the soul to shine beyond the body. You can perceive the energy of the body by looking with the sight that needs no eyes. Looking with your physical eyes, you will be able to see what lies within. There is a light that dances in the eyes of those that are truthful. Just as there is a shadow that lives in the eyes of those who are not. There is no way to hide the truth that lives in the eyes. There will be those that will try, but to one who knows how to see, it is not possible to hide.

The light in all beasts is pure, the beasts are not made the same way people are. They do not seek to be other than they are. It is the confusion that is created by oneself, when you try to be other than you are that creates shadows in the eyes. In the path of the growth of the person, all people will seek to be other than themselves, at some point."

"Why do people want to be something other than who they are?"

"Now this is a very good question. The home world we come from has a history that will be very much like the future that this planet will face. Since the beings here descend from the beings there, certain qualities shall be passed on. That is the inevitability. Most species that are equipped with a dualistic understanding of reality, go through a growing process that will take them to the edge of destruction or beyond. By the time our race had learned the truth of what we had done to our planet it was too late, and we had to leave. Your kind will follow in the same footsteps if they don't maintain the memories of the ancients.

Do you remember the bird we saw awhile ago, that was dancing trying to secure a mate?"

"Yes, just back there." I pointed as I spoke.

"People live in a way that makes them like the beasts, but they do not have the perception of the beasts so it causes problems for them. When a male loses a fight for a female, he starts to think that he is not good enough. The male will start to wonder why the female chose the other male and wonder what the difference is. If he thinks he knows what the difference is, he will start to desire that he is like the other male. Instead of seeing the good qualities he has, he will only see the qualities he does not possess. He then starts to compare himself to another, and this creates competition based on an illusion that there is not enough for everyone. What he wants is what he sees with his eyes, not always what he feels with his heart. Because of this, he believes he has to act against the other male to gain what he wants. All of these thoughts are contained within his own mind of course. He at some point, if his fear of separation becomes great enough, he may try to cause harm to the other male, in an attempt to gain the female.

All this is based on the illusion that his life would be better if he only had what he wanted. Because people often only use their eyes to see the world around them, it is in their nature to think they need more. If they had more food, if they had a mate, if they had more of something, that their lives would be better. In your world, this has not happened much because of the great understanding of what happened in our past. Here we have sought to create a reality for the people that is based on each individual having equal value, that was our priority. We in our existence have come to understand, people only think they desire more if they do not feel valued by others.

However that is all about to change. Orla is the one that will change it. There is always one. One who decides that their lives are more important than all others. All of this comes from fear. Fear that they are separate, fear that they will not know love, fear that they are alone. What they fear on the inside, appears on the outside as anger, rage, violence. In an attempt to create more self value they decide that other people need to see things the same way they do. If everyone saw the way they did, everything would be alright. When people oppose this way of thinking, they decide they have to make them think this way. So they start to try to convince them of why they are right, if that doesn't work they will resort to coercion, and if that doesn't work they will end up trying to control them. The need to control the lives of others for the betterment of the self, can only lead to self destruction. Growth does not come from creating all people the same. Growth comes from diversity. This planet flourishes because of the amount of different species. Tolerance comes from allowing for difference and variety. Tolerance leads to acceptance and acceptance leads to peace. Peace is the understanding that you are all things and all things are you, so the separation you were trying to control in the first place, is an illusion.

However in these controlling people, the emptiness that lives inside of them, is somehow greater and more destructive than it is in others. The more they indulge their fear, the more they are blinded by it. Soon the only life they know is to protect themselves from the illusion they believe to be true. That is the illusion that someone wishes to take something from them. So they take and take and take from other, hoping that the next thing they take will fill them up inside, but it never does. It is a very sad part of the nature of these people. And it all starts with the misperception, that you can see truth through your eyes, that reality is something that can touch. When it is believed that the world you see with your eyes is the real world, that is when the illusion takes over."

"I am not sure I understand. What is the real world? Is not that, out there, the real world? It is the only one I know of." Gnua smiled that knowing smile again. I wondered if she had heard that same question countless times? In that instant I suddenly felt I could feel the energies of all the women who had sat in my spot, speaking the same words.

"I have spoken to you of the difference of seeing with the eyes are seeing with the heart. Truth lies in perceiving with the heart. You have had many experiences now, that tell you, there is a great deal more to existence than you can see. Is this not true? With this being your understanding why would you think what you can see is all there is?"

Great, another question to answer a question. There was no way to win with this setup. No matter what, I knew I could not get out of this. I had to learn how to do this effectively one day, just so I knew how it felt to know what was going to be stated.

"I guess that is because it is all I have known. Because it is solid, I can touch it. It is right there before me."

"When you dream at night, do you think the dream is an illusion, or do you think it is real."

"I think it is real, especially if I am frightened, even when I wake up, I still feel as though the dream is real."

"Right. But the dream is not solid, it is not right in front of you. The dream happens in your mind. But you still think it is real. What we perceive to be real, is what we are told is real. This version of reality is learned behavior, and learned behavior is not always true. However there must be some truth in all things, otherwise we would not be able to perceive them at all. So just as you think, what you see in front of you now is real, I wish to offer this to you, this is only a very small part of what is real. Just as, the you that stands here now, is only a very small part of the you that is. What we are trying to teach you here is, to open yourself to perceive the more that you are. The more that the world is, so that you can see truth."

"I am supposed to learn all that from a garden?" Gnua laughed, and I could feel the tension release itself from my body.

"Each garden is a mini world unto itself. If you can learn to see what truly is here, then you can learn to see what truly is anywhere. Now I want you to try and see this garden as it truly is. Look beyond the leaves and the flowers. Remember all of life vibrates. Remember, how the cat sees? Well that is truth. The beasts see in a way that makes them a part of all things. They see how they are connected to everything else, they are a part of all of life. This is truth.

As you soften your eyes, or you can close them if you wish, do not ask yourself what is the truth. Ask the plant beings to reveal their true nature. Ask them to share with you, who they are, not what they look like. All of life exists on many different levels, you need to see the level that is most important to you in this moment. Now just relax, let the sound of the water carry you and ask to see who this garden really is."

I was slowly but surely getting familiar with this process of letting what was inside come out. That is the only way I could describe it. It never seemed to work if I tried to grab something from the outside and bring it in. Relaxing is the hard, part, to let go and not try to anticipate what will happen. To be empty but full. As I tried to stay aware of the process I was going through, while going through it, I started to feel somehow more alive, lighter. I started to feel as though everything around me was me, and I was experiencing it, not like I was looking at it, but as if I was part of it. I struggled to stay aware of who I was, while understanding what was happening. It was very difficult to be part of everything and separate at the same time, in fact it was impossible. When I allowed myself to be part of everything I could see myself sitting there, not as a person but as pulsing vibrating light. When I tried to be separate, I could see the plants as a wall of energy, and that energy seemed to pulse in and out depending on how hard I was grasping on to staying separate. The image I saw in my mind was there and then it was gone. In frustration I opened my eyes and there was Gnua sitting right in front of me, silent, eyes closed, seemingly in deep union with everything around her.

I closed my eyes again, I wanted to see how Gnua looked if her energy was part of everything. Quieting myself again, I just allowed my sight to come from deep down inside of me. A light started to eliminate the dark, I could see the plants and I could perceive myself, but I could not see Gnua, she was right in front of me and I could not perceive her. I opened my eyes again to be sure she was still there. There she was, still and peaceful in the same place. Again back I went to bring forth my sight. It was then that I could see a brilliant pulsing energy right in front of me. But the energy extended itself to all that was around us, and beyond, into the mountains and the sky above. I could see no end to the energy, I could only see different states of vibration. It was like looking at the mist. If you look at the mist as a whole it can appear to be a wall. But if you look closer some spots seem more see through than others. Gnua's energy was like that. In some places it almost looked solid, in others, it was very translucent and had a different quality. I studied her energy, so that I could ask more questions. I had not seen the sisters like this before, and I was curious. I knew what I was seeing was truth, but I wondered why we could not see this with our physical eyes. What was the sense in having physical eyes when they lied to us? The minute I started to think, I was thrown back to physical reality, and the world of solidity.

Gnua still sat in front of me, but this time her eyes were open.

"Your sense of perception is getting greater, but you still have not quite learned the truth of it. You have time and you will learn. You want to know why my energy appeared to be in many places at the same time? That is because it is in many places at the same time. I have been able to let go of the belief that I am contained by the being you see in front of you. I have the understanding that I am many beings in many places at the same time. We of the sisterhood, are in various stages of development, just as you are. You are different from the others that live outside the palace. Though Orla and your Mother came from the same place, they are different as well. I know you are about to ask what the difference is. So I will answer before you ask.

The difference is simply this, what is it that you choose to believe in? This is also the secret to the perception of reality. Let me tell you the story of what is to come, for it is the same story as what has already passed.

In the future as the people here become more and more separated, their search for meaning will become more and more desperate. They will grasp on to all forms of suggestion, playing them out to the end to find out there was no meaning in them. There will be wars, destruction, and devastation, not only of the planet but of their understanding of who they are. This will happen over and over again, each time it will appear to happen for different reason, but it will occur on the same planet. In the extreme, at the very end, the decision will be made as to whether the very existence of the people will carry on or not. With each war and plague that devastates this earth comes the opportunity for change. To live differently, to love more, to accept more and to grow. You see in the end, the final battle that is fought will not be a battle against one another, it will be the battle against themselves. The people will have gotten to a point where they feel there is no meaning in existence. There is no meaning in their lives or the lives of any other being. In their desperate search for the meaning of their lives, they will not be able to see what is directly in front of them. They will not be able to see that the meaning of life, is simply the power to choose to change their mind.

This has happened in some form on all worlds that are in development. There is no way to teach this to another, it is something that must be experienced. To change your mind is to change your reality. Your reality is just a projection of what you feel about yourself. Society on this planet will be devastated many times, and with each spiral upward the devastation will increase many times. In the end it will be decided whether the planet and all of its inhabitant will be released from their dimensional reality to go forth in a new understanding, or whether society will sink and the planet will start over again. This is pattern of growth. This is how the All experiences itself in constant levels of growth. This is how we die and are reborn on the same time thread. From the beginning to the end it is all connected. It could all stop in one beat of your heart, if you just changed your mind.

There will always be those that have the wisdom of the ancients but there will not be enough of them to tip the balance of energy. This is how it is meant to be. No one is to influence another against their will. Each of you will choose your life, even if it does not appear to be that way, this is the path of truth. This is something that you must learn and learn very well, for it will be at the basis of the decisions that you will make."

I was getting that feeling again that I really didn't want to go towards my future. It was getting late, we had spent the whole day in the garden and no time seemed to have passed. However, the long rays of the sun told a different story, one that said night was approaching. So we left for the mountain top, back to the temples and my white walls. I was having a difficult time separating everything I had learned that day from what I had learned from life. I believe my greatest difficulty was in believing that the future would not be what I had wanted it to be. I had to stop and think about what it was I really did believe about my life and what I wanted my life to be. Perhaps this is why I was created, not conceived. I felt very disillusioned and disheartened. I felt betrayed by my parents and the sisterhood. I felt like I was something and not someone. I was angry. I was hurt. I had no desire to carry on to a life that would not be mine. If I could not do as I wanted, why do anything at all?

Chapter Eleven

I could see the beginning of a new day starting outside my white walls. I was not sure I wanted to get up. I really did not want to hear more about duty or what I had been created for. That to me was to live a meaningless life. When I came to this place, I was young, I realize now, I had little knowledge of life. I have been here a long time, learned more than I wanted to learn, not only about life, but about what the future will be. I wasn't sure there was any reason to continue anything. If life was going to take the course the sisters told me it would, well then perhaps I should just let it go its own way, and I will go have a life somewhere else.

I lay there for while, trying not to think, but the harder I tried to stop my thoughts the more they flowed. I envisioned all kinds of futures, the ones I wanted and the ones I didn't. None of them seemed to make me happy. I did not want to be in the place I was born to be in. Freewill, they all talked so much about freewill, but I did not feel as though I had any. It seemed the decisions had already been made for me and I had no choice. I really just wanted to go back to sleep and not wake up.

It was midday and I still had not appeared in the courtyard. I was starting to wonder if they had not even noticed I was not there. I wanted to be left alone and at the same time I wanted someone to come for me. To at least check on me, I wanted someone to care. With that thought The One entered the room. She came to me and sat on the edge of my bed. She leaned forward and touched my face and smiled. It was a knowing smile. She was very soft and gentle with me. She sat there for a moment looking into me before she spoke. I could feel her gaze reaching into me, comforting me. The energy she offered was one of understanding.

"A life of service is a difficult life. It is a life that in the beginning you do not think is your own. I remember feeling this same way, when it was my time. You and I, we are very much alike, strong willed, and adventurous. Ever curious about the world around us, but wanting to go our own way. We are so sure we make better decisions than the universe.
Tell me now, how is it you envision your future, sitting at the head of your table?"

"Well, thinking of that just makes me feel trapped. Like you said it doesn't matter what I do, it will have the outcome it will have. I don't want to waste my life, doing something I don't want to do, if I have no control over it. That is not a life."

"Why do you think you have no control over the outcome of your life?"

"Well you said, I can't win. Things are rather predestined, and what I do will not make a difference."

"Well if that is what I said, that is not how I meant it. A life of service is a blessed life, when you can grow beyond yourself enough to see the powerful impact you have. The challenge most people have is they believe they have to control their lives and all the lives around them if they are going to make a difference. Most people see life as a win or lose situation. If they don't win then they lose. Life is never that straight forward. Life is always by degrees. The most powerful changes you can make are not always the ones you can see. True change happens within the people. That kind of change takes longer, and can happen over generations. It is true that in your lifetime you could make many changes by enforcing laws or making rules. But this is not change. True leadership is leadership that is based in service to the people. By doing what is right for the people, letting the people see, their concerns are your concerns. To lead the people means to lead by example, not by force. Loyalty is only ever created through respect. The people need to see, that you are the change they want in their lives. To be that change you have to live that change.   It is a sure sign that a society is about to evolve when those that rule place more and more restraints on the people. Always remember, there are two kinds of rulers, those that wish to expand and those that wish to contract. Those that wish to expand, rule for the people, those that wish to contract, rule for themselves.

"Well if I have to live as one of the people, then why do I have to be trained here in this place, away from the people learning to do things the people can't."

The One smiled a big smile, she really liked it when I used my mind to challenge her. "That is a good question.   Here on this planet, there are some different circumstances. If you were to leave the protected area, many of your people would die. The world beyond your area is beautiful, but it is wild and cares not for the life of your people.   The people are alive because we helped the world calm herself and stabilize. Your protected area is not part of the natural environment that has now been established on this earth. We maintain the delicate balance of cycles to create an ideal place to live. Enough rains to water the fields, the right temperature for things to grow and life to be pleasant. Never too hot and never too cold. There are no infestations of harmful creatures that would devastate the food supply. When the earth was first seeded, we had to create this perfect environment to ensure the seedlings could and would grow and survive. This was long before you came here. But all the beasts that are now out there, were once within your protected area. And this is how the people came to be part of your life. The people were created to help us maintain and care for all the seedlings til they could be placed into the other environment."

"Did we create the people? I was caught off guard by this unveiling. The people had always just been there, I had never really thought that at one point they had not been with us."

"No, the people were a gift, to help us, our bodies at that point were not well suited for doing a lot of the work that needed to be done, so the people were created by using different species, so that the others could successfully seed the planet. They have thrived here, grown and developed. They are separate from us, but still dependent. They have great intelligence and as they grow they are learning to understand the concepts that we teach you. In their future one day they will be like us. But they are a fledgling species and they are easily mislead. This is one of the reasons Orla has taken so many of them. It is very easy to change their minds for them. They do not have the ability to see the whole truth yet, they are simply not developed enough. We have however started to teach a small group of them. They are learning very well but they are limited by the density of their bodies. Still, they have great potential. So until they have developed enough to understand what it is we are teaching you, you are one of the few left that can take care of your protected area."

I was not sure what to say. I always got the feeling that no matter how much The One revealed to me, there was so much more she was hiding. Perhaps "hiding" is a little harsh. There was a great deal she was not yet willing to tell me.

The Others were not from here? I wonder why I had always thought they were from this planet or that they had come with the sisterhood? It was a difficult to change my perception so fast. Maybe that is why The One said change happens over generations. Maybe it is not so possible to change your mind that fast, perhaps you have to change your mind consistently, but by degrees.

"A life of service, is really about a of life of making subtle changes, about helping people be as happy as they can be. The happier people are, the easier it will be for them to make their own lives. In a life of service you have the opportunity to make real and lasting change. A life of service helps the people believe in themselves, and that they can create better lives for themselves. That is real power. Helping the people to empower themselves through education and love. This is what I am asking you to do. To take the special skills you are learning here and offer them to the people in a way they can understand them, and work with them. You are the last of your kind. After you, the Others will have to take care of themselves, and they will need knowledge and skills to do that. The members of the Counsel will be coming for the harvest. We are doing what we can to ensure a smooth transition, but we need someone that can move among the people, be with the people, so that the people can see a goal and a reason to become more than they are. A life of service is the ultimate challenge. The question is, are you up for it?" With that she hugged me and got up and left.

In that moment, I really wasn't' sure what I was thinking. My mind was thinking so many thoughts all at once, I could not focus on just one of them. The way The One put it, a life of service was an honorable life. I was still having some difficulty believing that. I had always thought life was about doing what you want to do, being who you want to be, having what you want to have. Isn't that the way it was? I remember watching my parents and thinking they had everything they wanted, but now I was starting to wonder. Were they just like me and they created the life they wanted, within a life of service? I didn't like life to change so much and so constantly. How was I ever supposed to understand something that was not going to stay the same. Why was everything changing so much right now, it didn't change like that when I was young.

"Yes it did, you were just very unaware of the changes, your parents saw no need to involve you in the decisions they made, but it is the nature of all things to change. Change or die, that is the way of the universe."

Wen stood in the doorway. Another of the sisterhood. I knew she had come to take me, to teach me. I did not want to go, I was tired and confused.

"Come, we must go now. You need to rise above this."

So I did as was commanded of me. That is how I felt, I was being told what to do. I could have refused her, but then I would just be putting off the inevitable. Let's get it over with. Off I went with Wen. We climbed, and climbed, up a small path that turned into loose rocks and sand. We climbed til it hurt to breathe, and then we climbed some more. We climbed til the blue sky turned to black and there was barely room for the two of us to stand together at the mountain top. There I clung to the mountain for support against the winds that tried to hurl me against the rock. It was cold, and I did not like it.

Wen commanded me to look out upon the earth. I was afraid to move, for fear the winds would grab me and pull me to my death. But I looked, and it was amazing. I could see the whole of the world. We were above all things. I had never been this high before. I could see the tops of other mountains, and the temples where the sisterhood were. It seemed like a tiny dot in the distance. I could not see the sisters but I could see their light. They looked like small balls of light that moved about. For the first time as well, I could see that their lights were of different colors and the vibrated in different ways. As I focused on that they started to look so different to me. Each one, was affecting the earth they walked upon in such a different way. They left small trails of light wherever they went and that light was absorbed into the earth. Far away I could see the land bridge that led to my home. There seemed to be activity there but I could not make out what it was. My eyes were not made to look across such distances.

After I had taken in as much as I could Wen spoke. "Is it not amazing! I love it here. This is not like any other planet in our system. You can look at the skies here and in all the dots of light that you can see, there is not another place like this."

Wen was realizing, I would not be able to hold on much longer, so she raised then lowered her arms very slowly. As she did this the winds died down to a breeze. I was able to relax my grip some. The cold also subsided. I was starting to be able to feel my body again. Wen was the Goddess of the Air.

"I do forget sometimes that the wind is more powerful than the body. The air, the winds, I just sometimes need to come here to feel their power, to feel what they truly are. The air is the most necessary and the most elusive of all. You cannot see it when it is still, yet you know it is there, cause you can breathe. Like the water, it is essential to the beings of this planet. Air is the energy that makes things move. Earth stands still unless moved by water or air. Even the waters can stand still if not moved by air. Air makes the bodies of the people work. They take in the air and everything moves in their body, cause it is pushed by air. Air carries messages upon it. The air never stops singing. Air carries parts and pieces of earth the to spots where they need to be. Though you cannot see the air, it has great influence on everything around it. There are wind rivers in the sky that are created by the winds that blow constantly. The great birds that soar endlessly spiralling upward, do so because the winds carry them. The clouds are dependent on the wind bringing them moisture from the sea. It is because of the wind that trees are flexible and the grass will dance in unison. To all beings who know how, they shall put their ears to the wind and wait for the wisdom that is carried on earth's breath. In times to come, you may wish to send a message to someone, but do not wish that message to be known by anyone but them.

To send this message you have to write in symbols known to you what it is you wish to say, and think of the person to receive the message. The wind will carry the message for you. You can write the symbols on sand or on stone, but you must put them somewhere that the wind blows. The wind shall lift them up and carry them. Vibration is received by the wind and reproduced as a wave, through to its destination. This has long been a secret used by us, the sisterhood. Why do you cling so fiercely to the mountain?"

"I do not have wings like the birds so that the wind will carry me, nor do I have your light body. I would fall to my death if I were to slip from this place."

"Oh, I thought that might be something you would like, you seem to think you have no future anyway. Perhaps death is more agreeable than a life that you are not in control of?"

I didn't want to have that conversation here, I just wanted down from this mountain. I didn't want to die yet.

"Well I am not sure I want to live a life of service. But I don't want to die at this moment. Lets leave." I demanded.

Wen smiled at me and nodded her head. She glided down the mountain before me, and I shivered and shook with every step. I was petrified of the rocks that slipped so easily beneath my feet. I was very happy when we got to the wider trail and the trees and plants welcomed me back, by offering me their branches for support.

"I don't really like the wind," I said to Wen. I knew she would not like that, but it was true.

"Well then this is your weakness, this is the weakness that can be used against you. All things that you fear, must be looked at. Why do you fear them? Fear is a warning system for your body. Fear allows you to know when there is a possibility of something harming you. But fear should never be understood to be your master. Fear is an internal sound, that sings with impending or probable danger. It puts you on high alert, tells you to pay attention to your inner and outer world. But that is all fear is meant to be. You need to listen to your fear, then assess the situation and proceed in awareness. Not run away and hide.

Up there on the mountain top, it was not the wind that you were afraid of, it was the fact that you did not think you had enough strength to withstand the push of the wind. If you had been stronger, you would not have feared the wind. Belief in yourself will eliminate most fears. Fear is a very intrusive companion. If you allow it too much control, it can exhaust you, then you truly won't have the energy you need, when a real problem comes along. Fear is often used as an excuse, to not experience the things you are meant to experience. Do not let fear rule your life, or there will be no life and you might as well have thrown yourself from that mountain."

By the time I got back to the white walls, I was exhausted. I just wanted to lay down. I wanted to feel the safety of the bed and let go of the fear that had invaded my being. I wasn't sure why I could not shake this fear. I was here, now, not on the mountain with the winds pushing me and pulling me. Why was I still afraid?

I was starting to feel that my journey today was not about learning of the air and the wind. I was starting to think it was more about learning of my weaknesses. Learning more about the thoughts I have been having. Perhaps I was not supposed to see life quite as casually as I had been. But I was too tired to think anymore, I would let sleep take me now. So I didn't have to think.

Through a fog, my Mother came to me. She stood before me exactly as she had the last moment I saw her. I ran to her and hugged her. She was real. This made no sense to me, and the expression on my face told her so.

"My child, it is so good to feel you. Yes I am real, and so are you. We are in an in between place right now. You can come to me in your sleep and I to you. We do not have a lot of time so we must go." she said in a voice so familiar, it brought tears to my eyes.

"Go, go where?" I asked. With no reply, she took me by the hand. I felt as though I was moving but I could see nothing that would appease the questions in my senses. We came to a point of light that grew as we stepped into it. We were home. We were beyond the land bridge back in the protected area, home of my Father, the land where I had lived my young life.

"Now I just want you to watch, we cannot be seen or perceived. We shall only be here for a moment so pay close attention to what you shall see." my Mother spoke intensely, this was not her usual manner.

I watched the scene before me. It all looked as it had before I left. The great stone pillars and the cool stone tile floors. The fabrics flowed in the afternoon breeze as they had always done. The colors played against the white walls of my home. The sun was high in the sky but the stone kept cool through the day. I could hear my Fathers voice, he was approaching. As he entered the main hall, I could see he was accompanied by a woman. She was very tall and moved with grace. Her hair was long and black, her features were pointed and she was very attractive. My Father spoke to her in gentle tones, and she smiled. He let go of her hand and left the room. As soon as he was gone the smile left the woman's face. She turned and motioned to another man who entered the room. In a voice that was just above a whisper, she asked the man, how the plans were coming. Would everything be ready in time? Her face then changed, she was not so pretty, her face was harsh, and angry. She said they had to move, before I returned home. He was weaker now, that I was not there. When I returned his strength would return. With a flip of her hand she ordered the man away. My Mother and I were once again in the dark.

"That was Orla, my sister, the Atlantean Queen. In his grief, your Father has offered her his devotion. Orla cares not for him, however he is blind to her intentions. She intends to over throw him and take possession of the house and the people. If the people do not do her bidding she will kill them. Orla cares not for anything but herself. It is very important you return home. You must save the people and the land."

Why did my Mother not say, I must save my Father?

"You hesitate at a life of service because you have no idea what that life really is. You only think you cannot do what you wish. These are the desires of a child, not the wisdom of the woman you are becoming. Would you see all that you have known, destroyed, because you want to do what you want to do? If it is all destroyed, what home will you have, and what is it you will wish to do, when there is no where to do it. You need to put these thoughts aside. Let go of the foolishness of your youth. If you wish to do something, to make a change, to fulfill your destiny, you will complete your learning and return home. I only pray it shall be in time. The One will not let you go til you are truly prepared to face Orla. She knows if you are not prepared than you may die also. I died so that you and the others could live, I knew I could buy enough time, with my death, that it would give you a chance to grow, and become who you truly are. I know you sense who you are, but I know you are afraid of living that truth. I will tell you one thing. If you do not at least try to right the wrongs that have occurred in my absence, you will go to your grave regretting the path that you chose. Then you will be destined to repeat it. I do not think the life you are living is something you wish to repeat. Go now awaken, and arise. You are a queen and a powerful woman. You must try to bring change or the end of our society is inevitable."

She disappeared back into the fog from which she came. For a second it was dark and then, there was light all around me. I opened my eyes to see the whole of the sisterhood standing around me.

"Now do you understand the importance of a life of service?" The One said as her gaze pierced into me, looking for signs of compliance.

"Yes, I am ready now. I will not let my Father down. He needs me. I need him. I will do what I must do, to remove Orla from my home, and return my Father to himself."

"Good, then we shall start the last of your studies tomorrow. Now finish resting. Soon you shall learn to weave."

The sisterhood turned and left, and I was returned to the darkness. Sleep was upon me, before I closed my eyes.

Chapter Twelve

In my childhood I had envisioned a life that looked like my parents life. I would grow and be paired with someone that I loved, would have a child of my own and live out my life in the land that I knew as my home. But as I looked back upon my memories, that was not what was meant for me, no matter what. The seeding of the earth had been very successful and at some point in the near future, other worlds would be coming for their harvest. That would mean building an entire society to accommodate the visitors and helping them harvest their seeds more than living my own life. As I took time to look realistically into what my future would be, I saw that no matter what, my life was never meant to be my own.

I rose before the sisterhood gathered to pay homage to the sun, I knew my time at the sisterhood was limited. Now that it had come down to it, I wasn't sure I wanted it to end. Life here was easy, easier than I knew it would be when I returned home.

I went to the Temple of the Sun to say my own prayers. To send a message on the wind to my Father, telling him I would be home soon. I gave thanks that the sisterhood had taken me in, and had been so kind to me, teaching me patiently, even when I did not want to learn. I was thankful for the Earth and the bounty that she had shown me.

In fact I was thankful for my life, even though I had not always been so and was very unsure of what the future held. In this moment I was grateful for the life I had lived. The truth was, I was not wanting to go into my future, but neither could I stay stuck. The fear of what could be was less than the fear of not trying. That is all I knew at this moment, I had to try, I had to change things. I did not want my Mothers life to be for nothing, and I did not want to see my Father ensnared by a woman with dangerous illusions. I was the only one who knew the truth, that could create a change. So onward I would go, even though it meant piercing the depths of unknown waters.

As I was leaving the Temple, the suns rays graced the day with their love. The sisterhood had gathered in their normal way to greet the day. I sat a short distance away and took in the ceremony. I wondered how truly old these ladies were? I wondered how many times they had done this ritual, because to watch them it would seem every time was the first.

I watched their movements as the dedication was passed from woman to woman. Their movements were synchronized and powerful. The energy flowed from one to another, no pause, no hesitation. Around the circle it went till it ended where it began. Life here was such a rhythm. I was realizing that the rhythm brought great security. It was the rhythm that allowed me to feel safe. I remember as a child always fighting the flow of things, but in the end it was the rhythm of the music, or my Mother rocking me back and forth that returned me to that place of peace, where all my troubles dissolved into dust. I think I had always fought the rhythm, for it was now in this second that I understood the power of the rhythm, and following its momentum. Being in the flow, allows me to stay peaceful and centered. I do not have to expend so much energy fighting my fear. You cannot push a river, if you try, you are likely to drown. Instead let that river carry you, and you can sail to new adventures.

I was starting to feel old. Even though I was barely full grown, I felt ages beyond my years. I wondered what other women my age were doing? Falling in love, having children, becoming wives? There would be none of that for me. I was on a different path. A path that was not my own, but still belonged to me.

Enaka was approaching me, I knew she was to be my next teacher. Enaka was one of the women, that I was not sure what it was she did. Some of the women had very specific duties, but Enaka seemed to do a bit of everything. I would be interested to discover what her teachings were.

"Are you ready?" Is all she said to me as we headed out once again. I had often wondered why none of my lessons happened in the courtyard. Perhaps it was a sacred area, not a teaching area. Perhaps I was just too novice to be allowed to learn there? Whatever the reason, it had crossed my mind a few times to wonder why.

I followed Enaka on a the path that led to the cliffs where my Mother and I had sat looking out over the plains. I loved this spot, it sat very high up, almost to the clouds. When you looked out over the plains you could see forever, right to the sea. It was a beautiful peaceful spot.

"Do you know why I brought you here?" Enaka questioned.

"No, I am not even sure what it is you do. Sorry." I apologized, and felt a little embarrassed.

Enaka smiled. "Well you are about to learn. What I do is a little obscure compared to the rest. The reason we came here is because there is so much open space, and what I must show you will be easier to see. As you look out before you, tell me, what can you see?"

I looked out over the open spaces again. I felt like my Mother was asking me this question all over again. I took in as much information as I could before answering Enaka.

"Well I see the plains that go forever, and in the distance is the sea. I see the animals that come here to eat, and at the edge of the plains I see the trees and the small hills that grow into mountains over there, in the distance. I see the birds that fly and the sky that is above them. I see some clouds and this spot here that we sit upon."

"This is good. Now, do you see what connects them all to each other?"

I wasn't sure I know what Enaka was talking about. I looked into the air, and then towards the ground looking for what I was supposed to see. I could see nothing. I tried harder squinting my eyes, trying to see the things that you can see with your eyes closed. But still I could not see anything. Enaka was laughing at me squinting so hard.

"I am afraid that won't help. But I will help you to see what I am talking about. Take my hand, I am going to allow you to see through my eyes. It is the way I see the world and it is also how I help the world." I took Enaka's hand and as I did, I felt a very warm sensation come over me. The warmth started to tingle and that turned to a buzzing feeling. The buzzing moved up my spine and to the base of my skull, then it felt like ants were crawling all over me. Then it disappeared. I opened my eyes to see the world before me as I had not seen it before. I could see the plains before me and the animals there, but they were communicating with one another. There was energy coming from the animals and going to the ground and the ground returned the message with information of its own. The birds communicated with the sky and the air. The sea spoke to the mountains and I could see there were energetic conversations going on within the sea. I supposed that was the creatures that lived in the sea talking one another or to the sea itself. Everywhere I looked, everything was connecting to everything else around it. Information flowing from one to the other and back again. A network, constantly in motion. Different species spoke in different colors. Green flowed into red and red flowed into gold and gold flowed into blue. Color flowed like streams and at the point where two colors met, there was a blending of the colors, like a tiny rainbow. It was beautiful. Where there had only been empty space before, now I could see it was filled with the colors of communication. The colored light that emanated from all things into all other things.

"Amazing isn't it?" Enaka said, sounding as entranced as I was. "Even after all this time, I still am humbled by what we don't think we can see. There are many beings that see this way all the time. In fact it is much easier for us, the sisterhood to see this way, than it is for you. We are closer to energy bodies, our bodies are lighter and vibrate differently from yours. It is important that you see this with your own eyes, that way you will know it to be true."

I kept looking in awe at the interactions between all species and what I didn't even think of as species. It told a story of intelligence and community that you could never describe with words. It told a story of co-operation between beings, whether those beings were animated or not. It was the truth of reality, that communication happens at all times, not just when we think it is happening.

"But how can all these things talk to one another?" I said.

"That is the right question. It appears that all these species are different from one another doesn't it?"

"Yes?" I replied, in a rather questioning tone. I wasn't sure if that was a trick question or not.

"Well you are right at least by appearances sake. All of these species are slightly different but created from the same elements, it is just the coding that makes them different. Their ability to communicate has nothing to do with speech though. True communication within all species comes from within the emotional centers of the being. Words are becoming more and more deceptive as the Others become more divided from the world they live in. You see the problem with communicating verbally is the words you use do not have the same meaning to all. This creates a barrier, especially if you assume another being understands what you mean. So all beings of the natural world communicate through emotional imagery. What they feel, their needs, their wants, their joys and their pain, are all expressed energetically to the world around them. The grass will understand the great honor bestowed upon it when a new life is born upon its green tips. And in turn that new life will honor the grass by feeding it. You see that spot where one species connects with another, you see that very colorful spot? It looks rather like a rainbow. "

"Yes," I nodded. I was truly enjoying this lesson.

"Well that is where I do my work, that is the point of connection, the point of flow. As in all things, at times there is a little help needed to connect a circuit of information. I repair those spots with the color that is needed. The color represents a certain vibration or frequency that is missing to complete the link. When it is repaired, communication can proceed. If these species were not in constant communication with their surroundings, most would die. You and your family and the Others that you care for, are different. You are in a protected area where that communication is not necessary. The things in your world are predictable. Out here, on these beautiful plains, the beasts need to know the best places to feed, when the clouds will cover the sun, and when the rains will come. Sometimes the rains come too swiftly and they can get washed away in floods if they don't heed the warnings of the clouds. Just as all beings here on this earth communicate, so do, all planets communicate with all other planets. There are planets out there that are based on anger, and planets based on love. Some planets are based on healing and other are based in pure intellect. Every variety that you can imagine exists around you. This is why earth is so special. It is a combination of all things. Planets like these are rare. A planet that has the ability to create more than two or three understandings of itself is a self aware planet. This is why the Council wanted to protect it so badly.

But we fear over time, we may not be able to maintain control of the balance here. You see it is the Council's practice, to never eradicate an established species. For that reason, other worlds have died, and it is considered a part of the natural turning of time. The council will only go so far to alter life.

All things flow into and out of one another, if there is a disconnection or a blockage somewhere, then all things will suffer. Every day, I watch the world to make sure things are flowing as they should. The elements have a cycle that allows for abundant growth, if one of them is out of balance the whole cycle suffers. The animals have cycles that flow with the growth and the decay of the land. If the land suffers so do the animals. If the animals suffer, then the land suffers. The land depends greatly on the animals to spread seeds and nutrients across its surface.

There is nothing that is not linked to something else. Now your species, and the Others, think of themselves as being separated from the rest of the species here on the planet, because they have lived in a protected space for so long, but this is not true. In the times to come the protected area will not exist anymore and the Others will be vulnerable to the elements and the beasts that roam free.

You must teach the Others respect for the land and to understand that the planet is alive and receptive to their needs. We teach a small group of Others, but you need to rule with the understanding that you will not just be a ruler, you will be a teacher. You must help them to honor the land and work with the cycles, so that they can continue to be abundant, and have an understanding of the interconnectedness of all life. Is this something that you are willing to do?"

"Yes of course," I replied. I had played with the children of the Others all through my childhood, I really didn't know we were different beings, until it was explained to me that our bodies received and processed energy differently than theirs did. They were not as advanced a race of beings as we were. So it was that we were capable of more control over our surroundings than they were. That is why we had to protect them. They were childlike and innocent, but also capable of great violence. It was said when they were created, they were given too much emotion, but that had to be, because it was the emotion that made them powerful and able to perform the tasks they were created to perform. I liked them. They were intelligent and had great understanding. They possessed great passion and skills. They learned very quickly and liked to laugh a lot. I would enjoy teaching them the necessary skills they needed to survive outside the protected area.

"Good Enaka replied. Now do you know how to repair a break in the flow?"

"No", I shook my head. I didn't even know the flow was so important till now.

Enaka smiled and said, "Ok well lets find one to repair. Look over there. See that little baby. If you look closely, the connection with her Mother is not very strong. The connection looks very fuzzy, thin, like it could break at any moment. If that connection breaks, the baby will die. Now, I want you to focus on the fuzzy area, and imagine it to look strong , with bold colors. Send the area love from yourself. See everything operating as normal. Visualize a strong bond between baby and Mother. In your mind I want you to imagine the flow into and out of all things as working perfectly, but with the Mother and the baby in the center. Don't try to fix, The One spot, just imagine, it is all working perfectly. Ok? Do you have any questions?"

I stopped to think about it for a minute, to see if I could imagine what Enaka was telling me to imagine or not. When I thought I had the right image, I described to Enaka what I was seeing in my mind. When she said that was right, I went to work trying to fix the disturbance in the flow. I closed my eyes and settled myself, I could see the animals down on the plain and the flow going from one to the other. When I got to the Mother and the baby, I saw the flow between then as strong and beautifully colored. It took several minutes to really feel that the flow was fine, clear, and moving as it should. When I opened my eyes again, Enaka sat there smiling at me.

"Very good" she said. "There may be hope for you yet"

I felt quite proud of myself. I was not sure that I would be able to see the flow without her help but I knew it existed and when you know something exists, it is easier to see.

"Well that was a good day, lets go back to the courtyard and see what the others are doing."

If you don't mind, I think I will stay here for a time. I would just like to watch life happen around me. I won't see things like this when I go back home.

"That is fine, don't be too late. The One worries if you are not back before the moon rises."

I nodded my head. Enaka rose and disappeared almost immediately over the ridge behind me.

I sat there watching the great lumbering beasts go about their day, eating the long grasses of the plains. It was so peaceful just to watch them. Every now and then there would be a disturbance at the surface of the sea. The water would boil and foam. I knew there were other beasts below its surface, but I was never fast enough to really see what made the water churn.

I thought about sitting in the same spot with my Mother, and how my future might be. I lay in the grass and let the sun warm my body. I knew

122

moments like this would be rare in the days to come. Then at the end of the day, I headed back towards the courtyard and the temples, my temporary home.

When I got back the ladies were buzzing about as usual. Busy with the chores at days end, before they settled into their usual evening session of discussion on this and that. I thought this evening I would join them, I really hadn't done a lot of socializing with them since I had been here. I was either too tired or too distant to be one of them.   And they had allowed it to be that way for me. Tonight it would be nice, it would be different, to just be one of them, not student and teacher.

Chapter Thirteen

In the evening the sisters liked to sit around a fire, talk and watch the flames. It is not that they needed the fire, but they were fascinated by it. On their home planet, they did not have fire in the same way. They loved the way it glowed and changed colors, seeming to dance to some unheard melody. Fire had a will of its own. The women did not need heat, or food, they did not need shelter. They lived in light bodies. Luminescent light, shimmering, glowing, and at time almost imperceptible, other times almost solid. Depending on what they were doing and what they were thinking, their bodies were constantly changing. Shifting like the sands at the edge of the sea.

They had told me that on this planet their bodies were not consistent, not in the way they were on their home planet. The shifting fields around the planet affected them in many ways. When they first arrived here, working with the energies around the planet was like trying to stay afloat in rough seas. However as earth calmed and the women became more adapted to working with their bodies energy flow and the planets energy flux, there were able to flow with the flux. Now the only way to know that the fields of Earth were changing was to look at the density of their bodies. It took constant maintenance to keep the balance, however it was less extreme for them now.

The darkness fell like a blanket of deep blue that covered all the land. The fire roared. In the light of the dancing flames, I could see the faces that had become so familiar to me.

Enaka, she taught me of the flow of life, and how all things are truly energetically entangled with all other things. Gnua. She was the gardener. She taught me to see how life really is. To look beyond what my eyes see and to perceive the truth and beauty that lies in front of me. Eawannu. Life sometimes needs a little help to get where it is going and this is what Eawannu showed me. The kingdom that lives within a kingdom. The little beings that assist in the growth of all things. Eluna, mistress of the water. I had never thought of water as a living being before Eluna. She helped me to understand that water is not just something you drink, but it is the carrier and transporter of wisdom. Tonn, funny little Tonn. She was the odd one out in the women. Most of them were tall graceful beings, but Tonn like the land she works with is a woman of substance. I do try to walk as though my feet kiss the earth after Tonn's lessons. Wen, the one that I found hardest to grasp. She oversees the air. She is the one I understand the least.

Her lessons made sense to me, however who she is somehow escapes me.

They all are so different but fit together like pieces in a puzzle. There is only one more sister that I must learn from and that is Chiana. She always seems to be happy and energized. She is also very youthful in the way she moves. When you are around her the world becomes even more alive and colorful. She is one of the older sisters but you would never be able to guess that. Her energy gives the illusion of fiery red hair and strong facial features, but with a smile that says ,"Lets go have fun". I really liked her and I was looking very much forward to learning what it was that she did.

Conversation was brisk around the fire, it always seemed to be that way. A lot of it was stuff I didn't understand. Things about how to improve efficiency in the way certain energies act and how best to dive into universal flow. I knew I had seen glimpses of all these things but to sit and talk of them technically was not within my level of capabilities. I was enjoying myself just watching everyone banter and bicker. The energy around the fire was lively and uplifting, it took me away from my concerns. Eventually The One wandered over to me. She sat next to me, placing herself gently against the ground, leaning her back against one of the many sacred stones in the courtyard. She must have seen the look on my face, because she started to smile.

"Are you surprised that I am casually resting against this stone?"

"Yes, I thought that stone was sacred. I thought sacred items were only used for ceremony? Isn't it disrespectful to treat them casually when they are held in such high regard?"

"I am very pleased with your progress. All the sisters enjoy teaching you. You learn well and are curious. However, with those questions, it has come to my attention that there are a few things that you do not yet understand. What I am leaning on right now is a rock. Just a rock. Yes it has been carved, and there are special symbols on it, but it is still just a rock. The symbols although sacred have no power, no more power than the rock. They are both important, but also irrelevant. I have lived a very long time, and I have never seen the symbols using the rock for their own purpose, nor have I seen the rock using the symbols for its own purpose. However when the sisters use the rock and the symbols, you have seen great things happen. Is this not true?"

I thought of many of the ceremonies I had witnessed, and yes it was true, but I had never before thought about why it was true. Indeed I had never before realized that the rocks and the symbols were doing anything.

"Well my young friend, things are just things, if they are not intended to be something greater than they are. The rock has no desire to be anything other than a rock, and the symbol's goal is to be a symbol. However if one of us intends that the energy of the symbol be revealed along with the power of the stone, great magic can occur. To become more than you are,

126

you must aspire to it. The stone will never be more than the stone, but because of our intent, the stone becomes aware of the power that it holds within it. Because of communication, the stone agrees to work with us. The symbols we use in some cases are like amplifiers, they allow a small energy to grow. In other cases the symbols can slightly alter an energy to be more pliable, or functional for what we are trying to accomplish. Nothing at all would ever happen though, if we did not intend it too. This is a very important thing for you to learn. You are going to be in many different situations in your future life, no matter where you are, or who you are with, nothing will ever happen, unless you first intend it too. There is a tremendous amount of power in life, and it is also true that some of the greatest power can be found in the smallest things. A word, a look, a thought, all these things contain infinite power. You can use that power with your intention.

Energy is just that, energy. It is all around us, every where we are. There is no place without energy. Energy is a non caring, non judgmental power. It does not care who uses it or for what, all it cares about is that it gets to experience, being used. In your future it is very important that you understand the power of energy, and how it is used, so that you do not misplace your understanding or your intention. To say that this rock created that tree would be incorrect, even though that might have been what you saw. To understand that one of the sisters used the power in the rock to help the tree grow, would be the correct understanding of the situation. The motives of others are often badly misunderstood, and sometimes purposely mislead. People do not always do what they say they are going to do, for the reasons they say they are doing them. Intention is everything. Orla is misleading your Father, with what he thinks are good intentions. Her motives are anything but good. These are the things you need to be able to understand in the people around you.

A rock is just a rock, until someone uses it for something else. That does not mean the rock has more power than it does, it just means that someone is able to use the power of the rock with intention.

Always ask the question, is this thing what it really is, or does this thing only appear to be what it is? Always examine the energy you feel around anything. Is the energy your are feeling natural to the object or is the energy unnatural to the object? This will tell you a great deal about how energy can be used. Energy is impartial and it does not strive to be right or wrong, if you remember this, your emotions will not be directed in the wrong manner.

When you allow for this, you can empower your focus correctly. In all situations, if you are working with beings that are not self aware, you are borrowing their power, not over powering them. You are asking for their cooperation to use their energy in a way they would never use it. They do

127

not sit back and wonder if you are good or bad, they just offer their energy freely. However it is different with beings that are self aware, the birds and the beasts. They have the right of choice and you cannot use their energy without their permission. They must agree with what you are choosing to do, this is where trust and respect comes in. The most important part of working with energy other than your own is in the deciding if what you are doing is good for the all, or not. There are times in life when you must do a tremendous amount of work for a single individual, especially when that individual is important to the all. However this will be the minority. Most of your life will be spent trying to decide if what you are about to do is for the greater good or not. Remember however, it is not always about making everyone happy, it is about what is best for their needs. You must be very clear that it is about "THEIR" needs and not about your own. Many fine rulers have lost their lands because they were unable to determine the difference between their needs and the needs of the people. I know this is a lot for you right now, but you will settle into it."

With that she squeezed my hand, and got up and left. I thought she would join the others but she went to the Temple of the Moon.

I did understand what she was talking about. I had seen my Father on many occasions make a decision for the people that he never would have made for himself. It had confused me at that young age. I had wondered who my Father was, because those decisions seemed so against his nature. But I now understood, it was for the good of the all. What I could not possibly know then, was, how hard some of those decisions would prove to be.

The evening passed quickly and I was tired, so I turned to sleep to fill my time. I remember dreaming that I was free. I was roaming in the deep forest, enjoying the smells and sounds that come in the wild. I thought I could sense another person there, but I could not see them. By his scent he was a man. I looked over the area, but still I could not locate him. I descended into a small valley that was heavily treed. There I followed a small stream that led me to the smell of smoke. A small fire burned brightly just ahead of me, and I could hear singing. It was a man singing by the fire, I came round the edge of the bush to the small opening in the trees, and at that moment, I woke up.

It was light out when I awoke. Even though I was awake, I could not shake the scent of the forest from me. I could still smell the smoke and the man. I wondered if it had been more than a dream. I lay still for awhile thinking about how that dream made me feel. I had not felt emotions like this before. I had no idea who the man was, or what he was doing in the bush. People did not live in the bush, they lived under the protective cover. All the speculating in the world would not give me any answers. So I got up and went out into the day. It was a glorious day. The temperature was just right with the bright sun streaming its rays down upon me. A gentle breeze blew and all felt right in the world. Even the dew covered flowers seemed to agree as they straightened themselves and nodded towards the sun. The small birds danced in the rays, as they bounced off the tiny droplets of mist that stirred as the light touched them.

"Beautiful isn't it. Morning is my favorite part of the day. Everything is fresh and new and it feels like the world is being reborn." Chiana spoke softly over my shoulder.

I hadn't heard her approach from behind so she startled me ever so slightly. I turned to smile at her, and was gifted with a joyful grin in return.

"Come we need to go discover what makes life, life." and she ran off in a direction I had not been before.

I hurried to catch her. She moved very gracefully but with great speed. She seemed not to take steps but to glide just above the surface of the earth, the effort it took to place and raise your foot was not present. We climbed high into the clouds, till the air turned to a putrid stench. The smell was so horrid it seized my ability to breathe and caused me to think I should die on that hillside. Chiana told me to just keep going, it did not smell nice but was important. So I continued upward to the flat topped mountain. It was here that we came to what appeared to be a mountain that has its top cut off.

"Long ago this mountain had a great crown, double peaks. It was beautiful. It stood majestic as it kept watch over all that was in its gaze. This was in the time that the earth was still restless. One day we felt the earth groan and shake, we knew she had pressure she must release, but we were not sure where she would do this. We were not living in the mountains at this time, we still lived beyond the land bridge on the island you call home. It was not long before the ground shook violently and the mountain exploded with a sound so loud it hurt our soul.

The top of the mountain, started to smoke and then there were sounds like a thousand thunders, and the earth came through the mountain. Everywhere there was smoke and fire, and a river of red ran from the mountain, we thought she would never stop bleeding. Days and nights it went on. Everything on the mountain appeared to be dead. No more did its peaks stand vigil over us. It was a vast deep wound. The earth had released her pressure, and after she was done, everything was covered in black. When the mountain had cooled, we came to see what was left. Standing here in this spot, we looked inside the mountain and we saw the same thing you see today. A boiling red river that flows to the surface and then disappears back inside the mountain. It is like a open wound for her, a place where she can release her energy, and not have to do so much damage anymore. "

"But there is such green lush growth here now? If it was all black, how did it turn to this?"

"That is why I have brought you here. It is time for you to understand the spark. The thing that makes life what you know it to be. If you look around you, you will see the trees and the bushes, plant life of all kinds, the animals that look back at you, the birds that fly above you and so many other forms of life, that you may not think of as alive. They are all here and living, they are all aware at different levels and they all have different perceptions of reality. Let me ask you a question, what do you think life is?"

What is life? I had thought about this before, but I have never been able to come up with one definitive answer. Life, what does it mean. To be alive? To be able to think? To feel? I had learned that all things are alive, even the rocks and the trees, but I still was not sure I thought of those things as being alive, like I was alive. I sat thinking for what seemed like a very long time. Chiana said nothing. She sat in a trance like state, waiting for me to speak. I knew speaking had nothing to do with being alive, nor did sight or perception. What factors were used to determine if you were alive? I had not seen a lot of dead things in my life. Some things looked the same dead as they did when they were alive, but you knew they were not alive. Movement was not the answer, for the rocks and the stones did not move by themselves. I could only come to one solution. To be alive is to know that you are alive.

Chiana opened her eyes and smiled that beautiful smile. "You are almost right about that. Since all things are alive in their own way, there really is no specific factors to determine life. Life has the most extreme variables known to us. It appears in all shapes and forms and at all levels of consciousness. There is no way for us to set some kind of margin that says, this is life and this is death except for one thing. This is the tiniest of all things. It is the spark of life. The spark is the single solitary point of consciousness that enters into structure to create life. It is nothing that you can see with your eyes or measure with a scale. It is a form of intelligent energy. It is a single point of light, that carries with it all it will need to know for its lifetime. It is a part of the All. A piece of universal awareness that has the desire to experience itself as something. That thing may be a rock, or a bird or a being such as yourself. Can you grasp my meaning about this?" Chiana asked as she watched me carefully to see if I would answer honestly.

"Well, yes and no. I can understand consciousness entering into something and it forming life. What I cannot understand is why you say it wants to experience itself as something other than itself, when it is already itself? Did you understand that?"

Laughing out loud, Chiana continued," Yes yes, of course. I remember being told this by my teacher and wondering the same thing. In our very limited perception of the All, we assume that it perceives the same way we do. I have come to understand that this is not so. Pure energy is just that. It may be self aware but there is no sensations, no feelings, no thoughts, no understanding of time. There is so much that we experience, that the All never would. So to understand that all forms of life exist in all different levels of awareness and perception, the All started to use its imagination about how life could be different than its current experience.

It is said that the All had its first feeling in the form of a tear, when that tear fell it created a world, and then another tear fell and another and another, till the sky that we see is filled with more points of light that you could ever count, and each point of light is a body of structure. Seeing all this made the All feel joy and with that joy came laughter. That feeling created the stars that shine light upon us, like the sun. The laughter generated joy, pure light and the light is what allows life to thrive here. The more the All experienced itself the more beings poured from it. None, more or less than any other. All were equal in life giving spark from the All. But as with many of the beings that exist through uncounted dimensions, as beings become self aware, they have the need to define themselves from others. And so it was with our race. When you define yourself as being more than something else, competition begins. The need to define oneself, the concept of MINE is born. You separate yourself from everything else with the misunderstanding that being self aware makes you better, or more important than other species you decide are not self aware.

When a species adopts this understanding, that it is separate, it starts to die. It may grow in numbers and develop great technology, but its spark starts to die. The spark is part of the All and when belief creates the illusion that it is separate from the All, its life force cannot function properly. If you took a teardrop and placed it in the sea, would you be able to tell the teardrop from the sea?"

"Of course not", I said.

"Right, that is what happens when the spark of life lives in a being that understands it is part of the All. What if you took a teardrop and placed it on a rock. Do you think it would last long?" Chiana questioned.

"It would be gone in a moment. But it would disappear back into the All." I smartly stated.

"There is a clever answer. Yes you are right. For all beings that believe they are separate, they return to the All, and rediscover the truth of life. However it seems that all young species have to experience great pain before they will allow themselves to understand love. I am the one that helps the spark of life channel its energy through creation. Love is the conduit for the spark. Over there is a nest of young birds. If the parents did not look after them they would die. It is the same with you. If you had not been loved, you would have died.

131

The spark of life needs a bed of love to ignite the flame of awareness. I infuse love into the things that need to be awakened by the spark of life. You were created because of the love of your parents. Not all things have that same love, but they still need to be given form. The only thing that keeps the universe together is balance, without that balance it would be torn apart, that means the All would be torn apart. This is what the All understood at a very early point. As more species became self aware, the less love there was, self awareness and love are not the same thing, at least not in the beginning. In the beginning, self awareness equates with the worst kind of selfishness, however at a later point, self awareness becomes selflessness.

Back to my point, the more self awareness there was the more love the All had to offer. This planet, this earth, has only begun its journey into self awareness. Orla is the first being that because of her self awareness, coupled with the feeling of separateness, shall do a great deal of damage to herself and others. The reason we consistently tell you of the connectedness of all things, is we do not want you to feel that separateness. You have already experienced it with the death of your Mother and the distance from your Father. But try to understand how an entire species feels that separateness when they cannot feel the All. The illusion becomes their reality and it takes many generations to discover they were never alone. The experiences you have had here, have taught you, that you are part of a greater whole, but no more and no less important than the whole. You are like the teardrop in the sea. You know you are the teardrop, but at the same time you are the sea. "

Chiana was then quiet. She sat once again looking forward into the space above the opening into the mountain. I knew everything she spoke of and had felt the connectedness to everything at times. It was still hard to see myself as connected to a twig, or the tiny ants that crawled on the ground. I knew the truth though. How could it be any different, after all, we all lived on the same planet, we breathed the same air and drank the same water.

I looked down into the mountain at the river of red flowing there. I wondered where it came from and where it was going? I had grown used to the smell to the point that I was not thinking about it all the time.

Chiana got up, and motioned for me to follow her. We headed back down the mountain and through the clouds again. She slowed her pace so that I did not lose her in the dense white fluff. As we were coming out the other side, I did not recognize where we were. It was all dark with points of light everywhere. It was like we had walked out into the night sky.

"Isn't it beautiful. I have always loved the night sky, with all the stars and planets. Everywhere you look there is life. Some of those forms of life you would not be able to recognize as life though. We become very familiar with our own reality and start to think other realities are not as real as ours. Because of this, we start to think we have the right to decide what is right and what is wrong. But that is not true. In this universe, there is no real right, and no real wrong. There is only balance. For everything that happens, every event, every death, every joy, every love and every hate, it is all just a balance point of something that is happening somewhere else. As you move through life, you will have experiences that you wish you did not have to have. We all do. However the more you can take from that experience and learn from it, the less pain you will experience. The worst thing you can do with a challenging experience is to label it wrong or right, bad or good. You can never tell what will come from an experience, some of the uncomfortable ones, lead to the greatest of joys. Do not be blinded by a moment of pain. Keep your eyes clear and open, to the spark of life that is injected into the moment. The spark of life that can lead you to a new experience, a happier one.

Each one of the lights you can see in the sky, they have all had endless sparks, but they started with only one. It is how we all start. We decide along the way, what we will create with that spark. No matter what this life brings you, remember, you will be the one to decide what it means to you, how it affects you. Nothing can hold you down if you don't let it. Allow your spark to shine as brightly as these lights, let everyone see you as a safe beacon, so that their sparks may join with yours. Most importantly, to those that would do you harm, send them love, they are the ones that feel the most separated. "

"Harm, what do you mean harm? Why would anyone want to harm me?" I turned to talk to Chiana, but she was gone. I didn't; know where I was. I reached down expecting to feel nothing but empty space under me, but instead I could feel a stone. I heard a noise from behind me and I spun around to see the glow of a flame just beyond the bushes. I was back at the courtyard. How? I do not know. The sisters were able to move through time and space in ways I would never understand. I made may way through the bushes to the fire. All the sisters were there chatting. Chiana was sitting beside The One and greeting me with that big smile.

"I bet you thought I left you out there in the night sky, all by yourself." she sort of chuckled under her breath.

" None of us would ever put you in any danger, we need you to stay all in one piece." The One chimed in.

The mood around the fire was a happy one, just as the day had started, it ended, in joy.

As I drifted off to sleep I could not get the image of the night sky out of my head and how many different beings were out there. How many different types of awareness? It was unfathomable. It did however bring me great comfort to think that I was not alone. That this planet, my little point of light in the sky was not the only one full of the spark of life.

Chapter Fourteen

Morning came too soon and I was comfortable laying still, watching the suns light play as it danced off the water in the alters. But the energy was rising in my body, I had a sense of anticipation, something was about to happen. Up I got and it would seem preparations were in full swing for something. The sisters were buzzing about, bringing great armfuls of flowers and fruit to the center of the courtyard. They were moving sacred stones into different positions, aligning them with one another. The One was standing in the center of it all offering direction. I wandered over to her and asked," What is going on?"

"Ah, tonight is full moon and we are going to celebrate the end of your lessons. You will be going home in two days, and we want to initiate you as one of us."

Going home? Those words hit hard. They impacted my body with enough force to make me stumble. I could see The One looking at me from the corner of her eye. But she did not move a muscle. She was just trying to judge how ready I was. The words I had been waiting so long to hear, had turned to words of dread.

"Maybe I should stay here awhile more. I am not sure I am ready? I am not sure I have learned enough?" I pleaded with her, not wanting to appear too desperate.

"Nonsense. You have been a very good student. Your Father needs you. You are ready. It will all be fine and I know you will be dearly missed by all of us here. You have no need for worries. Tonight is a celebration, let your heart be light."

By the end of the day the courtyard had been turned into a great flower garden. A small walkway had been created with tree limbs that were then covered in bright white flowers that sparkled in the sun. At the end of the walkway was the alignment of stones. Set in a double row, the stones had been layed out lengthwise. There seemed to be a pattern to the flowers, which I could not see from the ground. I went to the Temple of the Sun and climbed the side stairs, hoping it would give me enough elevation to see the pattern. What I saw was a spiral. The flowers had been arranged in such a way that they formed the same color pattern as a rainbow that moved inward towards the center. Birds and bees were flitting about, sucking on nectar and chasing little bugs that had been disturbed. The One looked my way and waved her arms for me to come down. I was honored that the sisters would go to so much work for me. It was indeed a little embarrassing. I should be the one celebrating them.

"We are all going to sleep now. It will be a long night and we want to have maximum energy levels. I suggest you get some sleep now as well." she said as she gently touched my hair.

I was not sure what she meant by a long night but I did feel suddenly tired. I did not know why, but I wondered if The One had altered my energy somehow, so that I would sleep. I barely made it to my white walls and onto my bed. I fell fast asleep. When I awoke, evening had fallen over the land. A dress had been left for me to wear. It was green with gold trim. Around the edges of the gold trim was a tiny detailing in red. It was very beautiful and very intricate. As I put it on, I was surprised that it felt like air, there was no weight to it at all. It felt almost alive as it lay against my skin. I felt different, wearing that dress, it is something I cannot really explain, I just felt as though all that I had learned was somehow within me as wisdom now. The dress made me smarter, more confident, aware of who I was at a deeper level.

As I went out beyond my white walls, I could see a fire burning in the center of the rearranged courtyard. The women were all present and standing waiting for me to join them. I stood hesitating, knowing this was the last night I would be able to be a free woman. I wanted to join the women, but doing so took me closer to the end of my time here. I paused, to take in the levity of my life, to be thankful for the moments it had offered me, and then, I went forth.

The One stepped forward to join me, the first of the ladies to offer their congratulations at becoming one of the sisterhood. The women formed a short but elaborate procession as they all went through the formalities of welcoming me. When they were finished The One led me to the beginning of the stone pathway that had been created earlier. There were small pots of fire on either side of the path all along the way to the end of the stone work. It was very beautiful with all the flowers reflecting in the light. Mesmerizing, I thought. The scent of the flowers were overwhelming me as the heat of the flame warmed the petals in the night air.

"I want you to walk slowly down this path. We are going to move around the fire in the center, as you approach us, wait for an opening and then step up on the platform that has been created. Just stand there and wait. We are going to be raising the energy for the initiation." The One gave me the instructions I needed to start the ceremony. I waited til the women started their slow rhythmic movements around the fire. I could hear the sounds they were making but I was not sure if it was singing or chanting. They all moved independent of one another but they moved in time with one another, each song coming from deep within them. The started slowly careful, but as the energy started to rise, the tempo picked up speed.

I walked slowly towards the center of the spiral, each woman was dancing in and out, back and forth. The steps seemed practiced and ancient, something they had been doing since time began. I could feel the energy coming from them and pulsing down into the soil, moving towards the center. As I got closer, even the air seemed to be alive, moving to their will, their desires.

I waited for an opening and stepped through it, I was not sure anyone even knew I was there, all the women appeared to be deep in a trance. The sound of their voices had taken them, their movements were pushing them closer and closer to merging together as one. I could feel the pulse of their passions, come up through the ground and vibrate below my feet. The energy felt like it was looking for me, moving slowly like a snake, sensing its prey. With such power as to make me scream the energy grabbed my legs, I could not move. The dress that I had been wearing, started to move, it was alive. The green coloring was morphing into all the shapes and forms of all living things, plants and animals. I could feel the intense vibration on my skin with each new form. The gold started to pulse and as it did, the red trim, started to form into a man.

The power of the energy that was moving all around me, was starting to move through me. I wanted to scream as it did, not for the pain, but for the images that were penetrating my mind. It was as though all the memories of all the women, were forcing themselves into me at one time. I tried to move but I could not. I could see that the dress was starting to unravel into a long string of images. Plants animals, things I had no idea what they were. One end of the string started to move, like it was searching for a point of entry. Piercing my skin, looking for the one spot to enter me. With a great thrust it pushed itself into me, forcing its way into the point between my breasts. I could feel it move into me. Like a long snake it went writhing and pulsing. As it unravelled into me, the dress disappeared.

There I stood in the center of the courtyard, naked. The gold trim from the dress had formed in the shape of a man that stood a few feet from me. I could not see who he was, only that he was a man. He reached out to me, but still I could not move.

The women were dancing around me now, at a fevered pitch. Moving so fast it was hard to tell who was who, they appeared to be moving in and out of each other, faster and faster, till they became one.

The One then appeared on the platform with me, even as I could see her dancing in front of me.

"The man there, he is the divine masculine the part of yourself that you need to merge with to be whole. You must let him come into you, for each woman must understand the power of the masculine that lies within the feminine, if they are to stand in the totality of their true power. In this way you will never feel the need to have a man in your life, so that you can be whole. In this way you shall be balanced and free yourself to love because of desire, not dependency. Allow him to enter you now." The One said to me in a very commanding voice.

The gold figure of a man approached me. As he got close, he touched me. I could feel strength, I could feel heat, I could feel powerful desire building up in me, the desire to absorb this energy. I felt like this was the part of me that I had been searching for, the part of me that, if I did not have it, I would not live. I opened my arms to embrace him and as I did, he touched my fingertips. The gold started to flow into my fingers, and up my arms. It was a joyous pain. The kind of pain that hurts but is so exhilarating, you don't care.

He flowed into me and through me, til every inch of my body had been penetrated. As I looked upon my naked self standing there, I could see the glow of the gold in my energy. I felt warm and alive. I felt powerful and full of love. I had never felt so much love. I could not hold back the tears that wanted to flow. The world was no longer just a place, it was a consciousness. It was my lover. It was all the self love I could offer. In that second an explosion of white light came from the center of my soul. It passed through all the ladies, it passed through the courtyard, and it kept going till I could see it no more.

I could no longer stand as my legs collapsed under me. With the last bit of light that hit my eyes I could see the women, they had fallen with me to the ground below them. My world went silent.

Instantly I could feel myself rising, lifting up out of my body. I looked below to see myself collapsed on the stone. Was I dead? Maybe I could not stand the intensity of the night? Maybe I didn't want to go any further in my life? I was not sure what was happening, all I knew is at that moment I felt free. I did not feel any of the obligations that had been imposed on me. I didn't feel the weight of carrying my body. I felt no fear. I only felt love and acceptance wrapping around me like a warm cocoon, spinning a living thread of light around my heart.

"You are now one of us." I heard a voice say. I turned to see a mist like figure of The One, looking back at me.

"Now you didn't think I was going to let you venture out here all alone did you? This is one of my favorite places. The world between the worlds. Here in this place you can experience the truest nature of your being. Here is where you and the All are one in the same. Here you are not encumbered by the trappings of the world. Here you are free."

"I did not know where I was, I thought I might be dead." I responded to her.

"No, you are not dead, you have a destiny to fulfill. I know you are very apprehensive to go home. You will be fine. It will be an adjustment, but events have already started to happen that will change the balance of power very soon. Orla is never to be trusted, no matter how indulging she appears to be. No matter how much she tries to prove her love for your Father. For her it is all a game, and she plays that game very well. You, however, will play it better.

Whenever you need me, you have but to call. I will always be watching from the temples. In the healing area behind your home, there is a crystal, it stands taller and clearer than the others. Whisper to it and I shall hear you. That crystal came from this place and it is still connected to this place, but do not let anyone else see you. No one other than your Mother knew of this stone. Use it only if the need is dire. When you awaken it will be morning, and you will spend the day with us. The sentinels are coming for you tomorrow morning, they will be waiting for you at the base of the mountain. Go now and rest, your body needs you to rejoin it."

I felt the impact as I slammed back into my body, I opened my eyes enough to see the flames before me, I was back on the cold stone.

The sun had risen its head long before I did. Even the sisterhood seemed slow in their movements this morning. The night before had taken its toll on all of us, and a little recovery time was in order. Thankfully the sun was out and the day was cheery. The mood was pleasant, but I knew all the women were a little sad as well. They were not sad just because I was leaving but they were sad because I was the last. A tradition that had been in place for as long as anyone could remember, was now over. I don't think I was able to really understand just how difficult that was for these women. These women had been trained as initiates and had spent their whole lives training more initiates, so what they were born to do was now, obsolete. I knew they were training some of the Others, but that was not the same. The others simply did not have same vibratory bodies, and they could not learn in the same way. So I was a little sad for these amazing women that had offered their lives to a cause.

The day passed quickly as we chatted with one another and talked about our time together. It was such a bittersweet time, knowing I was leaving the next day, but truly enjoying the moment. It was the first time in a very long time that I had felt like I belonged somewhere, with someone. I was grateful for that.

As the evening approached and the time came for me to rest my head one final time here in these misty mountains, where the sisterhood watched over all the surrounding lands, I was filled with intense knowing and awareness of just how much I had grown and changed, since being here. I had come here a little girl and would be returning as a woman. A woman ready to take the seat of my Father. A woman trained to rule. A woman who had knowledge of the future. A woman with a great many secrets. My question was, could I keep those secrets to myself.

Morning came and I was ready to leave. Saying good bye was so very informal. Each woman bid me farewell in her own way, but then went on about her business as though my leaving was of very little importance. I was a little disappointed but I knew they were trying to make it as easy for me as possible.

The One came to escort me down the mountain to my awaiting escort of sentinels. I still could not really believe I was leaving. My life was now opening into a new chapter. So much had passed and so many memories were made. I wondered if my Mother had felt the same when she left. We descended the mountain and at the base, a short distance away, I could see them, a group of sentinels sent by my Father. I would be so happy to see him again, but a little afraid as well.

"My child, it has been such a delight getting to know you. Now is your time. Time for you to return and to grow into your new role as ruler. Do not worry about your abilities, just practice what you know out of the sight of questioning eyes and allow the strength of the sun and moon to grow within you. Do not expect of your Father what he does not have to give. You may not understand this right now, but in time you will. He has not been the same since he lost your Mother and you are returning to a different man than you remember. However in return, he is receiving a different daughter than he knew as well.

Patience in all things, will carry you far. If you do not know what to say, say nothing at all. Remember, energies are at work, in this time of great transition and you are not expected to control your world, you are only expected to guide it through the transition. Do not feel pressured when it comes time to find a partner. All parents want their children to be happy and settled, this is not your path. You will choose a partner in a most unusual way, and he may not have the approval of all. This is not important. What is important is that you love him and you trust him, for he will be the only person that truly knows who you are. Above all else, know that we the sisterhood are here for you always. You remember the instructions I gave you to contact me. Go live your life in love and joy. Here, you will be greatly missed."

With that she kissed me on the forehead, embraced me, and then took two steps back. That was my cue to move forward. She was releasing me to myself, to my life, to my future. I cried as I walked to the sentinels. The looks on their faces was one of compassion and concern. They were my guardians now, at least til we were back in my Fathers home. I had been with the sisters so long, I was not sure I felt like I was going home, but rather that I was leaving it.

I was escorted by 12 sentinels. We stood very still as The One placed us in a protective shield that would allow the collapse of time, ensuring our trip home would be fast and safe. As we started to move forward, I looked one last time as this beautiful woman who stood there watching me leave. It felt as though my heart was being torn from my chest. I was leaving, but my love was staying with the sisterhood. As we passed from her sight, I could feel the child in me leave. The woman was now being birthed, as my new life lay ahead.

The energies were rising in me. I could feel the life blood of the wisdom teachings coursing through my veins. I was emerging from the cocoon of youth, carrying the wings of wisdom in my soul. I could feel myself growing with every step forward.

Then as if out of a dream, there is was, land of my birth, home of my Father. It lay sprawled out in front of me. My time had come.

Chapter Fifteen

I stopped the sentinels just outside the city. I had to breathe. I knew the minute I arrived I would be devoured by the welcoming of the people. I was grateful for their appreciation of me, but I needed time. Time was not a gift I was able to create for myself in this moment. So I just stood still. I listened to every sound, smelled every scent, felt the energy as it passed through me. I took long slow breathes, this allowed me to focus enough to slow time just a little. To give me that moment of space, before time stole me back again.

I could see the outline of the homes, in the back on the hill was my Fathers home. The curved roofs of stone, the grand arches and walkways. Higher up the hill behind the palace I could see the Alaria. There is where the calling crystal was.

The sun reflected off all the colored stones that the Healers used to balance the energy of the people and the land. Sacred water flowed from the mountains above into the giant cauldron, where it was heated by the sun. It then flowed to the baths made of giant slabs of healing stone. A separate waterway flowed to the center of the community where it followed a path into three concentric circles. The very middle of this space held the hollow stones that the musicians used to amplify and control sound on warm evenings, when they played for a devoted crowd.

My home, so long has it been since I had seen the green fields and waterfalls beyond. I could hear the hum of the people going about there business. I had forgotten how there was always movement here. Everything here was balanced, the wind never blew too hard, the sun was never too hot. There was always the right amount of rain. It seemed all so very controlled to me now. I had gotten used to the wildness around me living with the sisterhood. I liked the wildness, there was such truth in it. No pretense or illusion, just things as they were. I knew my life now, was going to be a game. A game of who can weave the greatest illusion of truth but not be bound to their lies.

I could delay no longer. It was time to step into another life, knowing the shoes would not fit. I motioned to go onward once again. In moments we were moving through the protective shield and were at the gates of my home.

There was my Father, standing waiting. By him stood Orla. It would take all I had not to reveal my extreme distaste for her. But for my Fathers sake, I would be nothing other that gracious. It was in this moment I realized, just how hard it is to restrain the wild beast that lives within me. I would have been so easy to let the cat out and destroy her, but that would have destroyed my Father as well. Whatever I was going to do, I must first decide how to protect my Father. He was my only concern.

The sentinels dispersed from their placement around me, I stood there, suddenly feeling very vulnerable, as I could see everyone and they could see me. My Father came to me. He embraced me with a hug so tight I thought he might break me.

"My daughter, my dear child, I am so happy you are home. I have missed you so much. There is so much to tell you. I have prepared a grand party for you. Tonight we will feast and dance and light up the skies with the joy of your return."

I looked at him closely. He was different and it wasn't just that he was older now, He felt different, the only way I can describe it would be to say, he felt hollow, empty, like the person that he had been was no longer there. He had been replaced with a lesser version of himself.

Orla had joined my Father quietly coming up to him from behind. She had mastered the pretense of submissive companion, but that is not at all how she appeared to me.

"Aeiya, daughter, this is Orla. This is your Mothers sister. In my time of heavy sorrows, she came to me and we grieved the loss of your Mother together. We found that in our pain, a mutual respect started to grow and that turned to understanding and admiration of one another, and now that has turned to more. Orla will be joining us here in our home permanently now. She will be my wife. I hope you grow to love her as I have."

My Fathers words were spoken honestly. He truly believed that which he said. Orla extended her hand to me. With my eyes I looked at her face. She was beautiful but it was a hard beauty. She had a strong and dominant face. Her hair was long and dark, she pulled it back from her face so it was tight against her head. It was as if she was afraid it would fight her for control, if she were to wear it loosely. She had scars on her arms, they had healed well, but they were still noticeable. And she was tall, taller than my Father, when she moved it was not with the ease of grace that my Mother had, but instead with a rather forced determination. I am sure she was more at ease with my Father than she was with me. She would be on her best behavior, knowing I had just returned from my training, she would know how sharp and raw my instincts would be.

"Aeiya, I hope we can grow in love as your Father and I have. That we can be friends. I am so terribly sorry for the loss of your Mother. I do want you to know, that my heart is open to you and should you need anything, I will do everything I can to help." She spoke her words with such empathy, I could almost have been tempted to believe her, if it had not been for the fact that when she touched my hand, pain shot up my arm. That pain was the pain of warning, it was a piece of her energy that was being rejected by

144

mine. I could feel her intent upon me. Orla was a master at being two people at the same time. One was imbedded within the other. Two completely different personalities. Both personalities were completely truthful to who they were, but opposite in every way. With the slightest bit of will, either personality could be offered to the outside world, without deception on the part of the person.

It was truly masterful in its deception, however, her energy could not tell a lie, and I knew now, I could never rely on the perception of my eyes. The only way truth could be perceived with her is by way of her energy. From this moment on, I would only see Orla through my cats eyes, and my cats senses, for the cat knew nothing but truth. As I thought of the cat, I could feel the wildness stir inside of me. I immediately turned my thoughts to something else. I did not want anyone to know of the animal that lived within me. That cat was my sanity, my privacy. The cat would be the only real life I had left and I wanted to be sure, no one else knew, not even my Father.

My Father reached out for my hand. I loved my Father so, I turned and hugged him. He looked at me with different eyes in that moment. His eyes were soft and welling up with tears. In that moment he seemed to see me as that little girl who left so long ago. The me that was his wife's child, my Mothers daughter. In that moment I saw my Father, the man I knew him to be, and then it was gone.

He took my hand and led me to the hollow stones where all the people had gathered. All the people that lived under the protective shield were there waiting for my return. I could see some of the children I used to play with, now they had families of their own. I realized in that moment just how long I had been gone. I knew then why my Father was so different. He had been hollowed out by Orla. She had been here long enough that she had carved the individuality from him. She had done to my Father what had been done to the stones, she had emptied him.

My Father led me up to the largest stone which stood in the middle of the group. This was the stone that important declarations were made from. "My beautiful daughter has returned to us. She is here, home safely. Tonight we shall celebrate. Tonight we shall gather in joyous union. I ask you all to join us here, to honor my daughter, today is the happiest day of my life. I will promise, a few surprises for those that join us tonight." my Father was bursting with pride as he stepped down off the platform. I looked around at the crowd and they were happy. It was always a joyous time when we gathered here, to hear the music and the songs. I loved the feeling of the vibration as the hollow stones gathered the sound and reverberated it outwards. As a child I would sit behind them with my back against their walls and feel the sound rise up my spine and down through the soles of my feet. It always made me laugh.

The memory of those moments warmed my return. I wandered around behind the stones to see the place I used to sit. Once again I placed my back against the cool smooth stone and slid downward, allowing the earth beneath me to connect solidly with my soul. I sat there trying to be in the present moment. Again life had changed so much and so abruptly, I was having a hard time keeping up. As I sat there, I became aware of eyes upon me. My first thought was Orla, but the vibration was different. The feeling was one of protection and nurturing, not of dissembling and destruction.

I lifted my head to see who was around me, but I could see no one. I placed my palms to the ground on either side of me trying to feel who may be close but unseen. Still nothing. Then I felt as though someone had placed a finger beneath my chin and was lifting it upwards. There higher up on the hill behind the hollow stones, up where the healers were, there was a woman all dressed in green, staring down at me. That is where the energy was coming from. It was her gaze that was wrapping me in protection. I did not know who she was, but I wanted to find out. I stood up, ready to go up the hill and find her, but she was gone.

"Aeiya, Aeiya, are you coming child?' my Father called out to me.

"Yes, I will be right there."

I took one last look, but she had disappeared. It would have to wait. I needed to be with my Father now. I turned and left the hollow stones behind as I joined my Father under the great carved stones of our home.

As my eyes adjusted to the light indoors, I turned my head upwards towards the false sky of my home. The ceilings were all carved symbols. Symbols of an ancient language, the language of the planet we descended from. I could never read the symbols, but my Mother would tell me that it told the story of our coming here and where we had come from, and how we survived here. The ceilings had been carved to honor the sky and the Universal Counsel and all that was above us, the energies that carried us here, and allowed us to make a home in this place.

I loved to watch the symbols through the day. As the sun travelled across the sky, the patterns of light would cause the shadows of symbols to change in shape, so that the whole story could not be told by just one glance. It would take an entire day watching the symbols change with the light. They would morph from one form to the next creating the story of our history, that could only be read by knowing how to work with the light.

It had been said that the key to understanding the birthing chamber was written in the symbols, but no one remembered at what point during the day, the knowledge would be revealed. I followed my Father through the openness of our entry to the inner chambers of our home. He led me to my room. As we entered the room I could see it had been changed. Some of my childhood things still remained, but it had been redesigned for a woman.

"It tore the heart from me to change this room. I will not lie, I wanted to think my little girl was coming back to me. But I knew, a woman would be coming back to me instead. Orla suggested that we create a space for you that would be befitting your status now. So we left all the things you loved as a child and opened up the space so that you would have your own chamber, your own privacy. I only hope that you like it, and if you wish to change anything we will do that. Welcome home my child. My heart is so much lighter now that I am here with you. I feel purpose has returned to me, life is flowing through me again. " With that he gently kissed me on the forehead, turned and disappeared into the shadows.

I entered into the room, that I had once called my own. It did not feel like mine now. I could feel Orla's influence in the room. I looked at the room through my cats eyes, and I could see those things that Orla had once owned that she had left here for me. Her energy imprint was all over it. I walked over and touched a beautiful doll. It was hand carved and the face was created in such a life like way. The clothes were elegant and it was obvious that the doll had never been played with.

As I held the doll, I could feel some of my energy flowing into it. My hands started to ache, and it felt as though the energy was being drawn from my arms out through my hands and into the doll. I dropped the doll as my hands started to cramp. It hit the floor with a thud. I stepped back from it, and the pain stopped. As I stepped towards it again, the pain started. I knew this was the work of Orla. There was something with the doll that allowed Orla to take some of my energy. I was not sure what to do with it, so I kicked it into the corner, out of sight.

I scanned the rest of the room for any other objects that had the same energy pattern, but there were none. I collapsed on to the bed. How was I going to do this? How could I live two different lives? I was not skilled at lying? I did not want to be here. I wanted to go back to with the sisters. I did not know what to do, so I cried. I lay on my bed and let the tears fall from my eyes, hoping that they would wash away my reality. Hoping that if I cried enough perhaps the images before my eyes would change from the carved ceilings to the great blue sky that I had lived beneath on the sacred mountaintop. My tears however, changed nothing.

I awoke a short while later. In its compassion, sleep had taken me from the extreme emotions I was feeling. It allowed me some time to find a temporary balance. A false composure that would allow me to get through the evening celebrations and to show the people I was grateful for there offering of love. As I slept a gown had been left for me. It had been layed out on the other side of the room. It was beautiful. All white, it hung to the floor. The front of the dress had been covered in tiny sacred stones, all delicately laced together by spun gold. The jewels followed the neckline down the curve of my breasts to the center of my body, then down to my hips, where it flared out in a gracefully curved line to the sides of the dress. I had never seen anything so intricately designed, not even for my Mother. All the stones on the dress were the same stones of power that were in my Fathers head piece. They were smaller stones cut in fine shapes, that matched the design of the dress. The stones in my Fathers head piece were large and raw. They seemed to have a life of their own, set in a band of metal that was brought from our home world. It is said the head piece was as old as the sisterhood and it held the energy and the knowledge of all those who wore it.

I knew my Father very rarely put it on. When he did, it was for special occasions, sometimes when decisions had to be made, or if the business was especially official. He did not like to wear it, he said it was full of memories that were not his own.

I reached down to run my hand along the stones and the fabric of the dress. As my fingers crossed the stones I could feel the playful tingles of their energies. They seemed to laugh as I touched them. The spun gold carried the energy from one stone to the other so the dress had the feel of being alive. The energy of one stone flowed to the next, all the way down the dress.

"The people love you so much that they made that for you, as a gift for your homecoming." Orla had come into my room, without me hearing her. I jumped as she spoke, her sudden appearance struck me from my moment of pleasure.

"It truly is beautiful". I could see her eyes, she was mesmerized by the dress. It had almost a hypnotic affect on her.

"I do hope you will choose to wear it tonight, it would make the people very happy. And I am sure you will look absolutely stunning in it. "

"I will be sure and wear this. I cannot believe the people made it for me. I must thank them for their kindness."

"Yes, the people love you, as does your Father. You must be someone very special. I am looking forward to discovering who you are," she said in voice, that sounded like a voice within a voice.

Orla walked towards the dress and reached down to touch it. As she got close to the stones, she suddenly retracted her hand as if in pain. I watched her face as a look of shock was quickly contained and controlled into a calm gaze again.

"Are you alright?" I queried.

"Oh, uh, yes. I just remembered there is something I must attend to." Her voice was rather unnerved, by what had just happened. She backed away from the dress and cast a stabbing look in my direction, then she turned abruptly and strode forcefully away.

I stood beside the dress, staring at it, wishing it could speak. I wanted to know what had just happened? Why couldn't Orla touch the dress? What did it do to her? It felt so good to me. I could hear Orla's voice in my head saying, "the people made it for you....."

The people made if for me. What people did she mean? I would have to find out more about this dress.

I could tell by the light coming from across the square, that evening was almost upon me. I could hear voices coming from just beyond the square. That told me that the people were starting to gather. As the light faded the night would be lit up by torches and light multipliers. It would be a good night. Music would make the air vibrate, the children would smile and the feast would be grand. Yes, it would be a good night.

As I picked up the dress, and readied myself to wear it, I could feel the delightful tingle. I slid the fabric over my skin, it was cool and I could feel the aliveness of it spread down my body. My skin started to vibrate in a most pleasant way. It reminded me of being embraced by The One and how she always made me feel safe and capable of anything. This dress made me stand taller, but more than that, it made me feel powerful, with a strength that knew wisdom.

As I looked upon a reflective surface I could see the stones sparkle in a pattern of many intersecting triangles. The pattern was reflected in my eyes. In that instant, I knew that everything was as it was meant to be in this moment, and that gave me comfort.

I stepped out into the cool night air, placing one foot in front of the other, making my way towards the hollow stones where the feast would take place. Along the way I stopped to talk with all the people, to thank them for the dress. Most of them had no knowledge of the dress, but thought it was beautiful. It did feel wonderful to be so welcomed by everyone. Perhaps being home was not going to be as terrifying as I had anticipated. I rounded a corner in the yard and followed the foot path that led to the square, as I looked up, there was a grand table spread with more food than any one could possibly eat. Piled as high as the people stood, foods of every type covered the surface. Children were running around with fruit in their hands, playing the games I remembered so fondly.

Just above and behind the table of food, was my Father's table. There he sat with Orla at his side, chatting with everyone that came by. My Father was in his glory. If it were not for the absence of my Mother, it would have felt like home. In that moment, there was much joy. Orla seemed to be genuine. She seemed to really care for my Father. I stopped to wonder if it were possible that she could change. Perhaps all she needed was the right environment and enough love to show her things could be different. I wanted her to be different, I wanted her to be able to change, I wanted to believe, inside of her, was a good, true woman, wanting to be part of a family. I just wanted things to be different than I was told they would be. I wanted to give her a chance to prove, she was not who she was.

"Aeiya, join us!" my Father called out to me.

My spirits were lighter, and I ran up the hill to my Father, embracing him, with the thoughts that maybe things did not have to be the way they were, maybe they could be different.

"Father, this is so beautiful and there are so many people here, Thank you. Thanks to both of you for welcoming me so warmly. " It felt good to let my guard down and to allow myself to just feel good.

"Why would we welcome you any other way. I love you, you are my daughter. Come sit here with me. I want you by my side when I make my announcements."

I did as my Father asked without hesitation. I gave no thought to what my Father would announce. His speeches were common at these events. They usually involved thanking the people and being thankful for all the land provided. My Father always tried to honor the people, he was very grateful to them for all their help. They were not just beings that we watched over, they were family and friends to my Father. We were not the same, but we were also not so different.

I sat looking out upon the crowds and was happy to be home in that moment. I had missed this place. I had missed the faces of the people ,I had missed my Father's face. I had truly missed the sound of the hollow stones and the way the wind carried the smell of the sea to my soul. I had missed my memories as well. The happy memories of playing in the square and in the fields, or trying to get the hollow stones to change the tone of my voice. The games of pretending that I was the overseer of all the people. I had missed playing the games that prepare children to become adults.

Chapter Sixteen

As the musicians started to play, I could feel their songs move through the stones capturing the air, luring it to dance with the pulse of their beat. The energy of the rhythm moved down through the great stone tiles that encompassed the water which flowed in circles around the square. Patterns formed on the surface of the water, dancing with one another in the pure joy of the moment. As the sound moved into the people, the beating of their hearts joined the rhythm of the song. People started to sway and move like trees in the wind, as their bodies pulsed in time with the sound.

I loved music, and how it made me feel. Music carried me to a place deep inside myself. It carried me from this moment in time, to a place where moments are not defined by time. It carried me to that place somewhere inside myself where I was free, where there are no rules and time is not something that I cared about. It carried me to that place where I could shed the skin that this reality forced me to wear. The skin that said "I was identifiable". The skin that said, "this is who you are supposed to be." The skin that betrayed the reality of who I was.

Music let me experience who I was. The part of me that cannot be seen by the eyes of the flesh. Music allowed me to experience the vibration of personality at the level of the soul. The patterns which formed on the surface of water told the story of what we all felt as the music played. The beautiful and articulate designs were the blueprints of our being. They were the truth of our life. Those sacred patterns were the geometry of our soul, and they danced within us, allowing us, for those moments to understand the truth of who we all are.

My Fathers strong voice grabbed me and shocked me back to the present moment. I had allowed myself to drift far away on waves of pleasure. But my Father had stood up and was starting to address the crowd.

"I am so happy all of you could join us tonight. This will be a night like no other. My daughter is home and for that I am thankful. I have love in my life again and for that I thank Orla. I have come to a decision, that has been a very long time in the making. Aeiya has returned to us from the Sisterhood where she was guided into becoming the beautiful and powerful woman I know she is. I give thanks to the Sisterhood for this. It has come upon me that I am not getting younger or stronger, and that overseeing the people is a task for someone who has the energy to do it. It is for this reason that I am passing the stone head piece to my daughter Aeiya. I know she is ready, and will be able to help all of us more than I can at this time. I will stay here as advisor to ease the transition. It is time for me to enjoy having a second chance at life now."

I was having a very difficult time processing what I had just heard. I think the crowd was too, cause all I could hear at that moment was whispers and gasps. I turned to look at Orla, there was anger on her face. She held her fists clenched tightly on top of the table. I was not sure if she was going to strike out. Her body seemed to have turned to stone and I could feel pain on my skin from her gaze as she shot a rancid look towards me.

I went to stand, but my Father motioned me to sit, he was not finished. I felt fear now, I was not sure what else he would have to say.

"Now, calm down, I have some other news, I would wish to share with you."

He turned to Orla and reached out to take her hand. As he looked deeply into her eyes, the words that I never wanted to hear, slipped from his lips, "Orla you have come out of the darkness to shed light in my life. Your love has awakened me and allowed me to breathe again . I did not think that I could love another, but I have been greatly blessed, and find myself deeply in love with you. I would ask that you be my partner in this life. That we come together in love and acceptance and leave our differences in the past. As we shall be together, not only shall our lives come together but so shall our two worlds. Let us merge, Atlantis and Lemuria. Let us end the separation that has been between us for far too long. "

My Father had given his pledge. Orla was trying very hard not to react. She was reeling from just learning my Father was placing me on the throne, and then discovering that my Father wanted her to be his wife. The wife of a counselor, not the wife of a king.

As Orla forced a smile and stood to meet my Father's eyes, I wanted to scream out, NOOOOOOOO. But I sat there silent, waiting like everyone else to hear her response.

"I love you, Edon, and I willing accept." With that, she threw her arms around him and that made the crowd rise to its feet and cheer with all its might. In that one precise moment, Orla had made herself a part of Lemuria. She was one of us now, and I am sure that was exactly her intention.

The illusion I had allowed myself to swim in, suddenly became a raging river and I was going over the waterfalls. I really wanted to panic, to run, to hide, anything that would take me from this moment, had to be better than the moment. I looked at Orla, and she was looking back at me. I knew what had just happened had not been part of her plan. She had been just as shocked as I. Perhaps, if I could calm myself and pull my energy back to me, I could use this moment to alter the balance of power. I contained myself and moved towards her and my Father. I embraced them both and offered the most genuine and heart felt congratulations that I could extract

152

from the vile and disgusting rage that was threatening to explode from every cell of my being.

Others quickly flooded into my Fathers space to offer their congratulations. I took the opportunity to disappear. I needed to put some distance between myself and the cause of my rage. As I moved away from the table I could feel Orla's eyes upon me, I did not turn around for that would have allowed her to see my anger, and that would have made me vulnerable. I walked away allowing her to think that I was stepping down to honor my Father and her, to offer my respect so they could have the moment for themselves. I moved away from the table, back behind the hollow stones, up the hill towards the healers. I moved as far away as I could hoping that my rage would start to subside, but it did not. I kept moving farther and farther away from the devastating scene below me, but all I could think of was I wanted Orla dead. How could my Father offer to merge the two worlds? She must have a much greater hold on him, than I had thought. He knew nothing of her world and he was opening our doors to it. What had he done? What was he forcing me to do? I was afraid. I could feel the fear cut through my body like a knife cutting through my flesh, digging deeper and deeper.

In the next moment, I opened my eyes, I did not know where I was, and it was a moment before I realized I was in my cat body. It was dark and I was not on familiar ground. I was somewhere in the woods, in the dense bush. I could smell the musky scent of the earth and feel the dampness of the dew under my paws.

There was silence. I lay down in the moss. It was soft and cool. I needed to rest. I needed to understand why all this was happening, but I knew I probably never would. It was then the thought occurred to me, when had I changed into the cat?

I had hoped I was far enough away that no one saw me transform. I was aware of the danger that I could transform, because of the extreme emotion I was feeling, but I really did not need the complication of being seen. There was nothing left in my life that would be my own now, all I had left was the cat.

The woods were calming me. Gently caressing the careening rage that had provoked my transformation. As the earth reached up to relieve me of my pain, I could feel the power of my cat self dispersing. I did not know where I was, and was concerned I would not be able to return home without my cat senses. I got up and headed for home as fast as I could. I think it was the adrenaline that allowed me to get as far as I did. But as morning was dawning, I woke in some small bushes in the hillside above the Alaria, the healers area.

I was happy to see my home, but wondering how I would get from this spot to my room without being seen. I then remembered the dress, that beautiful dress. I was ashamed I had lost it. I so wanted to know of it origin. To know the meaning of that dress could have helped me understand my life, just a little bit more.

What was that? In the bushes just above me, there was a noise. It sounded like something coming towards me. I was a little frightened that Orla had discovered me missing, and had sent someone to find me. So I hid, in the bushes. I could hear footsteps now, coming closer. They moved then stopped, like they were looking for something. Then I saw white fabric moving past me, it was my dress. I stood up to see who was carrying it. It was that woman from the day before. The one that had been staring down at me from the Alaria. Who was she, and why did she have my dress? I needed to know.

I positioned a couple of branches to cover me and ran cautiously after the woman in green. She was entering the area of the baths. I crept in behind her and watched as she went to the far side to a small bath area and filled the tub with water. Then she placed the dress in the water very gently. She used her hand to gently move the water back and forth over the dress. She was washing it, cleaning the fabric and the stones ever so carefully.

" I know you are there, you can come closer if you wish, I am not your enemy." her voice resounded with a light echo in the large hollow room. I stepped out from behind the stone pillar, still wearing my cloak of leaves.

"Oh my, well we had better get something to cover you up, we cannot have our new ruler going about, just wearing leaves." she said as she laughed and left the room. She returned almost instantly with a dark green robe, usually worn by the healers themselves.

"There, it is not as pretty as this dress, but it will work for now. How do you do, I am Tuallan."

"Thank you for the coverings, and thank you for retrieving my dress." It was all I could say to her, until I knew who she was, and how she knew where to find my dress.

"You should be more careful with this dress, it is very important to you. Do you know the story of this dress?" she asked. I could feel she was being as careful with me as I was with her. She was not aware of what I did or did not know.

"All I was told, was, the dress was made for me by the people. That confused me a little, most of the people I am familiar with, do not have the skill to craft such a beautiful garment?" I watched her ever so carefully, waiting for her to reveal something more of herself.

"You are a great observer. This will serve you well. You must get your emotions under control if you are to craft an illusion so elaborate that Orla will make a fatal mistake. That is what your intent is, isn't it?" a wry smile contorted her lips as she looked into me.

"Orla is about to be my Father's wife. why would I want to harm her in any way. If someone is going to harm her, I demand to know who, so they can be dealt with immediately. "

"Come now, perhaps the sisterhood should have schooled you better in the skills of lying to someone, other than yourself. You are not very convincing of that which you speak. But you are still young and you must practice this on everyone. That is what the royals do best, is it not, they allow lies to become the illusion of truth?"

Now I was not just angry and embarrassed, I was also feeling very insulted by this woman.

"Why would you speak to me this way, I have done nothing to you. I did not ask you to find my dress, or to get me this robe. I ...."

"Careful little one, your claws are showing. What are you going to do? Run to your Daddy and have him fix this? Or didn't you realize, Daddy doesn't' do anything without Orla's say now?" she was provoking me and it was working. It was all I could do to keep the cat inside. I could feel the blood coursing through me, my heart was pounding.

"Ah, so you do have some control. That is good. You must not ever let Orla see what lives inside you. She would reveal you and have you hunted down. Enough of this. I am one of the people that the sisterhood told you of, one of the humans that they have trained. I am here to help you and to protect you if necessary. I am The One's eyes and ears here in this place. Like I said I am not your enemy. But you are wise not to trust anyone here. Not even me, til I have proven to you, that I am who I say I am." she was nodding her head, watching me try to put all this into some kind of perspective.

"You were trained by The One? I know she told me that they were training some of the Others, but I never thought one of you would be here with me? I am happy you are though. What else do you know?"

"I know that everyone in the royal home is in danger. Orla wants to rule and she will do anything to get that headpiece. You see, we are not like you. We cannot change our shapes into other beings, and we are not able to control energies the same way you are. Our bodies do not vibrate the same way yours does. But we are still able to learn to work with the energies, and to see the world the way it is. We have to work harder and train longer than you, but we still understand the nature of truth, and how this planet works. I understand how you become the cat, even though I cannot do it myself. Orla does not understand these things in the same way. She considers you a great threat. She is afraid you will divide her and your Father, and he will take your side, and end her delusion of coming to power. The most important thing you could do at this point is to allow your Father to see what Orla really is. It is the only thing that can save this world. Do you understand what I am saying?"

I nodded my head, but I had no idea how I was going to reveal Orla as she was, without my Father becoming angry with me. I would have to lure her somehow into making a mistake. I would have to crack that shield she wore. That shield that projected the illusion of a loving elegant woman.

"I have a suggestion for you. Instead of trying to discover how to reveal her. Why don't you try to discover how she projects herself so perfectly? If you do that, then you will find out where the cracks in the shield are." she winked at me, as she said this.

She was right. To defeat her, I must understand who she is and how she is able to be two people at once. No one can master this so perfectly that there are no defects.

"Please, tell me the story of the dress. What is it about the dress that makes Orla walk around it. She doesn't seem to be able to touch it either? I cannot explain this." I needed to know about that dress, and why it repelled Orla.

"Of course, but first, do you know the story of how the Others came to be?" Tuallan asked.

"Well I know you were created to help us seed the garden. That in the future you will be needed to help harvest the garden as well. But that is all I know." I actually felt a little bit bad, that I did not know more about the Others. I had spent a great deal of time with them as a child.

"It is Ok, you were never supposed to know who we are, just how to deal with us. We are star seed. We come from the stars but are grown here on this planet. When we were created it was decided that we should look like you. It would be easier for us, if we looked similar to you, we would not feel so separated then. However since we were only meant to be a worker species, we were not based in logic. We were not supposed to have independent thought, or make decisions outside of a certain spectrum. We were however given great emotion. The ability to feel. It was understood that empathy binds people together. If a burden is too much for one, many will come to their rescue, and the work will get done, through co operation, rather that dominance. We were designed from pieces of you and the elements of this earth so we could thrive, and we could relate. Our emotion came from the star beings and our logic came from the earth beings. This is why we are eighty percent water and twenty percent earth. We were designed to feel what was needed, not to think about what was needed. It was not for us to make decisions on our own, we were just to follow them. To do what you are told, you do not need to think very much. Emotions like passion and desire , want and need were given to us, so that we would breed and become many. This is exactly what we did. We were given the ability to bear children within our bodies. It was a very practical decision, the best way to keep people working if they have children is if those children can be with them. It is also the best way to protect the children. It keeps people tied together, it is a kind of herd mentality. We do what we are programmed to do, and do not think about it. It is the way we are designed. We look for someone else to lead us, we do not feel the need to lead ourselves. We do not question the changes that are made around us, we just accept them. It is how we were designed, it is our nature.

When the sisterhood came to us, they told us that times were changing, and we needed to grow as a species. There would be a time in the future when we would have to think for ourselves and be our own rulers. This terrified the people. But the sisterhood were very reassuring telling us that we would never see those days, that they were many generations away. What the sisterhood wanted was to work with a small group of us, with our children, to develop skills in us that were latent. They wanted us to become aware of ourselves and our own capabilities. They wanted us to make our own decision and to be able to see the inaccuracies of decisions made by others. They wanted us to be able to fix problems and to become the architects of our own lives. And so it was.

Over several generations the sisterhood worked with a few families they had relocated to a secret place on the sacred mountain. At first it was very difficult for us to make any decisions. it just was not how we were created. With time and patience we learned that we are capable of making lives for ourselves. We are capable of learning the same things that you know, but in a different way.

We are beings based in feeling. The sisterhood taught us that truth cannot be seen, it can only be experienced. Truth cannot be seen, nor can truth be tasted, it cannot be heard either. Truth is a vibrational pattern that can only be identified when it is felt. If someone speaks the truth, you do not know it because you heard it, you know it because you felt it when you heard the words spoken. To experience life as it is, can only be done from a feeling level. Thoughts create a vibrational pattern too. But thoughts are recycled patterns, if they are not experienced from feeling. They are patterns that are sent to one another with preconceived beliefs. Those beliefs are not truth, they are just an opinion of a truth. So to live a life based on a thought, means you are actually living a life, based on someone else's belief. It is not, what truly is.

Are you understanding what I am saying?" Tuallan's gaze was intense. She was trying to judge my answer by my reaction.

"I am not sure that I do understand. I see the world as it really is when I see through my cats eyes. I see the patterns that energy forms and how it flows. It is in the same way I can tell Orla is not being truthful, because her energy flows against itself. Is that what you mean? "

"Yes just in a slightly different manner. You can see the energy , we cannot. We feel the energy. I know you feel vibration and pulsing, but that is not the same as what we feel. We have evolved tremendously as a species. We are now evolving as a race, and Orla knows this. It is why she is taking so many of us under her power, and training us how she wants us to be.

What you need to know is this, emotion was originally bred into us as a weakness. It was what made us passive and kept us breeding. The sisterhood has changed that, emotion is now where our power comes from. It is our strength. It is our intelligence. It allows us to be your equal. Emotion has given us our freedom.

It is what you must use, to lean the people in your direction, when the time comes. You cannot simply order them, for they will not respond. You must compel them. Do you understand that?"

That I did understand. It was true, for a very long time we had treated the Others like children. Showing them the way everything was to be done, Watching over them. Making the decisions for them if there ever was a dispute. They were not supposed to have independence, and they never appeared to want it.

"I do understand, yes. Regardless of what you may think of me, I am happy you are here. I am happy I am not the only one that carries the teaching of the sisterhood. "

Tuallan seemed to soften a little when I said that. She didn't seem so defensive. Perhaps it had been very difficult for her and her family to be different from the rest.

"Well most of the healers here now are the Others that have been trained by the sisterhood, but not all of them have been trained to the extent I have. So remember, if you need anything, let me know. I will help you. None of us want to see Orla get that head piece. It would be the end of reality as we know it. The future would no longer be guaranteed. "

She then walked over to the dress, picked it up and gave it to me. She motioned for me to put it on and go sit somewhere til it dried in the sun. I was not to show my face in my home unless I was wearing that dress.

I did as I was told. It was a while after I left that I suddenly remembered, she had not told me the story of the dress. I guess that was for another time. So it was, that I sat in the morning sun, til the dress was dry. Then I made my way down the hill and past some of the people still sleeping in the square, through the corridors and into my room. Then I crawled into my bed and allowed myself to sleep.

"Hey sleepy head, wake up." My Father's gentle voice was tugging at me. He was sitting on the side of my bed urging me to return to a waking world. I opened my eyes and smiled at him.

"Where did you go last night? I couldn't find you? I thought maybe you had run back to the sisters? " he laughed as he spoke, but he had no idea how close to right he was.

"I just went exploring. I didn't really feel like being around so many people. It has been a long time since I have been the center of attention. " I tried to make light of it, I have always hated the look of disappointment my Father got, when something is not right.

"Well I want you to get up and get dressed. Today it is just you and me. I want to spend the day with you. I want to get to know you again. So lets go wander through the fields to the sea. Lets just wander where our feet take us. I am sure you have a lot of questions and it is my duty to have answers for you. So come on now. Lets go." with that he got up and left. He would wait for me in the main entrance as he always did.

I did want to ask my Father a lot of questions, but I had not expected to, this soon. Choosing my words carefully would be a challenge. I knew he shared everything with Orla, and he would also share our day with her. But this may be the only opportunity that I might have, to plant the seeds of doubt about their relationship. This was my chance to change everything.

We had been gifted with a most beautiful day for our impromptu excursion. The sun was high in the sky and there was a gentle breeze blowing off the sea, giving the air that wonderful scent that makes you want to breathe deeper. The energy was light and I felt like a little girl again, wandering with my Father in the fields. For a time it felt perfect.

"I am enjoying this so much. I had forgotten how much I loved spending time with you. You have grown into such a beautiful woman. You have your Mother's grace, and her intelligence. I miss your Mother so much. Life without her was unbearable. I did not think I would survive it. You were gone and I knew bringing you back to be with me, was not the answer. I just did not want to continue without her. Then one day Orla came to the edge of the city. I was enraged. After countless years, for her to just show up now. But she seemed different, not so angry and destructive. She had heard of your Mother's passing and was requesting entry, for the purposes of grieving. I let her in. I thought, perhaps she had grown up. I believe everyone deserves a second chance. When she saw your Mothers things she became inconsolable. It was then that I realized I was not the only one who was in pain. I think it was this, that convinced me that Orla had changed. It is through this, over time and because of our grief that we found love. She is so good to me. She never questions me, she is very supportive and is always present . I have grown to love her very much. This is why I would wish that you take over my duties, and I could spend my life just as a man that loves a woman. Is this something you are prepared to do for me?"

My Father held me close and did not look at me when he spoke. I knew he did not want to see the expression on my face. He did not want me to answer that, I was not prepared. In my Fathers mind, if he didn't see "No" on my face then the answer was yes.

I was in no way prepared to wear the head piece, but I would do it to keep it from Orla. It was very difficult for me to see my Father as a weak and vulnerable man. He was not the same man I knew as a child. Yes he had always been fair and yes, he always gave second chances, but my Father was not a man that was easily duped. He was a man that was strong like stone and people were always leaning on him, he was not The One that did the leaning.

The only thing that made any sense to me, was that, the death of my Mother completely broke him. He was my Father and I would always love him as that, but he was by no means the same man. That was very hard for me to even consider, that the man I remembered and desired to be like, was here, right in front of me, but did not actually exist anymore. A cruel piece of reality, it was a severe blow to my heart. I knew I could not trust my Father, not because he would purposely betray me, but because he had woven such an illusion around Orla, that his version of truth was no longer his truth, but instead, Orla's truth.

The One had warned me. She was right to do so. She had told me I would be ruler, I just didn't want to believe it was happening so soon after my return. But still, seeing my Father's frailty with my own eyes, it was like a dream, a nightmare. My remembered reality no longer existed. The world changed when I was gone and I had returned to someone else's life.

I had always been taught that life was a continuum. One event was built upon another, and it kept growing til it was finished. It was linear, like an unbroken chain. But this reality had nothing to do with my previous reality. Somewhere, in my absence, my worlds got switched and the chain was broken, now it seemed to be up to me to fix it all, even though I had no idea how I was going to do that.

I turned to my Father with sympathetic eyes, "Of course Papa, I will do as you ask. I understand it was always going to be for me to wear the headpiece. My only concern is that I am still very young and I have not gained your great wisdom in dealing with the people. I will try very hard however, to attend to all affairs with wisdom and balance. How could I possibly deny you your happiness." Even though I said the words, I was not sure that I believed them. There was a big part of me that was screaming, "Why, how could you do this to me. This is not my mess, I don't want to clean it up. You are supposed to be the strong one, how can you dump all this on me. Can't you see what she is doing? Open your eyes. You are abandoning me, for a woman that has already betrayed you. What about me, what about my life, what about what I want? " My heart was pounding and I just wanted to run away, but I didn't.

I did not know how, and I did not know why, but I had chosen this path. I had to trust that is was the right one.

"Ah my daughter. My beautiful, powerful girl. I knew you would not let me down. So like your Mother you are. You will make a fine ruler. I know you and Orla will grow to love each other. My heart has been lifted, and I

160

can now relax into my joy. In one month we shall celebrate the passing of the headpiece from me to you. Come my child lets return and share this joyous news with Orla. You have just made her so very happy as well. She had no interest in ruling over the people. She wants a quiet life with me."

My Father was so animated he almost didn't seem real." I forced myself to smile and rose from the ground to join him. We walked for a bit and then it all got to be a little too much for me. I could feel the pressure rising in me. I knew if I were to face Orla in that moment, I would betray myself and she would know I stood against her.

"Father, I am very happy we have made this decision, but if you would allow it, I need a little bit of time to understand the complexity of my decision. Would you mind terribly, delivering the news yourself, and allowing me the rest of the afternoon to align myself?"

"Of course not, go do as you must. Enjoy the life you have now, you have earned that."

With that he picked up his pace and returned to his home, to deliver what he thought was wonderful news.

In that moment, there was one thought that was torturing me. It was the same thought that released me from my Father. My thought was," My Father had not really wanted to spend any time with me, he had only wanted to guilt me into taking over his life." The betrayal I felt as that thought took over my consciousness, started to consume me. I did not know this man at all. My Father would not have done something like that, my Father was not a dishonest man, my Father puts others before himself. I did not understand this man at all. Had Orla found some way to remove my Father from his body and replace him with something that she could easily puppet? I was so confused. I ran back to the sea. I sat in the wet sand, listening the waves pound on the beach.

In one month I would wear the head piece, and then I would be Orla's target. What would she do with my Father when he no longer wore that head piece? Would she reveal herself as she truly was to him then? Would he be able to take another blow like that?

I just did not want to be there at that moment. I lay still, as still as the sand on the beach, I wanted to be part of the beach, and let the sea carry me away, bit by bit. I tried to stop thinking. This just was not the life I had imagined for myself. Even when I knew my Mother had left, and I knew everything had changed, I thought I would still have my Father. But now I was alone, I had no one. I demanded that the sea take me.

The longer I lay there the more the sound of the waves obliged my request. The more I became the waves. Their energy passed through me as the water sifts through the sand. I could feel myself being disassembled, one piece at a time, drifting off into the sea, til I was no longer Aeiya. I was many pieces and many parts. Each part had its own story to tell.

My pain wanted to speak first. It told a story of how as a child, if my nightmares were not met with the immediate presence of my Mother, the feeling of abandonment would consume me. I would scream for my Mother, but she did not always hear me. Nor did anyone else. I was alone in those moments and those moments grew into their own life, that lived as a part of me, in the belief that I was alone in life. That there was no one that I could rely upon. No one would save me. No one would rescue me. If I screamed, no one would hear me. I just was not part of everyone else's reality. No one saw me, no one heard me. I was the invisible person. Not like others of my kind.

My lack of confidence was quick to jump in after my pain. You are not seen, because you do not deserve to be seen. What is so special about you, nothing. You take up far too much space on this planet so it is about time someone cuts you down to size. Who are you to think that you even have the right to wear that head piece? You, the daughter of a ruler, no, that is not possible. They are going to realize very soon that you are an impostor, and then you will be banished from the planet. You are no one and you never will be anyone. You mean nothing.

Fear dragged me to the bottom of the sea with it, before it would speak. This part of you feels as though it is drowning, so I will allow you to drown if that is what you wish. Whatever you fear I will offer it to you. I am your fear and I am generous to a fault, be afraid of anything and I will create it for you. Bringing your imagination to your reality, so that you can fully experience your fear is my specialty. Ask with a thought and you shall receive, is my gift to you. You should be afraid, look around you, there are no friendlies. You cannot see in the dark. No one is helping you. You should be afraid in the light as well, if the light is too bright it could blind you and steal your sight. Be afraid, be always afraid, for in that way you give me strength and I will grow.

Wait, don't forget me, I am your desires. I am what drives you. I live in your imagination as the life you are supposed to be living. You spend all your time comparing what you think you want, to what you you actually have. The gap between the two grows larger at every moment. You live in the gap, in a place of non existence. You cannot have or have not. You allow yourself nothing if it is not created in your imagination by your specifications. The more life offers you, the more you dismiss it as "not the right life." How you imagined your adult life to be when you were a child has created a blueprint for disappointment. How can you enjoy what is right in front of you, if you are always comparing it to something that does not even exist? You are very determined to not be happy and to not allow love into your life.

That was the voice that snapped me out of drifting endlessly. All of these pieces were part of me, part of the whole. They spent all of their time, arguing endlessly about how my life was so wrong. How could I possibly be happy? I was so separated from myself.

I was starting to understand the teachings of the Sisterhood now. So many of their teachings were about Oneness. It was in this moment as I brought all my pieces back together, that I understood the true meaning of separation. It was not the separation I felt from my Father or from the loss of my Mother. It was not that I was separate from the trees, or from the sea that was lapping at my feet. It was nothing to do with the distance between my self and the lights that brightened the night sky. The separation that I felt was the separation within myself. The argument of all my pieces. The constant bickering between pain, fear and desire.

It was the lack of self acceptance that caused all this internal conflict. I had been so wrong, and so conceited to think that I had mastered the ladies teachings. I was not separate from anything but myself. That separation within myself, was mirrored by my outside world. What was happening within me, became the world that I experienced. How was I supposed to want the life that had descended upon me? I may as well be crushed by a stone to the point where my lungs could no longer bear the weight of it. I understood what the problem was, but I had no idea of how to change it.

"Are you alright? We have been looking for you everywhere. I had expected you to return with your Father, but when he was alone, I was not sure what state you were in. We were not able to find you, so I contacted The One through the crystal. She told me where you would be." Tuallan came running up behind me. I was not happy to see her, but I was not wanting to be alone either.

"My Father and I used to come here when I was a child. I guess he thought he could ease the blow by bringing me to a familiar place, a place where we shared so many memories." I tried to speak without revealing my fear around all that had just happened.

"I am sorry, you have had to discover all of this, in this way. You must feel very alone. It is hard to discover the people you love and not the people you thought they were. Unfortunately everyone turns into the people they have around them. I think it must be a survival skill, adapting to your environment, ensures a longer life. It was your Mother that allowed your Father to be the man he was, now he has adopted Orla's energy, and that is why he cannot see who she is, because she is now the greater part of him. " Tuallan stated all this so plainly, like it was just fact.

It was the answer I had been looking for, Of course, my Father had absorbed Orla into himself, as himself. He was a piece of Orla now, just as I had experienced the pieces of myself. Why couldn't a person become a piece of someone else? It all made so much sense. How is it that Tuallan knew this and I didn't?

"Have you ever been to the baths?" Tuallan asked

"No, I have never been ill."

"Is that what you were told, that the baths were only for those that are ill? It is true, the baths can heal illness, but what the baths really do is heal separation. They put the pieces back together, by allowing you to remember your vibration as a whole. Have you not ever wondered why there are eight baths, all of different colors?" There was that smile again, that smile that said she knew more than I did. I really did not like that smile.

"I have often wondered just that, however I thought perhaps different colors healed different problems."

"You are right about that as well, but when you take the baths in sequence, they act to mend the separation inside of you. The conflict that all people face when their reality does not match their desires."

How did she know? There is no possible way she could have seen into me that deeply. Was it true that she could feel what I was feeling? In that moment I felt more vulnerable than I had ever felt. I tried desperately not to react, she must not know of my fear of being revealed. The Others were powerful and I had just dismissed them. I was wrong. I must be careful until I am sure, they can be trusted.

"Come with me now, I will take you to the baths, where you can experience the power and wisdom of the waters. Where you can be carried on the waves of sound. Allow yourself to let go of the battle that wages wars inside of you. Discover what Oneness feels like, and then you can practice keeping yourself in that way. Once you know the difference, you will not want to be separate again."

Chapter Seventeen

I longed to know that feeling inside of me, that feeling that I was one with myself. I was whole. The feeling that I knew myself and trusted myself, as I trusted the sun to shine and the rain to fall. But I did not understand how Tuallan would be able to show me anything that The One had not already revealed. It made me feel a little less of a person to think that Tuallan knew something that I did not know. As she had said, "Do not trust anyone." I took that advice to heart, and in this moment it was speaking loudly to me.

"Yes, I do want to know that feeling. However why would I have to practice staying that way?" I was honest in my query. I never really had to practice anything, I was shown a few times and the ability was automatically transferred to me.

Tuallan laughed out loud at me, and then she responded, "Yes, I forgot, the basic differences between our species. You just know, and we have to learn. Well this is good, it will be a new experience for you. This time you will have to do the same thing over and over and over again, until you learn it well enough that it becomes a habit."

"A habit?" I was not so familiar with habits?

"Yes, a habit. A habit is something that you do repeatedly, until you are so familiar with it, that it is an automatic response and you do not have to think about how it is done. A habit is a process that you absorb into you and it becomes a part of you. A habit is something that once it is absorbed you would not see it as separate from yourself, because it has become so engrained in you. Once a habit is established, it is hard to believe it was not always a part of you. Just as your Father is not a part of Orla."

The expression on my face must have told a story, cause the next words out of her mouth were,

"A habit can be a good thing or a bad thing, you must be wise enough to choose which, for once it has been absorbed, it is very hard to be rid of it."

She then walked away from the beach, motioned for me to follow, and seemed utterly uncaring as to whether I would follow or not. I just could not figure her out. She went from a moment of absolute empathy to being like a stone wall. I had no idea how she functioned within that range of emotion or lack of it. But she was right, it was the fundamental difference between our species.

We returned to the Alaria. It was one of those walks where I had really wished The One was with me and could have collapsed time. My feet were to heavy to pick up. Each step was a chore, so I was glad to arrive at the baths. I didn't really care about what they may do, at the moment I just wanted to rest. As Tuallan opened the duct to allow the water into the bath, I marvelled at the craftsmanship on the tubs. Carved from a single solid piece of stone, the tubs were completely smooth. They had been placed in a semi circle starting with red then orange, yellow, green, pink, light blue, dark blue, purple and finally a clear quartz crystal. They were beautiful. All the same stones could be found in the head piece that my Father wore. I knew they must have meaning but I did not know what it could be. The first bath was full of the pure water that flowed from the mountains. It was warm from spending the day in the cauldron. I removed my clothing and stepped into the bath. It felt so warm and wonderful on my skin.

"This is the first of 8 baths you will take. This tub vibrates to the lower areas of your body and to your survival instincts. Just relax and let the water flow over you. I am going to release the music to the stone, the vibration will move through the stone into the water and then through your body. You will feel the experience as memories. There will be no pain, only vibration." Tuallan was preparing me for a journey I could not have expected.

I lay there in the warm water. I could feel my body relaxing. The smooth walls of the tub beckoned to be touched. As I ran my fingers across the surface it felt like thousands of tiny little bubbles clinging to the side. My fingers allowed them to slip from their captive surface and find their freedom. Their dance of joy at their freedom gave the water a bubbling expression, a tingling on my skin. The joy that was released with the bursting bubbles was contagious. It passed through the water and into me, giving me a sense of ease that I desperately needed.

As the music started to play, the sound first came to me, not through my ears, but through the center of my body. I could feel it as an echo within the middle of me as it spread out from there in invisible waves towards my feet and my head. The sound was heavy, rhythmic and pulsing as it coursed through my flesh. Wave after wave moved through me until it centered itself at the base of my spine. I could feel its course change as my body seemed to absorb the sound, and it disappeared deep inside of me.

I felt the steady beat in the depths of my spine and it carried me on a current of memory, back to when I was a child. I was playing on the edge of the concentric circles in the center of the square. I was barely able to walk, but I insisted on walking on the very edge. My Father had been holding my hand. allowing me to gain my confidence. For just one moment he was distracted by someone calling his name, as he turned to reply I yanked my hand from his. I fell into the water face first. I must have taken water into me, cause all I remember is flailing my arms as fast as I could. I was terrified. In the next moment, my Father pulled me out, and I would be alright, no harm done. But that was not the whole truth that would occur over time. That small event was the event I had chosen as a message for my life. I would not be capable of doing things on my own. On my own I would not survive. I needed someone to hold my hand, if I was to make it through my life.

I opened my eyes and sat straight up in the tub. "That is not true," I screamed out. I can do it on my own."

Tuallan stood there, that smile on her face. "So you saw what you needed to see. That is what caused the first separation in you. Unfortunately for you, your parents reinforced it by coddling you for a long time after. They were wary of letting you do anything on your own that they thought could be the least bit dangerous. If they had let you carefully expand into your fear, this separation would have been healed. Are you starting to understand now, how this process is going to go. Each tub will take you through an experience, and allow you to heal a separation." she stood there nodding her head, waiting to see if I would nod mine in agreement.

I looked at her and nodded. I had no idea something that simple, that I had forgotten about, could have opened a wound so deep.

When I stepped out of the tub, my feet felt stronger on the floor. The whole lower half of my body felt more solid. I thought perhaps it was because of allowing myself to relax, maybe I was just feeling more balanced.

The next tub was ready and waiting for me. I stepped in and almost immediately the music started to flow. The orange stone felt warmer to me and lighter. The sound settled itself deep into my pelvis. It seemed to expand itself outward in a spiral that just kept turning. The music was quicker and more playful this time, not as heavy and rhythmic. This time the tones moved me to a dark room. I was older and had gone to visit one of my friends where the Others had lived. A new baby had just been born, his little sister, I remembered seeing the cord that tied the child to the Mother and asking what it was. He told me it was the bond that could never be broken, even when it was cut, it was still there, between all Mothers and their babies. When I questioned my Mother about the cord that had been between her and I, she told me there was no cord. In my mind, I thought if there was no cord, there was no bond. What ties my Mother to me? She could leave at any time and never come back, and there is no way for me to find her, no cord to lead me to her. For a long time after that, every time my Mother was gone, I wondered if she would come back. Then the day finally came when she didn't come back. She had abandoned me cause there is nothing tying us together. Again I came out of the water, spitting and sputtering. I had slipped just below the surface into the depths of that experience. Tuallan stood ready to drag me out if needed, but she waited, she wanted me to finish the moment.

167

"Did you see what you needed to see?" she asked quite gently.

"Yes, yes I did." I was shocked at how my second experience seemed to physically manifest my first experience. Once again I had slipped below the surface of the water. It was as though one experience was confirming another. I took a few moments to catch my breath and calm myself, then it was on to the next bath.

This stone was a bright translucent yellow. As I looked through the side of the tub, the yellow appeared to extend itself into the water, like rays of sunlight that streamed through open windows. It was beautiful.

As I stepped into this tub, I could feel myself being energized. The yellow was being absorbed by my body. I was starting to feel alive again. Awake and alert, I was ready to take on the next memory. The music was darting, piercing, high notes that came at irregular intervals. It reminded me of the insects that would dart over the edges of the pond that lay at the far end of the fields. They would flit and flutter in sudden movements. In my mind they seemed to move to the music that was vibrating through my ribs. My ribs felt like they were moving in time with the sound. Out they were pushed by the tones and into me they were drawn by my breath.

The scene in my mind fell upon the fields where I would run with the children of the Others. How I loved to run in those fields especially when the crops had grown above my head. There was no way to see where you were going. I would run and hope that I was headed in the direction of the edge, and my freedom. So many games were played in those fields.
I remembered one day a small group of us played in the field. We were all running about screaming and yelling. The crops were above our heads and the only way we knew where each other was is to call out, to make sounds. to giggle in pure joy. I was running and twirling, just for an instant I closed my eyes and wham, I ran into someone. We both landed on the ground and when I looked up, it was a little boy, he had hair the color of the sun. He smiled at me, got up and ran away. That was the first time I ever felt there was a difference between my body and the bodies of the Others, and in particular a boy. Something happened in that moment, we exchanged an energy, a look, a feeling.

I went home and told my Mother I wanted him to come live with me. I was determined, I would not give up. Everyday, day after day, I would assault my Mother with demands about this little boy. Finally my Mother told me, that at some point the games between myself and the Others, had to stop. I was not like them and it was not my position to live with them, it was for me to care for them. I threw a fit. I was enraged. I could not have what I wanted. I left my home and went to search for the boy. I never saw that little boy again. Even after repeatedly being dragged back to my home by my embarrassed parents. I only now realized that this event in my life created the foundation for me to believe that no matter what I want, I cannot have it. Desire for me, is something that is forbidden. Again the instant I understood the message, I was back in the Alaria. I was tired, I really didn't want to keep doing this. I protested to Tuallan.

"Fine if you want to stop, then stop, but you will have to start at the beginning again, later. This process has to be done in an unbroken chain, to be successful." she turned and walked away.

That confused me. Why wouldn't she try to convince me to go the rest of the way? Didn't she care? Doesn't she want me to stop Orla?

"Hey," I called out after her. "Why aren't you trying to convince me to finish what I started?"

"Your life is not my problem. I am not your keeper. If you want to quit, that is your decision. Don't you get it yet. You have to want to participate in your own life. You cannot expect everyone else to keep holding you up and pushing you forward. Why should we waste our energy on someone that can't commit to their own life? You keep insisting that this is all about Orla. It has nothing to do with her. Your life is all about you."

I had never been spoken to, by one of the Others in that way, in all my life. I was in my own life. I lived it every day. I woke up in my body, and went to sleep there. What did she mean, I wasn't participating in my own life? Tuallan reappeared and came to sit by the tub.

"Look, I know all this is very confusing for you. But you have to understand, you spend all your time wishing things were different, and thinking that all of this should not be put on you. You want someone else's life, but you will never have it. The fracturing that has occurred inside of you, is because you refuse to be alive in your own life. You are just there, in your body, sort of present when you are not imaging how it should be, instead of how it is. Is any of this sinking in, or am I just wasting my time?

I thought for a moment, and I knew she was right. but how did she know?

"How do you know these things? You do not live my life. You do not know what I feel."

"No, I don't and I don't have to. It is understandable that you are frightened. This is all new too you and very sudden. Maybe it is not the life you had imagined for yourself, but it is the only life you have. So you have a choice to make. You can stop running away and start trying to figure out, how to make things better, or you can walk away from these baths right now, and I will never bother you again. I will leave you to spend the rest of your life imagining what should have been? Your choice." Her words were firm and final. I remember that tone from my Mother, when she had had enough of my persistence.

"Alright, I will try, but I am not sure if I will be successful or not."

"Well that is not much of a commitment. You need to know this, there are those that try with the intent to try, and then there are those that try with the intent to succeed. I guess you have to decide which one you are."

The One had trained her well, she spoke in as many riddles as the great Mother did.

"Fine," I snapped, "Lets go to the next bath."

This stone was a beautiful light green. The color of new growth on the trees after the rains came. This water felt soft and gentle, though it was the same temperature as the other baths, it was cooler on the skin. My hands moved through the water with less resistance than before. The tones of the music started to flow through the stone. They flowed through the water and through my body. These songs were not jerky or jumpy, it was a constant tone that flowed into another tone and another and another, in a never ending cycle, moving together. So very peaceful it was, it carried me gently into my past.

I really do not remember a great deal from this bath. I know I had just come from the birthing chamber, and I was in my Mothers arms for the first time. I heard her voice and then my Fathers voice, I was surrounded by love. I felt warm and safe. As I tried to settle into that feeling I was ousted back to the Alaria.

"Well that is good, nothing is broken in that area. Next tub please. " Her instructions were short but very clear.

This was the pink tub, this one just simply felt like fun to me. I was looking forward to this bath. Even the water felt happy to me as I sunk lower in the tub. The music was joyful and bouncy. The kind of music you would like to dance to. A happy light step to its beat. I could feel a smile on my face, as I journeyed back to another place in my life. I was young and there was a gathering in my home. We were all dressed in fine fabrics. it seemed very formal, some occasion I do not remember. I wandered through the people that towered over me. There right ahead was Orla, she was talking to my Mother. The look on their faces said they were arguing about something. Orla raised her hand, she was going to strike my Mother. I ran over to stop her. In her reaction she hit me, and I landed across the floor. In that instant I knew the reason she had been banished, the real reason. I was not physically hurt, but my heart had been wounded. I loved Orla, I had been very close to her in my youth. I didn't understand how she could hurt me like that. I also knew instantly that learning to protect someone, meant that I would get hurt. Love was equal to pain. To stand up for myself or anyone else would put me in the line of fire, I would be the one to be sacrificed. Back to the Alaria I went. This was the hardest part of journey, it was so sudden, almost violent.

"Why does it have to be that way, when I come back. Can't you make it a little easier?"

"What you are experiencing is the release of the energy that has just been identified. The minute you see it, you let go of it. There is a physical reaction in your body. The energy that formed the fracture is gone and the

170

break is healed. It happens in the span of a breath. Do you really want to draw that process out?"

"Uh, no, I didn't realize that was what it was all about. I must admit I feel better now. I feel like I am stronger, more stable. I am thinking more clearly." I had really just discovered that in the moment. But it was true, I was better.

"Yes and it does get better yet. "

This tub was a beautiful light blue. Like the sky in the early morning just as the sun is rising. A soft blue, it made me want to touch its luminescence. I loved the feel of the smooth surface against my skin as I slipped under the waters surface. These baths were working at some level. I felt good. Better than I had felt in a long time. I knew the process now, so I waited for the music to start and just relaxed into it. The sweet sensual tones carried my consciousness to another time. What I saw before me was a medley of images. I was quite young in all of them. They all had one thing in common. I was trying to make a point, or speak my mind, perhaps I was demanding attention, I am not sure. In every image I saw, I was being ignored or worse, I was being shushed. I could feel that I thought what I had to say was very urgent, important, perhaps not to my parents but to me, and they were not allowing me to speak. The images started to rotate, they led to more images of the same thing. There were so many moments I had not been allowed to speak, I wondered how I had learned to talk. I truly did not know what the message was here. My confusion seemed to provoke another image in me. In this image I sat quietly in a corner. I was watching my Mother being busy with something. She could not quite see me from where she was sitting. After a few moments of my silence, I could see my Mother becoming frantic, she was looking for something. It took me a moment to realize that she was looking for me. That made me realize, perhaps there is more power in silence than there is in being to vocal. If silence makes people stop and give you their full attention perhaps it is the best way to create understanding through communication. And yes that was it, I was snapped back to the present moment again.

Onto the next tub. This one was a deep blue, like the midnight sky, with tiny flecks of gold in it. I recognized this stone immediately. This was the largest stone in my Fathers head piece. It was placed in the middle of his forehead, and the tiny gold flecks caught the light as he would turn his head. I loved this stone and always wanted to touch it. It drew me, into it. Whenever I went to the sea, I would run up and down the beaches hoping to find a stone like this, but I never did. Now I was going to be surrounded by it. As I released the weight of my body to the water, I knew this bath was different from the rest. The water was charged somehow. It felt alive, and waiting, wanting to pass me a message. As the music started to play, I could feel the ripples from the water move through my body. The water in the tub was becoming the water in my body. I was disappearing within the sound, my body melted away til I was liquid. My consciousness was the water. I could feel myself as the tide in the sea, and the raindrops speeding through the air on their way to the ground. I was being poured over a waterfall, to then I rose up as the mist.

Then something started to pull me, it was pulling me fast, pulling me backwards, back through time and space. I was pulled to a point where it was completely black. No light, no movement, no sound. As I looked around me, I could see a string, I picked it up and looked at it, I held one end in my hand and tried to follow it to the other end through the darkness. I could not see where this string led, so I started to pull on it. I pulled and I pulled, suddenly an image popped out of the darkness. I looked at the image but it was not familiar to me. So I kept pulling on the string. Another image came into view, but that was not familiar either. The more I pulled on the string, the more images, fell out of the darkness. Finally one came to me, it was an image of me pulling a string in the darkness. I did not understand what these images were all about.

A soft gentle voice spoke to me. It told me that all these images were of lives I have yet to live. It told me that all of my lives were attached by this string. The string represented certain lessons I had to learn, and that as I learned these lessons, they would lead to another lesson. My lives were lived in linear fashion but all at the same moment, so changing how I lived in one life, would change how I lived in all my lives.

The lives I had seen were all future lives, or lives that had not been completed yet. By making the right decisions in this life, I could alter or even shorten all the lives that followed.

I understood this and it came to my consciousness that, because of this, trying to do something for the wrong reasons is just not acceptable. To do something only because you are being watched, or because you think it is a shortcut, will never really work.

"The string is your consciousness and the images are the experience gained from the lives you lived. Everything belongs to you. What you do affects no other string, only your own." I knew then, I had to do, what I had to do, because it was all about me. Not because I had to please this person or get revenge on that person. I was the only person in my life, that my life could affect.

Back to the Alaria I went. Sometimes it felt like I had been dropped off the top of a mountain and slammed down with bone crushing shock back to earth. It took me a minute to shake that off. But I was ready for my next tub.

The next bath was the color of a lovely soft lavender. Standing at a distance the tub looked to be solid in color but that was deceptive. Once standing beside the tub I could see that there were veins of dark purple and

172

veins that were almost clear. In between these two extremes was every variation of purple that I could imagine. It was beautiful, like beings of a purple nation all coming together to dance in one spot.

Tuallan motioned for me to get in. She did not like it when I delayed too much between the baths. I am only to assume it had something to do with a congruency of energy. Once again the water was warm and nurturing. As the music started, my head began to buzz. It was as if my mind was part of the instrument and I vibrated within it, echoing out through my ears, and my eyes. I did not seem to hear the sound coming to me from outside myself, but rather it was like a thought that rose out of a feeling. The music was like a memory, it felt familiar. I felt like I was being gently lifted from the water and passed through the air by unseen hands removing me from myself. I felt unable to move, but I was not afraid. I felt no need to oppose the energy that beckoned me. In a place of darkness I felt myself expand outward towards all things. I had become non existent but existed in all things. I was not me, I had no self perception but I was understanding myself through all things. The energy seemed to flow through me, not just into me. I had the awareness that so many of the things I was experiencing, I had been those things, somewhere in time. As I was feeling the things that were most familiar to me, they seemed to line up in a line. In my mind they looked like beads on a string. Each existence separate and individual but all touching one another and aligned by the string. It was then that I understood, and that instant the awareness of the meaning of all those lives on that string flooded into me. My life, this life was all about the understanding that nothing was ever done to me. I was the sculptor of my reality. Choice was the clay that I used to sculpt my life. Every decision was a choice. I had spent a great deal of time feeling like decisions were made for me, because of the traditions of our people. In this moment I could see how I had chosen to be exactly where I was, right in this moment to learn the lessons of this life, so I could create a different life at a different time, and add another bead to the string. With that thought I was back, in the tub. This time, returning was not as violent as it had been. I had a sudden jarring awareness of being back in my body, it was as though someone had dropped me from a cliff with no wings.

I could see Tuallan looking at me, examining me, she was watching for signs that my experiences in the baths were changing me. I knew there was something specific she was looking for, but I had no idea what that was.

I stood there looking at the last bath. It was clear, no color. I could see the water on the inside of the tub, from the outside of the tub. As I circled to look for imperfections all I could find was what appeared to be bubbles buried in the stone. Tiny circles here and there that ran in veins. like a breath frozen in time. I was not sure where this tub would take me but I could feel the power of it, simply by standing near it. There was a very slow pulse emanating from it. As the pulse touched my skin I could feel a slight tingle. It felt like the air had formed fingers and was ever so gently caressing my skin with tiny flicks of wind. I lowered my body into this tub with anticipation. It was the last tub so it just made sense that a culmination of my experiences would occur here. This is the tub where I would be glued back together I thought. It would all makes sense now. I awaited the start of the music, but there was none. I waited a while longer, still no sound. I opened my eyes and no one was there. Tuallan had disappeared. I was not so sure what I was supposed to do now. The tub was relaxing and I thought perhaps I had misunderstood, perhaps this tub is not a part of the rest. So I decided to just rest and think about what I had just experienced.

My weight was gently supported by the water and I imagined that this is what the beasts of the sea must feel like. To not have to carry their weight they could fly through the waters as the birds fly through the air. As my thoughts formed, images took their shape and my inner landscape became a kaleidoscope of color and sound. It was so beautiful.

"This is the world you live in my child. It is how you perceive your life, before it is filtered through your thoughts."

It was The One's voice. I could not see her but I could hear her. I called out to her, needing her to hear me.

"Yes my child, I am here, come closer, follow my voice."

I could feel myself moving, drifting in a windless wind. There, just ahead I thought I could see some sky, and then greenery like there was on the mountains. Then I was in a small clearing overlooking the plains that led to the sea, and there just before me, sitting on a stone was The One. I ran to her, and hugged her. I had missed her so much. She felt safe to me, secure, all the things I had been missing since my return back to the royal home. It was just so good to be with her.

"I have missed you too. But what is this my understanding tells me, you have not been happy? Does it not feel good and right to be home, with your family? Are you not happy to sleep in your own bed again? Tell me child, what troubles you?"

I had the feeling she knew all the answers before I could give her any. However if my telling her my version would delay her leaving, I would talk as much as she wanted.

"Well going home is not what I thought it would be. Without my Mother, nothing feels familiar now. My Father spends most of his time with Orla, and I just feel like he has dumped the head piece on me, cause he can't be bothered to do his duty anymore and maybe he doesn't want to deal with me either. Orla has this magnetic hold on him and nothing can break it. My friends have all grown and have families of their own and duties to attend to. I feel like there are all these people around me, but I am completely alone." Does that make any sense? I knew I was whining, but I just wanted someone to care.

"Yes you are very articulate in your description of your circumstances. " The One smiled a brilliant heart warming smile as she spoke those words.

"Tell me, how would you have it be different if you had the choice?"

"Well of course my Mother would still be here, and if that were to happen, then Orla would be gone. I would have my friends look at me the way they once did, like I was one of them, not someone that was set to rule. I would wish to be carefree again, I do not want the head piece, even though I have agreed to take it. I want it to be the way it was. Is that asking too much?"

"Yes that is asking too much. Were you actually thinking that your life could stay the way it was? You were destined to grow up and you were destined to take the head piece. What does it matter if that is now, or later? What is it you think you will gain by waiting? Have you thought that, taking the head piece may give you the reasons you need to create a different community around you? A community based on a balance between your needs and the needs of the Others.? I think you are perceiving the head piece as a duty, but in truth, the head piece is a privilege. It will grant you certain abilities that you do not already have." The One had that look on her face that said she was telling the truth, just not the whole truth. I had become very familiar with that look over the years, it was usually the only way she could get me to do the things that were necessary.

"Abilities, what kind of abilities? How do they happen? Is there magic in the stones? Tell me more, what is it you are really saying, without using words to say it?" I had to laugh as I was saying these words. I knew what The One would tell me could not really not be translated into words. I would have to have the experience or the words would never express the understanding.

"To say there is magic in the stones is not really accurate. The stones hold their own vibration shall we say, and that enhances your own vibration. To tell you what abilities you can gain from the stones is not possible, because it has not yet been formed. The abilities you will gain, will be based on the abilities you choose to possess. So if you think there is something I am not telling you, you are right. I know the potential of what can happen, but not the actuality of what will. Only you know this."

"The last tub I was in, spoke of choice, and what that truly is. I am not sure why that plays a significant role in my life. Can you help me understand this?" I was somewhat confused about choice. I like the idea of having choice, but all things seem to come at a cost.

"Choice. Yes, This is the ultimate discovery of any life. Choice is the power to set in motion the circumstances that determine your future, based on a decision made in the current moment. Sounds simple enough, and it is very simple indeed. The hard part is being able to see the sequencing of events that follow the decision, and if they will create the future you think you want. We have all been in the position of thinking about our future and how we would like it to be. The complication of this is, we are assuming we will be the same in the future as we are now. That is something that does not occur. We may have the same interests, even some of the same likes and dislikes, but we ultimately change with every decision we make. So for you to sit here now and decide what your future should be, well, that would be a mistake. By the time you get to the future you had imagined, it may not at all be to your liking. The best thing to do to create a wonderful future life, is to make the very best decisions you can in the moment, and let life lead you. "

"You have obviously never worn the headpiece. You are expected to make decisions for the future, and force life to happen that way." I was a little disappointed that The One did not have something better to say to me, than, "let life lead."

"When you make a choice, you combine many different skills. There is the skill of thought, and the images that inevitably accompany it. Then there is the skill of will, what you use to implement the choice you have made. Then there is persistence, this is the energy you use, if your choice is not going as you had planned. Hopefully then you implement the final skill and the most important one, wisdom. You must always use the energy of wisdom to know when to change the choice that you have made. Not all choices are wise, and very few of them are permanent. Choice is the right to create your life from within your own being. But the true power of choice is the willingness to change your choice. I hope you are understanding what I am saying. So many of us have felt that once we have made a choice, we must stay the course, to the bitter end. This is not the way of wisdom. If upon your course of choice, you discover that the end will not be the appropriate outcome for yourself or others, then simply change your choice. Though this may not be something that you should do with a light heart, it is still the mark of a wisdom keeper. "

I wanted to hold her there, keep her with me, but I could see she was fading. I tried to hug her once more, but my arms fell upon smoke. I was pulled back through time and space, back to the warmth of the water in the tub.. As I settled back into the present reality, I was aware of Tuallan, she was there with me once again. She did not speak, she did not ask me of my journey, she only nodded in understanding. I had realized when I was with The One, that Tuallan had told me I would be going through a sequence of eight baths, however I had been through nine. I needed to know why she had lied to me.

"Why did you tell me, I would have eight baths and there were nine? What is your explanation for this?" I was a little demanding in my tone. I didn't want her to think I hadn't noticed. Tuallan looked at me with that wry smile.

"I told you, it would take eight baths to heal the separations within you. And that is the truth. The ninth bath was at the request of The One. The clear crystal bath seals the healing of the fractures within you and connects you to everything outside of you. The last bath connects you to the self that you are in all things. It completes the cycles of oneness within and oneness without. Is that enough of an explanation for you?"

"I suppose it will do." I did not like the feeling that she was one step ahead of me. For now I just wanted to return to my room, for rest and reflection. I left in silence, deep in thought. I returned to my room and my bed. As I lay down, I knew my understanding of choice would weigh heavy on my mind now. The understanding that I design my reality, by the choices I make, well that was a lot to consider. I needed sleep and dreams to ease the intensity of my reality. I closed my eyes and allowed the darkness to carry me away from this waking world.

Chapter Eighteen

The morning brought some much welcome levity to my life. The sun was bright, a slight breeze in the air everyone I saw returned my smile. It was such a great day, I decided to venture to the sea, and spend some time with the waves lapping at the shore. As I followed along the path, little birds sang and butterflies flitted about. I was listening to the whole world chatter with itself. Everything seemed to be in conversation with something else. I loved days like this, they reminded me of my carefree childhood.

It came to me that perhaps this is what I needed to do. I needed to find those moments that still live with me of what I would feel as a child. The lightheartedness, the joy, it need not be gone, I just needed to allow it to be. If I had discovered one thing in the baths, it was about allowing your life to happen. I had come to the realization that it had been me myself, that had removed the wonder from my life. I had come to focus so much on what I did not want, that the moments of joy which were right in front of me, could not be seen by me. I had determined it the wisest course of action, to make my decisions in the way The One had described. To do my very best at all times and let the future create itself. There was something extremely freeing about that.

Yes, my life was about helping and caring for others, but it was still my life. If I made the right decisions for me, then the Others would benefit by default. As I reached the shore, I could smell the salty air and feel the change in the light. Everything seemed lighter by the sea. I found a lovely spot where the rocks ended and a long stretch of sand was laid out in front of me. I sat on the rocks, watching the waves come in, creating animated designs in the sand as the water retreated back to the sea. With every wave, the sand would claim just enough water to create a new masterpiece, but the sand knew the water was not its to hold forever. So it held on just long enough to draw images from its imagination, of what life could be.

Most of the images were beautiful, but I could not make sense of them, only the sand knew the grace that it held when it experienced the water. I lay back and tried to imagine the world the way sand must see it. It must be such a sensual experience to have been still for so long and then, with the coming of the waters, to feel yourself move, to know what it is to brush up against other grains of sand. To, if only for a second, have your body surrounded by the softness of water. To be cleansed and cooled. I thought that water must be very exciting for the sand.

As I sat back up, I caught movement in the corner of my eye. I turned my

179

head and I thought I had seen someone disappear into the bush, down the beach. I didn't understand that. No one really came here without a reason. I rose, thinking I would have a better view standing on the rocks. Still nothing. So down the beach I went. I had to investigate. Perhaps one of the Others had wandered this way.

I could see footprints on the beach. It looked as though they had been walking towards me and then stopped. Maybe they did not realize I was there, and when they saw me they decided not to approach. The footsteps stopped, turned and then went back down the beach, they disappeared where the rocks claimed rights to the land from the sea. It was a mystery as to who it was. I did feel the stirring of curiosity in me. Someone knew I had been there, they had seen me, but I had not seen them. I would have to come here more often, perhaps this mystery person is someone I needed to know.

The day was passing me by and I decided to head back. Many more days would follow that I would return to the same spot, but never did I see anyone. The time was near for me to accept the head piece from my Father and Orla was not acting herself.

Orla was very adept at disguising herself although I am not sure that she knew herself enough to let anyone else know her. In some way, she was always eluding her own reality. It may have only been in tiny moments or in varying shades of solidity, but it was always there. So as the days for the exchange drew near, she became increasingly agitated. Her behavior was not noticeable by most. I believe I saw it because I was the one that was causing it. Any conversations I had with her became extremely short, she could not be still around me, her eyes constantly moved, as though following an invisible light. Something I found odd as well, she started spending blocks of time on the other side of the land bridge, just beyond the protective shield.

Why would she go out there? There had to be only one answer. She must have been meeting with someone. Perhaps someone from her own society was coming to meet her.
I attempted to talk to my Father about her unusual behavior, but when it came to Orla my Father had selective sight and selective hearing. He saw what he wanted to see, and dismissed the rest. It astonished me how he could explain anything rationally. I knew Orla was planning something, I could feel it, I just didn't know what. She did not want me to have that head piece. Orla wanted to rule, and if I received the head piece not only was she not in power, but then she would be bound to my Father. If there were any caring at all for my Father, it was not enough to make her want to be his wife.

In many ways it felt as if I were living multiple lives. In each life I played a different character and had a different purpose. It had become very difficult to differentiate, the variations of myself. There was no drastic separation between my roles, barely discernible shifts in perception defined how I managed being the daughter, the ruler, the adult and the child. I knew I was not so different from Orla. We even dealt with the same goal, although from totally different perspectives. She wanted the head piece and I did not, but I would do whatever it took to keep her from it. The One had told me to be able to stop her, I would have to be like her, I think this is what she meant. We were both living our lives in ways that were not completely truthful. Though we knew who we were, we both created persona's that would satisfy those around us, and allow us to keep our secret lives hidden.

I had one more day of freedom before I would wear the head piece and be expected to perform the duties of a ruler. I could feel a tremendous amount of tension around Orla. I needed to know what she was doing beyond the borders of the shield so I made the decision to follow her. She had been leaving most mornings and returning mid afternoon. I would go out to the land bridge early and wait for her there. Whatever she was doing was not to benefit my Father. Her energy field was very dark and heavy, not the kind of energy you would expect someone in love to have. I just did not know why my Father would not acknowledge her strange behavior. I had given up trying to coax him into seeing the illusion of Orla. There was no use, he was blind in her direction. Whatever this was, I would have to deal with it myself.

Early the next morning, I crept out beyond the boundaries of the city. When I was beyond the eyes of the sentinels, I could walk freely, but with caution. As I got to the edge of the protective shield, I could feel nervousness stirring in me. I had travelled beyond the shield before, but it was under the protection of The One. I did not fear the beasts that roamed wild as much as the unknown. I did not know exactly what I was looking for, I did not want to, not, see something.

I kept walking til I could no longer see the city. If Orla was hiding something she would have to come at least this far. This is where I would wait for her. I chose a spot high on a rock that was partly hidden by the trees. The light was filling the cracks in the cliffs as the sun climbed higher in the sky. It was a beautiful day, warm and breezy. Off in the distance I could see large white clouds drifting above the sea, lazily casting their shadow across the surface of the water. I could smell the earth that lay in the crevices between the rocks. Moss grew on the dark side of the walls, where it was moist and cool. Being here in this spot made me miss the mountain top that had been my home for so long. I could barely see those mountains from here, but I could feel them pulling my energy towards them. I wondered what the women were doing, but I knew they would be following their usual routine. Paying homage to the sun, before they went

181

about their chores. I was wondering if The One could see me. If she was looking down on me, ready to help if I needed it. I wasn't sure, but I was hoping that to be true. As time passed I could tell it was getting close to mid morning, so I nestled myself into the scenery, hoping Orla would not deter from her routine today. She did not disappoint me. It was not long before I could hear footsteps. There she was, hurrying along the road across the bridge. She kept looking nervously behind her, I wondered if she thought I was following her.

I let her get ahead, then I left my hiding spot to pursue her to her destination. We did not travel very far before I saw what my eyes did not want to believe. Just ahead was an area of broken rocks. At some point the mountain had given way and came down in a pile of boulders. The large stones were everywhere, and as Orla approached, people were coming out from behind the stones. First one then another and another, soon there were enough for a small army. Everywhere you looked you could see stones and the heads of people that had hidden behind the them.

Orla walked straight to one man, she embraced him passionately, she kissed him, and he returned the kiss. My heart started to pound, I was angry. I had known that Orla did not truly love my Father, but I had not thought her this deceptive. I needed to get closer to them, I needed to hear what was being said. She would not be here long before she headed back, if I was to figure all this out, I needed to be closer. With careful steps I was able to sneak around behind some rocks, as I strained my ears to hear, I could feel my body tense in rage. I just had to keep everything under control. Now was not the time for the cat to come out. I feared that Orla might be wise enough to identify the cat as me. I just needed to hang on for a little while longer.

"Are you ready, are we clear on the plan?" Orla questioned the tall dark haired man she had shared the embrace with.

"Yes my lady. We are ready to move, just say when." The man responded to her with a slight smile on his face.

"It is imperative that you get her, before she gets that head piece. Once it is on her head, whether she knows how to use it or not, she will have the power to stop us, Do you understand that? She must not get her hands on it. " Orla had become very animated as she spoke.

" I do understand we have been over this many times, I know what I am doing. What do you want me to do with the old man?" I could see the tall dark man did not like to be thought as inept.

"I don't care what you do with him, I would prefer him dead, but that may not help us in the end, just make sure he stays out of the way. Once that head piece leaves his hands, get him out of there, how you do it is not my concern. Everyone will be at that ceremony, so you will have no problem getting into the city. Just stay out of sight til I give you the signal, then don't let anyone or anything stop you."

"I am at your service my Lady, your will is my will. Soon the city will be ours." The energy coming off this man was venomous. He and Orla were a good match.

I could feel the heat of my rage threatening to burn my skin. In that moment I wished death to befall all of those that were against my Father. I had never wished something so vehement as this before. I could feel the cat coming out. I had to get further away, before the cat rose out of me, and sought to kill them all. I ran as fast as I could, trying to move silently. At this point it was more important to get away than to be heard. In moments I could feel the impact of my feet against the soil change. I looked down and my paws were cushioning the sound of my steps. I could feel how powerful the cat is and how easy it would be to kill Orla's followers. But no, I knew, it was more important for me to return to my Father. I had to stop this.

I ran as fast as I could to the edge of the city.   Orla needed to see me at the palace when she returned. I calmed myself, deep purposeful breaths, in and out. As my body diminished in size, I grabbed handfuls of grasses to cover myself. Hoping to slip back into society as a person in plant disguise. I was at the edge of my home and all I had to do was get past the last few sentinels. People were everywhere, busily preparing for tomorrows ceremony. I kept waiting for something to distract their ever watchful eyes, but they did their job well. I could not move from that spot with out being questioned.

"Need my help again, don't you?" Tuallan spoke suddenly but softly behind me.

"Oh, you should not sneak up on me like that. I need to get into the palace before Orla gets back. I have to talk to my Father immediately. Do you know where he is?"

"Yes, he is with the organizers right now making the final preparations. He has asked to attend the baths later with Orla, a purification right, before they come to a merging. I assume you are not going to let that happen?" Tuallan always intuited more than she actually knew.

"Well they may merge, but I do have to stop the ceremony, can you do something to get rid of those sentinels? I need your help. " I pleaded with her, time was growing short.

"Sure leave it to me, I will just tell them your Father needs to see them. OK?"

"Yes, fine, I don't care, just do it now."

"Ok, good luck." And off she went to distract the guards.

In a moment they turned and followed her as she lead them away. I made a dash for my room. Quickly I put on more clothes and went to find my Father. I must speak to him before Orla returned, but I still did not know what I was going to say. After looking in several different spots I found him out by the hollow stones making more preparations for tomorrows ceremony. My mind was frantically searching for the words that would invoke my Father's sense of loyalty towards me. I knew there were many things that could be said, but few of them would be considered sacred enough, to not be shared with Orla.

"Father, there you are, I have been looking all over for you." I greeted him with a big smile and open arms.

"Aeiya, I had been looking for you this morning as well. You were no where to be found, I was beginning to wonder if you had run away, like you used to when you were a child." He laughed as those fond memories became part of his present moment.

"No, of course not. There are times I would like to run away, however I realize you can never run from yourself. Since we create our own lives, running away seems a bit silly, cause we can never escape ourselves. "

"Is that wisdom I hear, passing over your lips child." he smiled through his words.

"No, I do not think it is wisdom, just a consequence of spending to much time with the ladies on the mountain top." his compliment had made me blush.

"Oh, speaking of that, I have a surprise for you. The One will be performing the Ceremony of Transition tomorrow. Does that make you happy?"

"Oh yes very much, but I thought she could not come down from the mountain, without harm coming to her?" I was now a little concerned, maybe what Orla was planning was more of a problem than I had previously thought?

"I do not know, she just assured me she would be here. Now what is it you were wanting to speak with me about?"

"Now that I know The One is coming, I would like to have the ceremony in a surprise location. A spot that means something to Mother. It would be in her memory and in her honor. Do you think this is possible Father?" I saw his features soften as his memory drifted back to my Mother, his wife, the only woman he would ever truly love. It was the only tactic I could think of that would not raise suspicion that he would agree too. It is also something I knew he would not want to speak to Orla about. Whenever my Mother was fondly remembered by my Father, Orla would become jealous and consequences would be forced upon my Father. I knew he would happily comply and hand the rest of the arrangements over to me.

"Oh, that is a lovely idea. What did you have in mind?"

"I would like to have a private ceremony, just a handful of people in a natural location outside of the city, Then upon our return we can start the welcoming and the festivities. I just don't want to tell you where I want to

184

have the ceremony performed. We will just get up at sunrise and go there. Is that alright with you?"

"I do believe in this case, it is whatever the new ruler of Lemuria wants." He smiled and hugged me. He almost seemed relieved, that I was taking over. Perhaps he could feel something was about to happen, but he could not quite place it.

Now all I had to do was choose a place that was close enough but also far enough away to be sure that we not be discovered. There was no place like this that came immediately to mind, so I headed to the sand by the sea. I would sit, be still and think. I knew that when I did not know what to do, I should do nothing. So I would be still and let the answer present itself to me.

The One had taught me well. It was now, after some time back in the world of every day existence that I was experiencing just how those teachings worked in a practical way.

As I sat there on the beach listening to the waves crash down on the shore, smelling the salt that the wind had grabbed from the sea and carried towards the shore, I could feel that I was not the only voice that needed to be heard on this problem with Orla. The sea spoke of its concerns about the misuse of power that Orla's people would carelessly throw about, over time.

The winds too, spoke their thoughts. They expressed concern about the lack of balance in Orla's desires. The land though, kept showing me images of blood being spilled. This is the most vile thing that can happen to the land when beings of the same species, attack and kill their own kind for no reason more than greed. The pain, the fear, the rage, whatever emotion was being experienced that caused the shedding of blood, it all drains into the land as well, and leaves an imprint that cannot be easily disbursed. Our flesh, is made of the elements of the land, and therefore it feels as we do. It experiences as we experience, for there is never any separation. The One showed me the power in this, when I lived on the mountaintop.

The sisterhood had many sacred areas for the purpose of communication. There were temples, rocks, trees, and pools of water that were placed in very specific spots to enable this communication. The One taught me of the veins that ran deep in the earth. These veins kept the earth in contact with itself. Messages were sent from one spot to another allowing her to keep herself balanced. If the land was too dry in one area, a message could be sent to another area, to start creating rain bearing clouds. Sometimes, earthquakes were necessary in one place to settle another. It was always about balance.

I was shown how this communication worked by placing specific elements within these veins. It is in this way that The One could know what was happening under the protective shield of my home, or in Orla's land of Atlantis. All planets have these veins and she had told me many times of the many temples that covered vast areas, not all of them could receive the same messages, but the temples were placed to be able to communicate among themselves. In this way, a temple sitting on an earth element vein could receive messages from a temple that was placed within the element of air. At times I had even heard specific voices as they travelled along these special veins. Once you knew what to listen for, understanding what was said, was a simple matter. All of life is a frequency, you must feel the vibration to speak the language.

The most important lesson The One taught me was, never rely solely on the physical senses. The senses exist in physical reality, and are part of that reality, therefore they are limited to that reality. It is the senses that exist beyond the physical that explore the greatest truths. The senses we have in our outer bodies, is where life can be felt as it truly is, before it is shaped by belief. The denser reality becomes, the more the physical senses perceive it. However once it has become tangible, then it has also become contaminated with some form of opinion. It is the complication of beingness in physical form.

With so many concerns about Orla coming from so many places I decided to hold the ceremony where all these elements come together. Right there on the beach. It was not far from home, but it was a very well hidden spot. Having made my decision, I wandered down the beach trying to calm my mind and pass some time. I was avoiding Orla, I did not want to see her before the ceremony, I did not want her to see that something had changed. If she felt something had changed, she would try to change it back.

I had gone a short way down the beach and there I saw footprints again. There was someone visiting the beach on a regular basis. I knew they were not of the royal house, it had to be one of the Others. I would say it was a man, based on the size of the print and the depth to which the print sank into the sand. For a second I thought I caught the scent of something, though I was not sure what, it was not something I was familiar with.

"My child." I jumped as The One spoke to me. I was so deep in thought, I did not know she was there with me. I ran over to her, but she stepped back. "Please she said, I would love more than anything to embrace you, but I cannot. I must be very careful of my energy reserves, till I can return to the mountains. It is so very good to see you. How are you holding up against Orla?"

"It is so good to see you as well. You have no idea, how many times I just wanted to run back to you, leaving all of this behind. I don' t know if I can do it? I don't know that I have the strength? Did you know she has her people waiting just outside the shield? It sounds as though she means to over throw us? Why is she doing all this? Help me understand, please?" I pleaded with her. I thought if I could understand all this, perhaps I would make better decisions as to how to keep everyone safe.

186

"It would be very difficult for me to tell you why she is doing this.   I can tell you in words, however if you have not experienced the desperation she feels, it would be most difficult for you to understand. Simply put she has been jealous of your Mother ever since your Mother was chosen for queen. Over the years of her exile, a dark energy has grown in her. It is a sort of theatre in the mind. She would sit and dwell on how her life would have been if she had been chosen. How wonderful and perfect life would have been for her. As time went by of course those thoughts transformed from day dreams into a life that she believed was rightfully hers, and that your Mother had cheated her of. None of that was true of course, but this is what happens when you give your mind the ability to think for you. Her anger grew as she believed more and more that she had been cheated, that anger became a desire for vengeance. She has convinced herself that if she has the head piece, her life will be happy."

"That makes no sense. Good rulers don't want to rule, they rule because they have a sense of duty to the people, they have honor and tradition behind them. They do not do it to make their lives happy, they must however believe that they are capable of making the lives of others better."
She was right, what she was saying about Orla was not making sense to me.

"Because Orla has allowed her life to descend into a sort of madness, she has also created a body very similar to the others. She is very dense. She is very solid. It is more difficult for her to experience the lighter energies, you and your Father do. She was made in the same way your Mother was, however living without joy creates a reality in which it is difficult to see truth. Truth becomes less and less visible, the more you believe your own thoughts to be true."

I have to admit I was getting a little confused. If you could not trust yourself, who could you trust? I knew The One was very aware of exactly what I was thinking. I just sat and waited for her to respond.

"Trust is a very interesting concept. What is trust exactly? What is belief? These things are very different concepts, however as we listen to ourselves more and more, we start to trust what we believe. This is a very dangerous path to walk. You would be better off asking a tree or a rock the answer to your question, you would get the truth, because the tree and the rock are not concerned about what you want to believe, they live in truth."

"What makes the difference, why do the tree and the rock live in truth but not us?" I wondered.

"This goes back to separation. The instant you see yourself as separate from the trees and the rocks you no longer see the whole truth. You are made of the same elements as all other things on this planet. It is because you have movement and language that you believe yourself to be different. As you have learned all things have a language, all you have to do is learn to speak it."

187

I nodded my head, that was a big lesson for me. Most beings around me, knew what I was saying even before I did, because they did not rely on words to communicate.

"Communication in beings such as yourself and the others can be easily seen, because of this it is assumed that you are better, smarter, more advanced beings than other life forms around you. What is not fully understood however is the quality of the communication. When trees and rocks communicate, there is no misinterpretation. Even the beasts that walk, swim and fly communicate more truthfully that the two legged beings of this planet. Words are our legacy of deception. It is very easy to communicate a non truth with words. The more people believe in words, the less likely they are to know the truth of real communication."

I was becoming very familiar with this truth. Orla was a master at words, and my Father loved to bathe in them. I was young compared to most of my kind, but I had seen the old ones, they did not speak much, but they seemed to communicate just fine. I understood why now. I was also getting a good understanding of the power of stillness, silence. To be with your own being was to communicate truthfully with yourself. I finally understood the power of that. All that time, The One tried to show me what the power of stillness was, and I never really wanted to understand. Now I did.

"I finally understand what you have been trying to teach me for so long. Truth in communication does not come in words, because words cannot accurately communicate truth. Words are created from the breath, as it passes through our throat and over our tongue. To be formed, words must go through many processes, too many for them to be pure. So even though they start within the purity of vibration, they become contaminated by form. Therefore they are never really true. So anything that can be spoken, cannot really be true. Is this what you have been meaning for me to understand." I smiled, because I knew the truth now.

The One smiled in return, there was almost a look of relief on her face. "Yes, I am very pleased. Now I know you have the wisdom to look beyond the words. Words originate within intention. However sometimes the intention is not the same as the words spoken, this is deception. The deception will show itself as a conflict in the vibration of the words, where the breath starts. If you are sensitive to this, you will never allow yourself to be fooled by words.

I look forward to seeing you in the morning, here in this spot. You will be a great ruler. Your time has come. It has been a long time since the power of the feminine has sat in this position. I will be honored to perform this ceremony."

With that being said, she turned and faded into the forest at the end of the sand. For the first time I could say, I truly understood, that the farther something gets from its point of creation, the more layers of deceptive illusion it will be wrapped in. This helped me so much to understand Orla. She was wrapped in many layers of self made deception, and I knew from my time with the sisterhood, those layers are not easily removed. The layers merge so seamlessly with who you think you are, that there is no desire to remove the layers. The layers become invisible. A great deal of guidance is needed to be able to perceive these layers. Time and persistence is needed to remove them.

I knew from that moment on, my perception of Orla would not be the same. I would see her as a woman buried beneath her layers of illusion. The only question I had left was, "Could she, or would she ever want to remove those layers?"

As I opened my eyes the birthing of a new day was heralded by the tiny streaks of lights across a dark sky. I had dreaded this day for a long time, but now, it was here and I was as ready as I could be. I knew the dread I felt would not stop the events that were about to occur. Knowing that, I would do the best I could to handle all of it with grace and understanding. The only unanswered question was Orla and how she would react to the change of location. I was hoping it would cause her to reveal herself, that would be the ideal resolution to this situation, but I did not hold to hope. The only thing I knew for sure, was this morning would reveal the true intentions of all. I dressed for the ceremony and went to meet the others in the courtyard, where the ceremony had been originally planned.

"As you know I have made a few changes for this day. It is my right to request a proper place of ceremony, based on my intention of rule. So if you would all please walk with me, I would like for us to go together."

My focus was on Orla, and her reaction. My eyes scanned her face for every movement. Her eyes were wide and I could see she was forcibly stopping her head from turning in the direction of her people. Her lips were clenched shut, for she knew, uttering her opinion in this moment was not wise. Her fingers tightly wrapped themselves around her thumbs in absolute defiance of freedom. I could feel her energy trying to wrap itself around my neck.

"My darling, are you alright?" My Father asked her. That seemed to break the evil spell she was stabbing me with.

"Yes, yes, I will be fine. I was just caught off guard, I was mislead to believe that we were having the ceremony here?" Her voice was cracking under the strain of a rigid throat.

"It is Aeiya's right to choose a spot that best represents how she intends to rule. She spoke with me yesterday, in fact I was relieved that she seemed to be actively taking part in her new position. I was delighted to grant her request." My Father looked at me, his face was full of pride as he imagined how his life had come to fruition through me.

189

"Of course, forgive me, I am not familiar with these traditions. I am dressed inappropriately, just give me a moment and I will change." she said as she let go of my Fathers hand.

"No, Orla, you are just fine, we will leave now, before anyone else wakes, this is to be a private and quiet matter. "

I called the sentinels to bring up the rear as we moved forward in procession towards the beach. I could see that every few moments Orla would raise her eyes and turn her head, she was looking for her lies to come into view. No figures were to be seen on the horizon, as the sun lit up the ridge, just as the light of my truth was illuminating Orla's intent.

I could see The One waiting for us on the beach. She was beautifully lit by the morning sun rays, that were gifted with a hint of blue as the sea offered its grace She motioned that I stand on her right and my Father stand on her left. Orla stood a few feet behind my Father with the sentinels at her side. The space behind me was empty.

"What we do here today is a simple matter. It is the giving and the receiving of responsibility from one to another. Edon, gifts his daughter with the Crown of Wisdom. He is now willing to let go of his expected duties and bestow them upon Aeiya with love. If you would both turn to the sun, we shall pay homage. To the sun, the activator of life. The spark of Illumination, he that warms the waters of the great Mother, we give thanks for your precious gift. We thank you for the energy of action, without you all of life would be still.

Now both of you take a handful of sand. Great Mother, she who offers her body to bring forth life, she who allows us to flow from the moisture of her soul, she who shelters us and who gives us form, she who allows us to experience ourselves through the mirror of her beauty, we thank you.

Now, Edon, you must wear the head piece for the last time. Thank it for all it has done and allow it to release your energy from its stones."

The One took the headpiece and placed it over my Fathers head. This ceremony was the first time I had heard it called by its proper name, the Crown of Wisdom. I was not sure why, but I was feeling a little anxious about wearing the headpiece for the first time.

The One could see by some invisible cue that my Father had done his job. She then removed the headpiece and I could see him waver slightly. Whatever he had done, had taken a great deal of energy from him. Seeing this did not help my anxiousness.

"Now my child, I am going to place this crown upon your head. I want you to envision your intention upon the land and its people. How it is you intend to fulfill your responsibilities to those that you oversee. The crown will adjust itself to your energy and will bring forth all the memories of those who have ever worn it. Be ready for this, it will happen very fast and you may not feel as yourself for a moment, but a moment is all it will take."

190

The One gently guided the head piece towards my head. I could feel the energy pulsing just above the top of my head. As the head piece came closer, I could feel pressure in my temples. My eyes started to darken and unusual scents filled my nose. I could hear voices speaking in languages I had never heard as I felt all the energy in my body trying to push out through the top of my head.

I just barely felt the band touch the skin on my forehead and everything went dark and silent. I had no idea where I was. My body felt weak, I thought I would collapse. Images started flashing before my eyes of past rulers in places I had never seen. This crown had come from the home planet. I was not prepared for that. I could feel the energy of the decisions that had been made flooding my mind, the emotion of them threatening to explode my heart. As the energy started to overwhelm me, I heard The Ones voice, "Breathe, just breathe. The energy of the headpiece is merging with your energy. You are fine. You will now be able to recall all the past decisions that have been made with the assistance of the wisdom of the stones. That's it, just keep breathing."

Light started to gift my eyes with sight once again. I could hear the sea gently lapping at my feet. I could smell the salt in the air. My Father was holding me in his arms. He must have known what would happen when I put the head piece on.

"There you are, back with us. There is no way to prepare you for that, so we don't try. I am glad you came back. Now you know the power of the stones." My Father hugged me warmly. That hug came from the Father I knew, the Father that I had grown up with. I relaxed into him, and returned his love.

The One placed her hand on top of mine and my Father's. In that instant I caught a glimpse of something, but I was not sure exactly what? The sharp painful image frightened me. The One realized my perception and quickly pulled her hand away. She knew what I had seen. Her eyes studied my face for understanding, but she saw none, only fear. She stood up and then stood back. She had not anticipated the power of the head piece to transfer her sight.

"It is done. The transfer of responsibility is complete. Edon, you are free to live your life as you wish now. Aeiya, it is now your gift to lead the people. May you both find love and peace, on your journey."

She turned and walked away. I wondered if I would ever see her again, it was the first time I have had that thought. I did not like the feeling, watching her walk away gave me. It was like seeing my Mother walk away for the last time. I felt very lonely in that moment, I did not feel like the ruler of the people.

"Ok, lets get you up and return you to the people for a proper greeting as the new leader. You are my daughter and you will always be, but now on

191

this day, you have become a great woman. Are you ready to walk that path?"

My Fathers smile warmed my heart and dispersed my loneliness.

"Come Orla, let us return to our people." My Father stood up and turned towards Orla. But she was not there. She was no where in sight. She had left during the ceremony. I was afraid she had gone to gather her army.

I ran past the sentinel towards the city. From my distant vantage point I could see Orla crossing the gate into the city, she was running towards the Alaria. I tried to follow her but as I crossed the city gates, I was swarmed by well wishers. I lost sight of Orla, as she disappeared into the forest behind the healing baths.

As the festivities got under way, I could not reign in my concern that Orla would reappear with an army. My Father was still unofficially performing his duties, moving through the people, thanking them for making his time with them the best part of his life. But he kept looking around, I knew he was looking for Orla. Every now and then his eyes would meet mine and I knew he wanted to ask why I had run after her, but the truth was, he did not want to know the answer. So he never said a word to me. For that I was thankful.

The celebrations went into the late afternoon, the people were happy, dancing, playing, rejoicing in rejoicing. There had not been a celebration like this in a very long time. Everyone was letting go, finding their inner joy, forgetting the properness with which they were supposed to behave. I wondered if this is what Orla was waiting for, everyone to be so relaxed that they could not put up a fight if they were asked to.

I needed a break, I needed to be in a quiet space for a moment. I excused myself and walked to the Alaria. I was hoping to see Tuallan, she may have been harsh at times, but she was always the voice of reason.

Standing under the tall arches of stone was Tuallan, I waved and smiled at her. She looked behind her, and then came running out to see me.

"Now is not a good time to be here. Why are you here, you are supposed to be down there with everyone else?" She spoke nervously, as if she were trying to hide something.

"I just needed a break, I like the silence of the baths, so I was hoping you would be here." I looked beyond her into the dim area that held the tubs, I could hear music playing, the same music that played when I took the baths.

"What is going on? Who is in there?" I pushed past Tuallan and entered the baths. There in the final bath was Orla.

"What is she doing here? Is she alone?" I was shocked and demanded an answer.

"Yes, I was trying to keep you out of here. I don't want you messing things up." Tuallan's response confused me

"What do you mean, mess things up? I am trying to make things right. You can't talk to me that way. There are things going on that you do not know about. You shouldn't be meddling in something that is not your business." I spoke sharply to her, mostly because I was shocked at her implying I did not know what I was doing.

"Well that is your opinion. I saw her going into the bush, so I followed her. She went over the ridge and spoke to some men that were waiting there for her. They argued, and then the men left. I wanted to know what they were talking about, so when she came back out of the bush, I asked if she would like to take the baths, as part of the cleansing ceremony. She agreed."

"So were you able to find anything out?" I asked, not sure if I would believe the answer or not.

"Very little. While in the baths she spoke of the head piece and wearing it. She also spoke of a man, Rojan. I think he is her partner. I think he may have been the man she was arguing with. The only other things she said was ...."

She was hesitating, I wasn't sure why. "Well say it, I need to know!"

"She said, Edon, never!. She seemed upset when she said that. It was like she was thinking something she didn't want to think. All I can tell you is, it wasn't good." Tuallan lowered her head as she spoke.

I couldn't help but wonder if she knew more than she was saying, but I knew that if she was, she would never tell me unless she wanted to. One of the worst traits of the Others, they purposely withheld information if they felt it would compromise them in any way. I never understood this. I could only explain it from what The One had told me, that they felt separation more than I did. I always had the feeling, they were somehow protecting themselves by withholding the details of the stories they told. Like their lives, if all the details weren't there, they were never left vulnerable to being known. Perhaps they felt, if they were not known, they would not be held responsible. After all they did identify themselves with their bodies, not their souls.

Irregardless, I now knew where Orla was, and I had to get back to the festivities before someone noticed me gone.

"I will inform my Father that Orla is alright. He is concerned."

"Your Father is the one that should be concerned." Tuallan had an odd tone to her voice, but she would offer no more.

"Thank you for your help. I will see you soon. If she says anything else, please tell me" I asked with gratitude in my voice. This always appealed to Tuallan's nature.

"Of course. Now go. The last thing I need is half the city up here looking for you.:"

I smiled and left. I was relieved that whatever threat, this man Rojan was to my home, it was not happening today. Perhaps I could enjoy some of the celebrations myself. It was the joyous part of becoming a ruler, and it would not last long.

I told my Father that Orla was fine, she was in the baths. He looked puzzled and relieved at the same time. He too chose to relax and enjoy the fun a little more. His demeanor however, was challenging for me to read. I was not sure if he was relieved that Orla was not here at all or if he was just happy she was OK. I had not seen my Father this relaxed since I had returned home. He was the Father I once knew. Warm, affectionate and laughing. I loved to hear my Father laugh. It was contagious. As the sun descended, the sky spoke the language of color. Deep reds, oranges and magenta's, graced our eyes. If color was sound, what we saw would have been the work of a master, crafting and weaving tones together to create the song of the soul. It was the perfect merging of the body of the Great Mother and the spirit of the Father. The gift of that evening was to see what love looked like if it were a song played in color.

As the last ray of light faded into darkness, the music started to play in the hollow stones. This was always my favorite part, of any celebration. The hollow stones allowed me to not only hear the music better, but to feel it move through me body. I went to sit directly in front of the stones, on the other side of the water that flowed around them. It may have been the influence of the head piece, but every tone that came from the stones became an image. Each sound told a story within time. Every beat followed itself through history, back to its origin. Before my eyes were images dancing with colors that all followed the tempo of thought, creating a pulse that vibrated through my being.

I was suspended in time, not moving forward or backward, but vibrating in stillness as time passed in memories before my eyes. All the memories contained within the stones, the knowledge, the wisdom and the experience of the lives that the head piece had shaped. We became one mind, one breath, one thought. I became we, and we were I, one endless chain of individual thoughts, that created a singular mind. I let it carry me, I let it create me, I let it become me. I was no more.

The sound of absolute silence forced me to lift the lids of my eyes and look around me. It was the middle of the night. The skies were lit up with points of light stretching to infinity. I could see the fog that hovered over the sea. The moon made it look like a cloud bubbling up from the ground. People were sleeping all around me. The celebration had ended and everyone had slept where they sat.

I wandered down the steps in front of the hollow stones, across the square and back towards the sea. I did not know why, but I felt called there. I had never walked the path in the dark, but the moon would help. I tread carefully placing one foot in front of another. As the forest opened up to

194

sand, I could feel the coolness of the sea air. The fog lay suspended just above the surface of the water. There was a glow on the water, the effect of the moon shining off the luminescent surface of the fog.

The sea herself was calm, steady, not moving but in constant motion. Somewhere past the point of my sight, I could hear a sea creature sounding. Calling its mate perhaps. The feeling here was so peaceful. I lay on the sand and released the energy I had kept controlled all day. That felt good, I could breath again. I could be myself again.

I lay and watched the stars til they faded from sight with the coming of the morning sun. I wished I could just stay there on that beach for the rest of my life. I could forget about my training and my duties. I could forget about Orla and Rojan. But it would also mean I would have to forget about my Father, and that I would not do. I rose, like the ruler I am supposed to be and went back to the courtyard. People were waking and starting to return to their homes.

I had assumed that Orla had collected my Father at some point and retreated to the palace. I am sure she spun some story of concern to answer any questions about her sudden disappearance. I would hear about it later. For now, I returned to my room and lay on my bed. There was nothing that needed my presence. Today would be a day of rest.

Chapter Nineteen

Time passed and life was quiet. I had merged my lust for freedom with my sense of duty. The head piece was starting to fit comfortably around my head. I was able to settle most of the small disputes that came before me. There were also those disputes that could only be managed, never settled. There were no real problems under our protective shield. Even Orla and my Father seemed happy. She laughed more around him and disappeared less and less. I felt like I was slowly being lured into a false sense of security. I was never sure if Orla's actions were genuine or not. In truth she seemed to warm to my Father. Her hand would linger on his shoulder. Her glances toward him came with a smile. She seemed to relax when sitting next to him. I was no longer so sure that she was the enemy.

I could do nothing but wait. I tried to keep my defenses sharp, I did find this rather difficult when there is nothing to defend against. My life felt like the adult version of my childhood. Mostly carefree, only interrupted by moments of chaos. The chaos added some excitement, a little something to create conversation with. In all, I was happy. It had been 5 years since the head piece has passed to me. In that time, I had grown and matured. Orla and my Father had grown close and I had not seen The One.

During one of my forays to the beach, as I sat on the sand watching the waves try to steal the beach back to the watery depths, I felt something I had not felt before. It was a buzzing in my head, and a stirring in my spine. It felt like energy was building in me. I was not sure what this was about. The One came to mind, but I did not hear her voice. A restlessness started moving within me. It agitated me like fear, but I was not frightened. It made me feel the heat of my body, but I did not sweat. I did not like this feeling. I left the beach and went straight back to the palace. I was pacing in the hallway outside my room when my Father came walking towards me. "Child, whatever are you doing?" I guess my demeanor was unfamiliar to him as well.

"I don't know what is happening, I have this sound in my head like bees that are crying and intense pressure here, in my back. I feel like I should be upset, but there is nothing to worry me. I am hot but it is not hot out. What is wrong with me?"

My Father could see how upset I was, but still he could not help but smile.

"You are fine. From everything you are telling me, your body is trying to tell you, it is time to take a mate. A partner in life. Someone who you are to discover love with. That is all." He just stood there smiling.

"What do you mean, a mate? Why do I need a mate? I have no need for a mate."

"Ok, but the feeling will only get worse til you find one. That is your choice." He laughed as he walked away.

As disturbed as I was by the anxiety I was feeling, it always amazed me at how my Father had learned to deal with me. Ever since I was a child, he knew he could not make me do anything. However he had a way of making it all seem like it was my decision. Perhaps he was preparing me even then for being a ruler.

I did not know the least thing about finding a mate. My Mother had never spoken of this to me. How was I going to discover what I must do? Did I ask all the men of the land to join me here, so I could pick one? Did I literally go out and find one? What was a mate supposed to do for me? Too many questions going around in my head, and no one to answer them. It was time to use the crystal in the Alaria. I needed to speak with The One, she would be able to tell me how to go about this. My Father was right, the feeling in my body was getting stronger. I was not sure how long I could take it. It crawled over my skin like ants with daggers on their feet.

"Tuallan, Tuallan, I need to use the crystal, I must speak with The One. Tuallan are you there?"

"What is wrong with you, you are behaving very strangely?" She looked at me with piercing eyes. She was always scrutinizing me. I had never quite decided if she was a friend or an enemy.

"I must speak with The One immediately. Why, does not matter, it is personal, but important. Now, right now." I was getting very demanding.

"Alright, just give me a minute." She moved a few things around to reveal the crystal. The crystal was never really hidden, however it was never put on display either. Tuallan always discouraged everyone from being interested in it. The crystal was only to be used for matters of great importance. Tuallan closed off the entrance so no one would walk in, then she came to sit by the crystal. She would hold the energy, while I called The One. After a few moments of trying it became clear that it was not working. I could not compose myself long enough to send the energy through the crystal. I was feeling very desperate.

"What is wrong with you. Look can you keep it together just long enough to hold the energy? I will call her, if you can hold it. OK."

"Yes, yes, fine."

Within seconds I could hear The One's voice. "Tuallan, what is it you need?" "

Nothing Mother, it is Aeiya that needs you."

Mother? I had never heard anyone address The One as Mother before. That caught me off guard, and it raised some concern in me. Those thoughts however were for another time.

"Yes, I need your help. My Father has told me it is time to take a mate. I don't want to take a mate, can you make this feeling go away?"

The One smiled, I could see her image faintly through the crystal. "No, I am afraid not. All of our kind become activated at a certain age. Indeed you are strong, for you have held it off longer than most."

"Tell me, what I must do. I do not want to feel this way. I do not want my people to see me this way." I could feel myself falling apart. I desperately needed answers.

"The best way for you to go about this, in a way that is unseen, is to follow your nose. In the evening after dark, move into your cat body and follow the scent that stops the energy pulsing in you. This energy will not harm you, however you will not be able to take care of the matters at hand till you find a mate. Do you have more questions?"

"You want me to find a mate while I am in the form of a giant cat? He will run and hide, thinking I am going to eat him."

"I know this is hard to understand, but it is one of those times you must do as I say, without question. It is not something that can be explained, it can only be experienced. No more questions, no more arguing. Just do this, and the sooner the better." the crystal darkened. The One had ended the connection.

Tuallan stared at me, but she did not say a word. She was still assessing the situation when I left the Alaria. It was late afternoon now, in a few hours it would be dark. I would do as The One said. I did not have any desire to become my cat self. It had been years since I was driven into that form. I knew right now, the way I felt, it was all I could do to stay in this form. My body wanted to become the cat. It wanted to be something much more primal, animalistic, wild.

The minutes passed with the speed of hours. I had barricaded myself in my room and left word not to be disturbed. Darkness was approaching, I could feel the wild growing in me.

While I still could, I thought it best to climb out the window and run to the bushes. I did not want anyone finding a large cat roaming around the palace, it would have spread to much fear. The darkness was swallowing the light and I could feel my heart beat faster, the moisture from my throat was drying up.

Within moments I looked down to see fur covered paws. I never remembered changing. I seemed to black out momentarily. But the instant I saw my paws, my world came alive through scent. It always astounded me how clearly life could be perceived when I had the senses of a cat. Nothing was hidden. The sense of smell was dominant however in this world. Most everything was identified by the vibration of the scent it gave off.

I paced in the under brush waiting for the people to disperse themselves to their homes. All the while I kept catching the scents on the air, looking for that one that pulled me in some direction. When I was sure I would not be seen, I moved through the palace grounds looking for a signal. Up to the Alaria I went, but I could only smell the land. Down, back through the courtyard across the fields, to the edge of the forest, my legs carried me. Still nothing. I always felt so much stronger in my cat body. Each step was carefully placed with full awareness. I was in the moment at all times. Not only was aware of my surroundings, I was my surroundings. I loved the cat body. I had missed moving about this way.

A gentle breeze came through the trees from over the sea. A scent caught my attention. It was like nothing I had smelled before. This was a scent I had to follow. It brought my body alive, it made the base of every hair tingle. I could feel a wave of energy move through me. I followed the path to the beach. As I turned and looked up the beach, I could see the scent in the sand. It looked like tiny little drops of gold, dotted here and there all the way up the beach. The light seemed to shine from within each drop. I wondered if someone had purposely layed a trail for me. Perhaps it was some kind of joke? Maybe someone was trying to reveal me? In the end it did not matter, the scent was pulling me. I had no control over the steps I took. It had a strong hold on me and it was not letting go.

I followed the scent up the beach, it then disappeared into the forest. I pursued, with each step, it seemed to get a little stronger. The stronger it got, the more an image formed in my mind, til I had built the picture of a man. But this was no man like me. This was a man of the Others. That would complicate things considerably. Still I had to follow the scent. I went through the forest, over hills, through valleys. There was a well worn path that I had never been on. I wondered what a man was doing out here. Especially a man of the Others. I had never seen one of them separate themselves from the rest of their kind. They all lived under the protective shield. Out here he was dangerously close to not being protected.

I could smell smoke, it was a ways off yet, but it was definitely smoke. He must have a fire going. Perhaps that is what he used for protection and light in the darkness. The scent was strong now. The scent had control of me. I fought to not lose myself to it. It was hypnotic, exotic. I wanted to live within this smell. I felt as though memories were being jarred from their hiding place but there were no memories with this man.

As I got close I could see a glow from the fire. It lit up the trees around him. I stayed well back in the forest. I did not want to be seen or felt. I needed to observe this man, before I approached. As he moved about the fire I could see he was tall. Much taller than I. His hair was the color of the suns rays as it reflected off the golden fall wheat. His eyes were the color of the sea when it changes, neither green nor blue, but a beautiful combination of both.

He looked out towards me, he hesitated. I knew he could not see me, I was too far away and it was very dark, but I think somehow he knew I was there. His skin was darker that the Others. This man lived in the wild, he had no home or shelter, and it had given him skin the color of the earth. He was beautiful. The scent matched the man. Seeing him was like having a vision, yet there he was, right in front of me. I had to get closer. I moved silently, one step at a time, making sure he could not hear me. The closer I was to him, the harder it was to keep myself composed. I could feel him from here. He made my skin vibrate. His energy passed over me like warm water from the baths, heating my body, making me feel alive. I could feel him slowly moving over me, leaving behind a fire energy that lit my soul. I was getting lost in the experience of him.

"Come into the light, I want to see you." He called out to me.

Panic seized me, it made me lower myself to the ground. How did he know I was there? I had been so careful. I could not appear to him this way. I was still in my cat body. He would be afraid.

"Come closer, I know you are there. I saw you that day on the beach. You are one of the Royals aren't you? Come, I will not hurt you."

I wanted to run, but I could not break the spell of the scent. When he spoke my body moved. I could not resist much longer.

"If you don't come here, I will come there. Come, don't be afraid." His voice fell upon my ears like the songs of the hollow stones. An invisible bond moved me forward. I did not want to move but I could not stop my body, the attraction was stronger than my will. As I drew near to the light, I could smell my own fear. Fear that he would see the cat and retreat. Fear that he would leave and I would not find him again, and worst of all, fear that he would reject me. I moved slowly, stiffly, but without stopping. The flames of the fire danced off my fur as I entered the light. This man did not move, he just stared at me. I did not sense fear in him. I stared into the depths of his blue green eyes and he stared back. He walked toward me, I tried to step back but my paws were frozen to the ground. He reached out and touched my face.

"I have been waiting for you, ever since I saw you on the beach. Why have you taken so long? You are so beautiful. Since I saw you that day, you are all I can think about. Sometimes I would go to the courtyard and wait behind the bushes, trying to get a glimpse of you. Now that you are here, I can breathe again."

I was very confused, he was speaking to me, as if I were in my female form, not my cat form. I was wondering if he could even see the cat. Perhaps something was wrong.

He ran his hands down the length of my body, as he did, it had a calming affect on me. I could feel myself wanting to change back. My skin was aching to feel his touch. As he moved around me, touching me, each fingertip felt like a warm soft breeze against my skin. The energy moved outward and collided into itself, sending chills down my spine.

In the next moment I became disoriented and I knew I was changing back to my female form. Seconds later I stood before him naked and a little unsure of myself. He stood there staring at me, taking all of me in with his eyes. It only whet his appetite. He moved towards me slowly, carefully placing his feet exactly where he wanted them to go. He was circling me. I stood motionless, I still did not know what he was thinking. His circles around my body, were smaller, tighter, closer to me.

Standing behind me, he lowered his mouth to my neck as if to taste me. I could feel the warmth of his breath, heating the surface of my skin. His face brushed across my hair, he was drinking me in. He came around in front of me, his body was so close to mine, it felt like the energy was bouncing back and forth between us. He placed his arms around me and slowly, gently lowered me into a thick bed of ferns. They were cool against my skin. The night air made the ground smell musky and sensuous.

He was on his knees, looking down at me from above. I had never felt so out of control. I reached out and ran my fingers along the outside of his thighs The light that shone from within his eyes burned brighter as he felt the caress against his skin. He thrust himself forward, stopping just short of banging into my head. His gaze was long and intense, he seemed to be searching for something within me. Ever so tenderly he placed his lips against mine. I could feel the heat growing between our bodies as the kiss intensified. My breathe came quicker, my heart beat faster. My skin was so alive I could feel the slightest movement of the air around me. The kiss was long and passionate, leaving me to feel exhilarated and exhausted. All I could do was look at him. The power of him, the beauty of him. I had never felt as alive as I did in this moment.

He then traced a line with his tongue, from my lips, down my neck, down my chest, to a point between my breasts. The conflict between cool air and warm tongue, came as extreme pleasure. With ever so much finesse, he started making small circles with slight pressure. Spiralling outward with greater pressure and then back in. I could feel a flood of energy building in the base of my spine. I could not contain it as it moved upward slowly, slithering like a snake. With each curve on its journey upwards it gathered strength and power. This man seemed to know exactly what he was doing. He knew he was drawing this energy forth. My body was limp with power and heat. I started to pant. Every emotion I have ever had was climbing up my spine in a river of pleasure. It kept building and building to the point where the energy met the tip of his tongue and it exploded out of me. We were forced apart by the power of the ecstasy. Engulfed by a cocoon of golden light, we floated side by side in ecstatic union of souls merging. There was no him, there was no me, there was just us experiencing each other as one.

I could see him for who he was and he could see me. We had been stripped of our personalities and layers of opinions. Here we were, with one another, completely naked souls, experiencing the pure love of each other in the truest form of bliss. I never wanted to leave that moment. We allowed ourselves to be completely taken over by the ecstasy and the purity of the truth of love. We let go of ourselves and discovered one another.

I awoke to the scent of ferns and flowers. At some point in the night I had been wrapped in ferns to protect me from the cool air. He then placed beautifully scented flowers all around me, creating a dome of exotic scents. It was a beautiful world to wake up too.

I looked around me to realize, I really did not know where I was. I had come at night, in my cat body. I was not sure I could find my way home, and when I did, how was I going to explain the lack of clothing and my disappearance. Still I felt so exalted in love, those were just minor complications.

My surroundings told me I was in a sheltered valley, not too far from the sea. The beautiful man that would be my mate was not in sight, but I knew he would not be far. The bond had been forged between us the night before and I could still feel him in me. I knew he was close. I sat up feeling the slight shock of cool air against my skin. The sun was rising as he came into view. This beautiful being whose light put the sun to shame. He came to me with love and reverence, fell to his knees, kissed me, offering me water. I took a few sips, the amount my body would allow.

I looked long into his sea green eyes. The color was so clear, so unlike eyes I had seen before. Around his pupils was a star burst of white light. It was hard to tell if it was coming out from behind the pupil or just part of the design of his eyes. The white seemed almost to pulsate as he changed his focus. This man was different than any man of the Others. There was something more to him.

"Good morning" he said in a voice that flowed into me. The smile on his face, told me he was remembering the night before.

"Good Morning. Thank you for covering me. It was very thoughtful."

"I did not want the cool air to touch your skin and wake you. You were sleeping so peacefully. I thought you must need to rest."

I could so easily have fallen back into those eyes and gotten lost for the day, but I needed information. If I was going to present him to my Father, I needed to know who he was. Unfortunately there was not time to waste. If I didn't return by the afternoon, they would send out sentinels to look for me. So dressed in a gown of ferns, I reached out and took his hands.

"Who are you? What is your name? Why are you living out here, alone?"

My questions came with no breath in between. I knew he could hear the anxiousness in my voice. He smiled at me, as if to calm me. Then he took a thoughtful breath and began.

"I am Torando. I have lived my whole life in the wild. Many of my people lived here at one time, but most left to follow Orla when she was banished. We, my people and I, we are not like you, nor are we like the Others, we are somewhere in between. When The One first started to create the Others, she thought that a race of beings that were half you and half them would be the best way to have the help that was needed. So she took pieces of many things on this planet and blended them together with parts of herself, we were the result. At first she was pleased. We were strong and intelligent. We could take orders but also make decisions. We helped to seed the earth, we worked hard, with no resentment. As time went on and the seeding of the Earth was completed, we wanted to create our own society, we wanted to create our world within this world. We wanted to be self ruled and make decisions for ourselves that would be best for us. We still wanted to help, if help was needed, but we realized that the decisions that were being made for us were not always beneficial to us. We are different than you, and that was not always taken into consideration.

The leaders of your world at the time did not want this to happen, so they forbid it. The more that was forbidden to us, the angrier we became. Eventually there was an uprising and many of us were killed. What was left of our kind were banished. A few of our kind were used to create the Others as you know them now. The Others look like us, but they do not have the same abilities to experience reality as we do. We were considered a threat to your predecessors and forced to live here, out beyond the shield, and take our chances.

We, however, survived. Once we were established we learned how to deal with the beasts. We learned what frightened them, and we also learned how to work with them. What we discovered was, frightening them just made them angry and got many of us killed. By working with them and gently educating them that they have their land and we have ours, we could live harmoniously. Some of the old ones, even had beasts as companions.

I am still here and the rest left to follow Orla. There were not many of us here when she came for us we are the last of our kind. Still I do not believe that anger can make things better. I have seen it for myself. Anger leads to death. I would rather have a death of my choosing than a death driven by anger. Anger can only be brought forth in the face of fear. So to say my people were angry would be a lie. My people were afraid. They were afraid to be the last of their kind, they were afraid to be forgotten, they were most afraid that they were not accepted by your kind. It was not anger that drove them to Orla's side, it was fear.

Now, I know why it was that I stayed. I am here for you. You are my mate, my partner, my love. I will stand with you no matter what. Your Father will not be happy, when you present me to him in his home. Orla will not be happy either. She will fear that my kind will follow me, if they know I am with you. Are you prepared to take on the burden of so much fear?"

He smiled lovingly at me as he gently squeezed my hand. I was in shock. I had no idea there had been another race of people. I had never heard it mentioned. I wondered if that had anything to do with why Tuallan called The One, Mother?

I was feeling rather overwhelmed, with this sudden re-education of my history. I knew he was telling the truth, it was in his eyes. His eyes were different from mine, and they were different from the Others. He was somewhere in the middle. I had no idea what I was going to do. I was the chosen leader now, but that did not give me the right to go against all that had been established, did it?

Why would The One do this to me, she must have known who I would find, who I would choose for a mate? Why would she not tell me of this race of beings? To many questions and not enough time. I had to get back home before they tried to answer their questions with the sentinels. I could do nothing about anything at this moment, dressed in ferns, so I would go home and see what I could find out, first. One step at a time.

"Torando, my love. For this moment, you must stay here. I need to go home and prepare myself to present you. I hope you can understand this. I do not want to put you in any danger, by presenting you inappropriately. I will return to you within a few days and claim you as my own. Then I will present you to my people, at the same time I present you to my Father. I just need time to create the opportunity. Please do not be disheartened with this. I must do this in a way that will allow me to stay in control. My authority must not be questioned about this. Please tell me you understand?"

My heart was bleeding to leave him behind. But there was no other way. The path must be cleared to claim him as my mate and that would take a few days.

"Yes, of course. It will cause me great pain to be separated from you, but that will pale in comparison to the life we shall live. I will wait for you here in this place. But now let me lead you to the beach, you can make your way from there. "

With that he swept me into his arms, and carried me out of the valley. He had incredible strength and he never seemed to tire. Along the way we spoke of our experience from the night before. The wanting it had created in our bodies, the passion that overtook our mind and our heart. Even speaking of it brought the heat back to our skin again, but there was no time to stop. There would be plenty of time to merge the energies of our love, to create the heat of our passions and allow them to explode into oneness, after we had been joined in the acceptance of the people.

At the beach, he gently placed my feet on the sand. He had managed to tie some of the ferns together so they made a natural and elegant covering for me.

He gently placed his palms against my neck. Just touching me sent waves of heat tingling down my body. I shivered ever so slightly. He smiled.

"I will miss you till your return. Do you know the path you will follow to find me?"

"Yes, I will not lose you now. It will be a few days and I will return for you. Gather your belongings and be ready to come home, with me forever. Torando, the only one I shall ever love."

He placed his lips against mine gently at first, but we could not help feeling the passion grow. The embrace was deep and powerful. I could feel the heat start to build at the base of my back again. I pulled away and smiled.

"If I do not go now, I will not go at all. Soon my love, soon."

With that I forced myself to walk away. I kept looking back to see him standing there. I had left a piece of my heart with him, for the further away I got, the more my heart hurt. The bond between us, could not be broken now. We had exchanged pieces of ourselves with each other, we lived within one another now. That is a bond that knows no bounds.

I strolled up to the palace, bare feet and dressed in ferns. Though I could hear no voices, I knew the people were in a state of shock. This is something they were not prepared to experience. There leader passing amongst them as a child of the forest. The energy of their thoughts pierced my personal field. The shock of it all made me smile, it was time for change. Tradition can be a practice of honoring those that came before, but it can also be a prison, that chains us to them.

I entered the courtyard to see my Father standing with Orla, they were discussing my whereabouts I am sure. I could see my Father's head turning towards me, not knowing it was me. Upon realizing it was his daughter, his eyes narrowed, his lips formed a thin line, and I could see his fists clench. I knew he was not happy. So I walked straight up to him.

"Father, I have found a mate. I have done your bidding. I will make all the necessary preparations to present him. Good morning Orla. I hope you did not worry after me. I am fine. I must rest now."

I walked away before either of them could say anything. The moment I was out of sight, I ran down the halls towards my room. I sealed the door behind me, and fell to my bed in joy. I may have been the leader of the people, but in my Father's presence, I still felt as a child. This was a good first step in liberating myself. It was time for me to embrace the position, I had been born too. I could feel my power growing inside me. I would allow it.

I took the rest of the day to rest and to think. To my surprise, I was not disturbed. I am sure my Father was trying to think of a way to deal with this, just as frantically as I was.

The more I thought about it, the more I wondered why The One had allowed me to pursue this man. It made no sense. It would cause many problems to add to the problems that were already present. It was true that Orla and my Father seemed to share some kind of bond, but I did not fully trust that bond to be true.

By the condition of my return my Father would have known, the mate had been chosen and it was not of our blood. To have a mate of another blood was forbidden. I would have understood this, if we had still been on our home world where there were plenty of mates to choose from. Here however we were a dying race. On this planet, a mate was about joy, not furthering our bloodline, for that would not happen. The One said she would no longer activate the birthing chambers, our time had come and I was the last.

I wondered if my Father would realize, by trying to enforce tradition, he was denying me my joy. It was in that moment that I started to realize, just how complicated this was going to be. My Father would be against me, Orla would be against me. The people would accept anyone I presented, that was tradition, even though they could reject him, they would not. These people were not the people of our traditions.

I had to stop thinking about this, I was getting angry, very very angry. I was not angry at tradition, I was angry at my Father, he would stick to tradition. I loved my Father, but he was rigid. He knew no other way.

In that moment, with that thought, I knew. I knew why The One had chosen to not give access to the birthing chambers anymore. Our race was to entrenched in habit. We were no longer flexible enough to evolve. I had learned that any race, any species that is not adaptable, will not survive. Our race was proof of that. Adaptability was Orla's power. She had broken with tradition and built an entire civilization outside of ours. Did I agree with what she did or how she did it, no I did not. However I could not dispute the power of change and the flexibility that change can bring. Indeed change brings death or transformation, and both are by choice.

I now had the full realization of the immense power that Orla held. Her power was not in her ability to deceive, her power was in her ability to adapt. Perhaps she and I were more alike than I cared to acknowledge. I understood what The One had been talking about long ago when I lived on the mountain top, when she said "I had been created for this". She didn't mean I had been created to rule, she meant I had been created to deal with Orla, for I had been created outside of tradition, I had been created to be adaptable. I wasn't sure if I admired the pure wisdom and foresight of The

One, or despised her for not telling me the whole truth. As I had been learning over the last while, The One had many hidden secrets that when revealed were still only half truths.

I still could not know what her reasons were. Only she would know that. My life felt deflated at the moment. I was just a link in a long line of events that tied everything together. How could she not tell me the truth? Was she afraid I would not co operate? If she didn't want me to know, then she must of been afraid that I would not play my part. Wait, if she was afraid I would not play my part, then this is not destined. I could change my mind. She knew I could change my mind.

That is what power is, choice. The ability to change my mind. It is so powerful that even The One fears it. The One is the most powerful being anyone on this planet has known. Why does she fear choice so much?

I clung to this thought as though it was my last breath. I was trying to force my eyes to stay open as if I were afraid no answers would come if they closed. But sleep has a will of its own and to sleep I went, still clinging to the question of the power of choice. Had our race been so patterned that we had forgotten how to change our mind?

"A very long time ago, we were children of the sun, just as Torando is now. Passion ruled us. We were sensory beings, for us living was to indulge in whatever made us feel the most. Power, passion, art, love. We became a race of beings controlled by our own addiction to stimulation. Life was no longer about wisdom and understanding the great secrets of the universe. We wanted more color, more sound, more passion. We forgot about the connection with the universe and replaced it with connecting our bodies. Our search for truth and love was replaced with an addiction to lust and fear. We became slaves to our desire for a reality of illusion. The physical reality of our bodies was more important than the connection to The Oneness. And so it was that we forgot about The Oneness. There were only a handful of masters left, that could teach the reality of existence. They had secluded themselves to the farthest regions of our planet. I was trained under one of these masters.

For lifetimes I trained and I learned and I watched our civilization destroy itself and our planet, because it had forgotten The Oneness. I learned from my master that all developing peoples follow this pattern of knowing, forgetting then remembering. Some survive it, but most don't. It became painfully clear, we were not going to survive. My master instructed me to leave the planet and come here. I would never have left the home planet, it was not my choice.

You want to know of the power of choice. This is the power of choice. Choice is the power that creates the universe. Choice is the birthing energy. Your choice belongs to you and no one can alter that. On my home planet, people were always saying they had no choice. But even choosing to not have a choice, is a choice. All they were really saying is, "I don't want to be responsible to manifest my thoughts as my reality." For creation is the power of manifestation at work, and nothing would ever be created if first, there was not a choice made.

So what is the easiest way to disempower a society, it is to make them believe they have no choice. How do you think it is, the Others stay so calm and controlled? They are under the belief that they need us to survive, they have no other choice. The beauty of that belief is, you only have to enforce it once, then it will be taught through generations. The Others were created to not question their beliefs, but what they do not understand is, their beliefs were given to them by us, they are not their beliefs, just suggestions.

Our race became so engrained in their own beliefs, that they became inflexible and were no longer adaptable. Yes we came here to this planet, that was change. However the society we created here, was identical to the society we came from.

Yes you were created different from the rest. You were created more like Torando. Freedom of thought and the understanding of choice. This is why you will never be like your Father and you cannot truly understand him. But it is also why you had to be deceived into believing you were like him, at least to this point. If not, you would have left long ago, and never accepted your responsibilities. But now you can use your adaptability and your own power of choice to bring about the necessary change that can ensure the memory of our race will live on in the lives of those that claim the future. You are more than a match for Orla. You can defeat her and bring together the Others and Torando's kind. Together they will recreate a new society, that will flourish here on this earth."

I awoke in the darkness, remembering the words of The One. She had been with me as I slept, giving me the answers I needed to make sense of my decisions. I had doubted her, but I now understood her reasoning. Was nothing ever as it appeared to be?

I knew there would be no way to bring all parts of my life together when it came to Torando. So I made a decision, I would go and get him the very next day, before my Father or Orla had anything to say about it. For anything they said would not matter anyway. Perhaps I should have just brought him home when I came back. However my desire for peace and lack of love for conflict allowed me to delude myself into thinking, just maybe I could convince them. This would not be the case. So this very morning just before the sun rose, I would leave and return with my love.

I set out under the cover of the pre dawn light. My intention was to have us both back by the noon time sun. As long as Torando was there, I should be able to accomplish this. If he was not there, I would have to wait. I went to the beach and followed the shoreline to the path he had made that led to the valley. Finding the entrance to the path took a few moments, it was very well hidden. I was thankful for the light that began to stream across the sky as I turned inwards towards the valley. Here the vegetation was lush and dark, bringing shade to even the brightest day.

My journey was drawing to an end when I could see the ridge on my right side and the river that was a short way beyond it. The land had flattened out and the trees were not as thick. It was just up ahead. I came to the circle of trees he had called home. I could see where he had slept but he was not there. Perhaps he had gone for water. I would sit here and wait til he came back. It could be a long wait, I had told him it would be a few days.

The sun had climbed high in the sky before I heard him returning. He was singing as he came up the path. There were no words to his song, only sounds and tones that created harmony. I was so happy to see him. I jumped up and startled him. But then he smiled a big smile.

"I thought you said it would be a few days?" an apt question considering the sudden change of choice.

"I know, but I came to understand very quickly, that waiting was not going to change anything, so I thought I would come for you immediately. What song were you singing? I have never heard anything like that."

"It has no name. We learned long ago, working with the beasts that if we were to keep harmony amongst us, we must let them know we were not sneaking up on them. So we started to sing as we walked, that way we were always heard before we were seen. It calmed the great beasts so much at times, that they would come to our fires and sleep as we sang. They seemed to like the constant rhythm of it."

"Are you ready to come with me, to my home? I am so happy to have you with me."

"Yes just give me a few moments to gather my things, and then we can be on our way." He was happy, but there was a tone in his voice, a hesitation. Life with me would be very different than he had known, and could be difficult for him. He was used to freedom, that is not what he would experience with me. At least we would have each other.
I wanted him to be sure, so I asked again, "Are you sure you want to come with me, I do understand if you have changed your mind?"

"I am not sure you do understand. We have been pair bonded now. Our energies have aligned, there can be no other mate for you or for I. It is simply not possible. Once I have attached myself to you, I can see no other. My energies simply do not allow room for another in my life. It is the way we were made. We choose once, and hopefully we choose wisely." It all sounded so matter of fact.

Whether he wanted to live with me or not, as far as he was concerned, there were no other options. He was driven to be with me. I could only hope it would make us both happy.

He had gathered his things and we started on the long walk back to the palace. We were in no hurry. I was hoping to take the time to get to know more about him. I asked about his Mother, he told me she was no longer living. She had been killed many years before in an accident. He said his Father died of a broken heart. He went on to explain that people that had been pair bonded, often did not live long after their partner had died. They just did not have it in them, the will to live. Half of their life had been taken from them, and the other half wasn't' worth living.

I really wasn't sure how I felt about that. I tried to explain to him that my Father lost my Mother and he went on to Orla. He in turn explained to me, that they were different, pair bonding wasn't their experience.

"Pair bonding is a part of us that comes from the beasts. I think it was meant as a means of control when The One put us together. A threat to one of us, is a threat to both of us. Your kind had to have control over our kind, the way it has control over the Others, or what would be the use of having an entire society around for no other reason than to help when needed. "

I guess I had not really thought of it in that way. The Others had always been there and I knew no different. I thought of them as equals, not as beasts of labor, but I was understanding more and more, that this is what they had been created for. That made me feel shame. That a society as great as ours had to have other beings created with control factors so we could command them. It is not the kind of society I pictured myself being a part of. But then again, I was different, The One had told me this many times. She had however never specified how I was different. It was getting to the point where I was starting to feel like a mixture of all beings here on this planet. I didn't' seem to be just like my parents. I was not just like Torando, nor was I like The One. My character traits did not match Tuallan's either. I really had no idea what I was.

What I did know was, I had followed the scent to my mate. My mate was going to make me happy and complicate my life incomprehensibly. I was the only one that would not feel threatened by his presence in the palace.

Orla was trying to hide having a mate of the same species. My Father would never fully approve of breaking tradition. Tuallan, well she just disagreed with everything. There is no way I could wrap my head around the full consequences of what I was doing, and then again, I really did not care. As we got closer to home I was not sure I was ready for all this. Part of me wanted to take another night or two getting to know him, so I could present him in a better light to my Father. Fear can mask itself as many things, and at this moment it was trying to mask itself as some twisted form of honor.

With the palace in site, I wanted to turn to Torando and ask him one more time if he really wanted this, but I knew it was no longer a matter of choice.

The energy of pair bonding would place him where I was, no matter what. That drive to be with me, left him decisively impotent. All I could do was hope all would be well.

We were close enough to home that I could see a formal reception line forming. The sentinels must have announced our approach to my Father. Anticipation morphed into anxiety as soon as I saw my Father's face, he was not happy, but he would do his duty. For he, like Torando, was bound to something much deeper than personal opinion. The sentinels had formed two lines leading up to my Father and Orla. People from the community were starting to gather as well. Word would spread very quickly now, there would be as many onlookers as well wishers. I grabbed Torando's hand and started towards my Father.

I could see my Father grab Orla's hand at the same time. I suddenly had the feeling he was mimicking me. He was the rebellious child in this instance. Something didn't please him and he was going to do his duty, but then let his thoughts be known.

"Father, may I present Torando, he is to be my partner." I know protocol was to ask for a blessing, but this was in no way traditional, no blessing was necessary, I was already in the position of ruler.

"Torando", my Father reached his hand out and tipped his head toward my new found partner. Torando seemed unsure as he shook my Father's hand. He was resistant. That is something I would speak to him about later.

"This is Orla, my Fathers partner."

"Oh yes Orla, how are you? Very nice to see you again" Tornado spoke earnestly. However my Father had no idea how the two of them would possibly know one another. This caught him off guard, I saw him spin his eyes towards Orla and she tried to ignore the stern gaze.

Right then, in that very moment, I knew the facade that had coated my world with a false reality was cracking. Secrets were starting to ooze from the cracks. When things are discovered they can never truly be buried again. Everyone's energy was changing very quickly in that instant. Shields were being raised. Thoughts were being thrown like spears. Minds were searching for the answers to questions that had not even been posed.

As I looked around to acknowledge the crowd that had gathered, I could see they were feeling the tension, although they could not pinpoint exactly what it was they were feeling, it made them nervous, restless, like a herd of beasts that we being hunted, they were getting ready to run.

"Thanks to you all for welcoming us. This is Torando. He is to join me in my life. We will make a formal announcement later, with a time for celebration to follow. "

With that we turned and walked towards the palace. All I could hear were individual words that escaped the loud whispers racing through the people.

Confusion ruled the day. Life was no longer supposed to make sense, they just had not realized that yet.

In all people's lives, there comes a moment individually and collectively, when life simply stops being what it has always been. This was one of those moments. Everyone would now be forced to have an opinion on Torando, the circumstance and the lack of tradition. Everything that had been the same since we began our stay on this planet would now change, and that would cause a chain of events that would determine what our society would become.

It is rare we can see that moment of change as it happens, but if we can, we can harness the energy of it, without getting caught up in it. That is where I stood. I was drinking in the energy of chaos, and turning it back out as power. It was the first time in my life, I stood as a woman in command of herself, not looking to anyone for approval. I did not question the action I had taken, even though I could not know the consequences it would bring.

Once inside, we wandered through the palace, I wanted Torando to get familiar with his new home. My Father accompanied us, but he did not say much. Mostly he just smiled and nodded his head. Orla walked two steps behind him at all times. I knew she was trying to create a just cause for knowing a man of a species that my Father had written off as forgotten. That however was a problem that belonged to them, I did not want to deal with it til it was forced upon me.

My focus was Torando and creating a seamless transition from me, to we. It was important that he feel this was his home now, for him, there was no going back. Within three days we would have the joining ceremony and the celebration that followed. I would simply go forth as if everything was normal. Everyone would have to get accustomed to my version of normal.

Traditions become traditions, not because it is the best way to handle a situation, but because someone refuses to do things differently. All I had to do now, was start my own tradition.

I showed him to the room which would be his own til the ceremony. He was a little overwhelmed with everything. I knew he just needed some time. This was a very different life than the one he was used to. Quiet, was a rare commodity here. I too needed a moment. Tomorrow I would have to deal with putting together a ceremony I knew nothing of. Simple, is all I wanted. I knew very soon in the future, a simple thing like trying to breathe could be complicated, so for now, simple was the only answer. The ceremony was not officiated by anyone, it was really a ceremony for the people. Traditionally it was meant to create security, knowing that the line of royals would be continued, and a nation would have direction and leadership. Now however, the people were not our people and the line of royals would not be continued. The ceremony would be a personal one. A statement between Torando and myself, a commitment of love. It would mean more to us, than it would the people.

I have always loved the morning. It is the time when clarity comes a little easier. I decided upon a small ceremony in the courtyard. Torando and I would speak words of commitment to one another. What we felt at that time. I would have my Father wrap the sacred bindings around our wrists and that would be the whole of it.

Traditionally the ruler wears the headpiece when this ceremony takes place. This is so the partner commits themselves to the ruler as well as the partner. I did not want that for Torando. I wanted it to be him and I, two beings here in this place, in this moment. My decision felt right to me as I sat and watched the sun rise from the white stones that served as sitting places. Stones had been cut and arranged in different levels so people could sit and watch the day at the edge of the courtyard. Trees had been skillfully placed so that as the sun followed its path across the sky, shade was offered to all levels of the seating arrangement.

As a child I had spent many days sitting watching the people come and go, from these stones. They were familiar to me, they had their own stories to tell. Women would come here to trade their skills with each other while the men would sit and talk. It had been a meeting place since we had established ourselves here. This is where the ceremony would occur. It had been a gathering place for the people, now it would be a gathering place for the heart.

The sun was nicely cradled in its blue surroundings and the noises of people starting to go about their day filled the air. I could feel a tingling starting on the surface of my skin, the energy was coming from behind me. I turned to see Torando standing there, quietly watching me. I motioned for him to come sit with me.

"Ah, we are greeted to a new day with the warmth of the sun. Did you sleep well?' I asked him.

"I am not accustomed to sleeping in such a soft place, but yes, I did fall to sleep midway through the night. Do you like being shielded from the stars? Many times I opened my eyes expecting to see the lights of the night sky and they were not there. That was the most difficult thing for me."

I had never thought about not seeing the stars. "It will take some time to adjust, I know. It is nice though, to not get wet when it rains." I was giggling as I spoke. I loved how he made me feel, and how he made me forget. Forget that I was responsible for these people, forget that I wore the headpiece, forget that I knew so many things I did not care to know. I loved how he made me forget. He slid closer and put his arm around me, I lay my head on his shoulder. We did not move for some time. Then he said, "Have you decided what kind of ceremony you want?"

Pleased that he cared what I thought I responded, "Yes, just a simple ceremony, right here. We should say what is in our hearts about joining with one another and then my Father will bind us. That is all I want, nothing more."

"Do you think you Father will bind us? He was not happy when we arrived."

"My Father is bound by tradition, it does not matter what he wants, he will to what is expected. It is what he knows."

"Well my love, I am going to leave you here to finish your thoughts. I am going to wander and meet the people. I would like to feel a little more familiar here in this place."

With that he kissed me and left. He would stop and speak to everyone in his path. He was trying to become one of us.

The thought of my Father doing what he knew was disturbing to me. The thought that he was rather incapable of altering tradition because he wanted something different for himself or his people was truly bothering me. I couldn't help but wonder why he just could not do something different? Why was I so different from him? I was the progeny of he and my Mother, I should have been the same, but I was not. I went back to hearing The One say, I had been created for this. Every time I thought of her saying that, the words got bigger. She was saying so much more than she was letting me know.

As happy as I was to have found Torando, the thought of him having to give up his life and the way he lived, was not a pleasant thought for me. All because of an invisible bond that would not release him. I wondered if he had thought about the future with me, and what that would bring? I wondered if the love he felt for me was a reaction to the pair bonding, or if he would have felt it if there was no bond? I was being flooded with feelings of doubt, and I had no idea where they were coming from. Why were they happening now? It was too late to change anything. We had bonded and I had introduced him to the people. But what if all this was a mistake? What if he was not the only one that I could have found? Perhaps I should have continued to look? All these questions would not change anything, so I decided to silence my mind and finish making the arrangements for the commitment ceremony.

Later that day, Torando and I decided to go to the beach and watch the sunset. We sat on the sand and watched the sea swallow the sun. The glorious rays left over as the sun said good bye to the day painted the azure sky with a depth of emotion only life itself could interpret. I sat looking into Torando's eyes, realizing they were not the same color as I had originally remembered.

"Why are your eyes so blue now? They were the color of the sea when I first saw you."

"My eyes mirror what I feel. They will always be shades of blue or green but the intensity of the color is meant to match my emotions. Don't your eyes change color?" He looked at me quite puzzled by this.

"No, my eyes stay the same. I guess it is one of the differences between us. What about the star burst of light behind the dark center of your eyes?"

"That will tell you how much energy I am directing beyond my self, also it will tell you where the energy source is coming from. If I am drawing energy from the stars, it will be silvery white in color. Energy from the sun will have a golden tinge to it. If the energy is from my heart is will be silvery pink. I have been told, this was done so that our creators could tell what we were thinking. What about your creators? How did they create you?"

"I am not sure of the exact process. The essence of my Mother and Father is placed in a birthing chamber with the elements of this planet. My Mother, Father and The One join together energetically and project that energy to the essences in the chamber, and I am created. Although The One has told me many times that I was created different. I have never been sure of what she means by that. I do know I am different from my Father. He sometimes seems incapable of thinking for himself, he always does, what he has always done. I am not like that, I want things to be different, than they have been." I knew at that point I was thinking out loud, looking for someone to tell me it was OK to be different.

"I understand. Our kind were designed to deal with constant change. We were created to take what is and make it into what will be. So we look for the difference in something, not for the similarity."

"So when you pair bond, you are looking for differences?" I was feeling a little confused by that statement. I had known that the pair bonding was a control factor in the creation of their species, so I was not sure what it was that he was saying.

"Not exactly. We seek differences outside of ourselves, pair bonding is all about, inside of ourselves. We look for a mate that is as much like us as possible. This way we fit together. It is easier. Do you understand that? It is a hard thing to explain."

" I think so. If you find someone who thinks the same and acts the same, there is less trauma in the bonding process. It keeps the status quo of things."

"Yes, that is the idea of it." He was smiling at me.

"How is it, you and I are so alike. I am not sure I see that part?" I really wanted to know what he was going to say. I felt we were so different.

"On the outside yes we are very different. But on the inside we are very similar. We are more like the beasts of the forest than the people who live inside the carved walls. We cannot stand to be chained to ideals or traditions. We have a desire to be free at all costs. This earth, this planet we live on, makes more sense to us, than our own species. We have both learned that communication does not happen with words. Communication is an experience that comes from action. That is why we don't understand our own species so much. What they say and how they act on what they are saying, do not usually match. We, both of us, would prefer a life of roaming the hills and sitting by the sea, than what comes from the tradition of pomp and circumstance. Neither one of us, will be here for a long time, it is simply not in our nature."

I did agree with what he said, even if I would not tell him so. I would have asked him what he meant by, "not being here long," but the truth was I didn't want to know. It was enough that he felt we were the same. That was what I needed to hear right now, it made me feel a little easier about the ceremony. I let go of the feeling I was forcing him to do something he did not want to do, and allowed for the possibility, that this was all happening the way it was supposed to. I relaxed into his arms and in silence we discovered we understood each other perfectly.

The energy of the bond between us was growing. It felt like a thick cord that ran from his heart to mine. The energy that pulsed along the cord was the beat of our hearts going back and forth to each other. It was a comforting feeling. He was becoming a part of me very quickly, and I a part of him.

I saw my Father for the first time in two days as he was leaving to attend to something. All he did was nod his head and moved quickly beyond me. This caused me great pain. I had wanted my Father's blessing even though I did not expect to get it. I wandered down the corridor and into the light of the sun. I stood there letting its rays fall upon my face as though they would wash away the memory of a life I did not want to lead.

"Are you already for the ceremony tomorrow? Can I offer my assistance with anything?" Orla came silently up behind me. I could feel her coming but I knew she was trying to startle me. She wanted me off my guard.

"Everything is done, thank you. I appreciate the offer." I said without turning around. I knew that was just a question to open up a conversation I did not wish to have right now.

"So where did you find Torando?"

"I think you know where I found Torando, the same place you found Rojan." It was out of my mouth before I could stop it. I had not wanted to say anything at this point. I could feel her starting to panic behind me. I thought it a wise idea to turn and face her, just in case she would stab me in the back. As I looked into her eyes, they went from panic to a stare that was cold and angry. She had hoped her life would not be revealed, and now that it was, she would turn to anger as a way to shield her lies.

"Rojan, how do you know anything of Rojan? That was many years ago. It is not of your business. I would ask you to keep my business to yourself. It has no place being discussed here in this place. That is a discussion that would cause great harm to your Father. Neither one of us want that. Do we?" Her eyes had narrowed to small slits.

"Yes many years ago. But time has a way of collapsing in on us, when we least expect it. The walls of time are made so you can see through them. But just because you can't see those walls, doesn't mean they are not there. There are many secrets living within these walls now. I wonder, how long will they remain hidden?" With that I walked away.

I had no idea where all the anger suddenly came from in me. I had for a moment glimpsed a person I did not know as myself, but that lived within me. It frightened me. I wondered if the bonding with Torando had anything to do with this? More than that, I wondered what Orla would do now? Her secret was no longer hidden. She knew I was aware of a lot more than she would want me to be. I may have unwittingly caused a problem, where there had been none. I needed to speak with Torando about this. Perhaps he knew more about Rojan than he had said. I needed to know all he knew. So I went to find him. I did not have to look far. He was just beyond the courtyard watching some children play the same games that I did as a child.

"Torando, I need to talk to you." I could see he understood the urgency in my voice. He rose and came straight to me.

"Come lets go over here, it is more private. I just spoke with Orla. It slipped out that I knew about her and Rojan. The look on her face frightened me. It was like something evil in her awoke when I mentioned his name. You must tell me everything you know about him. Please." The look on his face told at least part of the story. He did not like Rojan.

"Rojan was different even as a child. But he was the kind of different that got a lot of people hurt. His games were not about including the others, his games always put him at the top, no matter who got hurt in the process. As he got older, he would start stories that would cause problems amongst us. We started to mistrust each other. He made us believe that some of our tribe were going to enslave the rest of us. In truth it was he that wanted to enslave us.

When Orla was banished, Rojan found her and her followers wandering helplessly in the forest. Some say he saved her life from one of the wild beasts. The stories that surround that time are all different and there is no way to know what is true.

Rojan and Orla pair bonded as you and I have. He is bound to her. Because of her status as one of your people, he agreed to help her regain this place. He vowed vengeance on all of your kind. But Orla's ambitions were much bigger than that. She wanted her own city to rule. So she convinced Rojan that they would rule together if he would help her build a city of their own. They would build a grand empire together, amass a great nation and then return to over throw your city.

This started the warring in our tribes. There were some of us that did not want to follow Rojan and Orla into their imagination. Rojan tried to enslave the people. Many resisted, many were killed. A very few of us escaped. They must have given up, hunting us down at some point. Because the day came when Rojan, Orla and the people they had taken, left the forest and I never saw them again, til a few years ago.

I was out gathering food one day and saw a small group of people by the land bridge, they did not look like your sentinels. I was careful to conceal myself as I got a closer look. It was Rojan with a group of trained warriors. Orla joined them and they were discussing how to make war on the city. I left there and never went back to that place. This was long ago, many years.

I know Orla has a great city beyond the land bridge and over the mountains. I have heard her say that she has ordered her people to build cities all over the land as they find suitable places to inhabit. She is the only one of your kind left. However she has been pair bonding with my kind and the others that she took with her. I have heard it said they are strong and capable of independent thought.

These are the people she is ruling over. She is using them to build cities all over this Earth. She wants to rule this earth. I do not know why she has not over thrown your city yet. She has plans to stop the harvest unless her terms are met. Beyond this, I do not know anything. I tried to stay as far away from them as I could. I wanted nothing to do with them. Darkness and destruction is all they leave in their path."

I was having a hard time believing all of this. Cities? All over the earth. How was she finding enough people to do this? Did she think she could just take over the city, and we would give it to her? Our sentinels are strong and they would fight. Or would they? If Orla has trained men to kill, perhaps the sentinels would not be enough. They knew nothing of war. The sentinels were more of a formality than protection. There had been nothing here for them to protect us from. I realized just how vulnerable we were. If Orla wanted to take the city from us, she could.

"Thank you for telling me all this. I don't know what to do about it. Orla seemed to be bonding with my Father in these last few years. She seemed to be more content and happier. I had thought maybe she was becoming one of us again. But when I saw that look in her eyes this morning, I saw the old Orla. I knew she was still there."

"Perhaps you should talk to your Father about this. He has seen much more than you have. Maybe he could help?" Torando offered, but he did not know my Father.

"My Father died when my Mother died. The man I call my Father, is very different than the man I grew up with . He has become very dependent on Orla. That is why I now wear the Headpiece. He no longer wanted the

219

responsibility, and I did not want to see Orla ruling beside my Father. I knew Orla wanted the city, but I had no idea she wanted the planet. What am I supposed to do with all this?"

Torando did not know what to say, so he had the wisdom to say nothing at all. He simply embraced me. It is all he could do. And so we sat there, watching the day pass us by. We sat in silence. Him knowing there was nothing he could do to make me feel better and me, wishing life were different than it was. At the end of the day Torando broke the silence.

"This is a circumstance in which nothing can be done at the moment. You do not know if what you said this morning will affect anything because Orla does not know what she is doing herself. So the best thing you can do is wait. Be as prepared as you can, but you must wait. Doing nothing is the most powerful thing you can do in this situation.

If you try to prevent something unknown from happening Orla will see the weakness in that. That is Orla's talent, seeing the weakness in all things. That is how she has manipulated your Father. She knows he does not step beyond the boundary of tradition, so she uses that to keep him where she wants him to be.

The people here, know nothing of tradition. So you will not be going against their memory in anything you wish to do. The only person who knows you are breaking tradition is your Father. It is his conditioned response to routine that has put him where he is now. And isn't that all tradition is, conditioned response to routine? When you came to this world, there was nothing here. Over time the world was calmed and seeded. Everything grew so now there is all this beauty and life. If tradition was the right thing, everything would stay the same. Change is the thing that brings beauty and life to us. Change is growth, change is love. How much would we miss in our lives, if things did not change? So come on. Tomorrow we have our ceremony. That will bring happiness to all the people. I know it will bring happiness to me."

He hugged me, pulled me to my feet and grabbed my hand. He walked quickly towards the palace and took me with him. I felt as though he was pulling me through life at the moment. I had only just found him, but he felt irreplaceable in my life. Finally someone that cared enough to take care of me. I could feel the love for him flood my body, it pulled me closer to him.

Perhaps he was right. Maybe this is something I can do nothing about in this moment. I should be aware but not waste my precious time on creating something that I do not know to be true. It was Orla's move now. I was just going to have to be patient and let her make it.

The next morning as I entered the courtyard, all I could see was an ocean of flowers that had been layed out for us by the people. The courtyard was covered in flowers, the white stones were covered in flowers, the hollow stones were covered in flowers. The scent was overwhelming. Torando came to stand beside me, I knew in that moment he understood the devotion of the people to us. It was an astonishing sight.

As we started towards the stones a little girl came up to me and offered me one white flower. She was so beautiful and the pure joy of being escaped from her eyes as I smiled and thanked her. We moved through the people and made our way to the the place I had chosen. My Father stood there with Orla. I could not read either of their faces, I was to involved with myself. We chose a small area to stand in which was a little higher than the crowd. I waited for Torando to voice his commitment, with hope that I could express myself properly when the time came.

"Aeiya, the instant I saw you, I knew we were the same. Somehow it was the desire of The Oneness to separate its love and place one half in you and the other half in me. Until we found one another I could not be whole, I could not truly love, for I was only loving half of all possibilities. Now that you are here in my arms, I know what it is to love all of me. It is not when we speak that I hear your love, it is in the silence that I know your love. For this reason I am yours and yours alone for as long as we are both here. I will love you as no other can. As the stages of our life change, our love shall grow stronger. It will lift us up when we fall, and give us rest when we do not sleep. I shall receive your thoughts as my own, and with wisdom return them. You are as my own body, please allow my love and devotion to nourish you until we return home."

I looked at him, I had tears in my eyes. He was so eloquent and sincere. I could feel his gaze within me. My heart grew larger.

"Torando. When I set out to find a mate I did not know who I was looking for. But you found me, and I could have chosen no better partner. Your heart beats within me, within my own heart. I could know no other. You have filled my senses. Until you came to my life, I believed I would have to face everything on my own. But now I understand the meaning of love. Love is sharing all that I am with you. I can be myself with you, because that is who you love. Your love has set me free, I can fly again. I love you for that. I love that you are able to see me as I am, in all forms, and the forms don't matter. I wish to bind myself to you." It is all I could say as I held the tears back.

"And I wish to bind myself to you."

My Father approached us and took a beautiful rope of flowers that had been lovingly made for us by the people. He placed my hand on top of Torando's and then wove the rope around our wrists and hands several times.

He looked at us both and simply stated, "By this earth, you are bound." It was done. We had committed ourselves to one another. I turned to the people to offer them thanks.

"Thank you so much for all the beautiful flowers and for welcoming Torando into your hearts. I look forward to many years with him. Now lets get on with the celebration!"

As Torando helped me to step down from the stones I could hear music starting in the hollow stones up behind us. The people were starting to disburse so they could all find their favorite spots to celebrate. Tables had been laden with food and flowers, and the children ran about freely. It was a very happy moment.

As the music wafted through he air, all I could think about was escaping. Escaping with Torando, somewhere quiet and private. The last few days had been a whirlwind of activity. I did not want to celebrate, I wanted intimacy away from prying eyes. The look on Torando's face told me he was thinking the same thing, so I grabbed his hand and we ran as fast as we could towards the forest. I was hoping we would make it before being seen by anyone.

As we disappeared into the lush greenness of the forest, I could feel the leaves on the trees sweep away my stress. The forest, the sea, the mountains, they had all been safe places for me. Places where people could not put demands on me. Places that were full of love and nourishment, of giving back in a way, that no person could. Torando let a sigh out of him and I knew, he was feeling better as well. We found a place beneath a giant tree and collapsed to the ground. There we lay silent with our bodies entangled. We did not need to speak. We needed to feel one another silently. We needed to feel the pulse of the great Mother pass up through the earth and through us. The cool mosses beneath us were soft and as our body heated them up, they released their smell gently scenting the air of musk. We knew eventually someone would come looking for us, and we had every intention of returning to the celebration, we just wanted a few moments alone. As we lay there listening to the sounds of the forest, off in the distance I thought I heard voices. I turned to Torando to see if he had heard them too. The puzzled look on his face said he did.

We slowly maneuvered ourselves to a better vantage point. Not to far away Rojan stood speaking with Orla and a few other men. I hadn't thought Orla had seen him in a very long time. Perhaps I was wrong. We could not hear what was being said, but both Orla and Rojan were acting as though they were agitated. My moments of peace were being interrupted by anxiousness. It was never a good thing when Orla was speaking to Rojan. I wanted to walk straight up to them and demand to know what they were planning, but Torando placed his hand on my shoulder. He knew Rojan better than I, so I stayed where I was.

A few moments passed and Orla headed back for the party. Rojan took his men and headed in the direction of the land bridge. My false sense of safety had been placed directly in front of me again. Would life never be simple? In my frustration, I rose to my feet and started back towards the party, Torando followed me silently. I had the feeling he wanted to tell me something but he did not want to make the moment any worse than it already was.

The celebration lasted long into the night. I was not enjoying myself knowing that Rojan and Orla were talking again. I had hoped for my Fathers sake, that Orla had let go of her petty pursuits.

Torando, seemed to have a great deal of fun, talking with the people, dancing and feasting on the many foods that had been prepared. At the end of the evening, we were both exhausted and left for our chamber. We would now share my room since we were bound. We crawled into bed, into each others arms and fell asleep. An uneventful end to a day that had brought significant change to my life.

As morning broke, the golden rays of sunlight streamed through the air and lit up the room. I lay there watching Torando sleep. He made me feel so much safer in my own life. But with that thought it also made me wonder, why I needed him to feel safe.

The One had taught me to question everything, especially my own thoughts. "Your thoughts are not a part of reality. " she would say. "Your thoughts are your imaginings, they are what you use to create a reality that is not based in truth."

As the warmth of the sun stirred Torando to life, I could feel the warmth of his love stirring inside of me. As he opened his eyes, I opened my heart. I could feel the energy of love flowing out to him, like a river gushing after the spring rains. It was that love and the love that I felt returned to me, that made me feel safe.

"Good morning." he said in a voice soft and low. I could feel his voice penetrate my being. It sent a current of energy across my shoulders and down my back.

"Good morning. It is a beautiful day to wake up to. Did you dream?" I asked Torando.

"Yes I did dream, but I do not remember what now, seeing you, has wiped my memory of all other things. Nothing matters as much as you. " His eyes lit up when he was speaking the truth of his heart.

The only thing I could do at that point was smile and curl into him. Words had no meaning. Warm and safe, we drifted back to sleep.

Bang! Bang! Bang! The loud noise of someone wanting to enter my room awoke me from a sound sleep.

"Aeiya, are you awake, you must come at once! Aeiya!" The voice was cracking, like they were in a state of panic.
"I will be right there," I called out.

I quickly dressed and ran out to the large gathering room. Many people were standing there, something had happened. They were all looking at something beyond themselves, out towards the mountains in the back of the Alaria. I rushed to my Father's side.

"What? What is it?" He lifted his arm and pointed to the hills. Everywhere there were people standing with weapons. Just standing there, not moving, not speaking, just staring towards us.

As my eyes scanned all the faces, trying to make sense of what was happening, there in the middle was Rojan. He had placed himself on a rock. He wanted to be seen, he was making a statement that he was in charge.

I stepped forward, not sure what was going to happen, I called out to him, "What do you want?" I did not want anyone to know, I knew who Rojan was, I was afraid it may put Torando in danger.

"I have come for Orla, she is bonded to me. Edon has taken her from me and I am claiming her back. This matter must be settled now. Orla come to me, we can end this right now!"

I looked at Orla who seemed to be half hiding behind my Father. I had no idea what was really going on, just the day before she had met Rojan in the forest. Why wouldn't she go to him now?

Torando came up behind me and placed his hands on my shoulders. As I turned to look at him he was focused on Rojan.

"Can you see his energy?" he whispered to me in a quiet voice.

I tried to quiet myself, to see his energy. All I could see were patches of black around him. In my mind he looked ill. Something was wrong with him, even though I did not see this with normal eyes.

"What you see is what happens when the pair bonding is severing. Rojan is dying, His energy is leaving him and going to Orla. They have been apart so long, that is the only way he can be with her, if he attaches his energy there. That is what pair bonding is."

Even with the threat that stood before me, the thought that entered me was, I now know what pair bonding is. It is the inability to live without the other. The severity of it frightened me much more than Rojan standing there in a weakened state.

I looked towards my Father, he was in shock, he had known nothing of Rojan. He did not know why this was happening.

"Go to him Orla. Go figure this out" I demanded Orla fix the problem she had created.

"No!" She yelled back at me.

"Can't you see you are putting everyone here at risk. This is your problem, you must fix it." I didn't want to say that I had known of her association with Rojan. I felt like it was the only advantage I had in this situation.

Orla did not move, and it started becoming clear to me why. If she went to him, she was admitting to the pair bonding. If she stayed at my Father's side, she would keep my Father's loyalty. This is what they had been planning in the forest. I felt she was trying to find a way to bring Rojan into the palace. She wanted him there for some reason.

"What is your name I yelled to Rojan?" I did not want to give myself away. I could tell Torando approved, cause he squeezed my shoulders.

"I am Rojan, leader of the people of Atlantis, and Orla sits at my side on the throne." He stood taller as he spoke those words, he was speaking his truth. I did not however think those words were Orla's truth.

"Rojan, leader of Atlantis, if you agree, we shall meet with you to speak of your concerns, at midday in the Alaria. Do you agree?"

"Yes, I will speak with Orla, I do not want Edon present." He jumped down from the rock and disappeared into the forest.

No one said a word. We were all in a state of disbelief that this moment had just happened. It was my Father that broke the silence.

"Orla, who is that man?" There was no anger in my Father's voice, only the hint of a broken heart.

"His name is Rojan and he was with me in Atlantis, however, what he and I had was over a very long time ago. He knows this, I do not know why he is doing this?"

That was too much for Torando. He spoke angrily for the first time.

"You are very well aware of what pair bonding is. You knew exactly what you were doing when you came to him and bonded with him. You wanted all my people to follow you and you used Rojan to get what you wanted. Now you want something else so you are using Edon. Fix this Orla. I do not want to have to stand against my own people, but I will. And I will stand against you as well!" Torando was furious, I had no idea he was capable of such rage.

I could see the defiance in Orla's eyes. She had no intention of fixing anything. They would meet and speak, but it was all part of the plan. A plan I knew nothing of. She has purposely done this to Rojan to make him desperate enough to wander into our territory. Rojan knew he was dying, and like all frightened beasts he would do anything to save himself, even if it meant war and killing his own people. There would be no reasoning with him. He wanted one thing and one thing only.

Amid all of this, my Father looked like he was about to collapse. It was all too much for him. He was not able to process all of this information at one time. I am not sure he was even able to understand that there were so many stories within stories. All he knew is someone wanted to take his love from him, and he didn't feel able to stop them. As I stood and looked at my Father, for the very first time, I saw a defeated man.

I called to the sentinels to help him as he stumbled. They took him back to his room. As I watched Orla, she looked upon him as if she no longer had use for him. I wanted to have her removed from this place, but I knew it was not the moment to do so. Her leaving had to be my Fathers decision, otherwise it would kill him.

I returned to the bed chamber where I found Torando pacing furiously back and forth.

"What are you doing?" I asked. His behavior was almost frightening me.

"This is my fault, it is all my fault, I never should have come here."

"What are you talking about?" He made no sense to me. His presence here had no relevance to what just happened.

"You must understand. I was a threat to Orla. This would not have happened if I was not here. The minute she saw me, she was afraid her secrets would come out to you and your Father. So she forced her hand and she did it fast. Before anyone could see it coming. Can't you see? She wants this place and she will do anything to get it. That was the beginning of something more. Something that will bring this place to an end, so that Orla can rule. My being here has put you and everyone else in danger." Torando was beyond consolation. He left, heading towards the beach. I wondered if he would return.

I did not want to think it, but I knew he was right. I had known for a very long time that Orla wanted Lemuria. Those long years ago that I had followed her. I knew then, but I did nothing. I had wanted to believe that she and my Father were making a life for themselves. It seemed so real. Something changed all of that. Could it possibly be that Torando was right? Simply by his presence here, she became that threatened? He knew her history. He knew what she was capable of. She would have believed that he was the only one that knew the truth.

All of a sudden I was afraid for Torando. If Orla thought he was the only thing standing between her and what she wanted, I knew she would do anything to get rid of him.

I quickly dressed and went after him, I did not want him to be out there by himself. I ran down through the courtyard, and past the stones where we were bound. I kept running along the path through the fields to the beach. My breath was growing thin, but I could not stop running, Past the edge of the forest, I could hear the water now, I was close. As I came out from the darkness that the leaves held to themselves, the bright sunlight blinded me for a moment. I shielded my eyes from the sun to see better. My attention was drawn to my left. Far up the beach there was a commotion, something was happening. I ran towards it, as I did, figures of men were scattering.

I fell to my knees a few feet away. It was Torando, he lay on the beach. He did not move. He was covered in blood. I dragged myself to him. I kept screaming his name but he did not hear me. I put my head to his chest, I could not hear his heart. I could not feel his energy. He was not there. His body was lifeless. I could not stop the pain from seizing me. I was frozen, I could not move, my being was encased in a tomb of pain. Why?

What reason could this possibly serve? He was the only person that ever truly loved me. Why would he be taken from me? I could not stop screaming from the pain that encompassed me.

Sentinels must have seen me leave the courtyard. Moments later they came up behind me, they must have followed the sound of my screams.

They picked me up and they picked Torando up. I remember feeling like I was moving through the air. I was watching Torando's body as they carried him home. I wanted to be with him. I did not want to stay here. I tried to let go of my body, I tried to follow him, but I was not allowed to. The extreme exertion of it all, pulled the energy from my body. I could not stay conscious.

I awoke to blurred faces around my bed. I could identify some of the voices, easier than I could see the details of their face. Then I heard the voice of The One. She was here. It was a dangerous thing for her to be here with me. Maybe I was not in the palace, perhaps I was back on the mountain, home, where I should be.

I sat up and demanded, "Where am I?"

"Hush now, Lay back down, You are home, here with your Father. Tuallan is here too." The One's voice was calming. I would rather have been on the sacred mountain.

"Leave, everyone get out. I need to speak to The One." I could barely speak, but I wanted to be alone. I had to get some answers.

Everyone left the room. The One sat on the edge of the bed holding my hand. I could tell, it took a great deal of energy to be there with me. She was putting her own life at risk, trying to save mine.

"Why did this happen? Can you do something about it? I want him back? They killed him because of me. It is not his fault. I want her dead. Why? Why? I don't understand?" I could not contain my tears. Every one that dropped from my eyes felt like acid running over my skin. I wanted my life to end. There was no reason for me to go on.

"Death is a part of life, whether it is just, or not. Orla knew if she could draw Torando out, away from you, that he would be vulnerable. She knew he would blame himself for this, Rojan's stand against you, this act of war. But this is not the time for you to give up. You are in terrible pain now, but time will ease the pain. Time will do nothing to ease the memory, however it will allow you the distance you need to rationalize the release of your pain. You have been asleep for three days. Torando was sent home. He made the crossing to expand his being. He is fine. You will continue to feel him around you, it takes time for the pair bonding to dissipate. For now you must rest. When you are better, in a few days, I have made arrangements for you to come to the mountain. There I can show you things, that I cannot here. Until then, do not speak to anyone of what has just happened. Alright?"

227

I nodded my head weakly. Go home to the mountain, of course I would go home.

I could feel sleep taking me, I gave myself to it. I was hoping I would not wake up.

The next morning however, I opened my eyes. I needed to get up. My body wanted to move. I was still in such pain that movement was difficult. Every step felt like I was being stabbed with daggers. I managed to get myself to the hollow stones. The circular pools in front of the stones were filled with water from the Alaria.

I slipped into the waters, they were warm and felt good against my pain. I let myself float around the concentric circles, breathing only when necessary. The sun was threatening the dark skies with its light. The birth of a new day threatened to place more time between myself and my love for Torando. To keep him alive and here with me, was to keep the pain in my body. To let go and allow time to do its job, was to risk not feeling his love encompass me.

I knew this was the wisdom of the universe playing itself out in my life. Trying to keep alive a love that was no longer here, no longer present in this moment, would cause the deterioration of my being. To allow the love to move to my memories, where I could hold it dearly would allow my being to stay in the present. I knew it was the difference between seeing something before me, or allowing something to follow behind me.

Pain is a great persuader. If I was to go to the mountain, to try and find some peace, I could not do it in this much pain. I was not allowed to die, so I must do what I can to live.

I brought the memory of Torando's face to my heart, with that came the flood of his love.

"I love you so much. Nothing can change what I feel for you. I am so sorry I did not protect you. I should not have let you leave. I will never forgive myself for that. I am not allowed to join you right now. I know I will be with you again, when the time is right. I hope you understand that I can't hold you in front of me. I must allow you to find the place in my heart, where you can stay til I join you. There is where you must stay, so that I can live on, to care for those around me. I cannot live without you, but I can' keep you present. Please understand. I am setting you free here in the sacred waters of the Alaria, the waters that find their home in the mountains. They will carry you to the sea, and from there you will cover this earth."

With that I allowed his energy to be released from my cells. I kept his love in my heart but I set the possession of him free. My body started to ease as I did this. Much of the pain left and headed towards the sea. As the pain left, the love of him moved into the empty spaces. I could feel his love as though he was right there in front of me. I tried to embrace it as much as possible. As my tears disappeared into the waters, I understood we are all just tears. Each one of us, a single tear that merges back into the sea of the universe, when we are called home.

I found some comfort in that thought. That, once the life leaves our bodies, we have another, greater family waiting for us. It is the family of our consciousness. It is the body from which we were plucked as a single cell, placed in a different reality and encouraged to grow. To learn, and ultimately to understand at no time were we ever separated from our family. We are born to understand that we are not alone. We come to this place to meet all the beings upon it. The ones that look like us and the ones that don't. Around us at all time is life. Life that we should be identifying as being just like us. But we don't do that, we still continue to choose to feel alone. We wait and we search for that one person that we have decided is like us. Then we place an inconceivable amount of pressure on them to be our everything. In our minds we have convinced ourselves that this one being, is the only being that is like us, and the only being that can give us the love we give them.

So now instead of being all alone, we are alone with one other being. It is no longer, I am alone against the world, now it is we are alone against the world. The ridiculousness of this made me laugh. It felt good to laugh. I wondered what Torando would think of my thoughts. He never understood separation. He had the sight that allowed him to see oneness, even when that oneness included energies he did not want to be a part of.

I knew The One had taught me all of this, and that I had not forgotten it, I just had not put it into practice in my daily life. Had I not wanted to be part of everything? Did it not make me feel special enough, if I was no different from everything else? Why could we not be special and stand beside the next being in their specialness? Fear. Yes that was it. Fear wanted us to be more special, than everyone else. Fear that we would not be seen. Fear that we would not be loved. Fear that we were not good enough. Fear that we were not like the rest. I understood just how ironic it is, that we spend so much time trying to be like everyone else, that we isolate ourselves even more, to the point where all we can see is separateness.

Just laying here in the water thinking, was good for me. Since coming back here, from the sisterhood, I had not taken nearly enough time to be alone with my thoughts. My love for Torando was giving me this gift now.

"You are going to get all wrinkled if you stay in there much longer." Tuallan's voice yanked me back to the present and out of my blissful drift across consciousness.

"What, you shouldn't sneak up on me like that. I was trying to ease the pain." I replied, not yet sure whether I was back and present or not.

"Yes I know. Aeiya, I am so so sorry about what happened. I loved Torando, he was a beautiful person. This earth will miss him." Tuallan's voice was so genuine.

I had not thought of that, that the earth herself would miss Torando. But I understood this to be right. I am sure he was one of her favorites. He loved the earth so much, I am sure she returned that love.

"I am supposed to go with you to the sisterhood. The One told me you would be leaving to go there in a few days, when you felt better. I am supposed to make sure you arrive safely. Is that alright with you?"

"Yes, of course. I am looking forward to spending time with the sisters again. I need to do that right now. "

I let Tuallan help me from the waters, and I returned to my room. I did feel better, but I still needed to rest. Only time could help me now.

Days passed and with each one I felt a little stronger. I spent most of the time in my room or wandering by the hollow stones. Tuallan had come to see me a few times and we talked of Torando, but no one else spoke of him.

I knew either my Father or Orla had forbidden his name to be mentioned. Whether they thought it would be easier for me or they were using this moment to exert their own will, I do not know.

On the day I was to leave for the sisterhood, one of the Others, a young girl came to help me with my things. I had seen her working here many times,, but I had not taken to much time to get to know her. She was bright and well spoken. Her smile lit up the room and her energy said she was genuine in her thoughts.

"Ma'am? Miss Aeiya?" she started. I turned to her as I heard her speak to me. It was not often that the Others spoke to me by name.

"I wanted to tell you how much it hurt us all that Torando was taken from us, and from you. It was not right. If you need us to fight, we will. I was supposed to give you that message." She spoke, but with a little hesitation.

"Thank you. I do miss him terribly. I am not sure what you mean by fight?" I truly was puzzled by her use of the word.

"Ma"am? The war that is coming? My people all know that Rojan is going to come and take what he wants. We all know Orla is going to help him too. Hasn't anyone told you this?" she looked at me with great concern on her face.

I was not aware of any of this. Perhaps something had happened while I slept and that is why The One was requesting my presence now. I did not have any answers for her, but I did appreciate her concern.

"I am sure whatever is going on can be worked out. Don't you worry about it, but thank you for your concern. It really helps me to know that someone else misses Torando." I could not stop the tears from welling up as I spoke. I did miss him. I missed the connection.

It had come to my understanding that the connection I had with Torando, had allowed me to connect with the rest of life. He was my conduit. He was the permission I needed to not feel alone. I understood that relationships may start with two people but they are the path to connecting with the world. The very fact that one being wants to connect with you on such a deep level, means there are more that will as well. Perhaps not in the same way, but with the same depth.

For my species, children did not come from our bodies and I had wondered why there was a necessity for bonding with one specific individual. I knew now it was simply to place a security net around your heart. That security was the key to opening your heart to the rest of life. To allow all the love that is out there in all its form, to have a place within you.

I was ready to leave. I saw Tuallan descending from the Alaria to join me. I had thought my Father would be here to see me off. He was no where in sight. He knew I was going, and I would not be gone long. I assumed he was not concerned.

"Are you ready?" Tuallan said in her very straight forward manner.

"Yes, let us be gone." And with that we struck out on our own. No sentinels to accompany us.

Chapter Twenty

As my Mother before me had done, I collapsed time to concentrate space. Our movement from the island across the land bridge to the base of the mountains did not take but a few hours. Without this the trip could take weeks. That is time I did not have.

I wanted to breath the mountain air and sit with the sisters again. I did not want to have to wear the head piece or be the ruler of anyone. I was secretly hoping I would not have to return to the palace. I could enjoy living out my days with the sisters.

At the bottom of the mountain where the entrance to the sisters is hidden, I decided to say my good byes to Tuallan.

"Thank you for accompanying me. Are you going to be alright on your own?"

"What do you mean, I am coming with you? Didn't The One tell you that?" She was a little agitated with my statement.

"No she didn't. How are you going to go up the mountain with me?" I didn't think the Others were capable of such journeys.

"I have been up the mountain several times. Just signal The One we are here and she will bring us up." Tuallan stated in a voice verging on angry.

"Signal The One? What are you talking about?" I had not heard of such a thing.

"Ok, stand here. Just use your mind and tell her we are here. Forget it, let me do it. That is how I go up every time." Tuallan closed her eyes and I could see she was concentrating. Within moments I could feel us rising upwards passing the low lying clouds. Up past the prying eyes of anyone who would do us harm.

We arrived at the landing on the mountain top. A few short steps and I would be home. Tuallan ran off in a hurry. I was more hesitant. I was happy and excited, but nervous. I did not know what kind of reception was in store for me. However, placing one foot in front of the other will always take you to your destination.

I came into view by the Temple of the Sun. There, where so much had happened the last time I was here, stood all the ladies in a circle waiting for my return. There was one spot left open in the circle, it was meant for me to join them. I had forgotten I had been initiated as one of them. They were not waiting to receive me, they were waiting for me to be the last link in the flow. I dropped my things and took my place in the circle. Immediately I felt the energy flow through me. The energy that had passed through each one of the women carrying a piece of them into me as it did. I in turn allowed pieces of myself to flow into them.

This was the energy of truth. They felt, what I felt and I felt what they felt, it was the only way for complete communication. It was the merging of hearts and thoughts to create a single mind capable of solving the problems at hand.

As the energy coursed through us picking up speed. I could see Tuallan sitting by the Temple of the Sun, her eyes were closed and she was relaxed, deep in prayer.

As the circling energy pulled me deeper and deeper into it, I could clearly see the faces of all the women. The One, Chiana, Wen, Tonn, Eluna, Eawannu, Gnua and Enaka. Each spinning before my eyes. Their thoughts were my thoughts and my thoughts were theirs. The speed of the energy went so fast that at one point I thought I saw all the faces of all the ladies, disappear into The One. The One looked directly at me. I had to look away. The gaze was too intense.

The energy suddenly stopped. It had held us all rigid, unable to move so when it stopped we all stumbled backwards a step or two, trying to regain our balance. All of us, of course, except for The One. I was not sure what I was feeling, but it was different than before. There was a distance this time. The way she kept looking at me, like there was something she saw that I did not. I decided I was probably making it all up. The One could be very formal at times and it would be different tomorrow.

"Aeiya, dear sweet girl. How are you? We are all so sorry for your loss" Chiana embraced me as she spoke for the others.

"I have so missed being here with all of you. Thank you for your prayers and you concern. I will be fine, time is on my side." I said feeling the love they were sending to me. Enaka came and sat beside me, bidding me to sit as well.

"Welcome home. It is not the same around here with you gone."

"That is true, no one messing things up all the time." Tonn said with a big smile on her face.

"Oh, leave her alone, she just had to find her flow." Eluna said, winking her eye at me.

"So tell us, how did you meet Torando?" Eawannu asked. That question caught me quite off guard, but it was a welcome one. I did want to talk about Torando. I needed to talk about Torando.

As the ladies all gathered around me, I related the story of our meeting to them. Telling them of my searching for him in my cat body, and wondering if he could actually see the cat when I met him. Then I told them of the amazing energetic exchange, the likes of which I knew, I could not ever experience again. They all seemed very pleased with my story telling skills.

234

"What did your Father think when you brought Torando home with you?" Wen asked.

"Well I did not think he was going to accept it. He met us with clenched fists and a mouth that did not want to open to speak." I laughed as I remembered that moment. It all seemed so far away, only the feeling of Torando seemed close now.

The talking and laughing went on into the evening. I talked of Torando so much he felt alive to me again. I was home, with the people that cared about me. For most of the evening Tuallan sat in prayer. Only after dark did she rise from her spot and retire to a bed. To stay in one spot for so long, was a discipline I did not think the Others could master. Tired, sore but feeling somewhat elated, I disappeared graciously to my white walls. I had healed more in the past few hours than in the many days before this. That is when I realized, that is what all the talking was about. Talking lovingly about Torando allowed me to move his energy out of my energy field. The vibration of my voice literally shook his energy from all the spots that I had hidden from myself, hoping to hold onto a piece of him. Yes, these women were wise. Where there were dark corners filled with the grasping of thoughts, now these corners were filled with love. Most of the pain had been removed from my body. I was hoping after a good nights sleep, the rest would be gone as well. I closed my eyes as the dreams of Torando came to collect me. We were together again, reunited swimming in a sea of love.

Morning came too quickly. I wanted to get up and go to the Temple to honor the rising of the Sun, but I had slept too late. In fact it was the afternoon by the time I had returned to physical reality. I had needed the deep rest that can happen here. I did feel much better as I got up and went outside. The warmth of the sun felt good on my skin. This was the world as I enjoyed it. The ladies were buzzing about doing their normal routines. Tuallan sat with The One and was getting some kind of instruction on something. Here I believed I could lose myself and the painful memories. I moved about among the women, helping as I could and just generally feeling at home, feeling a sense of belonging. The day was short lived for I had gotten up so late. Before I knew it, We were all sitting around the evening fire after the sun had gone down.

"I have always wanted to know why you ladies have a fire in the evening. You don't need it to see or for heat. Why do you light a fire?" I asked curiously.

"It is a beacon. A source of energy for the soul. A reminder that life comes from the elements and after it burns brightly it will return to the elements. A fire is a way of honoring all of life and the cycles they follow. For none of us live outside of the cycles. The cycles are the blessing that bring change. They are a gift. Fire is a gift symbolic of the cycle of change." Gnua explained. She loved the fire and the way it danced with itself. She knew fire had no one to please, and no one to fear. Fire knew the secret of life.

"That is beautiful and it makes so much sense." I said appreciatively. I sat and thought about that. The cycle of change. It happens to all things I thought. Those that are most resistant to it, are those that live life in fear. Those that understand and welcome change have a certain flow to them. I had seen it in my own people and in the Others as well. Fear and flow, seemed to be part of the basic structure of personality.

" You are feeling much better now aren't you?" Tuallan had come to sit by me.

"Yes, thank you, I am. I did not know, so much emotional pain, could be held by the body as physical pain. Life is a lesson, I will never stop learning." I laughed as I thought of being an old student, still trying to grasp simple concepts.

"That is the secret of all things. Every time we try to grasp a concept the concept evolves to something more. We can still be grasping the same concept at the point of our death as we are trying to grasp now, however it has evolved with us" The One joined us in conversation.

"Very few things in this Universe change in the way we think they change, they are only perceived differently because we perceive our life from different angles depending on where we stand. All life forms go through similar cycles as they grow and mature. Whole societies travel together through cycles of change, til they come to understand the power of the individual. When an entire society becomes as important as one individual, peace will be the prosperity that is pursued." As is typical of The One, with that statement she got up and left.

I turned to Tuallan, shrugged my shoulders and laughed. Tuallan looked at me and smiled. She knew I just needed to not care at the moment. I stayed up late that night watching the fire, every now and then I had the sense that the fire was watching me. That was a feeling I shook off. It was a feeling that unnerved me a bit. It felt like there were many eyes looking at me from the other side of the fire, watching me, looking for weakness, judging me. Had I not shook it off, sleep would have eluded me.

Morning came as it always does and I joined the sisterhood to honor the sun. My body was feeling normal again. The pain had gone. I was grateful for that. Missing Torando was something that would be with me for a long time, I accepted that. It was not as crippling as the pain.

As the women went on with their day, I went to speak with The One. She sat silently in the Temple of the Sun. She seemed fixated on one of the large crystals that spun the light into the dark corners of the temple.

"Did you hear me calling you?" She asked without moving.

"Yes. I know you wish to speak with me. So I came to find you."

"Come, sit here with me." She patted the empty spot beside her.

"I am having a hard time understanding why I am here. I understand you have allowed my body to heal. Thank you for that. But I know it is more than that. You could have healed me from here. There is a reason you have brought me all this way." I looked at her, and she kept looking straight ahead.

"Yes, you are here for a reason. I did not have the energy to stay there with you and guide you through what you need to see. Here I can help you and there will be no one to interrupt the process." Her words were heavy as they crossed her lips.

"What do you mean process, I thought I had gone through all the processes necessary?"

"You did and you excelled at them. The process I speak of now, was not part of your time here before, because the path you walked then, was a different path. The path you walk now was unforeseen at that time. No one could have known. I look into the future often and it follows a specific path, until someone changes their mind. Then the path changes. The path changed when you and Torando found each other. You had seen each other many times but the connection had never been made. I had hoped it never would. That connection changed the direction of time." I could hear the sadness in her voice, but still I did not know why.

"What do you mean, changed the direction of time?"

"As you move about, and go through your days, you think you are travelling through space. You stand at this point and you want to go to that point, you take as many steps as required, and it feels like you are travelling a distance from here to there. But this is not true. Space is the illusion of time. Tell me, when you came here, did you feel like you were travelling through time or space?" She finally looked at me, when she asked that question.

" Well, you taught me to collapse time, so I guess I was moving through space?" I really did not know how to answer that.

"You did not answer my question, again, did it feel like you were travelling through time or space when you came here?"

"Well the feeling coming here was like the passing of time, the collapsing of time makes it difficult to see the space I am in. So I guess if I cannot see the space I cannot feel it"

"Right. The space around you is something that is determined by the physical senses. When you cannot determine specific points of identification, the space becomes irrelevant. Time becomes the marker that you experience"

"Then why do I collapse time, to get through space. That does not make sense, if space doesn't exist without time?" I was pursuing this, I had to make sense of it.

"Space is a by product of time. It does not really exist. The mind is made in such a way that it has to fill all empty spaces. So if we were to remove the mind from the nature of time, space would cease to exist. The mind uses spatial concepts to place context into our lives. Without this we would be able to see all of our lives on the same time line at the same moment. Time allows for space, however space does not allow for time. You can also think of it this way. Time is the domain of the heart. Space is the domain of the mind. Memories may be recorded by the mind, but they are remembered through the heart. As you go through your life, you will discover, memories only become memories, if there is feeling attached to them. Do you understand what I am saying?"

" I think so. You are not really trying to help me understand the concept of space and time you are telling me all this because it has something to do, with what I am going back to. Right?" The One smiled at me. Nodding her head, she said, simply, "Yes."

"I have been around for so long, there are times I complicate things when they do not have to be complicated. I think I can ease into telling you things you may not want to hear, by telling you the consciousness concept behind them, but that is not always the case. You are going back to a different world. It will no longer be easy to live your life there."

"It has not been easy to live my life there since I went back. I have never been comfortable, at least not till I met Torando. He made life there much more bearable. The truth is, I do not feel like I belong there. I feel like I belong here. That is someone else's world. I don't understand how they continue to function the same way they always have functioned. I don't want to go back, I want to stay here. " I knew I was pleading with her, but I could not stop myself.

The One smiled tenderly at me, like a Mother smiles at a child just before she pulls the thorn from your finger. The smile is intended to make the pain easier, but it doesn't work that way.

"You must go back, you must finish this time line. The start of the next chapter depends on it. You see, there are always people that live in critical moments in time. Unknown to them, their lives are what allows time to continue on the same path. It is like the hub of a wheel. All of the spokes are dependent on the hub holding them in place. Without the hub, they serve no purpose. At this point in time you are that hub. All potential futures on this planet stem from your life. You are the last of us. Another species must take over this planet and the cycle must continue. The cycle must stay intact. However, you must prepare for what is to come. " Her voice was stern and direct. There was no option available.

"What do you mean, what is to come?"

"What do you think is coming? Tell me what is it you feel." I knew this game, this is where you try to empower someone, by allowing them to tell themselves the bad news. They take it better than you telling them, because they answered their own question and that seems less threatening to them.

" I think we are going to war. I think Rojan and Orla are going to force us to give them the head piece. We shall probably end up as their servants. Is that about right?" I answered, even though I did not want to.

"That is close to right. When you went home the first time, it had been foretold that you would be assigned a mate and the time line would continue as it had for years to come. Your Father changed his mind and wanted nothing to do with your life anymore. The time line started to separate at that point. When you discovered Torando, the separation was completed. His line of people can go nowhere with your line of people. However his line are breeding with the Others under Orla's rule. That has assured the fate of the planet. You now have to willingly let go of your position to complete your time line."

"Give the head piece to Orla! I won't do that. I will burn it or bury it before I do that!" I was not ready to hear anymore of this. What she wanted me to do was just not possible. Orla had killed my Mother and stolen my Father from me, and she wanted me to just hand over the head piece. No, I would not do that, not even for The One.

I left the Temple and then left the courtyard. I headed for the place my Mother and I had sat and talked before her death. I could not stop the tears from flowing. Why would she ask me to do something like that? It was wrong.

I sat overlooking the plains in the exact spot I had shared with my Mother. I kept thinking if she were still here, things would be different they would be better. Why was all of this falling on me? How much more of my life could they take from me? I had known I would spend my life with Torando and they took that from me, without a thought. No one cared for me. No one wanted me to have a good life. I was a tool being used in some game of the universe. I needed it to stop. I needed it to end. I wanted to be happy, but they kept taking my happiness from me.

I sat and I cried till even the tears were taken from me. Then I was numb. I did not know if I would feel again, if I could feel again. I had always seen The One as a surrogate Mother, and now she is asking this of me. I felt betrayed. How could she care for me, but yet, still ask this of me? I continued to rage and cry into the night. I did not fear the night, I welcomed it. Perhaps the beasts that roam the dark to find their prey could put an end to my suffering. On and on I went til exhaustion conquered my rage, and then sleep quickly, quietly overcame me. As I slept, the dream world came to my consciousness. In my dream Torando and I were children. We were running through the same fields I used to run through. It was a warm, bright sunny day and we kept running and running til we finally came to the end of the fields. One way took us to the forest and the other way led to the beach. We bickered back and forth for a moment trying to decide where to go from there. Torando then turned to me and took both of my hands in his.

"Its your choice, you know. It's your choice." That is all he said. With that the dream faded. When I awoke that dream was still with me. His words were resounding through my mind, repeating themselves over and over.

It was still dark as I sat and listened to the sounds of the night. All things that are present in the day are also present at night, but we perceive the night in a very different way, than we see the day. We are beings that are designed to move in the daylight, to use the light of the sun to see. It is not in our nature to be able to see well at night, because of this the darkness unnerves us.

When I would travel at night in my cat body, I never experienced that nervousness. I could see as well as I saw in the daylight. The night brought a certain sense of safety, like a dark blanket that protected me from the prying eyes of the day watchers. My cat body was not who I was, it was only one small part of me, useful in very specific situations. I had to live my life as who I was, how I felt and what I appeared to be to everyone else.

With time and distance, sanity was also arriving. I knew I had to go back and talk to The One. I needed to know more about why I was expected to hand over the head piece. I knew it was not a request, it was an expectation. That was the duty of my life, I was always expected to do the appropriate thing, whether or not I agreed. The truth of this matter though, was that, I already felt like it was so far beyond me, that I was just a tool. I was just one more event in a long line of events that would someday be part of the stories told by old men when they wanted to quiet the children.

I followed the path along the edge of the mountain back to the temples and the courtyards. There in the dim light of the last flames of fire daring to flicker, sat The One. She had waited for me to return. As she sat there, her heart was heavy and her brow was troubled. This was not an easy thing for her. I had never seen her as alone as she was in that moment. I went and sat down beside her.

"I am sorry, for not being able to give you the respect you deserve. I am sorry for not being able to hear your words. I have had too much pain recently and I just could not take any more in. What you are asking of me, is very difficult. I have been thinking, and have decided I owe you the respect of hearing why it is that I must do this." I spoke softly and genuinely to her. I did not want to upset her, and I did not want to be upset." She turned to me and forced her lips to smile. She looked like she had aged tremendously over night, that is how she appeared to me.

"I know I have asked you to carry a great burden. I am not asking for myself. It is the will of life that I ask this. I have watched many worlds rise

240

and fall and rise again. This one shall be no different. Through the course of history stories are told of acts of courage and bravery. People that have lived or died for causes they believed in. Most stories follow a similar pattern. There is always a hero. Someone that has come from a somewhat unknown place and risen to greatness, because of their acts of selflessness. These acts in whatever form they take, happen against insurmountable odds, and affect whole societies, if not worlds. The stories are told till they become legends, and those legends grow in magnitude with time.

The truth of history in all worlds is that these incredible stories that are told around fires at night, are just that, stories. They all have bits and pieces of truth to them, enough to make them believable. The truth of history is that no one would really want to hear the truth. Societies, indeed entire worlds are changed by continuous small acts and decisions made by everyday people. And there are always two types of people that bring forth these changes. There is the person who is wanting to grow and expand and the person who is wanting to contain and contract. These are the people that change history.

We can all be either one of these people at any one point in our lives, however we cannot be both at the same time. It is always at the climax of the moment, that we make up our minds, which one of these people we are. It is the moment in your life that you become your truth. It is the moment of your life that the accumulation of what you think, becomes what you feel. There is no way to predict which one of these people you are, because there is only one way to find out. You have to live that moment, it is only then that you will know what truth is to you.

Those are the moments that change worlds. Those are the moments entire societies are built upon. Most of those moments go unseen by those that tell the stories of history. These moments happen everyday to everyone, and then they are forgotten. Your moment is coming. You will have to make a decision, whether you want to grow and expand, or whether, you want to contain and contract. It will not be a conscious decision, because you will not have time to think about it. It will be a reactive response to a highly stimulating event. What I want you to think about until that time comes is this, what makes one person grow and expand and the other contain and contract?"

I could see in her eyes, there was so much more she wanted to tell me. For whatever reason, she never would. For as much pain and suffering that I had endured in my life, I suddenly understood how horrible it must be to carry the knowledge that The One carried. To know what is going to happen and to know you must stand back and watch it happen. That must take great courage. To have the wisdom she had attained in her life, she must have met with great pain.

We sat in silence for the rest of the night. That silence was the most

241

intense conversation I had ever had. Decisions that I was not yet aware of were being made. Life was choosing a direction. History was being made. And none of it happened with a single spoken word.

I decided to stay a few more days. I just wanted to enjoy being there. I wanted to spend time with the women that had raised me, taught me and cared for me. I wanted to soak up as much of the mountains presence as possible. Perhaps I would carry it all back to the sea with me.

I thought about what The One had asked me to do. There was only one way I knew how to do that. I started to strip away all the other voices that were in my head. The voice of my Father, my Mother and of Torando. I stripped away the voices of the children I knew when I was a child. The voices of the women here on the mountain, too were stripped away. I stripped away all the voices I could remember hearing, I even stripped away the voice of The One. When all the voices were gone, there was silence. I had not realized that no matter what I did, what I thought or even what I said, there was always another script running in the back of my mind, commenting on everything I did, thought or said. There was always someone else's voice there, telling me, "I was right" or "I was wrong". The sound of the silence was profound. In the end there were still two voices left. There was my voice, the being that I am. Then there was the voice of my mind, the personality that I portray.

I tried to divide my time over the days to come between being sociable and been silent. At first it was a battle to keep all the other voices out of my head, but they soon learned they were not welcome, and they left me alone. The two voices that were left were harder to deal with. The voice I was most comfortable with was the voice that was demanding, confrontational, judgmental and quite condemning. The other voice, the voice of my being, was loving and supportive. That voice did not expect anything of me. It did not tell me what was right or wrong. It did not demand I make up my mind.

I started to understand that in my entire life I had been acting out a role. I was born to this family and placed in this position, so my behavior was expected to be like this or that. But that is not at all who I was. The more I stripped away the voice of the role that I was playing, the more I could see the many faces I had worn as the being that I am. It was through this that I started to understand what The One called a time line. I wore personalities the same way clothing was worn. If the cloth fit the circumstance the purpose was served. Once the cloth no longer fit, it was discarded, and there was more clothing placed in front of me to choose from. All of it, everything, all the moments that string together to create a life, they are all about the feeling that the experience created. Experiences that had no feeling were not remembered.

I became extremely amused by this. For all the voices in my head, and all

242

the opinions of those voices. none of them mattered. The truth was in what is felt and experienced, words simply cannot compete. I understood then that the thing we call life, really isn't life at all. What we call life is what we perceive life to be and perception is just a matter of opinion. Perception is reality that has been filtered through the inconsistencies of the mind. It has been filtered through all those voices, and opinions.

So I made a vow to myself. I decided to start looking at life as it is. To see what is before me, without the filters of my perception. Without having an opinion. Without judging something or someone to be good or bad. I just wanted to see what was there, not what I decided should be there. I no longer wanted the voices that had been in my head all my life to influence the rest of my life. I wanted to be free.

Freedom, that's it! That is what freedom is. Freedom is no longer needing to be attached to all those voices and all those opinions. Freedom is allowing others to have their opinion, but not adopting it, because you don't know what to think yourself. Freedom meant stripping myself of all the personalities I wear as clothing. Freedom is understanding the difference between who you are, and how you act. Knowing this, I let a huge sigh escape from me. I think I have been searching for freedom all my life, but never really knowing what it was, enough to find it. I felt in that moment, like I didn't have to think anymore. The me that needed the answers to come by thinking them, just melted away.

Later as I sat with the women around the light of the fire they appeared different to me. Not that they looked different or even acted different. It was more the interaction between them that made me take notice.

As they chatted to one another and moved their hands and bodies, there seemed to be a cord of energy that ran through all of them. It was the same cord of energy running through all of them. I had never seen this before with anyone. We all have our own energy that moves through us and interacts with all things around us, but this was like one energy that animated all the women.

By the light of the fire, the energy was easy to perceive, as it got darker farther from the fire, I could not follow the cord, or where it led to. The cord seemed to just disappear into the darkness. I sat and tried to rationalize if what I saw, was what I saw. It really did not makes any sense. Tuallan noticed my behavior was a little odd as I was trying to see where the cord came from.

"What are you doing?" She asked in her point blank manner. You could trust that Tuallan would never mince words.

"I thought I saw something, but it must have just been shadows." I did not want her to know how my perception had changed since stripping myself of the voices.

"The firelight can play tricks on your vision. I have always thought that is entertainment for the fire. It manipulates us that way. It draws us in. And then just when we think we have caught the illusory monster, poof, it is gone. The fire wins again." She walked away laughing. I knew she was laughing at me, but I did not care. Tuallan was one of those beings I could never truly decide whether I liked her or not.

I was looking around for The One, but I did not see her. That was unusual, normally she sat out at night with us. There was a faint light coming from the Temple of the Moon. Silhouetted in the doorway I could see her, standing there looking at me. She was beckoning me. I wandered over to the Temple wondering what it was. Inside the temple I thought the light would be coming from a small fire, but it was not. The light was coming from small crystals that sat in the four corners. No bigger than my palm, these small clear crystals, lit the whole temple. I touched one of them expecting to feel heat, but there was none. There was no noticeable feeling of anything. If anything, I thought I could feel an aliveness coming from them that I had never experienced in any stone before. I knew stone to be conscious and to store memory, but to come alive like this, that was not something I expected.

"How are they doing this?" I was excited and my question verged on demanding.

"Inside all beings there is light. A great and powerful light. Most just choose to not let it shine in the presence of others. You see, when someone shines their light brightly, others take notice. Those others may not always want to see the light. So they will do what has to be done to suppress that light, sometimes even at the expense of the life of The One bearing the light.

All beings shine their light in different degrees, but to be safe on this planet means you must blend in, if you stand out you will be noticed and that could be dangerous. These crystals contain immense power. Each one could provide light for your entire lifetime. Light like that is very powerful and if that power was ever used inappropriately there would be mass destruction.

When I was very young and just a student, my teacher showed me what I am showing you now. He asked the crystals to reveal themselves, and so they did. I was so fascinated by the light that came from within, I had to discover how he made it happen. For many years I did everything I could to make the crystals light up. Then accidentally, one day I happened to be meditating close to one, I was opening my heart, and sending love to all things, and the crystal lit up and sent its light back to me. I knew what the secret was then. But that still did not satisfy me. I wanted to contain that light, Oh, my intentions were good, I thought if I could contain the light we would no longer have to make fires. We could light our homes at night, all we needed was a crystal. Many more years of my life passed and everything I tried, failed.

One day I took the crystal to a very dark cave, deep underground. I had wondered if I could get the rocks to absorb the light and perhaps give off a constant glow. I placed the crystal in the middle of the cave and asked it to shine, and shine it did. It lit up the whole space. But the light seemed to get continuously brighter and brighter. It didn't take long for the walls of the cave to start vibrating. The light continued to move outward, constantly expanding, and as it did it became too much for the cave and the walls started to crack and shake. I ran out from there just in time. The chamber exploded outward and then it collapsed inward.

Many people had homes that were close by. I did not know that the cave was part of many interlinking tunnels and rivers that ran underground. The collapse of that cave set off a chain reaction that kept going for a long time. The whole area became unstable and many homes were lost. A few people lost their lives because of me. I was temporarily banished. I had to pay penance for what I had done.

The only way I could redeem myself was to understand what had happened. Why did that cave collapse because of the light? I spent the next many years of my life alone and this is what I learned. Light once activated, constantly expands and vibrates. Light can infuse the things around it with light if it is received, however not all things are ready to receive the light. In an enclosed space like that cave, when light is rejected, it turns back in on itself, even though it continues to expand, and at some point, the expansion is to great for the containment, something has to give. This is what is happening in our world at the moment. Light is pushing against a resisting force. The resisting force will fight back, but the light cannot be contained, something will give."

I knew she was talking about Orla and myself, but I did not really want to know more. I was tired of planning and scheming about how to deal with Orla. My entire adult life had been all about how to deal with Orla. It was all my life was about til I met Torando. I did not want to see harm come to my Father because of her, but I did not have the strength to care about her anymore.

"When something starts a pattern of expanding beyond itself, the pattern does not stop. It is the nature of the Universe. Containment is not possible. Even though it may be thought that something is captured, it really isn't. Light consists of the same energy as your spirit, no matter what, you will continue to expand. Wisdom is not the ability to contain light, wisdom is the ability to direct it. Wisdom happens when you understand that life is not about what is happening around you, it is what is happening in you."

I smiled. I knew then that I was not going to get another Orla lecture. I was getting an approval of sorts. The One was telling me, that I had found wisdom in no longer caring about what Orla was, or what Orla did. My life belonged to me now. Now I could consciously direct it. I nodded to her and left. Nothing more needed to be said. I went to my white walls and slept a very deep peaceful sleep.

The morning seemed extra beautiful as I joined the ladies in honoring the sun. With each breath I felt my heart expand. I was feeling more love and contentment than I had ever felt. I moved through the day, helping here and there, and taking time to experience life. I knew I would soon have to return home, but that was not going to stop me from loving the moments I had here.

The next few days passed with great speed, but I found my self able to maintain a kind of time suspension within the moments. I was fully present in every moment and I discovered that this created a form of personal timelessness. Being fully present meant that I experienced myself in my surroundings as they were exactly in that same moment with me. I did not think of the next moment, nor did I think of The One just passed. I experienced every moment as it was, without any attachment to another moment. This allowed me the experience of knowing that time was passing but I did not feel it moving. My physical reality was always in the current moment, so it had no perception of time at all. In those few days I was able to understand the sisterhood more completely than I ever had.

The time had come for me to return home. I knew I would be returning to a different world. Not because everything there had changed, but instead because I had changed. I could not see the world the way I once did. Whether the reality be beautiful or painful, I saw things the way they were. I did not want to return to my duties as ruler of my land. I no longer felt that was who I was. I was not a product of lineage, I was a constantly expanding point of light. The Head Piece was what contained me. I just couldn't allow that any longer. How I would tell this to my Father, I had not decided yet. We would just have to find another way.

Tuallan and I said our goodbyes and we set off home. The trip was quick and uninterrupted. I did not see anything unusual so I was not expecting anything to be different, but I was wrong. Upon arriving at the other end of the land bridge, the first thing I noticed was, there were no sentinels standing there waiting. That had been the tradition since the shield had been in place, but today, none stood waiting.

As we walked into the courtyard, it was quiet. People were there going about their business, but it was quiet. Anytime previous to this, the moment they saw me, they would have come to welcome me. This time, even though I was standing there with them, they did not appear to see me. I was a little unnerved by it all, I didn't know whether this was happening because I was seeing things differently or they were acting differently.

"What do you think is going on?" I asked Tuallan. I wanted to make sure I was not the only one that thought something was not right.

"I don't know, but whatever it is, Orla is behind it." Tuallan just stared straight ahead as though she could not believe her experience.

My next thought was for my Father. I ran to the palace and started searching for him. I finally found him far in the back, sitting at a table, staring off into the empty air.

"Father" I yelled as I ran to him. He slowly turned his head and looked at me.

"Aeiya, my beautiful girl." He reached his hand out to touch my face. He seemed to have no energy, no life in him.

"Father, what has happened here?"

"Change has come to this place. I never thought it would be this way. I could not stop him. Orla tried to stop him, but.............."

"Stop who? What is going on? Where is Orla?" I felt myself frantic. I wanted answers. What had they done to my Father?

"Rojan came with his army. They came into the palace and took the Head Piece. Orla tried to hide it, but he took it from her. Some of the sentinels tried to stop him, but he just killed them. He has taken over, and we are under his rule. I can't believe he just killed them.........."

My Father seemed to be in shock. He could not comprehend the violence of it all. He had never experienced violence, not like this.

"Where is Orla?" I demanded to know.

"I don't know. He took her. I have not seen her in days." My Father had crumbled under the stress, he was a broken man.

"I am going to find her, stay here." I needed to know what was going on. I left and headed to the Alaria. I had to let Tuallan know what had happened. As I entered the Alaria, I could not believe my eyes. The baths had been destroyed. Tuallan stood there crying.

"Why, why would they do this. The baths heal people. They make the world a better place." Tuallan said through streaming tears.

I walked to her and held her. "It is because they make the world a better place that they destroyed them. They will create this world in their image now, and that will not be a healing place. "

I did not know what to do. I was afraid for my Father, afraid for Tuallan, afraid for my people. I didn't know how to stop this.

"Can you get yourself back to the mountain? I need you to tell The One what is going on. Tuallan do you hear me?" I shook her, I needed to know she was listening to me.

"The One already knows. She told me that I would be coming back to a different world. It would not be the place I knew, and I would not want to stay. She sent me back to get the great crystal that is hidden in the palace. She said it needs to be protected now. Orla and Rojan are looking for it."

The great crystal? I had no idea what that was. I remembered my Mother telling me of secrets that had been passed from ruler to ruler, but she never told me what they were or where they lay.

"Do you know where it is?" I asked Tuallan.

"Yes, The One told me to bring it to her."

"Ok, lets go get it, then lets get you out of here." I hurriedly escorted Tuallan back to the palace. I did not know where Rojan or Orla were, I just knew I had to get the crystal out of the city.

I turned to go into the palace and Tuallan pulled away from me.

"What are you doing, we have to get that crystal?" I yelled at her.

"The crystal is not in the palace, it is in the garden."

She seemed to know exactly where it was, so I followed her, trying to keep an eye out for Orla or Rojan on the way.

Beyond the courtyard, there was a large central garden. It was used by everyone. All people were welcome. The plants that grew there were different than the plants that grew by themselves in the forest. They were stronger, more vibrant. Some of the flowers had petals that would change colors. It was a special place that drew everyone and everything to it. But until now, I had never thought there might be a reason why. I kept watch and Tuallan moved into the garden, towards the center. She disappeared behind some of the plants and I could hear her digging. In moments she reappeared.

"I got it she said. Lets get out of here."

We walked quickly towards the land bridge. I didn't want to bring any attention to us by running. At the edge of the city where the shield ended, I figured we were safe.

"Let me see it." I held out my hand as Tuallan reached into the bag.

From the bag she pulled a crystal so clear it seemed I was looking through air. As she held it colors would pass through the center and then out to the edge. It would then release the color into the air, like mist. I reached out to take the crystal and as I did, the colors turned to purple and red. The crystal was not shaped like other crystals. The ends were not pointed. This crystal was round and felt warm to the touch. It felt as though it were alive and responded to my touch. When I had a thought the crystal would react to that thought with color and light. I watched it for a few minutes and then my thoughts turned to Orla again. The crystal turned dark but as the darkness moved through it, it was transformed to light and released. I had another thought about Torando's death. The same thing happened but with different colors. I did this a few more times, with other negative thoughts. It was always the same thing, darkness turning to light. I realised then, why this crystal was so important to The One. This was the crystal they used in the birthing chambers, to create life. The birthing chambers were pure energy. This was the crystal that directed and transformed the energy. That is what Orla wanted it for. She wanted to use it. She wanted to activate the birthing chambers again. She wanted to create a new kind of person. I was so caught up in my discovery I didn't hear their approach. If it hadn't been for Tuallan stepping backwards, I would not have known. I lifted my head to see Rojan and his men racing towards us. I grabbed the crystal and stuffed it in Tuallan's bag. I pushed her backwards, away from me as hard as I could.

"Go, go, get out of hear I screamed."

She scrambled to her feet and started to run.

I threw myself into Rojan's path. His men came around him and ran to grab Tuallan. Just as they were about to grab her, The One collapsed time and she disappeared into the light. She had gotten away.

Rojan had me by the throat, holding me against the rocky ground. He kept raising me just enough to slam my head back into the ground. His eyes were wild and crazy, but he seemed to take great pleasure in my pain. I thought he may kill me.

"Rojan! Let her up." Orla's voice shattered his focus, and he released his grip. Orla walked up to me and grabbed my arm. She hauled me up off the ground, and then violently pushed my arm back towards me.

"Where is the crystal?" Her words were violent.

"What crystal?" I was not going to tell her anything.

"That is not wise. You know exactly what crystal. The crystal your Father told me about. How we were all created. Now tell me where it is!"

I knew she would not give up, and if my Father had told her about it, I could not lie.

"I don't have it. Tuallan took it. It is going to The One." I said as bravely as I could.

Orla exploded in rage. She was angry enough to make Rojan's men take a few steps back. Yelling and waving her arms wildly, I did not know what she was going to do.

"You are going to get it for me. Take us there right now."

"I can't. I don't know how. The One has always brought me to her. I cannot do it on my own." I had told the truth, but I did not expect to be believed.

"We'll see about that. Bring her" she ordered.

Rojan's men grabbed me and we started back for the palace. We got to the courtyard and Orla gave her next order.

"Kill them." It is all she said as she pointed towards the small group of people on the other side of the gardens.

"No. leave them alone, they have nothing to do with this."

The men looked at Orla, she just nodded her head. With no other thought, the men murdered the people. They struck them down as though they meant nothing. I did not believe what I saw. I could not look and turned away. Orla grabbed my face and turned me back.

"This is your fault, it is all your fault." she spoke her words quietly, but specifically.

"I can't take you there. I don't know how." I cried out. I couldn't stop myself from crying. It was my fault that those people were dead. I should have done something to protect them. I should have refused to come back to this place.

"Well if that didn't work, I know something that will."

Orla grabbed me by the face and dragged me into the palace. She dragged me to the small area in the back where my Father sat, numb to the world around him. As she let go of me, I dropped to my knees. I knew she meant to kill my Father. Rojan walked right past her and up to my Father. He stabbed him in the back as he sat there.

Orla ran to Rojan and hit him across the face with her weapon. Rojan fell to the floor, bleeding.

My Father lay on the floor, barely breathing. I ran to him.

"Father, Father." I lifted his head to my knee.

"I love you, I will always love you." He reached to touch my face but he didn't have enough strength.

As his eyes turned towards Orla, he reached out to her and in a weak voice said, "Aleeya?"

Then with all the strength he had, he smiled and looked at Orla, but what he saw was my Mother, Aleeya.

That so enraged Orla that she took her knife and plunged it into my Fathers heart.

She grabbed my hair and threw me against the wall. All I wanted to do was get back to my Father one last time, but I hit the wall so hard, I could not see. When I regained consciousness, Orla was pacing around the room, ranting about my Mother. How she was glad she killed her and how my Father deserved to die too.

I raised my head from the floor and said, "Alright, I will take you there."

Orla's head snapped around. "Well it is about time."

She had her men pick me up drag me back through the palace. When we got to the courtyard, she stood me up, and forced me to walk. She was making a statement to anyone that would oppose her.

It was a very long walk back to the land bridge. The only thing I could see was my Father laying there calling my Mother. His love had never been for Orla, it had always been my Mother. Orla was the closest thing to her, and that is what he clung to. There was some satisfaction in that for me. I did not know what I was going to do when I got to the land bridge. I was hoping The One would come for me. I was hoping she would know I was there. I knew she could stop all this.

"Stop there." Orla commanded me.

"We are not close enough, we need to be further onto the land bridge. I cannot connect from here. " I pleaded with her.

"I have decided I should let you go. After all, you have relinquished your rule. You will not oppose me now. Everyone you know is dead. Everything you love is dead. You killed them with your arrogance and selfishness. You deserve to spend the rest of this life alone. "

In that moment, something changed in me. The distance between Orla and I started to fade. I saw Orla stripped down to what she is. I saw Orla as me. I saw all the years of anger and discontent take shape and form in her. All the years I spent wishing life were different than it was, I saw how that shaped her. I saw all the times I could have been nice to her, or offered a loving word to her, I saw how that sculpted her reality. I saw how all my choices were my choices. My whole life I have not wanted to be here, til I met Tornado. I saw how my life had affected everyone around me and I had not cared. I also saw how it was all supposed to be exactly the way it was. It was what I had to learn. There was no other way, but I did not know that till now.

One more thing came to my knowing as well, it was the day Torando said, "we will not be here very long." I knew now, what he knew then, that all of this was playing out exactly as it was supposed to. I had done what I came here to do. The second I had that thought, I could feel myself expand. My point of light started growing immensely. My heart could no longer be contained by my body as it expanded outward towards everything. As my energy grew I experienced everything that my energy passed. their pain, their sorrow, their joy. A piece of me stayed with them, and I took pieces of them with me.

In that moment facing my death, I should have been angry or frightened, instead I found myself feeling the most profound love I ever had. I knew that Orla was just a piece of me. A piece of me that I had denied. A piece of me that hadn't found love. A piece of me that just wanted to be seen. I got down on my knees, I needed to be closer to the earth. Then I offered this to Orla.

"I have watched you for a long time. I have seen you change and then change back. I do not know what made these changes. What I know now is that you think you can take what it is that you want. I am here to tell you, that is not possible.

You choose to kill but you do not want the blood on your own hands. You think you have power because of this, but you do not know what real power is. You think that by taking the lives of some, it will give you control over the lives of the rest. The power you seek comes from pain but real power comes from the understanding that you have no need for power. The only experience that brings this enlightenment, is love. The force that you use to control others, is the force that you lack to control yourself. I know now what truth is, and you cannot take what is not given. You feel the need to have my life so badly, but you do not understand, you can only lay claim to my body. So I am giving you my body, I cannot give you my life for it is not mine to give. I am part of all things. One day I hope you will understand this.

I wish I had it to do all over again. But without knowing what I know now, I would do it the same. I want to apologize to you. I should have loved you more. I should have accepted you more. I should have forgiven you more. You and I are the same. I am sorry I did not see that before. I am sorry you did not have the life, you thought you wanted. Perhaps you can have that life now. I want you to know, I offer you all the love I can. I would ask you to love yourself, to be good to yourself. I would ask you to have hope. It is your life and it is your choices that create your life. You are a good person that just got lost. Find that person again."

I shuffled around on my knees so that I was facing the sacred mountains. There at the end of the land bridge, I could see The One, she was standing waiting. She raised her hand to me. As I raised my hand to her, I heard Orla scream "No". I felt the pressure in the back of my skull.
My eyes went dark. I went home.

Orla ran to Aeiya's lifeless body. She collapsed and cried. She had not wanted her dead, She really wanted no harm to come to her. It was more important to her that she be seen taking power from Aeiya. She did not expect to feel remorse and pain at the loss of her niece. Orla was now the last of her kind, and she was not prepared for how lonely that made her feel.

The One had been standing there helpless to change the events that had unfolded. In a daze of desperation thinking that she could alter Aeiya's senseless death, The One stepped out from her protected space, but Tuallan was there to stop her.

"No, you must not. You knew this was her path. You cannot change this, you cannot bring her back. The world needs you, I need you. Stop. Think. Are you willing to throw everything away for something you cannot change?" Tuallan pleaded with The One.

The One quietly stepped back into the energy field. She fell to her knees and wept. She allowed the overwhelming surge of emotion to take her. Aeiya had been more her daughter than any other initiate. When Aeiya was created, The One had offered a large piece of herself to the new child being created in the chamber. No one knew this. Aeiya was to carry on the line, she was the last hope. Now, she was gone. The One was not sure she wanted to continue. Why continue if there is no hope?

Tuallan knew what The One was feeling, so she dared to speak. "I know you feel there is no hope now. I know you are in pain. Nothing will ever replace Aeiya in your heart and nothing ever should. But you can still help steer this world to a better place. You have taught me that all of life cycles. Change is inevitable. It cannot be stopped. Sometimes change feels good and sometimes change is unbearable. But change is the only constant we have to depend upon. It is now that we have to depend upon it the most. Now we have to use this time of desperation to prove that all we know, all that you have taught me is true, we must believe that the next change to come will be for the good. This is what you have taught us all. As bad as this is now, the times to follow will be equally good. We cannot give up now, there are too many of The Others depending on us. We must show them that there is hope and that they can learn to be more than they have been taught that they are. They can rise up and be people who are self governed. They can make decisions for themselves and make their lives great because of it. We must teach the people that they are not here to do the bidding of those in power, that they have a right to create their own lives because they are as powerful as those that would rule them. But we must do all of this from a space of love, so we don't become like Orla. The people have the right to know that they have a choice, and that choice is the real power in this world. Together they will set themselves free from those that would use them as slaves. It is time for the people to inherit this world now. It is time for us to become who we are meant to be."

The rousing speech made by Tuallan, moved The One. She was right. The Others had so often been dismissed as not much more than intelligent animals, but Tuallan had proved, their intelligence lay in the power of their emotion. She had bridged the gap between using emotion as a control factor and discovering the power that emotion truly holds. The One could see this now. Teaching The Others would be a challenge, because they learned in a much different manner than all previous initiates did. However, what they learned about they could also build upon. This was something that was difficult for Aeiya to do. She either knew something or she didn't. It was difficult for all of her kind to take something she had learned and create from that point, a pathway to other lessons. The Others used emotion to do this. The One was starting to see, The Others could become a great society, they could learn and evolve into what The One was herself, over time.

"Tuallan, I am in mourning and that will take a long time. However I will not abandon you or your people. You are much stronger than I have thought. It is time now, you are right. We must teach as many as we can. I will need your help to create a society of people that understands the great teachings. Together we are going to teach your kind to be Wisdom Keepers. Go now, gather together all those you know that would qualify for this quest. Bring them to me on the mountain. We will start immediately." With that she rose and started to make her way slowly back to the mountain top. Each step she took was taken consciously to honor Aeiya's life.

As she walked she thought about the journey that lay before her and the sisterhood. The race that had once been created as beasts of burden were about to inherit the future. There was great hope in this for The One, because this species had proven itself to be both intelligent and compassionate. They were capable of independent thought, the most important ingredient in the development of any truly enlightened society. Some had learned to question their minds and the images that their eyes saw, and override them with the truth. That quality was the quality that all societies who survived their own ignorance possessed. This day had brought great sorrow, and the mourning process would be ongoing, however out of the darkness of this moment, the light began to erupt. The Others had the spark within them. A spark so strong that it could ignite a thousand universes. Yes, this ending brought about a new beginning for the Earth, a new age, a new energy. Those who were once slaves and only dared to taste freedom, would now gorge upon it. The One felt the flame of hope in her heart. That flame had been ignited in her by The Others. The cycle was now complete, the student had taught the teacher the most basic lesson, life is not to be dwelled upon, it is to be alive within the flow of change.

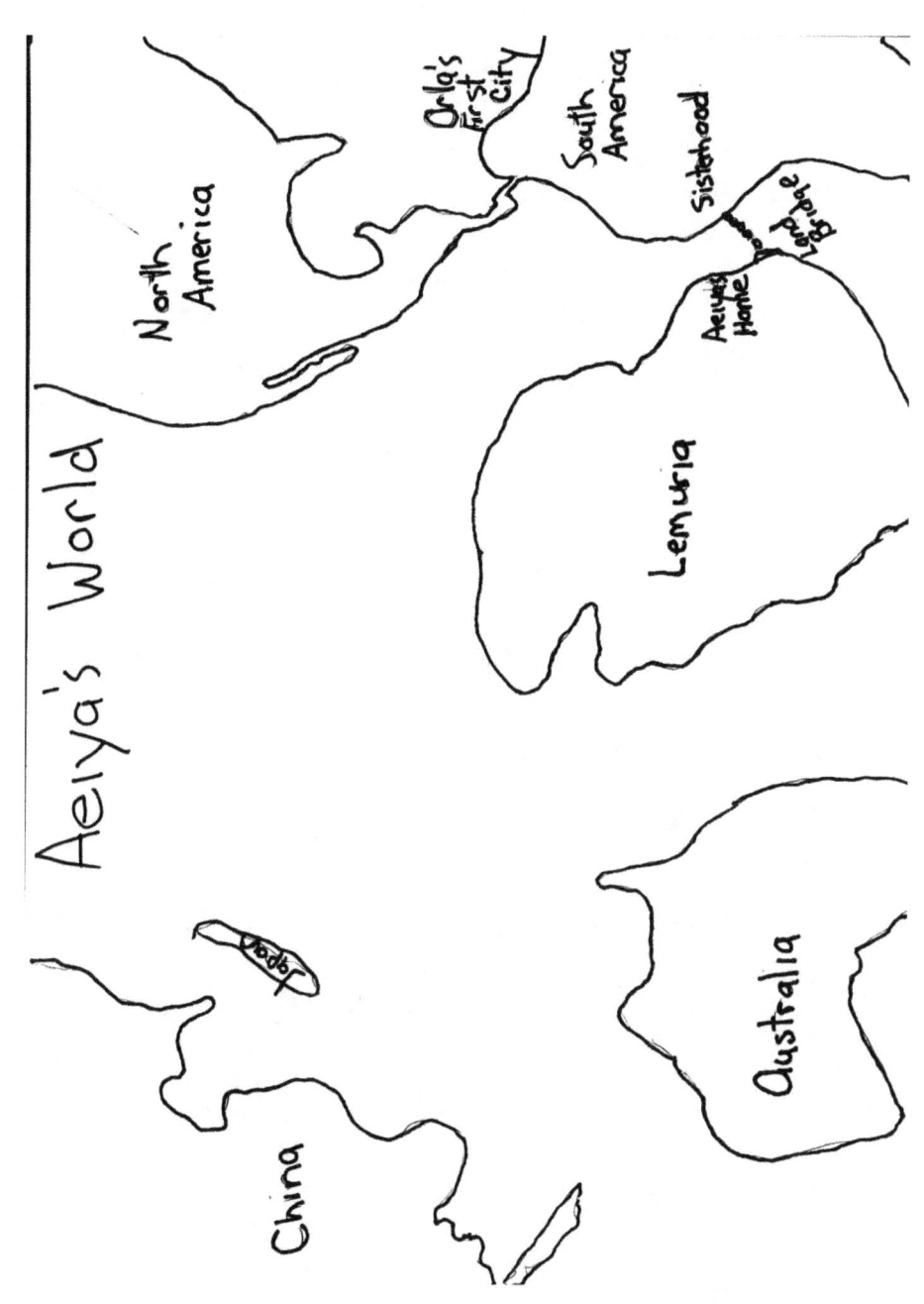

Aeiya's World

North America

Orla's First City

South America

Sisterhood

Lemuria

Aeiya's Home

Legienne

China

Jade

Australia

To contact the author:

for questions, comments or orders

please go to Facebook, type Rose McMullen

or email:

taonow1@hotmail.com

The Hollow Stones is available on

Amazon

For an autographed copy with a personal message

please contact the author

Follow Rose McMullen on Twitter

@seeofenergyme

Or occasionally on Tumblr at

http://www.tumblr.com/blog/quantumquandry

www.ingramcontent.com/pod-product-compliance
Lightning Source LLC
Chambersburg PA
CBHW070105030726
47506CB00002B/604